THE NOBLE REBELLION

Joshua G. Fensterstock

THE
NOBLE
REBELLION

Joshua G. Fensterstock

ARPress
45 Dan Road Suite 15
Canton MA 02021
  Hotline: 1(888) 821-0229
  Fax: 1(508) 545-7580

Ordering Information:
Quantity sales. Special discounts are available on quantity purchases by corporations, associations, and others. For details, contact the publisher at the address above.

Printed in the United States of America.

ISBN-13:   Softcover   979-8-89676-076-4
                 eBook   979-8-89676-077-1

Library of Congress Control Number: 2025907699

Contents

PROLOGUE

As the sun baked the desert sand, Sultan could see the wind blow in the waves of heat that radiated from below his sandals. He stood outside the mouth of the cave in which he lived since the Americans began destroying the al-Qaeda network. With all eyes focused on capturing Osama bin Laden, the Syrian-born Mohammed "Sultan" al-Fassad managed to survive in the caves of the Pakistani mountains. He was nothing more than a mere soldier in bin Laden's army, yet he never believed that suicide attacks were the best way to combat the American threat to the Muslim world. And he was not alone.

Sand began to rise in the hills in the distance. Sultan looked out to see if it was caused by the desert wind. He broke the silence in his native Arabic, "Ah, Emir! Your promptness never fails!" Saed "Emir" al-Fassad was Sultan's younger brother; he was loyal to Sultan as only a brother could be. Emir longed to join his brother in the al-Qaeda camps in Afghanistan, mostly to prove to Sultan that the stutter that plagued his speech since birth did not hinder his ability to fight for Allah. The Americans destroyed his hopes.

Sultan managed to get word to Emir of his whereabouts. Abandoning bin Laden proved to be the wisest move Sultan could make. He was no longer a "hot" target, and he could strategize as bin Laden did while having Emir carry out his orders on the outside. Sultan did not have bin Laden's financial resources, but then again, thanks to the Americans, he did not need them. Anything of bin Laden's that the Americans did not find remained in the hands of people in Sultan's situation: Namely, men who were on the run and looking for an American target. However, they realized that the rules of the game had changed. Bin Laden's death would refocus the Americans' attention on them.

Silence was the newest weapon for these fighters. Sultan communicated his orders only to Emir, and only in person. Emir contacted remaining al-Qaeda soldiers at large and convinced them to go along with Sultan's plan. With bin Laden in hiding he was the perfect diversion. The Americans did not have the resources to track "cold" leads, and Sultan's first order made certain to keep his profile frigid: The only method of communication about his vision would be oral and in-person. No technology. No cell phones. No e-mail. No landline phones or faxes. No family members were to be informed. And most importantly, no questions were to be asked.

Sultan smirked as Emir's truck approached. The cargo was precious, as Emir was ordered to deliver an Indian passport with Sultan's picture and new identity, and more importantly, the colonels for his new war. Twelve al Qaeda soldiers still at large agreed to help Sultan. Emir, Sultan's second-in-command, was bringing them to meet with Sultan face-to-face to discuss the first stage of implementation for the new Jihad.

As they unloaded from the truck, Sultan greeted each of them with a tight hug and three cheek-to-cheek embraces: right to right, then left to left, then right to right again. "As-salaamu aleikum," he said.

"Wa aleikum salaam," the colonels each responded in turn.

First was Omar Qaferi, a Lebanese national who learned cruelty from Hezbollah guerillas. Qaferi was followed by two men feared worldwide: Mohammed-Abdul Nasir's inflexible wooden leg, which replaced the one he lost when his suicide bombing attempt went awry in Israel just three years prior, thumped in the truck as he prepared to make his way out of the rear fuselage; as he exited, Rahim Ishmael adjusted the patch covering his left eye socket, a remnant of his three days spent tortured by bin Laden himself for insubordination during his first day at the al Qaeda camp.

Qaferi, Nasir, and Ishmael were the only experienced soldiers Emir could muster. They had access to enough of bin Laden's resources, which was ultimately all Sultan needed. Of the remaining colonels, only Yousef bin Ramsi, Mustafa al-Abo, Ahmed Il-Nabu, Mohammed Yasir, and Abu Saed Hussein had any training in bin Laden's camps. However, none of them was a target for the FBI or the CIA.

Sultan welcomed the men on whom he would rely into his meager cave where they eagerly consumed the feast Emir procured for the occasion. They spoke ill of the Americans throughout the meal. "They think they can subdue the will of Allah?" Qaferi asked. "They will feel the wrath of Allah through my sword! As many as I can find!"

"Not if I first cut all of their throats in the name of Allah!" Nasir retorted as he slapped his wooden appendage to enhance his presence.

"Ha! If bin Laden could hear you all now," began Ishmael. "No one has taken more Americans in the name of Allah than him. And only together, in Allah's name, and bin Laden's name, shall we taste the blood of revenge!"

With that, all of the guests cheered. They continued airing all of their complaints about American policies, especially toward their Palestinian brethren. Each one explained what he would do if he caught an American soldier; not a single one would comply with the Geneva Convention. When the company exhausted their appetites, Sultan stood and the formal business of the meeting began.

"My brothers," Sultan began in Arabic, "today is the first day of our eventual triumph. I would like to first thank all of you for your bravery. Allah will reward you and your families for your courage. Emir, you have made this day possible, and for that, I must especially thank you before all present." With that, all of the men applauded.

Sultan continued, "The Americans have destroyed the great army of bin Laden, but they cannot destroy the will of Allah. Our Jihad continues, and I will share with you how.

"You each possess a portion of what is left of bin Laden's money. We will use it to pay our way into the United States, and then we will destroy it not from without, but rather from within. We have 'Our Man' on the inside. He has provided us with the necessary identifications and access codes to eliminate all of the leaders of the American government in one glorious battle. We will destroy them at a time when they are the center of the world's attention.

"After the attack, I will remain in Washington and control their weapons from the Pentagon. You each have an assigned city to command, as you will. We have over one million soldiers each with their own personal arsenal inside America as we speak. They are waiting patiently for our attack. Emir has given you an address to report to in each city. That is the rendezvous point for our men in each city. We are only taking the coastal cities, to prevent international assistance from reaching the American people. The middle of the country will be crippled." Sultan unraveled a map of the United States on the table in front of them. He pointed as he explained, "We will take: Boston, New York, Philadelphia, Washington, Charlotte, Atlanta, Miami, New Orleans, and Houston on the East Coast; on the West Coast," he moved his finger to the other side of the map, "Seattle, Portland, San Francisco, Los Angeles, and San Diego."

"Are there any questions?"

PART I

The King's Gambit

CHAPTER 1

The livery car emerged from the Queens-Midtown Tunnel. There was no greater frustration than rush hour traffic on the Long Island Expressway. Max Noble, the thirty-two year old newly elected member of the House of Representatives, now realized that he should have used the Long Island Rail Road to get to his first public appearance since taking his oath of office just after the New Year, two weeks prior. He knew this for sure: Never keep one thousand registered voters who paid five hundred dollars per plate in suspense, for they will never let you live it down.

"I can't believe you, Maxwell Noble!" she started. Valerie Mintz, Max's wife of two years, who happened to be the most popular model in the industry, was less than pleased with his newfound success, mostly because it stole the spotlight from her. "I told you to pick me up from the city at two. What time do you show up? Four! Now we have to sit here! My Burberry skirt is going to wrinkle! We're going to miss your dinner, you know?"

"We'll make it," Max replied. "Just relax." The two stared out their respective windows for the rest of the ride. The silence was eerie.

Valerie was the right-now girl, not the right girl. Max knew that from the day he met her. His hair was jet black, and closely cropped; hers was long, blonde, and lively. His eyes were mahogany; hers were steel blue. He was the publisher of the trend setting magazine, *Intensity*; she was a young model looking for a break. They were perfect for each other's careers. She sold his magazines, and he made her dreams of being a cover girl come true. After a year of dating, he asked her to marry him. The engagement lasted another rocky year, but the wedding went off without a hitch.

Valerie's career took her all over the world. Max was faithful, but needed something to occupy his time. The magazine was a success; he bought a house on Long Island and quickly became involved in the things going on in the neighborhood. He preferred the serenity of Long Island to the noise of New York City at the end of the workday.

Knowing that Max ran a successful magazine, Jack Armstrong, the Chairman of the Nassau County Democratic Party, took an immediate liking to him. Republicans had controlled Long Island for nearly a century. The combination of poorly timed scandals and Armstrong's leadership allowed the Democrats to make inroads. While Armstrong's organization had taken the local towns, he had yet to send someone to Washington. Max was the perfect candidate: young, wealthy, hardworking, Jewish (in a predominantly Jewish Congressional district), and one-half of the most perfect marriage in America. At least, it appeared that way.

Armstrong asked Max to run for Congress on a Sunday evening in April. The nominating convention was the next month. Valerie, who was in town for the evening, was excited about the idea of having a candidate for a husband. It would put her at the center of a new stage in Washington, a town not known for the beauty of its temporary residents. She failed to realize the strain it would place on her career and her marriage.

Campaigning was hard work for Max and Valerie. At the train stations in the morning while shaking hands with commuters, Max promised to improve the mass transit system. Next, he went to the campaign office to discuss the day's strategy with Bob Dalton, his campaign manager. All Armstrong knew of Dalton was that Max insisted on following his every bit of advice, and that he was a mammoth, intimidating man. Dalton was Max's biggest supporter. He was also a veteran of Vietnam; as far as he was concerned, the war was still raging. Although he was a registered Conservative, Dalton agreed to back Max's run for Congress because he was a political outsider, and the regime could never be trusted. Dalton sent Max to different neighborhoods to walk door-to-door during the day. When Max was done, he, Dalton, and Armstrong would meet to talk about fundraising for the campaign; it would take nearly two million dollars to win. Following a brief nap, Max would go to different civic meetings, sometimes until midnight. The next day brought a similar routine. Even when she showed up to help, Valerie never saw Max.

The hard work paid off. November brought victory. Valerie became nothing but a memory to Max. When she confronted him about it, he resigned to silence. Her only purpose now was to be a prop on his arm for the rest of his political career.

Thus, continued their car ride to dinner.

* * *

The car pulled up by the rear entrance to DiCarlo's. Owned and operated by the Corvalo family, the most powerful organized crime syndicate on Long Island, DiCarlo's was the forum for every political gathering for Republicans and Democrats. The unwritten rule was that every incumbent held his or her fundraisers there, and the restaurant took a percentage.

Dalton smoked his cigar in the doorway lost in the clutter of his own thoughts. Steam rose from his bald scalp in the winter night. His eyes were hidden behind his sunglasses as if to shadow the whisperings in his head. Politics was a dirty business, and no one was to be trusted. He hoped Max realized that by now. If he didn't, Dalton was going to be his drill sergeant. This neophyte would not fall victim to dissention on Dalton's watch. As the car came to a halt, Dalton extinguished his cigar on the heel of his size fourteen cowboy boot. Slowly, he strolled over to the rear car door, glancing around as if his head sat upon a swivel.

Dalton opened the door and extended his gigantic hand. "Valerie, you're beautiful as ever. When are you gonna drop this bum and give me a try?"

"Just as soon as you do the same, you big oaf," she quipped as she kissed his bearded cheek. She pulled a facial hair from her lipstick, and complained, "Bob, you know, what you lack in hair up top, you more than make up for with that bushy thing." With that she pivoted, and went into DiCarlo's. Dalton flipped her "the bird" as she strutted down the concrete catwalk. The glass door slammed behind her as she rushed inside.

"There's no way this marriage is going to last until the end of my term," Max declared as he stepped out of the car.

"Maxie, that may be the best thing that could ever happen to you," Dalton replied. "Trust me, you can find pussy that smells a lot better than that skank."

"How do you really feel, Bob?" Max asked sarcastically.

"Actually, I don't think this was such a good idea."

"What wasn't?"

"This dinner."

"Why not?"

"I don't know. It's too soon. Everybody loves you right now because you're the new guy. But the people change their minds with a drop of a hat. One fuck-up tonight and you could be the laughing stock of Long Island, Washington, hell . . . the whole fucking world!"

Max laughed out loud. "Bobby! You kill me. No way

I can fuck this all up in one night. Jack is here right?"

"Shit, yeah!"

"Good. Then all I have to do is find him, get my cues on who the 'honored guests' are, and give one hell of a great speech. Easy as pie."

"Better you than me. I'd tell half those old farts to shove their money up their ass!"

"That's why you stay out here." Max reached into his coat pocket and pulled out a cigar. "This should keep you company while I'm inside," he said as he handed the cigar to Dalton.

"Knock 'em dead, Mr. Max!"

"Only for you, Mr. Bob!"

Max turned, and made for the door. Valerie stood in the doorway shivering as she waited for him. "Hurry up! I'm freezing," she whined.

"OK, I'm here. Let's go," Max answered as he hurried Valerie inside to the coatroom with his right arm. They took off their coats, checked each other's appearances, and plastered on the most insincere smiles they could muster. Hand-in-hand, they entered the dining hall.

The hall's ceiling was covered with a reprint of the Sistine Chapel. Michelangelo would have fumed if he knew that his life's work was replicated in such an unholy place in one day by a team of wallpaper hangers. Max hated the tackiness of DiCarlo's, but Armstrong insisted that if Max were to be considered a real player in this game, DiCarlo's would have to be his arena.

"Valerie, you look stunning as always," Armstrong pronounced as he approached the couple. The crowd began to applaud. "And Max, so happy you could join us." Armstrong shook Noble's hand, pulled him near, and whispered in his ear, "Tommy Corvalo, table three; Bill Worthington, table eight; and Elizabeth Magnuson, table nine."

Max stepped back and waved. "Thank you, thank you," he shouted over the applause as he wound his way through the room shaking hands with every person on his path. When he reached table three, he made certain to stop, and personally thank Tommy Corvalo, the "street boss" of the Corvalo crime family. "Mr. Corvalo, you're the greatest!"

"Welcome, Congressman Noble," Corvalo replied.

"Mr. Corvalo, please. You get to call me 'Max.'"

Corvalo smiled, kissed Max on both cheeks, and raised his glass. "Salute!" he exclaimed as he drank his scotch.

Max continued his stroll. Bill Worthington was the managing partner at Worthington, O'Donnell, Katz, and Brown, the largest law firm on Long Island. He bought four tables, totaling twenty thousand dollars. "Mr. Worthington," Max started, "thank you for all of your support. Please call me whenever you're in Washington. Do you have my home phone number down there?"

"No," he replied. "But call my office on Monday, and leave the number with my secretary. I'll be sure to take you up on that offer." Max knew that he would, and it wouldn't be a completely social call either.

Next, Max made a b-line for table nine. "Elizabeth, you look radiant," Max proclaimed. Elizabeth Magnuson was a high-profile power broker and the heiress to the largest real estate development firm on Long Island. Not a single office building or apartment building went up without her approval. Worthington began his career as her attorney. "I wouldn't be here without you."

"Oh, stop, it Maxie. You got here on your own. I just gave you a leg up. But when Bill told me that we were seated next to each other, I knew that I had to wear something special," she answered. Max, puzzled, looked at Worthington.

"Oh, Liz, I'm a happily married man. You know that," Worthington interjected.

Awkwardly, Max turned to Magnuson, "Well, we aim to please."

"And you have," she replied as she winked at Worthington. "You have, indeed." Max just smiled and nodded and made his way up to the dais.

The podium stood at the center of the dais, between Armstrong and Max's seats. Valerie, of course, warmed Max's other side. Armstrong stood, and approached the podium. "Ladies and gentlemen, good evening. At this time, let us all take a moment to rise for a moment of silence to remember our fallen brothers and sisters brave enough to risk their lives preserving democracy in the United States Armed Forces, to be followed by the Pledge of Allegiance." The audience unquestionably complied, remaining perfectly silent until Armstrong led them in reciting the Pledge of Allegiance.

"Thank you," Armstrong began as the guests took their seats. The light beaming on the podium made it difficult for him to see the crowd. He shaded his eyes with his right hand. "Wow! That light is bright. Can we turn it down? No? OK, Max, you'll have to deal." The crowd laughed. "Ladies and gentlemen, we come together tonight to congratulate Congressman Max Noble, a dedicated, diligent Democrat, desirous of defending democracy." There was a pause for a standing ovation. "His tenure has lasted two weeks, and he has not done anything substantial yet; otherwise, I would have more to say." The crowd laughed heartily once again. "So, instead of listening to all of the wonderful things I will be able to say about Max one year from now, let's let him tell you himself." Applause broke out again. "Ladies and gentlemen, Congressman Max Noble!" exclaimed Armstrong over the second standing ovation of the evening.

Max stood at the podium. He was shorter than Armstrong, but not terribly short. He was a man of modest stature. He reached up, and adjusted the microphone as his supporters took their seats. He held out his arms and smiled as they continued to applaud. He squinted to avoid the pain of the lights on his eyes. Fortunately, he had his speech memorized.

"Thank you. Thank you," Max patiently responded. "Ladies and gentlemen, thank you for letting me represent you. The people truly govern the United States of America, as you have proven. I will not let you down!" Another ovation broke out.

When the jubilee subsided, Max continued. "There is no greater honor that can be bestowed upon me than your accolades. I was elected to speak your minds, and to vote your hearts. However, I must utilize caution in doing so, for these are dangerous times, and we do not always agree as to the best course of action.

"Enemies lurk both without and within. Security is more than a word: It is a mantra. We must protect life at all costs, and challenge those who seek to destroy it. No longer can we afford to stand idly by while plans are in motion to cause our towers to burn.

"However, we are also governed by the Constitution, and the ideals upon which it was founded. The rights of all Americans must be protected. No citizen should have his or her privacy invaded in the name of 'security.' Due process must be afforded to all, regardless of whether or not they seek it. That is the price of freedom, and a sacrifice we must make.

"America cannot be destroyed from without. Our enemies know this. That is why they seek to attack us from within. But they cannot, and they will not, pierce our defenses!"

An ovation broke out once again. Three ovations and Max had yet to finish the introduction of his speech. It was a good night, until the shots rang out.

* * *

Dalton heard three gunshots. Visions of Vietnam flashed before him. He threw his cigar to the side, and ran into the dining hall.

It was chaos. The guests were scrambling, not knowing if the gunman was still present. As Dalton made his way into the madness, a short white man with a blonde goat-tee, and a mullet ran straight into him and fell to the ground. Dalton looked down, and saw a gun lying next to him. He reached out his oversized paw, and grabbed the stunned chap by his throat. Dalton lifted him up toward the ceiling. "Did you get him?" Dalton growled as he tightened his grasp.

"N-N-No," the gunman replied in fear for his life. Tears ran from his eyes as his face turned beet-red from Dalton's grip. With that, Dalton dropped him to the ground, and punted his head as if it were a football. The gunman went unconscious immediately. Dalton threw the limp body over his shoulder; he picked up the gun and placed it in his pocket. When the police arrived, Dalton would hand them everything but a confession. He carried the culprit to the dais to survey the damage for himself.

"Bob!" Armstrong shouted. "Bob! He's all right! He's fine!"

"I'm NOT fine!" Max cried.

"What did this fucker do?" Dalton asked. Looking down, he saw the horror. Valerie's lifeless body floated in a pool of her own blood. Blood was seeping out of the two holes: one in her chest, the other in her neck.

Max held his wife's head, and wept. Guilt consumed him. He was the target. "I couldn't see through the lights," he said through his tears.

Dalton looked toward the back of the room. It was an obvious tactic. Blind the enemy so he can't see the shooter. "Fuck me!" he muttered as he shook his head. He should have checked the room, and he knew it.

"I heard the first shot, and I just stood there," Max sobbed.

"Valerie's maternal instincts took over," Armstrong interjected. "She knocked him back, and took the next two bullets for him."

"I'm sorry, Max," Dalton sympathetically stated. He had not seen a bullet-ridden body up close since his last tour of duty. However, it was not a sight one easily forgets. He knew that Max was now as much of a veteran as he. This night would haunt him forever.

Dalton had just received an unsolicited promotion. Now, he would not only have to teach Max how to be a politician, but also how to deal with the death of his wife. There was no telling what damage had been done. The dust would take months to settle. By the time re-election came around, Max would have to pretend this night never existed. The challenge seemed immediately impossible. To Dalton, that meant it was improbable.

"Why?" Max screamed as he sobbed. "Why? Why?"

* * *

The police finally arrived. They began their investigation by sectioning off the crime scene. Dalton handed them the gunman and the gun. The officers pulled Max away from the body. They took statements from Max, Dalton, Armstrong, and all the other witnesses who remained on the premises. Two officers in navy windbreakers placed a sheet over Valerie's body. It immediately became saturated in her blood.

CHAPTER 2

The President of the United States was sitting at his desk in the Oval Office when his Chief Domestic Policy Advisor, Simon McKenzie, entered trying to catch his breath.

"Mr. President," he began, thankful for the opportunity to pause while he waited for President Cole's acknowledgement of his presence. Cole nodded. "It's all over the networks. Congressman Noble's wife has been killed in what appears to be an assassination attempt."

"Two days before the State of the Union?" Cole replied. "Who claimed responsibility? Hamas? Al Qaeda?"

"So far, no one," McKenzie answered. "But the State of the Union harps on how secure you've made the nation. While I believe you have, Mr. President, it may be construed as insincere to harp upon it, in light of today's events."

Cole leaned back in his chair pondering the question. Thomas Jackson Cole served three terms as Governor of Missouri. A die-hard Republican, Cole towed the conservative line all the way. He was anti-abortion, anti-gay marriage, anti-working class, and anti-Noble. Not that he knew Max Noble, personally; however, Noble was a Democrat who campaigned on the opposite positions. Now, Noble would be the center of the media storm, stealing it from the State of the Union. Cole knew the only move he could make would be to show sympathy.

"Let's see who carried out this attack," the President said decisively. "If it was a recognized terrorist organization, as I suspect it was, we can be sympathetic to Noble, and keep the emphasis on security for the future."

"Yes, sir, Mr. President."

* * *

McKenzie sat in his office with Janet Marks, the President's Press Secretary. He was preparing her for the President's position on the Noble issue, in case any reporters asked questions at the daily noon press briefing. It had not changed since his conversation with the President the prior night. Only now, the suspect had been fully identified.

"Billy Ray Johnson of Alabama drove up to Long Island to kill a Jewish Congressman because he wanted to prove himself to the Ku Klux Klan?" McKenzie asked in disbelief. "That can't be right."

"Apparently, he confessed," Marks replied, citing the facts from the Nassau County Police Department's press release. "According to the Nassau Police Commissioner, 'Johnson admitted to killing Valerie Mintz-Noble. His intended target was Congressman Max Noble. Johnson left Alabama two days prior after being denied admission to the Ku Klux Klan because his courage had been questioned. He believed that killing a prominent Jew would prove his worth.'"

"This country is fucking sick," McKenzie replied. He was a Republican who believed that taxes were too high, and he feared that a Democratic Congress would destroy family values. But even in his vision of America, biased attacks could not be tolerated. "Have we talked to Justice about an FBI investigation?"

"Attorney General Taylor won't issue a public comment until he gets word from the President," Marks replied.

"Well, that's the first time he's ever said that. Do you

think it has anything to do with the fact that he is from Alabama?" McKenzie queried with a hint of sarcasm.

"If I was in his position, I wouldn't touch this with a ten-foot pole. You'd better believe that the Klan knows where he lives."

"But if the President doesn't order an FBI investigation, the Jews will be all over him crying anti-Semitism. I'll get an answer from the President. In the meantime, tell the press that, 'The President offers his deepest condolences to the Mintz and Noble families, and in particular, Congressman Noble. As a gesture of good faith, he is formally excusing the Congressman from the State of the Union so that he may properly grieve the loss of his beloved wife. The President also believes that there is no room in America for violent acts of discrimination.' How does that sound?"

"Perfect," Marks replied. "I especially like the part about excusing him from the State of the Union. It shows the President's compassionate side. What about the security message in the State of the Union?"

"I'll find out about that when I talk to him about the FBI probe."

* * *

"Come in," Cole called.

"Good morning, Mr. President," McKenzie brightly offered.

"Good morning, Simon. Where are we on this whole thing?"

"Well, Mr. President, the good news is that Janet is going to tell the press that you are excusing Noble from the State of the Union so he can grieve, and that discrimination cannot be tolerated."

"That is good news. What's the bad news?"

"The Attorney General won't start an FBI investigation into this Johnson guy or the Klan without a direct order from the President."

"Barton Taylor was always a pompous ass!"

"Janet and I think it has something to do with the fact that he's from Alabama, and he is afraid the Klan will retaliate in his yard."

"So be it! That's the price of public service. Get on the phone with Taylor, and order the investigation into Johnson's story. Tell Janet the same thing. Going after the Klan can be his decision, and he can pin it all on Johnson acting alone if he wants. Either way, there'll be justice at the end of the day."

"What about the security portion of the State of the Union?"

"This is an isolated biased crime, not a terrorist act. The American people can still rest easy. Leave the speech as it is. The United States is still the most secure nation in the world."

"Yes, sir, Mr. President."

* * *

"Yitgadal, v'yitgadash, sh'mei raba," Max prayed. The Hebrew words of the Mourner's Kaddish, the Jewish prayer for the souls of the dead, were more chilling on his bones than the frigid January winds. Over his shoulder, he could hear the sobs of Valerie's mother; he could feel the rage radiating from her father. As they stood graveside, the guilt mounted on Max's conscience. Gravity pulled the tears from his eyes, but they froze on his cheeks before they could flow.

Valerie's coffin was lowered into the ground when the service was over. Her father grabbed the shovel, and hoisted a clump of soil onto his daughter's casket. He never thought he would be tucking his daughter permanently away with an earthen blanket. Mrs. Mintz screamed when the thud sounded as the dirt landed. Max took the shovel from Mr. Mintz; the stare between the two was colder than the temperature.

Max piled three massive heaps of dirt on top of the coffin, one for each bullet intended for him. While Mrs. Mintz heard three thumps from the earth, Max heard the gunshots again. He fell to his knees and wept when he had finished the ceremonial burial. Cameramen and photographers from the press and the paparazzi, who stayed far enough away as not to interfere with the funeral (although their presence made most feel uncomfortable), filmed and photographed the fallen Congressman on the ground. Armstrong and Dalton cringed, as they knew that would be the image associated with the name "Max Noble" throughout the United States. Max remained prone for a few minutes. Finally, Dalton approached him, and lifted him up by the shoulder. "Come on, Max. Time for us to go home," Dalton assured Max as he led him to the limousine. Max sobbed audibly.

Max rode in the limousine with the Mintzes. It was not a pleasant ride. Valerie's parents thought the world of Max until this tragedy. Now, they resented him; they held him accountable for their daughter's death. Despite Valerie's own fame, they felt that it was Max's run for Congress that brought danger to her. Politics brought more than fame; beliefs were involved, and emotions ran high. Fashion brought fame without hitting the panic button.

Armstrong and Dalton rode in the car behind the limousine. They knew the torment the ride with the Mintzes would bring to Max. Max did not grow up in a conventional household. When he married Valerie, the Mintzes took him in as their son; it was the first time he experienced life with a normal family. Now, they would disown him.

Armstrong was worried that Max would turn inward. He and Dalton were the only people left in Max's support system. They were his only family now.

"You know, we're going to be the ones who take care of him," Armstrong relayed to Dalton.

"Yeah, I know. We'll do whatever we have to do."

"Bob, we need to watch him closely. Mentally, I don't think he can handle it all. He loses Val. And then he has to learn to be a Congressman? He's not cut out for it."

"He's a lot tougher than you think. He knows how to survive."

"Well, I'm going to stay with him. I'll watch him. But you have to make sure his people don't desert him."

"They won't. That's a promise. But it's going to be a lot harder once that shot of him on his knees hits the papers."

"Yeah, I saw that, too. It makes him look weak. How do we counteract that?"

"For now, we do nothing. Let him heal. Time is our greatest ally. Give him a month to lay low. Then, when he returns to Washington, we bolster his image by showing him as someone who is dedicated, and diligent. When reelection rolls around, he'll be stronger than any other incumbent in Congress."

"At least the President excused him from the State of the Union. That should take the public eye off for a while."

"Cole only excused him to bolster his own image as a compassionate, caring individual," Dalton stated adamantly. "He didn't do it for Max. He'd have rather seen the bullets hit Max. There'd be one less liberal for him to deal with in the House." After an awkward pause, Dalton chuckled. "You liberals! You always make us conservatives look like we have no heart. Go smoke your weed, and cry me a fucking river!"

"Why did you help Max out, again? Oh yeah, you don't trust Cole. That's right!"

"No, I said I don't trust Republicans. Cole is the Commander in Chief. I support any man given power by the Constitution. I fought for this fucking country to protect your fucking Constitutional rights! I support the Office of the President regardless of political party. But since the Republicans have controlled both houses, there have been a lot of injustices. They've reneged on every promise they've ever made! No tax cuts. No welfare reform. Increased deficits. And a blind war against an enemy we can't find. When you told me you had a new guy who I could mold into someone who would do right by the American people, I had to swallow my pride and support a fucking liberal Democrat!"

"And how does that make you feel?"

"Fuck you!"

"Good! Glad to hear you're still on board!"

"Fuck you!"

"Does that mean you'll back Max's reelection bid?"

"Fuck you!"

Armstrong chortled. He knew that Dalton would stick with Max. He was a blowhard, and he had to have his occasional meltdowns. But when push came to shove, Armstrong knew that Dalton was loyal.

"Truce?" Armstrong offered.

"Fuck you!" Dalton bellowed.

"Will you at least watch the State of the Union with Max and me tonight?"

"Fine," Dalton replied.

CHAPTER 3

The fanfare blasting through Max Noble's television was almost regal. It was the introductory music to the broadcast of the State of the Union. Dalton hated watching the "liberal" media; he preferred a network with conservative leanings. "Do we have to watch it on ABS?" he asked referring to the American Broadcasting System. "Bill Leach is such a fucking pansy," he stated, referring to ABS' number one anchorman who brought most Americans their nightly and breaking news.

Armstrong sat next to Dalton on the black leather couch in the study of Max's home. Max was in the bedroom at the end of the hall, but he was aware that the only two people in the world who gave a damn about him were in the other room. Armstrong leaned toward Dalton and whispered, "Bob, maybe just for tonight you could keep your opinions to yourself. For Max's sake."

From the other room, Max yelled, "The First Amendment shouldn't take a backseat to my feelings, Jack. He can say whatever he wants in my house." Max made his way into the study, taking his seat behind the mahogany desk. "No matter how ignorant it is," he stated as he shot Dalton a look that could kill.

"See," Dalton gloated, "he has a little 'conservative' in him." Dalton flashed a gigantic grin as he placed his hands on the back of his head and reclined, savoring every moment of his pyrrhic victory. Armstrong looked at Dalton, then at Max, and shook his head in disgust.

"Good evening," Bill Leach began through the

television speakers, "I'm Bill Leach welcoming you to this broadcast of President Cole's State of the Union Address to the United States Congress."

"Do you think we'll get any mention?" Dalton asked.

"I don't want people to feel sorry for me, Bob," Max replied.

Bill Leach continued. "For the first time ever, the Congressional chamber is filled with every member of Congress, including the Vice President and the Speaker of the House of Representatives who will be seated behind the President as is the custom; every member of the President's Cabinet; all nine Supreme Court Justices; each of the Joint Chiefs of Staff; and the head of every federal agency. President Cole must have something of great importance to announce since anyone who is anyone in this great nation is here tonight. There is quite a buzz in the air."

"Is he fucking kidding?!," Dalton inquired as he jumped off the couch. "Not everyone is there! The most important Congressman ever to be elected is sitting right here with me on Long Island!"

"Relax, Bob," Max cautioned. "I haven't done anything to make me 'anyone who is anyone' yet."

"I don't give a flying fuck! I told you Leach is a fucking pansy! He can't even get his fucking facts straight."

"Bob!" Armstrong exclaimed as he raised himself to stare Dalton in the eyes, "Get a hold of yourself! Just sit down and watch the damned speech. Let these fools have the nation's undivided attention. Max could use a break from the spotlight for a little while."

"He's right, Bob," Max agreed. "I think I'm going to lie down and get some sleep. Let me know what the big announcement is in the morning."

Armstrong looked worried. "Are you sure? We can

gag Bob with duct tape to keep his mouth shut."

"Try it, hippie!" Dalton joked.

Max chuckled. "It's alright, guys. I'm just exhausted. A good night's sleep should take care of everything. Let yourselves out after the speech, and call me in the morning to wake me." With that, he left the study and made for the bedroom to get the rest he desperately needed. He couldn't help but think to himself how ironic it was that he would get the rest he needed knowing that Valerie would not be there to bother him in the morning. When he reached the study doorway, he paused and turned to his friends, "And guys," he said almost weeping, "thank you."

"You're welcome," they said together. When they heard the door to the bedroom close, they turned their attention back to the television. While Armstrong wasn't looking, Dalton changed the channel to his favorite conservative network, the Satellite Broadcasting Network, which was more commonly known as, "SBN." "Sucker!" Dalton taunted.

"Whatever makes you happy, Bob. I'm too worried about Max to care about this stupid speech anymore."

"Fine, but you're still watching it with me."

"As long as you keep your voice down so Max can sleep."

"Deal," Dalton declared as they shook hands and took their respective seats on the couch.

"Mr. Speaker, the President of the United States," and thunderous applause rang through the television.

"President Cole," explained Harry York, the news anchor, "has entered the Congressional chamber and has begun shaking hands with his allies from both sides of the political aisle. It is remarkable how great of a man the President is that he has been able to work with the

Left. Tonight's announcement, whatever it is, will surely be criticized for all the wrong reasons by the liberals."

Armstrong shot Dalton a menacing look. "Don't say a word, Jack," Dalton warned. "I don't want to hear it."

"And now, ladies and gentlemen," York continued, "President Cole is taking the podium, and SBN is proud to bring you the State of the Union Address."

Dalton and Armstrong stared at the television screen. "Thank you," Cole began. "Thank you. My fellow Americans, tonight is a historic night for this great nation. Because of our brave soldiers and their valiant and relentless battles in the war on terrorism, our nation is more secure today than ever before." A five minute and twenty-six seconds long standing ovation ensued. Then, the screen went black.

"What the fuck?" Dalton wondered aloud. He grabbed the remote and flipped the channel to ABS. It, too, was black. He flipped to every major channel that carried the national news. Their broadcasts, too, were entirely black. "This is fucked up. How can they all have lost the signal at the same time?"

"Do you think they lost the satellite signal?" Armstrong asked.

"Must have," Dalton stated. "There is no other logical explanation. Call it the soldier in me, but I am worried that something else may have happened."

"Don't be ridiculous, Bob. Cole just said how secure the nation is."

"Never trust a politician, Jack. They're all a bunch of fucking liars looking to boost their poll numbers with some good sound bites."

"Even Max?"

"No, he hasn't had the chance to join their club yet. He's not 'anyone who is anyone in this great nation,' remember? Fucking Leach!"

* * *

Dalton spent nearly two hours exhausting every avenue to find out what was happening. He sat at Max's desk surfing the Internet and calling every person whose phone number was stored in his cell phone. There was nothing on the Internet other than conservative bloggers and conspiracy theorists blaming the "liberal" media for a boycott of the President. He would have loved to believe that, but the fact that SBN went black, too, contradicted that theory. The longer it went on, the more he sensed that something was terribly wrong.

Without warning, the picture came back. "Oh my God!" Armstrong exclaimed. "Bob, look at this."

Dalton made his way from behind the desk and stood next to the couch. "What the fuck?!" The camera was focused on the vacant podium in the Congressional chamber. Behind it the bodies of the Vice President and the Speaker of the House lay slumped in their chairs, each with a bullet hole in their forehead and their blood and brain matter splattered on the American flag behind them. Dalton recognized those entry wounds from Vietnam; they were killed at close range. "What the fuck is going on?!"

"I think I am going to be sick," Armstrong replied. "Where the hell is the President?"

The camera began to pan the chamber. The lifeless body of its assigned Member of Congress occupied each floor seat, and the guests in the audience who applauded from the mezzanine were also motionless. Bullet holes riddled the columns and balcony. Each aisle was filled with men wearing all black, including black ski masks, standing single file, each at attention with his AK-47 machine gun resting comfortably on his right shoulder. The camera completed its circle of the chamber. Only this time, one of the men in black stood behind the podium.

"Bob, they've annihilated the entire government!"

"No shit, Jack! Anything else you want to share with me?"

"Well, they actually missed someone," Armstrong stated. Armstrong and Dalton looked at each other. Their heads turned simultaneously toward the bedroom. They knew that as soon as the gunmen figured out that Max was alive, they would be coming for him. Armstrong broke the silence. "Max is in danger."

"Absolutely. But these fuckers are gonna have to kill me first!" Dalton reached under his left shoulder and pulled out his revolver. He ran to the window and began to survey the grounds. "It's quiet out there, now. We'll have to wake him and move him."

"Wait, this guy is about to say something," Armstrong noted pointing to the television. The man behind the podium placed his gun on the floor next to him and removed his ski mask. He was a man in his late thirties of Arabic descent with a thick, but short, beard. The look on his face was uncompromising and angry.

"Infidels," he began, "your President expresses his regret that he could not introduce me himself. But he is still with us tonight." The man reached down and held up the decapitated head of President Cole. The gunmen all cheered and fired their weapons in the air.

"My name is Mohammed al-Fassad. I am your Sultan of the new Islamic Republic of America." Again, the gunmen cheered and fired their weapons in the air. "I am hereby taking control of your government's operations, including all operations at your Pentagon. My Caliphate shall control your cities. Each of my Caliphs now has direct control over a region of the country. Do not attempt to resist; we have over one million mujahadeen. The Caliphs now control Boston, New York, Philadelphia,

Washington, Charlotte, Atlanta, Miami, New Orleans, Houston, Seattle, Portland, San Francisco, Los Angeles, and San Diego. From the Pentagon, I will be monitoring all of your actions by satellite.

"We have all of the records of every soldier and police officer throughout the land. Each of you is being given the opportunity to surrender at your local post office by noon tomorrow. Those of you who choose not to comply will be hunted down and publicly executed along with your families. Make no mistake; any efforts toward insurrection will be crushed immediately. Before this broadcast, I ordered all of your nuclear weapons to be targeted at your cities. Just as you have held the world hostage for decades with your weapons of terror, you are now hostages of them." The gunmen saluted Sultan with cheers and fired their weapons in the air one last time before the television screen went black again.

Armstrong's and Dalton's eyes met in awe. "Bob, what are we going to do?"

"We're not going to sit by idly while this asshole tries to take over our country!"

"Bob, he has taken over the country."

"Then we take it back!"

"How? We can't take on a million-man army!"

"Let me handle the military ops, Jack. You just wake Max and get him ready to be sworn in."

"Sworn in as what?"

"President of the United States."

CHAPTER 4

Armstrong roused Max from his slumber. Placing his hand over Max's mouth and his finger over his lips to indicate the importance of silence, Armstrong whispered to him, "The big announcement never came. You're in grave danger. Bob went to get the car. We're getting you out of here." Puzzled, Max attempted to speak. Armstrong quickly interrupted, "We'll explain everything in the car. Get dressed. Pack a bag. Let's go."

Armstrong led Max out of the house while Dalton waited in his black sport utility vehicle with the engine running. Out of paranoia that snipers could be anywhere, Dalton told Armstrong to make Max cover his head with a black overcoat to avoid having any movements detected by night-vision scopes. When they reached the car, Max went to sit in the back seat; Dalton made him lay prone on the floor.

Finally, Max broke the silence. "What the hell is going on?"

"We're taking you to Judge Vineri's house," Armstrong answered.

"Alright," Max replied in a state of confusion. "Why are you taking me to see the most senior judge on the Second Circuit? I know he's my constituent, but I don't think he likes midnight house calls. Most constituents don't."

"I called him to tell him that we're on our way," Dalton offered. "He couldn't be happier to hear from me."

"Listen, guys," Max stated sternly, "cut the crap. Jack, you said I'm in danger. You make me sneak out of my own house with an overnight bag while covering myself with a black coat, and now you have me stuffed on the floor of Bob's car, and the most powerful judge in New York is waiting for me. Somebody talk to me!"

Dalton steamed, "Max, for your own fucking good, shut the fuck up and trust us! The judge will explain everything. The world has changed in a split second, and I hope you got enough sleep through it to keep up."

Armstrong tried to comfort Max as best he could. "Listen, just go with the flow on this one. I promise you, it is the last time you will ever be 'out of the loop.'"

* * *

Judge Arthur Vineri sat in his personal library awaiting the arrival of Congressman Max Noble. The Italian-American was the chief judge of the Second Circuit in New York, making him one of the most powerful judges in the nation; especially, since the Supreme Court justices had just been murdered. On the desk in front of him sat two open books: A pocket-sized copy of the Constitution of the United States, and the New Oxford Annotated Bible. He glanced back and forth between them looking for an overlapping passage.

Nothing. Neither made sense. And neither was relevant anymore. But people placed all of their faith in them for centuries. Though ceremonial at best, Judge Vineri knew that the forthcoming ritual was the most important moment in American history. He knew that the presidency must not be allowed to remain vacant one moment longer.

Judge Vineri, a former editor of the Columbia Law Review, had the text of the Constitution committed to memory. He had ruled on Constitutional law questions for thirty-one years, almost as long as Congressman Noble's entire life. The thought caused him to chuckle wryly. There would be no need for the book at the ceremony. As a devout Roman Catholic, the same could be said for the Bible he studied for years in Catholic school; however, its presence was required to add solemnity to the recitation of the Oath of Office. He wondered aloud which passage was most appropriate for the moment, "One Samuel Sixteen? Very possible," he noted, referring to the anointing of King David. Suddenly, through his window, he saw headlights appear at the driveway gates. He looked up at his wife, Mary, standing in the doorway in her nightgown and bathrobe.

"Why don't you let the young man decide, Dear," she asked her husband of forty-seven years.

"Do you think he is as well-versed in the Bible as I?"

"Arthur," she retorted, "no one outside of the cloth could make such a claim. But should he not be tested? He may yet surprise you."

"Oh, Mary. When I die, they will speak of my wisdom in my eulogy."

"Don't say such things at times like these, Arthur!"

"Let me finish!" he scolded. "The truth is that you are my wisdom. I owe everything in my life to you. You give me strength when I should have none. You give me courage when I am afraid. Tonight, I will break the law," he paused, ". . . technically. But at your insistence, I believe it to be the right thing to do. Ironic, don't you think?" The doorbell rang throughout the house. "Come, Dear. We have work to do."

Judge Vineri turned to attend to the business at hand. Mary grabbed his arm, looked him in the eye, kissed him, and told him, "I love you." Together, they descended the grand staircase into the foyer.

Moving the curtains next to the majestic oak door, Judge Vineri looked to see who was calling even though he knew who it was. His eyes lit up upon gazing at Max Noble, the next President of the United States. He hustled to open the door. "Please, please, come in. It is a great privilege to have you in my home Mr. . . ."

"Ahem," Dalton interrupted as he cleared his throat.

"Ah, yes," Judge Vineri replied, "I take it that you have given me the honor of breaking the news to him."

Armstrong replied, "Well, your Honor, we felt that you are the best suited to explain the, um . . ." Armstrong stumbled as he searched for the words, "legal ramifications."

"Where are your manners, Arthur?" Mary chimed in. "Mr. Noble, may I take your coat?"

"Of course," Max replied. He cordially thanked her as he handed her his black overcoat.

"Please forgive me," the judge begged. "Mary has been reminding me to watch my manners for forty-seven years. I don't know where I would have ended up without her."

"Ahem," Dalton interrupted again as the men followed Mary into the house. Judge Vineri closed the door.

"Oh, dear!" the judge exclaimed as he looked at Max in awe. "I guess that in all of the night's events, I have forgotten how horrible this day has been for you, Congressman. Please accept our deepest condolences on the tragic loss of your beloved Valerie."

"Thank you, your Honor," Max replied humbly, "In many ways, I feel that Valerie's death has saved me. It is as if I have a new opportunity . . . a chance to begin anew and devote myself to a higher calling."

"You should mourn the loss before offering messages of renewal," Mary suggested.

"To the contrary, Mary," the judge retorted, "I believe

that the ability to embrace a new beginning is the greatest asset Mr. Noble possesses given the circumstances."

"Your Honor, what am I doing here in your lovely home?" Max inquired.

"We are getting to that. Patience is another virtue a man in your position must possess."

Armstrong laughed. "We're still working on that one, your Honor."

"Very well, then. Let's sit in my library, and I will explain the, what did you call them, Jack, 'legal ramifications?'"

"Yes, your Honor," Armstrong replied.

"Bob, will you be joining us?" the judge asked.

"With all due respect, your Honor," Dalton began, "you have two witnesses in Mrs. Vineri and Jack, here. I've always believed that three is a crowd."

"Suit yourself, Bob," the judge replied. "But remember, you are giving up a front row seat to history."

"Thank you, your Honor. But I have my own work to do while you do yours. Otherwise, we won't have a history to speak of. I'll show myself out, and I will be back to pick Max and Jack up in the morning." Dalton made his way back to the door. He surveyed the grounds through the glass next to the door before opening it.

"Bob," Max pleaded, "where are you going?"

"Judge Vineri will explain everything, Mr. Max. I'll see you tomorrow. Sleep well. You're gonna need it." With that, Dalton left.

"Would anybody care for some coffee or tea?" Mary asked.

"Some decaf tea would be terrific, please," Max replied.

"Nothing for me, thank you," said Armstrong.

"I'm fine, thank you, Dear," the judge informed her. Mary left to prepare Max's tea and to allow the men to attend to the business at hand. "Well, gentlemen, follow me." Judge Vineri led Max and Armstrong to his library. Each man sat in a chair facing the judge, who stood behind his desk. The judge leaned on the edge of the desk looking down at Max, his arms supporting his torso like a lion purveying the savannah. "Congressman Noble," he began, "the worst has happened, and as there is much to explain to you, I will cut to the chase. You are now the President of the United States."

"WHAT?!?!" Max reacted. The shock caused the chair to jump with him.

"Relax, Max," Armstrong said in a soothing voice. "We're all going to help you with this."

"How is that possible?" Max wondered aloud. Mary walked into the room to bring Max his tea. He thanked her and took a sip, and she left the men again. He tolerated scolding his palate to relieve the cottonmouth that came over him.

The judge began explaining the turn of events that unfolded after Max went to sleep. He emphasized that it was highly unusual for every member of the government to attend the State of the Union for just this reason. He expounded how it was possible that President Cole wanted them all there to illustrate that the government was immune from harm; however, he surmised that, "The irony of that theory is too great to be a reality."

"The only plausible explanation was that someone orchestrated this from inside the government, and that the 'Sultan' and his men knew that this would be the time and place for a single, coordinated strike," the judge continued.

"Who could help from the inside?" Armstrong asked for clarification.

The judge stared at the floor for a moment. "It had to be someone who was in a position to influence the President. And you can rest assured that this person is still alive, and probably calling the shots from behind the scenes."

"But how do we know who the traitor is?" Max inquired.

"In time, his or her identity will become clear," the judge offered. "In the meantime, you must understand that your presidency will be extremely limited. The Constitution, through Article Two, Section One, Clause Five, and the Twenty-Fifth Amendment declares that the Vice President succeeds the President. This is common knowledge, and more importantly, common sense. In 1947, Title Three of the United States Code, Section Nineteen, was enacted to set forth that if there is no Vice President, then the Speaker of the House of Representatives succeeds to the presidency; if there is no Speaker, then it is the President pro tempore of the Senate; if there is none, then the Presidency succeeds to the Cabinet members."

Max stood and walked over to the window, staring at his ghostly reflection in the glass. "When does it succeed to a Congressman who has been in office for almost three weeks?" he asked.

Judge Vineri's voice grew bolder. "Under normal circumstances, it doesn't."

"Max, you are the only elected member of the Federal government left alive," Armstrong offered. "You are the only one who has any claim to the presidency."

"A claim that is tainted, nonetheless," the judge interrupted. "In addition to this question, you are not truly eligible for the Presidency because of your age; Article Two, Section One, Clause Four requires that the President be at least thirty-five years old. I apologize that all I know is that you are not yet thirty-five; how old are you?"

"I'm thirty-two," Max replied. "I'll be thirty-three next month. The twenty-second."

"Washington's birthday, you know?" the judge asked rhetorically.

"Yes, but that irony is reality, your Honor," Max quipped.

"Touché," the judge answered. He hated all of the quick-witted attorneys that appeared before him over the years. Yet he admired the quality in Max. "As I was saying, your presidency will be limited. In a few moments, I will administer the Oath of Office. I would imagine that as soon as word of this reaches the Republican Party, a lawsuit challenging your authority on both grounds would be filed. I have spoken with the senior judge of each of the Federal Circuits. Given the crisis facing the nation, we have all agreed to ignore, through various measures of red tape, these lawsuits for one year or until you remove this 'Sultan,' and whomever his person on the inside is, from power and restore our democracy."

"So, I have one year to lead our army to victory, and then I will have to relinquish the reigns because I am not eligible to do that in the first place, and there is no law that says that I should?"

"There is another wrinkle," Armstrong added. "You don't have an army to lead just yet. The 'Sultan' has demanded that all soldiers and police officers surrender to him or he will hunt them down and kill them and their families."

"You're joking, right?"

"Unfortunately, he's not," the judge grimly added. "And most, if not all, soldiers and police officers will probably choose to protect their families."

"How am I supposed to get an army that will take back the country in a year?"

"Why do you think Bob left so abruptly?" Armstrong suggested.

"I see," Max replied. "Is there anything else before we all break every law I will swear to defend?"

"We just need a second witness," the judge replied. "Mary!" he called.

Mary came into the room, beaming with pride. Max could tell that the judge's courage to participate in this rebel plan originated in her.

Judge Vineri reached over his desk and picked up the Bible. "Any particular passage I should turn to, Congressman?"

"Exodus Three Thirteen," Max said without hesitation.

"The burning bush," Mary offered, taken aback with his knowledge of the Good Book.

"It seems appropriate," Max replied. "It seems that God has sent me to answer this calling. And what better mantra by which to lead than His name itself, 'I Am Who I Am.'"

"Very impressive, Congressman," Judge Vineri stated. "Exodus Three Thirteen it is, then." The judge turned to the chapter and offered the book to Armstrong to hold during the ceremony. "Whenever you're ready, Congressman."

"Let's do it," Max said without hesitation. Armstrong held the book chest-high. Max walked over to him and faced the judge. Trembling, he placed his left hand on the open pages of the Bible and raised his right hand so that his open palm faced the judge.

"Ah, your full name is . . ."

"Maxwell Abraham Noble."

"Repeat after me, then," Judge Vineri instructed. "I, Maxwell Abraham Noble, do solemnly swear . . ."

Max repeated, "I, Maxwell Abraham Noble, do solemnly swear . . ."

"That I will faithfully execute the Office of President of the United States . . ."

"That I will faithfully execute the Office of President of the United States . . ."

"And will, to the best of my ability . . ."

"And will, to the best of my ability . . ."

"Preserve, protect and defend the Constitution of the United States."

"Preserve, protect and defend the Constitution of the United States. So help me God."

Judge Vineri extended his hand to Max. "Good luck, Mr. President."

CHAPTER 5

Dalton pulled up to the gates of Don Vito Corvalo's estate. The boss of the New York Mafia owned a twelve thousand square foot mansion on six acres of land complete with sixteen bedrooms, seven bathrooms and a five-car garage; somehow, he never paid a dime in property taxes and no local official dared to ask why. Three of his lower-level soldiers stood guard. Each wore a custom-tailored suit underneath a wool overcoat. From their pant legs, Dalton could see that one donned a blue suit with a pinstripe; one wore a solid gray suit; and the last one was dressed in a beige suit. The men in blue and gray were tall and brawny, and the man in beige was short and round; their guns swelled their overcoats under their left arms. The man in the blue suit recognized Dalton, and walked over to the driver's door of the car as Dalton rolled down the window.

"Bobby! I shoulda known! Can you believe this shit with these fuckin' towelheads?"

"What can I say, Boots?" Dalton replied. Pete "Boots" Ambrosino was Dalton's favorite of all of the Don's thugs. He earned his nickname from his choice of wardrobe as a street punk growing up in Brooklyn: Every day, regardless of the weather, he wore t-shirt, a backwards baseball cap, sweatpants, and a pair of oversized work boots with the laces wide open. "We're gonna have to kick some sandnigger ass!"

"Boots," the man in beige interrupted, "who is this fuckin' guy?" He reached his hand into his jacket and placed it on the handle of his gun.

"Cool your jets, you fuckin' hard on! This is Bobby Dalton. You know, Dalton Industrial? Bobby gave me my W-2 for the first two years after I got out of the Pen."

Dalton interjected, "My crews worked on every bridge and tunnel in New York. If it wasn't for me, and Don Vito of course, you fat ass would be stuck on this fuckin' island!"

"Who you callin' fat, Tubby?" the man in beige asked.

Realizing that the situation was about to get out of control, Boots stepped in. "Everybody fuckin' relax! We're all on the same side here. Bobby, this is Jimmy 'the Peach' DeMartino, and that's Joey 'Bam Bam' Santucci – watch it, he's got a short fuse."

Dalton waved to Bam Bam and shook the Peach's hand. "Nice to meet both of you. Why do they call you the Peach? You some kind of fuckin' fruit?"

"Why you mother fucker!" the Peach raged, again reaching for his gun. Boots and Bam Bam each grabbed one of the Peach's arms and threw him to the ground.

"Chill out, Peach! He's fuckin' around." Turning his attention to Dalton, Boots explained sternly, "Jimmy only has to shave that fuzz on his face once a month. So he's fuzzy and round, like a fuckin' peach! Get it? Now, what the fuck are you doin' here?"

"What do you think I'm here for, Boots? I need to speak with Don Vito."

"About what?"

"Boots, you know I can't tell you that. If Don Vito wants, he can tell you."

"Yeah, you're right." Boots went into the guardhouse and picked up a phone. The Peach picked himself up off the ground. Bam Bam put his hands up gesturing for the Peach to calm down. Boots opened the gate and told Dalton, "He'll give you fifteen minutes. Park in front and wait for him in his office. He said you know where that is."

"Of course I do, Boots. I was meeting with Don Vito while you were still in baby booties!" Dalton started to drive up the driveway to the main entrance to the mansion.

"You mother fucker!" Dalton heard faintly behind him. He was unsure if it was Boots or the Peach. But it did not matter to him. The Don agreed to see him, and he was much more important.

* * *

"Bobby, are you in trouble again?" Don Vito asked as he slowly descended the spiral staircase in his bathrobe to greet Dalton at the entrance to his office off the foyer. He was an older man in his late seventies with flowing silver locks and a deep suntan, despite the January cold; an eighteen carat gold crucifix dangled from the thick gold chain around his neck. The house was grand, and the artwork was exquisite. The lavish marble floor would have cost a hard-working man a fortune; Don Vito took it from a "bust-up" job when a poor, foolish mason could not resist the ponies. Dalton removed his hat out of respect upon hearing the Don's voice and stuffed it in his coat pocket. The only man he dared not insult was the Don.

As the Don approached, Dalton reached out and gently grabbed both of his hands. The men exchanged kisses on each other's cheeks. "I think we're all in trouble this time," was all he could reply.

"Are you afraid that these guys are gonna mess up business?" the Don began. He slowly ambled around the room. He pointed to the open chair in front of his desk, and Dalton immediately sat like an obedient puppy. "Because I'm not. They want money and power, but they realize that they can't have either. We'll get by without interference from the Feds now."

The Don sat down in his desk chair. He opened the cigar box on his desk – Cubans, of course – and tilted the box toward Dalton to take one. Avoiding insult, Dalton obliged. Don Vito pulled a cigar cutter from his pocket and cut off the ends of Dalton's cigar; after taking one for himself, he prepared his as well. Both men sniffed their treats. "Ahh," Dalton started, "now, this, is freedom!" The Don lit Dalton's cigar followed shortly by his own.

"These guys come near my operations, and they'll be wishing they flew a plane into a building!"

"Well, Don Vito," Dalton interjected, "these new events have changed the dynamic of things."

"I know. As I've told you, Bobby, it's great for us."

"Look, it's great that there'll be no Feds. But these guys are gonna shut everything down. They can't run a government. No government equals no services like trains or buses. No services equals no jobs. No jobs equals no money. Eventually, that hurts us." Dalton, done with his analysis, placed his cigar back in his mouth.

"Hmph," the Don grunted as he puffed his cigar and pondered the suggestion. "You know something, Bobby? You're right! How did I miss the big picture? We gotta get rid of these fuckin' guys. At least with the Feds you know where you stand. They arrest you, indict you, incarcerate you, but business goes on. These fuckin' guys ain't gonna play that game. They gotta go."

"That's my plan."

Don Vito started laughing so hard that his cackle could have woken the dead. Once he composed himself, he asked, "You have a plan?"

"I do. And a good one at that."

"This I gotta hear!"

"We start our own army."

"I fought in Korea, Bobby. My fighting days are over."

"I don't mean you and me. I mean everyone else we can get together."

"Bobby, listen," the Don began in a calm and collected tone, "soldiers go through months of training. They get paid to put their lives on the line. You can't pay them, you have no guns, and they have nothing to fight for. These guys are obviously well financed, and they have the entire American arsenal at their disposal. Not to mention that they gotta be pretty sophisticated to pull off what they just did. Name one time in history when a gang of rag-tag weekend warriors overthrew a well-oiled fighting machine. At least I can get guys close to their leaders and take them out."

"You're right," Dalton replied. "I can't pay anyone. But you're wrong about the rest. I got plenty of places to get guns. And we've got our freedom to fight for. Besides, I don't want your guys involved at all."

"Then what the fuck you doin' here?" Don Vito sounded insulted.

"These guys are putting all the cops behind bars. I need someone to run protection in the streets. That's where your guys come in."

"You want my guys to be the cops? What's in it for me?"

"Well, someone has to maintain order. And I can get you, personally, absolute immunity for all of your enterprises until the day you die."

"Oh, yeah?" the Don asked, with is interest piqued. "How's that?"

"I'll get the President to make it happen."

Don Vito cupped his hands around his mouth to amplify his voice. "Bobby, the President is fuckin' dead!"

"Not the new one. Not the one who will overthrow this well-oiled fighting machine you think is out there."

"Did I miss the election in the last two hours? What the fuck are you talking about?"

"They missed someone. Someone who is close to us, and me, in particular."

Don Vito's eyes lit up. "Maxie!! Maxie's alive?!?!" he exclaimed.

"You bet. He buried his wife this morning. And," he said looking at his watch, "he should be taking the oath of office right about now."

"Bobby," the Don stated as he looked down and shook his head, "Maxie is a great kid, but he don't got the juice to lead an army."

"You just watch, Don Vito. This kid's been through shit before. You know, that crap with his father. He came through like a champ. He'll do it again."

"Running that trashy magazine is one thing. Leading an army is something else."

"Trust me. He can do it. I may need to take a couple of your guys and put them on special detail to protect him."

Don Vito leaned back in his chair. He smoked his cigar in silence for nearly a minute. It was the longest minute of Dalton's life. Finally, he stood and announced, "Okay, Bobby. I'm in. We'll make sure that people stay calm while you and Maxie send these mother fuckers to meet their virgins or whatever. And when you're done, I get to run my businesses without any interference from the Feds. Take the three stooges out front."

"Do I have to take the Peach?"

Don Vito laughed. "Yeah, he's a fuckin' hothead, and if you don't take him, I may kill him myself."

Dalton knew deep down that the Don was not making and idle threat about the repugnant thug. "So, you wouldn't mind if I accidentally shot him during a training exercise?"

The Don laughed again. "Bobby, none of those guys are made or even close to bein' made. Why do you think they're body guards? Because I don't give a fuck about them."

Dalton breathed a long sigh of relief. He stood and leaned over the desk to kiss the Don on both cheeks. "Thank you, Don Vito. You won't regret this."

"I know. Now go and get these fuckin' guys."

"You got it." Dalton turned and began walking out of the office. He put his hat on and looked back at the Don. "The Revolution."

"What?" Don Vito asked.

"You wanted to know one time in history when a gang of rag-tag warriors overthrew a well-oiled fighting machine. The American Revolution, that's when."

CHAPTER 6

Lester Noble stood at the window of his corner office on Park Avenue staring southward toward the Empire State Building. Almost as if gloating, he reminisced about all of the hard work and long hours he put in to building his media empire, which to Lester was as magnificent an achievement as the building he ogled. Lost in his own thoughts, he ignored his intercom buzzing.

Ingrate, he thought.

"Mr. Noble," Anna's voice quivered through the speakerphone, "Max is here."

"Tell him I will be with him in a moment," Lester replied. *What does the little shit want now?*

Lester sat at his glass-top desk. Looking at his reflection in his chrome desk lamp, he made certain his tie was perfect. He picked up his phone. "Anna?"

"Yes, Mr. Noble."

"Send him in."

The mahogany doors opened slowly. Max entered the room wearing jeans ripped at the knees and a Grateful Dead t-shirt with several small holes in it obviously put there by flying embers from cigarettes or whatever else Max was smoking throughout his college years. His hair was long; it passed his shoulders and he made no attempt to comb it. He gestured to hug his father, but Lester remained seated and counter-offered a more formal handshake. Accepting his lesser status, Max shook his father's hand and sat in the chair facing his father's desk.

"Maxie, my boy!" Lester exclaimed, "To what do I owe the pleasure of this visit?"

"Good to see you, too, Dad," Max answered with a tone of disdain. "I graduated college, you know."

"I heard. And I was elated that you graduated in four years. Do you have any idea what that place cost me?"

"You know, most fathers are proud of their sons for getting an education. All you give a shit about is how much I cost you."

"Cut the crap, Maxie. What do you need now?"

"Need? I don't need anything. I want something."

Lester let out a monstrous laugh that would have rivaled Vincent Price's more famous laugh from his early horror films. Composed, he said, "Maxie. Maxie. Maxie. You're a college graduate now. You don't get anything else from me – EVER!" His volume increased as he rose from his chair and began pacing behind his desk staring out at the city, never once looking at Max. "You see, Maxie, now that you're an adult, you need to find a new source of income. My wallet is no longer open to you."

Max remained seated. He hated his father, and with good reason. Max's mother died when Max was only three; Lester shunned the responsibility of rearing him, leaving that duty to Max's godfather, Bob Dalton, his deceased wife's dear friend. Unable to shake his legal responsibilities, Lester always provided for Max - grudgingly. The only contact Max ever had with Lester had been when he needed money. Now, Lester made it clear that their relationship had ended. "Dad, I want a job at *Power Today*."

Lester unleashed his Vincent Price laugh again. "What could you possibly offer the crowned jewel of my empire?"

"I was a business major and I took some journalism

classes. I know how to write."

Lester was less than convinced. "Listen, Maxie, a few journalism classes and a bachelor's in business just doesn't qualify you to work for my empire. You're not Noble material."

Max expected his father to say, "No," but for Lester to deny that they any relationship existed between them was unforeseen. At the age of twenty-two, Max had not yet learned to control his emotions. "Not Noble material? I have your fucking DNA, Dad!" Max roared as he leapt from his seat.

Lester spun around quickly to look his newest enemy in the eye. "And that's all we have in common!" Lester yelled back. Irritated, Lester continued, "You have no skill that will help sell magazines, and therefore, you are of no benefit to my empire!"

"Stop calling it that, you fucking megalomaniac! You sell magazines and newspapers! So what?! You don't contribute to society at all! You're the one who is worthless!"

"Get out, Maxie! And don't ever come back!"

"I'll be back, alright! And the next time you see me, you'll be the one pleading for a job!"

Max turned and stormed out of his father's office. As he headed for the elevator all he could hear was his father's Vincent Price laugh.

* * *

Despite having a college degree, the only job Max could find was working construction for one of Dalton's companies. Without his father's money behind him, Dalton insisted that he learn the true value of hard work. Max was humbled; he accepted the job knowing that Dalton would not steer him wrong. He complained about the hours and about working outdoors in the stifling summer sun. Dalton laughed with each gripe and always replied, "It's good for you, Maxie."

One bright summer morning found Max working on a renovation project in Long Island's luxurious East Hampton. It was the home of Elizabeth Magnuson, the heiress to Long Island's largest real estate development company and the highest grossing broker on the island to boot. About fifteen years Max's senior, Elizabeth loved to watch her "boys" at work around the house while she tanned by the pool in a different piece of revealing swimwear every day.

"Boys," she would call as every member of the crew craned their necks in hopes of catching her attention and being her choice to do whatever it was she wanted them to do. More often than not, it was taking time to refill her glass with her drink of choice. She took an instant liking to Max; maybe it was his long hair or maybe it was that he made a good drink. Whatever the reason, almost half the time she called, she would give the chore to Max.

One day, Elizabeth called Max by his name. "Maxie, could you come here a moment?"

Max put down the nail gun in his hand and walked away from the gazebo he was working on by the pool. "What can I do for you Ms. Magnuson?" he asked as he strolled over to her lounge chair. He instinctively reached out his hand for her glass, but quickly realized that it was nearly full.

"Pull up that chair and have a seat," she said as she pointed to a patio chair a few feet from her. Max did as he was told. "Maxie, is this a summer job for you?"

"Well," he replied, "I'm hoping to find an indoor job for the winter, if that's what you mean."

Elizabeth laughed. "No, silly. I meant are you happy in your current profession?"

"Oh," he said with an awed expression. Max looked

around and lowered his voice so that none of his coworkers would hear his answer. "Honestly? I wanted to work for *Power Today*, but they didn't hire me. They said I wasn't Noble material."

A puzzling look replaced Elizabeth's generally jovial expression. She leaned closer to him. "Aren't you Les Noble's kid?" she whispered.

Embarrassed, Max responded, "Yeah." He quickly deduced that Dalton told her who he was.

"Well, did you tell him what they said?"

"Didn't have to. He's the one who said it."

Elizabeth's mood suddenly shifted to pure anger. "Listen to me, Maxie. Les Noble is the biggest piece of shit in the New York social scene. He fucked my friend Karen, got her pregnant, told her to get an abortion, and instead of paying for it directly, he gave her twenty-five thousand dollars and made her sign a confidentiality agreement so that it wouldn't get out and ruin his reputation. You're a better man than that."

Max blushed and shied away momentarily. Then he turned back to her smirking. "Thanks, Ms. Magnuson, but I don't know if that's . . ."

Elizabeth interrupted, "Maxie Noble, you get to call me Elizabeth." She peered over her sunglasses so that Max could make direct eye contact with her. Once she caught his gaze, she winked.

"Okay, Elizabeth." Calling a homeowner by her first name while the job was still ongoing made him feel awkward. "As I was saying, I don't really like my father, but he makes every decision in 'his empire,' and he'll be the first to tell you that."

"Ugh! Les and his fucking 'empire,'" she countered. "Maxie, I'm going to make a suggestion. Hear me out before you respond, okay?"

"Sure," he responded realizing that there was no harm in listening to a woman who shared the same sentiments toward his father.

"You should start your own magazine, one that will rival *Power Today*. Les doesn't know shit about how the world is trending. He's washed up. You're young, Maxie. Not to mention smart and handsome. I'll back you all the way, but you can have complete creative control. We'll split the profits fifty-fifty. What do you think?"

"That's an intense offer considering that I've never worked for a magazine before. How am I supposed to run one?"

"We'll bring in someone as your right hand man who knows the biz inside and out. You're a Noble for crying out loud! You're Les Noble's kid! The public, and more to the point, advertisers will trust that you grew up around the 'empire,' and that this is second nature to you. We'll have to cut your hair and polish you a little, but I'm willing to bet you clean up nicely. Then, once we're on top, we'll make a move to buy *Power Today* right out from under Les' 'empire.' How does that sound?"

"I don't know. That's a really intense offer." Max thought for a few minutes while he stared at his coworkers laboring away in the sweltering heat. Finally, he looked back at Elizabeth. "Could you handle being part of that intensity?"

"Without question. I like intensity." She looked off at another one of her "boys." "Intensity. I like that word. Wouldn't it be a great name for a trend setting magazine?"

Max laughed. "Sure, why not?"

* * *

Elizabeth hired the best public relations firm in New York to handle the launch promotion; her friend, Karen Sommers, happened to be the firm's owner as well as the same woman whose life had nearly been ruined by Lester's lapse in judgment and abominable ego. They say, "Hell hath no fury like a woman scorned," and Karen was living proof. She poured every resource she could offer into promoting *Intensity*. And she did it all for half of her normal price. Destroying Lester Noble's "empire" was more satisfying to her than fattening her bottom line. She could taste how sweet her revenge would be.

Karen's work paid off instantly. Modeling agents were badgering Max trying to get their clients on the cover of the premiere issue of what Karen was hyping as "the hottest trend setting magazine ever seen." As not to burn any bridges, Max set up photo shoots for every model whose agent called. While he was careful not to promise any one of them the cover, he did promise that each model would be featured in the premiere issue.

Some of the models were in awe of Max, or at least they acted like it. He was young and handsome, especially with his new haircut and wardrobe courtesy of Elizabeth. Each model was aware of the buzz around *Intensity* and Max; most of them tried to placate to the young publisher in hopes of clouding his unproven professional judgment. The harder they tried, the more obvious they were. Max would not be fooled. The coveted cover would go to the one model that made no attempt to pretend to be impressed by Max's potential.

Valerie Mintz was new to the business. She had a portfolio filled with bathing suit modeling pictures, most of which seemed amateurish at best. Max saw the potential in her pictures, and he knew immediately that his new magazine would make her the next supermodel. He also knew he had an uneasy feeling in the pit of his stomach every time she was present. Her beauty was completely natural; he could see no signs of cosmetic surgery. Her intellect and wit could be seen every time her eyes came into contact with the camera's lens. A hint of cynicism could be detected from her body language; Max thought that to be her greatest attribute.

After the premiere issue was released, Max asked his new cover girl to join him for dinner. Valerie hailed from a small town and a humble family. Fine dining was something she was taught about, but she never actually experienced it herself. Max's insistence on taking her to the Rainbow Room atop Rockefeller Plaza made her somewhat uncomfortable; she loved the feeling.

Their night began with small talk, but the conversation slowly wound its way into deeper topics: Max shared with her his motivation in starting *Intensity*, and how the death of his mother due to ovarian cancer caused his father to send him to live with his godfather. Valerie, in turn, only offered that her motivation to become a supermodel was driven by her desire to wear the clothes she saw in magazines but could never afford. She took very little interest in Max's upbringing, but he passed it off as part of her sarcastic attitude toward the world. The night ended at his thirty-fifth floor apartment on Manhattan's Upper East Side; having exchanged their passions, Max knew that he had a woman to share his life with for the first time since his mother passed away. He reveled in the feeling. Valerie did not notice.

* * *

"How do I look?" Max asked Valerie in the elevator on the way up to Lester's office.

"Powerful, baby. Powerful," she replied as she grabbed his suit jacket by the lapels and kissed him.

"Ahem," Elizabeth interrupted. "Let's not get Maxie unfocused here, Val. This is a big day for him."

"I can't wait to see the look on Les' fucking face when Max tells him the big news," Karen added.

"I'm sure he's already heard it, but I'll bet you he's

not expecting this visit," Elizabeth retorted. "Now Bill," she added looking at Bill Worthington, "have we gotten confirmation that the trades are finalized?"

"Just before I arrived," he answered. "Noble Enterprises, Inc., with you and Max as its sole shareholders purchased fifty-one percent of Noble Publishing, Inc. at forty dollars per share at the opening bell. Les never saw it coming; he didn't make any attempt to drive up the price. Just remember, Max, as a minority shareholder, Les will have certain rights so you have to make him feel somewhat included in the process. Otherwise, he can slap you with a derivative lawsuit that will drag on your cash flows and P&L."

The elevator door opened. "Thanks, Bill," Max replied. He didn't understand half of what Worthington said, but he knew that he would have to use every bit of tact he could to tell his father that he was taking his company and his job.

Max and his entourage stepped out of the elevator and Max led them down the hall toward Lester's office. They walked past the receptionist's desk without breaking stride. "Mr. Noble is in a meeting and he can't be disturbed," Anna yelled at them.

As they approached the door to the office, Max could hear his father screaming at someone. Lester knew. Max put his hand on the doorknob, took a deep breath, looked at his friends, and said, "Here we go." He turned the knob, and pushed the door into the room.

Lester had his entire executive staff in his office. It was a standing-room-only berating of them all for allowing the takeover to happen. When Max walked in, Lester snapped, "What the fuck do you think you're doing?"

"You're in my office, Dad," Max stated confidently. "It's time for you to leave."

"This is my empire! You have no business being here."

"To the contrary, Mr. Noble," Worthington chimed in, "over the years you sold a majority of your shares to various banks to raise capital to build your 'empire.' Max's company bought those shares this morning. You are only a minority shareholder now. And at a meeting held by the majority shareholders this morning, you were terminated as CEO, and Max was named President and CEO of the company. So, as he said, you're in his office, and it's time for you to leave."

Lester knew that Worthington was right, but he would never admit it. "Who the fuck is this guy? Pee Wee Herman?" Les chided while pointing to Worthington's bow tie. "And who are the other majority shareholders who made the genius decision to give control of my 'empire' to my idiot son?"

"That would be me," Elizabeth smugly explained as she entered the room.

"Elizabeth?" Lester could not believe his eyes. Karen entered the room right behind her, followed by Valerie. Lester squinted, trying to place them in his memory. Karen looked familiar, but he couldn't remember why. He recognized Valerie only from her pictures in *Intensity* and those strewn throughout the tabloids with Max. "Glad to see you brought all your bitches with you, Max. Now playtime is over. I don't know what makes you think that you can do this to me. I have rights, and I intend to make your life so fucking miserable that . . ."

Max heard enough. The time to fight back had come. He raised his voice to a level Lester had never imagined was possible, and it intimidated him. "That what, Dad? Is it possible for you to make my life even more miserable than you already have? You couldn't wait to get rid of me after Mom died! You sent me to live with Bob, who is more of a father than you ever were! You kicked me out of here once already, and you took everything from me in the process. But in the end, I managed to make it on my own, Dad!" He lunged at Lester as he yelled.

All Lester could do was cower in fear. No one had ever opposed him before. His ire continued to rise. Lester Noble would not give up without a fight. "You made it, Maxie? I don't fucking think so! You got a rich bitch to give you some money. You put together a trashy magazine, and you're banging the model whose face is selling them for you! YOU haven't done a fucking thing worth being proud of!"

Max noticed Lester's left eye beginning to twitch. Then Lester began to rub his left arm. "Think what you want, Dad," Max began, "but it doesn't change the fact that I am here and your career is over. It's MY 'empire' now! And there's not a goddamn thing you can do about it. You're useless! Washed up! And the whole world will be celebrating your departure. Now, if only I could get you out of my life completely . . ."

"Why you," Lester started as he went to tackle Max. But as he lunged forward, he began to gasp and he dropped to his knees.

"Someone call 9-1-1!" one of Lester's executives yelled. "He's having a heart attack!"

Max looked down at his prone father. Lester's face was turning from red to purple. "That's right, Dad. You are going to die, aren't you?"

Lester nodded in agreement as his gasps became shorter. Finally, he collapsed. His executives gathered around him; one of them began to perform CPR. It was useless. Lester Noble was dead.

Max sat in Lester's chair. He spun around and looked out the window. He began to laugh that same Vincent Price laugh that he remembered from his previous encounter with his father. He quickly caught himself, remembering how much he hated that laugh. When he composed himself, he spun the chair back to face the executives. "This marks the end of the 'empire.' We're going operate in a manner that will inspire creativity and freedom of expression. The only way to do that is to start with firing all of you. So, as my father once told me and I am sure he would tell you now if he could, 'Get the fuck out of my office!'"

As the executives left, the paramedics entered with a stretcher. They worked on Lester for nearly a half an hour before they took the body from the office.

Max stayed behind with his entourage. Sitting at his father's chair, he asked, "How did I do?"

"Marvelously," Elizabeth answered.

"You were so sexy, baby," Valerie added as she jumped onto his lap.

"Max," Worthington interjected, "did your father have a will?"

"Not that I know of. Why?"

"Well, if no one produces a will to probate, all of Les' possessions, including his forty-nine percent of the shares in the company will be yours."

"Baby, it's all yours now!" Valerie exclaimed.

"Congratulations, Maxie," Elizabeth added. "Now don't let us down." She winked at Max and tapped Worthington and Karen on their shoulders signaling them to follow her out of the office. She closed the door behind her to give Max and Valerie some privacy.

"Baby, I'm so proud of you," Valerie began. "That must have been hard for you to do."

"Actually, it was easier than I anticipated. I don't even feel a drop of remorse that he's gone. He was such a bad person that I feel like the world is better off without him."

"Well, you're a much better person than he is. And

you're going to accomplish much bigger things than he ever did."

"I love you, baby," Max stated almost catching Valerie off guard.

"I – I love you, too, baby," she reluctantly replied.

"Will you marry me?"

"You're serious?"

"Of course," Max said, puzzled by her hesitation. "I couldn't have done any of this without you. And I want to share it all with you. Everything in my life will be yours too until the day we die."

Valerie began to cry. "O – Okay," was all she could reply.

* * *

The lights. Why were they so bright? Max couldn't see anything beyond the podium. He squinted to do his best to keep the lights out of his eyes. He would give his speech by memory.

As he spoke, he quickly glanced at Valerie seated next to his empty chair adjacent to the podium. She was completely disinterested. She never accepted his decision to follow Armstrong and Dalton's advice to run for public office. She knew that their marriage was on shaky ground. Now that he was a Congressman, it would only become worse. At best, it would be a political marriage in which there would be no contact between them except for strategically timed photo opportunities. It would probably kill her modeling career as well.

The lights. They were really getting to him. He continued speaking, but all he could remember was the lights clouding his vision. Then it happened. Valerie tackled him.

Bang.

He still couldn't see passed the lights.

Bang.

He looked at Valerie. Blood.

Bang.

He looked at her again. More blood. What just happened? Is she going to . . .

"NO!" Max exclaimed. The room was dark. He was lying in bed. But it wasn't his bed. "No! Valerie!" he yelled as he began to cry. "It's my fault. It's all my fault."

Suddenly, the door opened and the lights were switched on. Mary Vineri stood in the doorway. She ran to Max and began to coddle him like a toddler. "Shhh. Shhh. There, there. It will be okay."

"Is everything alright?" Armstrong asked as he came running into the room followed by Judge Vineri.

"I can't do it," Max sobbed. "I can't do it. It's all my fault. She's gone and it's all my fault."

"I'll take it from here," the Judge stated.

"What are you going to do, Arthur?" Mary asked.

"I have counseled all four of our children through the trials and tribulations of life. Not to mention all of the advice I have given from the bench in my career. I think I am more than qualified to talk to the President about this. And that is not open for debate, Mary."

"Oh, Arthur," she retorted. "Sometimes you can be so pompous." She let go of Max and made her way to the door. "Come with me, Jack. We'll put up some tea for the President."

"Okay," Jack complied. Feeling the need to be included, he stated, "Max, I'll be downstairs if you need me."

"Thanks, Jack," he replied. "And thank you, Mrs. Vineri," he yelled to her. Jack closed the door behind him as they left.

"So, explain to me how you think that Valerie's death is your fault," the Judge demanded.

"She never wanted to get involved in politics," Max began. "She said that people get too emotional about it, and that it would bring us down. She was right. I spent days pleading with her and wearing her down to let me do it. She was reluctant, but she gave in."

"I see. So you feel guilty about her death because she had to be convinced to serve the greater good?"

"I guess you could say that."

"Well, then. I would argue that destiny is what caused you to follow your heart. It was destiny that you would be offered the opportunity to seek public office. It was destiny that made you convince her to go along with your ideas. It was destiny that you got elected. And it was destiny that she was taken from you. And destiny is something over which we have very little control. We carry out God's will, that's all. That will may change based on our actions, but in the end, it is all God's will."

"But if I listened to her, I wouldn't have run for office and she'd be with me here today," Max began to sob again.

"And there would be no hope in either of your lives that freedom would be restored in our nation."

"That's not true. Someone else would have stepped up to be the President."

"I disagree. We cannot rue the confluence of events that leads us to certain points in our lives. Valerie may have needed convincing, but if she were adamant about her feelings, she would have let you know it. In a way, her sacrifice was her destiny, and she knew that. You see, not only did she agree that you should run for office, but you are only here today because she sacrificed herself. If not for her death, you would have been at the State of the

Union. And the she would be the one mourning you. In the end, she chose to give her life to save yours. Destiny, you see, dictated all of this."

"It can't be my destiny to be the President. How am I supposed to lead a war? I have no military training or experience. I'm half the age of most of my constituents, who only represent one four hundred and thirty-fifth of the nation's population. It can't be left to me. I'm not ready."

"All of this is true. But like it or not, the recent events in your life have placed you on this path toward your destiny."

"Then what is my destiny? Am I to take back the country and serve as President until we elect someone better? What if I don't want to be President?"

"Mr. President," the Judge made certain to emphasize that he had taken the oath of office. Max did not respond. "I have no crystal ball. While I believe in God, I do not communicate directly with Him. I cannot tell you that I can see the future. But I have been around long enough to see when people must act. And that is your destiny, Mr. President.

"Whether or not you seek to be elected is a matter for you to decide," the Judge continued. "But unless you act now, there will not be a time for that decision to be made. The only things certain are that Valerie gave her life to save yours and that you are the only remaining official of the Federal government, as we knew it. Therefore, Mr. President, you are destined to restore our democracy so that you may make that decision. Freedom is rooted in choice, and you must make a choice now to allow others to be free later."

"But what if I fail?" Max asked.

"You will have plenty of help, Mr. President. I believe that Mr. Dalton is making certain arrangements right now to ensure that you do not undertake this task alone. Your responsibility is to embrace your role. Do that, and you will be successful in your task."

"How can you be so sure?"

"Faith, Mr. President. Faith. I have faith that God has delivered you to us safely, and that you will achieve your destiny. You need to develop that faith, too. And I have something for you that might help."

"What is it?"

"Let's have some tea, Mr. President. Then I will show you."

"Thank you, Your Honor."

"No, thank you, Mr. President."

CHAPTER 7

"Boots, Peach, Bam Bam," Don Vito called from behind the front door to his home, hiding in the warmth while his bodyguards stood outside in the cold.

"Yeah, boss," Boots replied. "What d'ya need?"

"Come inside, all three of yas," the Don replied. The bodyguards followed orders, excited to have the opportunity to spend five minutes in the Don's presence and, more importantly, to get out of the bitter winter air. As they shook off the cold, the Don explained, "Dante and Paulie are on their way over. When they get here, you three are going with Bobby, here." Dalton stood behind the Don and nodded.

"What for, boss," the Peach asked.

"He'll tell you later," the Don answered. "For now, just go with him and do what he says as if he was me. Do you get me, Peach?" the Don asked as he stared the Peach square in the eyes.

"I got it, boss," the Peach answered with a hint of emasculation in his response.

"Good," the Don replied. "Because if Bobby tells me that you gave him a hard time about anything, I'll fuckin' kill ya myself. Coppice?"

Boots stepped in between the Don and the Peach, interjecting, "No problem, boss. We got it. Bobby's the man. End of story."

"Good," said the Don, acknowledging that his message was received. "Now, I'm going to bed. Go call your wives, girlfriends or whatever, and tell them that I'm puttin' yas on a big job, so you won't be home for a while. Bobby," he said as he turned to Dalton, "they're all yours. Good luck." Without further delay, the Don climbed the spiraling staircase and retired to his bedroom. Dalton looked out the window and saw a car pull up. Two men, who seemed to have been aroused from their sleep but still managed to put on their best suits, exited the car.

"Okay," Dalton began as he looked at Max's three new protectors. "You heard the man. Go make your calls and meet me at Commack Diner in an hour. We'll get some coffee, and I'll fill you in on the new job there."

The men nodded, obviously surprised and confused.

* * *

Dalton sat at a booth in the Commack Diner vigorously shaking three packets of sugar substitute. The small cup of coffee in front of him steamed. The waitress glanced at him, noticing his thoughts were elsewhere.

He had not been on a mission since his last tour in Vietnam. Then, he took orders from his commanding officer, Lieutenant John Sharpe, who was often regarded as a brilliant field commander. Sharpe had a knack for assessing the situation, studying the terrain and implementing the perfect strategy to achieve victory. Dalton lived his entire post-military life trying to equal Sharpe's analytical skills.

The mission at hand was simple: First, the situation. Max had to be kept safe. Dalton knew he could trust the newly procured protection crew, but the threat to Max — the same threat that killed Valerie — had to be eliminated. The Aryan Brotherhood would not allow a Jew to be the Commander in Chief of the United States under the present circumstances; it would be an abomination of everything they stood for.

The second part of the mission, the terrain, made things more complex. Dalton knew a few of the Aryans from his local chapter of the National Rifle Association. Often they would try to recruit him for their cause. They would tell him to join them for their bonfires – a twisted tribute to one of their Nazi heroes' rituals where they burned every book they could find – in the woods on the eastern end of Long Island. Foolish braggarts, all of them, they would boast to Dalton about their smuggled weapons cache that they had waiting for the right moment for their army to make their move, not realizing that they divulged its location. Dalton knew that they would be gathered there this night to prepare for battle. Only he would not, could not, allow this to be their war. Surprise would be the key to victory. What Dalton struggled with was how to get close enough to their rally in the woods so that he could take them out – all of them. He only hoped that Don Vito had given him at least one brain in the crew to help him plan.

"You gonna stop shakin' that sugar, Sugar?" the waitress asked.

"Sorry, honey, I – I forgot about it," was all he could reply.

"No sweat, Sweetie," she answered with a wink. "It'll taste better in your coffee, though. That's all."

"Thanks," he said as he ripped open the packets of sugar substitute and poured them into his coffee. A quick splash of half-and-half from one of the mini containers in the bowl in front of him, a stir with his teaspoon, and the beverage was ready. He slurped as he sipped it, raising his eyebrows from the burning sensation on his upper lip. "HOT!" he exclaimed.

"Well, you didn't ask for iced coffee, did ya?" the waitress sniped sarcastically. Just then, he saw his crew walk in the front door. Boots led the way, followed by Bam Bam and the Peach. One thing he knew for certain:

If there was a brain among them, it certainly wasn't the Peach.

"Over here, guys," he yelled across the diner. "Three more cups of coffee for my friends, Toots," he ordered the waitress.

"Bobby, I only drink tea," the Peach yelled back. His smirk signaled that he was clearly unaware of the gravity of the situation.

"Sit the fuck down, Peach," Dalton sternly retorted. "You're drinking coffee like a man tonight."

The Peach opened his mouth, but before he could say anything, Boots interfered, "Look, guys. Obviously, some shit is goin' down. Bobby, just tell what the fuck it is, we'll do it. End of story and no questions asked."

"Yeah," Bam Bam's bass voice boomed as he stared at the Peach. The message clearly received from his compatriots, the Peach slumped into his seat at the booth. Bam Bam sat next to him while Boots settled in next to Dalton.

"Alright, guys, I'll explain," Dalton began. "But no interruptions. You got me?"

"We got you," Boots answered for the three of them.

Dalton leaned in toward the center of the table and lowered his voice, "You guys know what happened tonight. Those fucking towel heads came over here and killed everyone in the government that could stop them from taking over. Or so they think. They missed one guy. That guy is being sworn in as the next President as we speak. Your new assignment is to keep him alive. You with me so far?"

"So we're like the new Secret Service?" Boots asked.

"Cool, do we get earpieces?" the Peach inquired loudly. Boots could only roll his eyes at the stupidity of the question.

"Shut up, Peach!" Bam Bam yelled as he slapped him upside the head.

"Yeah, you're the new secret service," Dalton continued.

"Who is it?" Boots asked.

"Max Noble," Dalton answered. The three men nodded. "Now, there is a credible threat to his survival that we have to take care of first. The Aryan Brotherhood is going to make a move against these towel heads. The problem is that they won't fight with Max because he's a Jew. After what that K-K-K guy did to his wife, we can't let them anywhere near him. Nothing can be left to chance. So when we finish our coffee, we're heading out to Moriches to take 'em out."

"How many we talkin' about, Bobby?" Bam Bam asked.

"Don't know. A hundred. Maybe two hundred."

"What's the plan?" Boots asked.

"Don't know that either. There's another component. These Aryans claim to have a weapons cache, which will probably be close to where they are. They brag at my NRA meetings that it's enough to arm a small force. We're gonna need to take it with us to use against the towel heads. So, there's too much risk of destroyin' them if we use bombs and Molotov cocktails. Any suggestions?"

"We got a couple Uzis in the car if we can get close enough," Boots offered. Dalton felt relieved that his instincts correctly pointed to him as the brains of the operation. "We'll probably be able to take 'em out of commission in a few minutes. Then we'll do it the old fashioned way." Boots raised his hand putting his index and middle finger to his temple and raising his thumb as if it was a gun. He moved the thumb down like a hammer firing the bullet. "Bam! See ya later ya skin headed bitch!" He paused and looked around as Bam Bam and the Peach nodded in agreement. Dalton was stoic. "Can we get close enough, Bobby?"

"We're gonna have to."

* * *

The dirt road into the woods reminded Dalton of his nights in the jungles of Vietnam. It seemed to wind endlessly. The only difference was that the trees surrounding it were bare in the winter's cold. Dalton drove slowly while Boots, Bam Bam and the Peach examined their Uzis.

"You guys took the bullets out, right?" Dalton asked. "This road is a little bumpy. We don't need anyone in this car getting shot."

"Relax, Bobby. We're just makin' sure they're clean," the Peach responded while blowing in the gun's chamber to remove any particles of gunpowder that may cause a misfire.

Ahead in the distance, Dalton saw a dim light. He immediately shut the headlights and slowly brought the car to a halt. "Okay, this is it," he said. "That's the bonfire up there. Everybody knows what we're doin', right?"

"Yeah, we got it," Boots replied. "Bam Bam and Peach are going up the left flank, and you an' me are goin' right."

"Right," Dalton confirmed. "Just make sure we don't shoot each other."

"Not to worry, Bobby, we're professionals," Bam Bam reassured him.

"Ever kill anybody, Peach?" Dalton asked.

"Popped my cherry at sixteen," the Peach replied. "How about you, Bobby?"

"Not since 'Nam," he replied. "Not since 'Nam." It had been quite some time since he killed a man. Bam

Bam was right: The others were professional killers. This mission was just another day at the office for them. He realized that for all his talk about killing the enemy, he wasn't the same person he was during his tours of duty. He began to question whether or not he'd still have the ability to pull the trigger when the moment arrived. "Alright, enough bullshit. Let's go." He pulled his revolver out of his shoulder harness. He opened the chamber, checked that it was loaded, and spun it back into place. "I'll fire the first shot. Then you boys do your thing."

The men split up according to the plan. They crept slowly toward the bonfire trying to make as little noise as possible. As they neared, they realized that they could have made all the noise they wanted. The only thing audible was the sound of the Aryans repeatedly chanting, "Sieg Heil! Sieg Heil!" When the bonfire came into full view, they could see the Aryans, their backs staring at the four of them, saluting their leader with the Nazi salute.

What would Sharpe do? Dalton thought to himself. *The leader is the immediate threat. Take him out and the boys will get the rest.* He walked up until he could clearly see the outline of the leader's body against the background of the bonfire. *Just like the range*, he told himself. He looked around. The dark of night and the bodies of the Aryans were the perfect camouflage from the leader's line of vision. Boots, Bam Bam and the Peach stood at the ready. The leader stood approximately one hundred yards from him. *It's now or never.* He took a deep breath. *Let the war begin.* He aimed his gun.

Bang! Bang! Bang! Bang! Bang! Bang!

Dalton unloaded all six shots, each hitting their target in the torso. *The range paid off,* he thought.

Caught by surprise, the Aryans turned to find the source of the shots only to be greeted by three flashing lights and the rat-tat-tat of the Uzis. One by one the Aryans dropped to the ground; blood flew through the air.

The shooting finally stopped. The Aryans lay on the ground; some were already dead. Others moaned in pain and could only cough blood as death neared. Boots, Bam Bam and the Peach took out their handguns and began to make their way through the bodies. They shot anything that moved.

Suddenly, one Aryan sprung to life. By his slim frame and his acne, it was obvious he was barely legal to vote. He punched the Peach in the face with a hard right hook knocking him backwards. The Aryan ran directly at Dalton.

"He's all yours, Bobby!" the Peach shouted, his own blood trickling from his fattening lip.

The Aryan let out a hellacious yell, his right fist raised and ready to release a second blow. Dalton, expecting the punch, dodged the attempt and countered by hitting the Aryan on the back of the head with the butt of his gun. The Aryan's body went limp as he fell to the ground unconscious. "I'll take care of this one," Dalton said. "You guys finish the rest."

Boots, Bam Bam and the Peach continued to make their way through the prone Aryans. As Dalton removed his belt and began binding the live Aryan's hands with it, he could hear the sound of the boys' guns. To their credit, they followed Dalton's orders, and were meticulously annihilating any Aryan that remained.

"That's all of them, Bobby," Boots announced.

"Only about fifty of 'em by my count, Bobby," Bam Bam commented. "What happened to 'one hundred, maybe two hundred?'?"

"I guess there weren't as many as I thought," Dalton answered. "It's a good thing. That wasn't easy."

"Ah, that wath a pieth of cake," the Peach retorted

through his fat lip. "Now wha'da we do?"

"Well," Dalton answered, "we wait for this one to wake up." He pointed to the unconscious and bound Aryan at his feet.

"Why do we do that?" Boots inquired.

"He can lead us to the weapons, if they really exist."

* * *

The Aryan slowly fluttered his eyes. The smell of smoke emanated from the smoldering bonfire. In his bleary state, he could barely make out the faces of the four men surrounding him. A quick review of his recent memory reminded him that they were not his friends. He began to squirm on the frozen ground; there was no escape with his hands and legs bound.

Bam Bam was the closest to the Aryan, and the first to notice his movement. "Where ya goin', ya Aryan fuck?" he asked as he kicked him in his midsection.

"Fuck you!" the Aryan defiantly answered.

Bam Bam reared his leg back to kick him again when Dalton called out, "Leave him alone. He's a prisoner now, and the rules of war state that he must not be tortured."

"Prisoner?" the Aryan asked, confusion abounding in his question. "I'm on your side! I want to kill those fucking sandniggers just as much as you do!"

"Oh, I realize that," Dalton replied as he kneeled down to look the Aryan square in the eyes. "But you want to kill our new President, too. That makes you a traitor. So, my friend, now you are a prisoner of war and you will be treated as such."

"Are you out of your mind old man? The President is dead! Everyone is! We have to kill those sandniggers and take back our homes! Once we're in charge, we can get rid of the niggers, spics and kikes, too!"

"You forgot the gooks and faggots," the Peach added sarcastically.

"Yeah, them too," the Aryan agreed. "Think about it. It'll be the perfect world. Pure white Christians waiting for Jesus to return and bring peace to the world."

Dalton began to chuckle. "How old are you, son?" he asked.

"I ain't your son," the Aryan responded. "You're the traitor! A pure white Christian killing the only people who can stand up to those sandniggers. You're going straight to hell!"

"What's your name?" Dalton asked ignoring the Aryan's remarks.

"Timmy," the Aryan answered. "Timmy Hicks. And I'm nineteen."

"Well, Timmy Hicks, I'm Bob Dalton, and I'm fifty-eight. Do you know what that means?"

The Aryan shook his head to signal his negative response.

"It means that I'm your elder and you will respect me because you don't know shit," Dalton explained. "Now, Timmy, you've obviously never met a Jew . . ."

"Why would I want to?" the Aryan interrupted. "They're just after my money! Those fuckin' kikes!"

Boots, who had taken up position behind the Aryan, smacked him upside the head. "Shut the fuck and listen to Bobby, ya Aryan fuck!" The Aryan focused his eyes on the ground. Dejection was beginning to set in.

"Thank you, Boots," Dalton acknowledged. "Now, as I was saying, you're being held as a prisoner because you want to kill the new President, who happens to be a Jew."

The Aryan looked up in disbelief. "Huh?" was all he

could conjure as his question.

"Well, my young Aryan friend, those towel heads forgot that a racist fuck like you tried to kill Congressman Noble. He is alive and well, and he has been sworn in as our new President. So, until you accept that, and until I believe that you won't try to kill him, your Aryan ass will remain in our custody."

"If I'm a prisoner, I have rights! You can't just do this to me!"

"There ain't no judge or jury here," the Peach told the Aryan, leering at him hoping that he would try to escape so that he could avenge the sucker punch. "Bobby's in charge, Aryan. If he says you're a prisoner, you're a fuckin' prisoner!"

"How long have you been a member of the Aryan Brotherhood?" Dalton asked as the interrogation continued.

The Aryan, remembering the bump growing on the back of his head, began to realize that he was no longer free. There was no point in resisting any longer. "I just came down tonight. Jimmy Clark's been in it for a while. He came to my house and told me that their army needed pure white Christians like me. So I came down. I swear I'm not like those guys."

"Sure talk like 'em," Bam Bam noted.

"Yeah, Jimmy talked like that all the time. And Mr. Peters was sayin' all that shit before you guys showed up, too."

"Well, listen up, Aryan," Dalton continued. "I'm not releasing you just yet. We're gonna take you to meet the President, and we're gonna let him decide what to do with you. I will remind you, though, that the punishment for treason is death."

The Aryan's eyes began to well up with tears. He

swallowed hard as he thought about the possibility of facing death. He could not accept such a sentence simply for being in the wrong place at the wrong time.

Dalton noticed tears beginning to flow down the Aryan's cheeks, a sure sign that fear began sinking in and causing a stinging sensation on his skin in the brutal cold. "I'll tell you what, though. If you cooperate with us, I'll be sure to tell the President. He's pretty understanding, a trait very common in Jews. He may show you mercy. Do you understand me?"

"Um-huh," the Aryan replied as he nodded affirmatively.

"Good, then we can continue. Did Jimmy say anything about giving you a gun?"

"Yeah, he said that after the bonfire, we were gonna go to the shack to get our guns."

"Do you know where the shack is?"

"Yeah, it's down the hill just passed where the fire was."

Dalton, Boots, Bam Bam and the Peach all looked out in the direction of the Aryan's description. It was too dark to see if he was telling the truth. "Bam Bam, Peach, go check it out." The two men drew their guns in case of a double cross and headed off to investigate.

"What else do you know about the guns, Aryan?" Boots asked.

"Nothin', I swear. We were just gonna take some and go find some sandnigg – I mean some Arabs to get back at 'em."

"See," Dalton commented, "does that make any sense? You would have killed a few innocent people with no plan for attacking our real enemy. Your Brotherhood would have accomplished nothing."

The Aryan realized that Dalton had a point.

"Bobby, you gotta come see this!" the Peach shouted from the distance.

"You got him?" Dalton asked Boots.

"Yeah," Boots answered as he pulled out his gun. "Don't try to run, Aryan, or I'll put two in ya. Doesn't sound like anyone will mind anymore."

"Don't go anywhere, Aryan," Dalton said, satisfied that Boots was in control of the situation. "I'll be right back." Dalton stood up and started for the shack.

"They were ready for World War Three, Bobby," Bam Bam explained as Dalton approached the entrance to the shack. He took out his keychain and activated the small flashlight on his key ring. He pointed it into the shack to see the inventory.

Bam Bam was right. There were enough guns to arm an entire battalion of troops. By his quick estimation, there had to be thousands of assault rifles and close to one million rounds. There were a few cases of rocket launchers, grenades and even uniforms. Dalton knew that they were lucky that the Aryans were better smugglers than he estimated.

"We'll have to come back for this stuff tomorrow with a semi," Dalton mentioned to Bam Bam.

"My brother-in-law drives one for the Teamsters," Bam Bam mentioned. "You want I should call him down here tonight? He'll do anything for me."

Dalton paused for a minute. "Are you guys numb from this cold, yet?"

"No," Bam Bam answered.

"I'm good," the Peach concurred.

"Okay, call him. You two stay here, help him load the truck and bring it to my house. You know where I live?"

"Yeah," Bam Bam replied. "I drove Don Vito there for that barbecue fundraiser you had for Max last summer."

"Perfect. I'll meet you guys there at dawn. Good?"

"You got it, Bobby," Bam Bam answered.

"No sweat," the Peach added.

Dalton returned to Boots and the Aryan. Without breaking stride he said to Boots, "Pick him up and put him in the back seat. We're going."

CHAPTER 8

"General, our commanding officers are contacting us from all over the globe," Lieutenant General Chet Rogers reported. "They are awaiting your orders, sir."

All eyes in the operations center of the Pentagon, commonly called the "Hub," focused intently on General Daniel Harmon. With the murder of all of the Joint Chiefs, Harmon was the *de facto* commander of the United States' armed forces. A middle-aged man known for his intellect and quiet demeanor, Harmon had the reputation of being a master strategist lacking the charisma required to serve as one of the Joint Chiefs himself. After spending hours in solitude in his office pondering the night's events, he emerged to Rogers' greeting. "Tell them all to follow Sultan's instructions. They should surrender their arms where he directs. He said that he is coming here to control his operations, and we will not resist at this time."

Flabbergasted by Harmon's response, the men in the room remained silently at their posts frozen in awe. "We're not going to prepare to defend the Castle, sir?" Rogers inquired referring to the Pentagon. "I think I speak for every man in this room when I say that we won't let them take it, sir."

"No, General," Harmon replied nonchalantly. "I said that we will surrender control to Sultan when he arrives. That is an order."

Rogers, several years Harmon's younger and much more dapper, disapproved of Harmon's decision; however, he would not dare question the highest-ranking member of the military in front of others. Rogers poorly disguised his contempt with his reply, "Yes, sir."

Harmon recognized from Rogers' tone that his authority was in question. He knew that if he did not win the trust of the men at this moment, he would never gain it. He announced to the room, "General, when you have four stars on your uniform instead of three, you can give the orders," Harmon began pointing to the fourth star on his uniform, a clear critique of Rogers' rank. "But before you give them, you must look at the consequences. I have spent every moment since this atrocity occurred in my office analyzing the situation. Do not think for a single moment that the gravity of the situation is lost on me. If we opt to defend the Castle, there will be casualties. At this moment, the nation has no democratically elected leader, and we all answer to those elected by the people. Right now, we cannot afford any more losses. Your lives and your knowledge are too valuable to our nation's survival. When Sultan arrives, we will follow his orders and serve at his pleasure. When the time is right, we will make our move."

His soliloquy worked. Every head in the room nodded in agreement. "General Rogers," he continued, "select three men and meet me in my office to begin planning our next move."

Relieved, Rogers loudly replied, "Yes, sir." Turning to the soldiers at the communications console he said, "Gentlemen, you heard the General's orders. Tell our men around the world to stand down."

* * *

Harmon's office was decorated with photographs from his tours in Vietnam. Younger and slimmer, he was Colonel Harmon back then. Even with the military's humiliation at the hands of the Viet Cong, no one ever imagined that the American government would fall without resistance.

Rogers knocked on Harmon's door. Three men followed him; none were below the rank of Colonel. "General, we're here," he announced.

Harmon rose from his desk and welcomed the officers in. "Who do we have here?" Harmon asked rhetorically. He could put a name to every face at the Pentagon.

The first man to enter announced, "Major General Thomas Norton."

Harmon laughed, "I know who you are Norton. I know who all of you are. I do have a sense of humor, you know."

Apparently, Norton didn't. He began to turn red from embarrassment. "Sorry, sir." The rest of the men squirmed, finding Harmon's ease with the situation discomforting.

"Here's how I see this, gentlemen. When Sultan arrives, we'll welcome him in. He will most likely have his top people with him, but they will need our help to run their operations out of the Hub. They aren't a sophisticated military, after all. We will befriend his men, and learn what we can about them. Once we figure out their weaknesses, we'll be in a position to advise them to our advantage."

"Sir," Rogers responded, "This plan may take some time. What about the American people? What are they to do in the meantime?"

"They should follow Sultan's orders, as well. I have a feeling that he will have his men dispensing their idea of justice without trials."

The intercom on Harmon's desk began to ring. He reached over and picked up the phone's receiver. "Yes," he answered. "Let them in and show them to the Hub,

Captain. I will meet you there." He hung up and turned to the officers, "Well, gentlemen, Sultan and his men have arrived."

* * *

Harmon entered the Hub to find every American kneeling on the floor with his hands on his head. "Sultan, I presume?" Harmon announced.

Sultan turned to face the voice pointing a gun in Harmon's direction. "Who are you?" he demanded to know.

"General Daniel Harmon, at your service, Sultan. I am the ranking military officer in the United States, thanks to your rampage this evening."

"Nice to meet you, General Harmon. Do I have your complete cooperation?"

"Absolutely. You have the cooperation of every man in this room. In fact, I think you can release them, now."

Sultan lowered his weapon. "Good. You will show me around my new headquarters, then."

"Most certainly, Sultan."

"Very well," Sultan replied. He turned to his men, and spoke to them in Arabic. The men lowered their weapons and the Americans returned to their posts.

Harmon and Sultan began down the corridor, talking to each other as two generals negotiating the terms of a complete surrender.

* * *

Two hours passed since Harmon convinced Sultan's men to release his. The Arabs spent the time learning from the Americans how to operate the Pentagon's advanced weaponry and computers. There was a certain air of disdain, but Rogers and his men knew to keep to

Harmon's plan.

A light on the secured communications panel began to flash. "What is that?" asked one of the Arabs.

Rogers walked over to the console and answered, "It's one of our secured lines. Someone is attempting to contact us from one of our bases."

"How do you answer it?"

"Pick up the phone, press the button and talk," Rogers instructed as he went through the motions of his instructions. "It's not a hard concept for the twenty-first century."

Responding in anger to Rogers' tone, the Arab punched him in the face, grabbed the phone receiver from his hand, and warned, "We are not idiots. You would be wise to show us more respect now that we are in charge." He began to speak into the phone, "Yes, who is this?"

The answer came through in Arabic. Rogers watched the Arab's eyes light up as he carried on the conversation. "Go get Sultan," the Arab ordered Rogers.

Rogers obeyed rubbing his jaw where the Arab's punch landed. Moments later Sultan returned to the Hub; Harmon immediately followed. "What is going on?" Sultan demanded to know.

The Arab holding the phone answered, "It is Emir. He wishes to report to you."

"Can we put him on speaker?" Sultan asked.

"Of course we can," Rogers replied. He walked over to the communications console and flipped a switch on the panel. "Go ahead, Sultan."

"Emir, report," Sultan ordered. Emir's voice began to respond through the speaker in Arabic when Sultan stopped him. "In English, Emir. I want our American friends in the room to hear this."

"V-V-V-Very well, b-b-b-brother. We have taken the cities as you have instructed. The C-C-C-Caliphs have all reported in. All p-p-p-police and soldiers have surrendered as you have instr-instructed, and here in New York, we have taken the d-d-d-diplomats at the United Nations as h-h-h-hostages for insurance. I have established our headquarters here in the Empire S-S-S-State Building, and we have tapped into the secured communications line through F-F-F-Fort Dix in New Jersey. V-V-V-Victory is ours, brother. Your p-p-p-plan was genius. Be sure to tell Our Man that his help will not be forgotten."

"Rest assured brother," Sultan responded, "he is aware and pleased with our progress. Tell the Caliphs to begin securing the cities. Shut down all means of public transportation. Block all bridges and tunnels. Freeze all activities at the ports. Institute curfews. Now we will see how Americans like being confined to their homes as they have done to our occupied brethren."

"It w-w-w-will be done, brother," Emir assured him.

CHAPTER 9

"Mary's always yelling at me to clean this place out," Judge Vineri explained as he and Max descended into the dark basement. A loud crash echoed up the stairs as the Judge knocked over a pile of boxes in his search for the light switch. Finding it, the Judge illuminated the room with a simple flick.

Max was astonished to see the Judge's messy basement. He had assumed that a man of the Judge's stature would surely have every aspect of his life in perfect order. Instead, the basement contained all of the undesired items the Judge and Mrs. Vineri had accumulated in their lifetime; there was no discernable order, either.

"I know it doesn't look like we care about these things," the Judge rationalized, "but every item down here has a story associated with it. To some, these are things that have little or no value. To Mary and me, however, these trinkets are priceless." He picked up a dusty chalkboard that had some faded, yet un-erased, pictures still on it clearly drawn by a child. "Hmmm," he said as he shook his head remembering when his grandson drew the picture for him. "Priceless."

"Your Honor," Max interrupted, "what exactly are we looking for?"

"I told you. Something that will help you to restore your faith."

"Shouldn't I talk to a rabbi or someone of the cloth for that?"

"Your problem isn't that you lack faith in God, Mr.

President. It's that you lack faith in your own abilities."

Max stared in amazement at the Judge as he continued to rummage through the piles of boxes and memories. The Judge had articulated that which only Armstrong and Dalton knew. And Valerie, too, but . . . .

"You see, Mr. President, you are a natural leader," the Judge continued as he carried on with his search. "You have a charisma and an aura that people are drawn to. It is a power that only few possess. So far, it has brought you success only with the help of others. You must learn to harness it and control it, so that you may use it to your advantage. In time, you will." Turning his head to face Max, he said, "But time is short, Mr. President."

Suddenly, Max heard a screech of metal on metal. Before he could move, the Judge had unsheathed a sword and held its blade at Max's throat. The gleam of the fluorescent light off of the blade had Max's full attention. The sword was roughly a meter long with wire wrapped around the cherry wood handle and a gold hilt and guard. "This, Mr. President, is what we were looking for."

"It's a thing of beauty, Your Honor," a mesmerized Max replied. He placed his finger on the blade and moved it away from his jugular vein. The Judge placed the handle in Max's hand. Max adjusted his grip several times until it felt comfortable. He stepped away from the Judge and swung the sword in the air. A feeling of empowerment came over him.

"Yes, it is. This sword dates back to the American Revolution. I bought it at an auction in 1979. There were rumors that Washington himself used this sword in combat. But when the auctioneer could not verify the fact, the price dropped significantly. A dispute broke out as to whether or not it was an American sword at all because the blacksmith did not mark the blade. Fortunately, I did my homework. You see, most swords used in the American Revolution were actually forged in Europe. If anything, all the Americans did was finish the handle. The cherry wood handle signified its American origin to me. I figured Washington and cherry wood – it could have been his. I bought it for five hundred dollars on the opening bid."

"If this sword is that old, will it survive a battle?" Max asked.

The Judge laughed. "Well, listen to you. Ten minutes ago you didn't know if you were the right man for the job. Now, you want to know if the sword will hold up in battle?"

"Well, I mean . . ."

"Mr. President, Bob will make sure you know how to use it. You are not battle ready yet. But you will be."

"Right, I'm sorry," Max apologized.

"Don't be sorry, Mr. President. The sword is already doing its job. Now, you are ready to do yours."

* * *

The sound of car doors closing drew Armstrong's attention from the television. He leapt off the sofa in the Judge's living room to the bay windows and pulled the curtain to the side. He recognized the portly figure walking from the driver's side of the SUV; Dalton's profile was Hitchcock-ian. The other two men were strange to him. One of them was holding a gun to the other's back nudging him forward to the doorway. Armstrong looked at Mrs. Vineri who was sitting in her armchair knitting her husband a sweater. He explained, "Bob is back, and he appears to have company. We should go get the Judge."

"I'll go get him," she replied. "You'll see to the door please, Jack?"

"Of course, Mary," he assured her. "This should be interesting."

Mrs. Vineri proceeded to the door that led to the basement. She peered down the stairs into the unsightly mess. Shaking her head she yelled, "Arthur, are you done pretending to clean that mess up?"

"What, dear?" the Judge yelled back.

"Don't play deaf with me. You know how much that debacle bothers me. I can't believe you took the President down there."

"We'll be right up, Mary," was all that the Judge could respond without raising her ire.

"Well, hurry up. Bob is back, and Jack said it looks as though he has guests." The doorbell rang.

"I've got it, Mary," Armstrong yelled from the foyer. He opened the door. Dalton walked in rubbing his arms as if to shake of the cold. He was followed by the Aryan, whose arms were still bound behind his back, and Boots, who continued to keep the barrel of his gun buried in the Aryan's back. "Who are these two gentlemen, Bob?"

Dalton responded, "It's okay. They're with us."

"Both of them?" Armstrong wanted to be assured.

"Ah, Bob, so nice of you to return," the Judge welcomed as he emerged from the basement. Max followed with his new sword hanging from his waist on his left side. "And whom do we have here?"

Dalton began the introductions, "This here is Boots," he began tapping Boots on the shoulder. "He is the head of Max's security detail. And this is a traitor we captured plotting to kill the President."

"Hey!" the Aryan shouted, "That's not true!"

"Sounds like you have someone who wants to plead 'not guilty' to the charges, Bob," the Judge offered. "Let me ask you, son," he continued as he questioned the Aryan, "Are you an American citizen?"

"Yes," the Aryan replied.

"Well, then, as a citizen, you are not an enemy of war and, therefore, are entitled to certain rights. Tell me, were you read your rights after you were taken into custody?"

"No," the Aryan answered.

"Then you are free to go."

"Your Honor," Dalton protested. "He's a neo-Nazi who will kill the President because he's a Jew! You can't let him go!"

"And you, Bob, have forgotten what it is this impending war is all about – restoring the freedoms protected by our Constitution. This man is an American citizen accused of treason, not a prisoner of war. Therefore, you, as an agent of the government, are required to inform him of his Fifth and Sixth Amendment rights. Since you did not do this, any evidence you may have collected is tainted and cannot be used at his trial. So, you see, Mister . . ."

"Hicks, your Honor, and I tried to tell him that I had rights," the Aryan added.

"Right," the Judge acknowledged, "Mister Hicks was right. And he is free to go. Now untie him immediately."

"Your Honor," Boots interjected, "He did try to kill us and run."

"And you would do well to put your gun away and keep your mouth shut. Something tells me that you weren't exactly a model citizen this evening," the judge chastised. Boots shook his head and looked down at his feet. "Now, put that gun away!"

Boots complied.

Dalton hated losing, but he knew he could not argue the law with the Judge. "Your Honor, can't we ask Max what he would do with him. It's his life on the line, here."

"Let him go," Max responded without hesitation. Dalton was astonished not only by the answer but also by how quickly it came. "The Judge is right. If we value what we're fighting for, then we must live by those laws." There was an air of confidence in Max's voice that Dalton had never heard from him before.

"Fine, Max," Dalton acknowledged as his faced turned red from his rising blood pressure, "but if he tries anything, don't say I didn't warn you." Noticing the sword at Max's side, he asked, "What's this thing?"

"The Judge gave it to me," Max replied. "He told me you'd show me how to use it, too."

"He did, did he?" Dalton looked at the Judge who nodded.

Max walked over to the Aryan and looked him in the eye. "Do you want to kill me, or do you want to help me kill those guys who have destroyed everything our nation stands for?"

The Aryan, overwhelmed with the situation, answered, "I never wanted to kill you, sir. But I would love to help you kill those sandnigg . . . those guys."

"Good," Max assured the Aryan. He reached behind him and untied his hands. "Now, shake on it, like a gentleman."

The Aryan complied, and shook Max's hand.

"Well, I hate to break up this love-fest," Dalton stated snidely, "but I have to meet the rest of Max's security team at my house at dawn."

"Yes," Armstrong interjected, "and we need to get Max home so that no one finds out that he is the President until the plans are in place to go on the offensive. For now, he is just a man sitting *shivah*, and his guests will be arriving shortly after dawn."

"Then we won't keep you," Judge Vineri

acknowledged. "Mr. President, you know your charge."

"And I am ready to accept it, thanks to you," Max replied.

"Great," Dalton added, "now let's get going."

The five men – Max, Armstrong, Dalton, Boots and the Aryan – got into Dalton's SUV. They drove out of the Judge's driveway leaving the Judge and Mrs. Vineri at the door watching as the car's taillights faded into the horizon.

"What are you thinking, Arthur?"

"I don't know, Mary. We've done all we can. Now it's up to him to do the rest."

"Is he up to it?"

"We'll find out, won't we?" With that, a tear came to his eye and he hugged his wife.

* * *

Dawn broke as Dalton's SUV approached Max's house, the morning sun reflecting off of the rear view mirror and into Dalton's eyes. The adrenaline from the night's events was wearing off, as was the caffeine from his coffee hours before. Between the sunlight and the drowsiness, keeping his eyes open was Dalton's next challenge. He quickly glanced around the car to see: Max was sleeping in the passenger's seat; Armstrong gazed out the window behind Max and was nodding in and out of consciousness; Boots was clearly making every effort to stay awake in the middle seat as he kept his gun pointed at the Aryan, who was sleeping behind Dalton. To keep everyone awake, Dalton began with idle conversation. "What's the weather supposed to be today, Jack?"

Partially roused from his pseudo-slumber, Armstrong replied, "Cold, but sunny."

"Yeah," Boots added, "it's been cold a lot lately."

Silence followed as they pulled up to the corner of Max's block. "So, boss, what's the plan from here?"

Dalton stopped the SUV at the stop sign and waited there for a moment while he thought. It took every ounce of energy he had to do what they did that night. Now, he had to answer, and answer quickly. His only problem was that he had not thought of what the answer should be. "We'll drop Max and Jack at the house; let them get some sleep. People will be stopping by the house all day – remember, he's still mourning."

"Will he be safe there?" Boots wanted to make certain.

"He'll be fine there," Dalton assured him. "The only other people who know who or where he is are the Vineris, Bam Bam and the Peach. Word that he's the new president won't travel that quickly. But people are going to look to him for answers, anyway."

"I'm almost afraid to ask, Bob," Armstrong chimed in, "but what are you going to do?"

"Boots and me are going back to my place. We'll take that Aryan shithead with us to keep him in our sights. I don't care what the Judge said. He's still a threat in my book. We gotta meet Bam Bam and the Peach at my place with the truck after we drop you off."

"Um, Bob," Armstrong interrupted, "who are Bam Bam and the Peach, and what truck are you meeting?"

The exhaustion caused Dalton to forget that he neglected to tell Armstrong and Max the details of his travels. "Right. For now, let's just say that Bam Bam and the Peach are on our side. They're Boots' friends who will be looking out for Max's personal safety. As for the truck, don't worry about that just yet. Trust me, Jack. That's all I ask. We'll get some quick shuteye at my place, and then me and Boots have to go see someone."

"We do?" a surprised Boots asked.

"Yeah, we do. There's another guy out there whose help we need."

"And who would that be, Bob?" Armstrong demanded to know.

"John Sharpe," Dalton replied.

"And he would be . . . ?" Armstrong trailed off.

"Sharpe was my lieutenant in 'Nam. Last I heard he was the colonel in command of the base at Mitchel Field. He was brilliant, and we're gonna need his brains to raise our army and plan our attack."

Skeptically, Armstrong pushed, "If he was so brilliant, why is he a colonel and not a general at your age? And what makes you think he didn't surrender like that Sultan guy ordered?"

"I don't know why he never went higher than colonel. But his rank is irrelevant, now." Dalton turned to face Armstrong despite the glare from the rising sun straining his eyes. "And he would never surrender to anyone."

* * *

Armstrong and Max were able to get four hours of sleep before people from the community began arriving at Max's house for *shivah*. While he could certainly appreciate the ancient Jewish custom by which the community would mourn with those who lost loved ones for one week following the funeral, he could not help but keep thinking about the events of the previous night. Valerie's funeral less than twenty-four hours prior seemed like a distant memory. Maybe it was because the Mintzes refused to sit *shivah* at Max's house, or maybe it was because their marriage had ended years before her life did, but for some reason Max almost forgot that these people in his house were there because of her death and not because he was the new president – a fact of which only Armstrong was aware in that crowd.

Nevertheless, Max could hear the whispers. While they greeted him and offered their condolences for Valerie's death, Max knew that, if it were socially acceptable, they would hound him with questions about the country's future. He could hear it in their whispers; the murmurs about "poor Max" echoed in his ears. It was nauseating him.

Their standing in the community did not matter either. Jeff Schonberg, the rabbi from Max's congregation, led the gossip in one circle. "He has to do something. Duty calls," he explained.

Jane Sherman stood in between the rabbi and her husband, Lenny Sherman, a multi-billionaire who spent nearly ninety hours per week at his real estate development companies to avoid her. She normally spent more time complaining about how difficult it was to be Lenny's wife as she got her weekly manicures at the chic salon than she did talking politics. Today, she had an opinion. "He's just a kid, rabbi. And with his wife gone, he's not up to it."

Lenny countered, "Honey, if somebody doesn't do something, my property values are going to drop and you can kiss the good life good-bye."

Each group of people spread throughout the house had similar conversations. "He can't do anything," was the popular sentiment. Max needed air. The pressure was building.

Only Armstrong knew what was truly bothering him. He walked over to the crate Max was sitting on as part of the *shivah* custom to signify his mourning. "Max, come with me. Someone is outside to see you."

"They don't want to come in?" Max queried. "It's freezing outside."

"Well, she's a little embarrassed," Armstrong explained.

Max shrugged and stood to follow Armstrong

outside. He relished the opportunity to leave the house. As they walked, the only thought to come to Max's mind was, *She? Elizabeth? No, she would walk right up to me in front of everyone. Who then?* They walked out into the cold. Max, jacketless, folded his arms close to his torso for warmth.

Standing in the driveway was a shorter woman wearing a teal ski jacket with a black scarf, black ski hat and black gloves. The dark accessories accentuated her blonde hair and pale skin; the ski jacket matched her eyes.

"Behave yourself," she scolded the young boy facing her. "I told you that this is something I have to do." The child wore a black ski jacket that matched his hair and his red scarf with the matching hat and gloves drew attention away from his dark brown eyes.

"But, Mom," the boy whined as he tugged at the bottom of her jacket. "I wanna go to Joey's and play video games!"

"Stop it, now!" she demanded. Reluctantly, the boy complied. As she looked up, she noticed Max approaching. "Max, I am so sorry for your loss."

"Thank you," Max replied automatically. Shivering, he looked her up and down. He searched his memory to determine who she was. His eyes lit up when he realized. "Roxy? Is that you?"

She laughed aloud. "Yeah, has it been that long?" She jumped on him and hugged him tightly.

"It's been what? Ten years?" Max thought out loud.

"A little longer," she replied. "We were still in college. But it's good to see you."

"Wow! I never thought you'd be here."

"Well, I figured that you would need a familiar face to help you out a little."

"Jack Armstrong," Armstrong introduced himself.

"I'm sorry, Jack," Max apologized. "This is Roxanne Fidelis. We dated back in college."

"Well, it's Roxy Miller, now," she explained. "And this is my son, Zachary. Say 'hello,' to the Congressman, Zach." Zach hid behind her. "He's a little shy. But it's nice to meet you, Jack. Thanks for bringing him out here. This would have been a little more awkward inside."

"Nice to meet you, too," Armstrong echoed. "Now, I suggest we go inside before we all catch a cold."

Max kneeled down and looked Zach in the eyes. "It's nice to meet you, Zach. You can call me 'Max.'"

Zach looked away, but mumbled, "Hi, Max."

Roxy took Zach by the hand and they started to walk back toward the house. "So, you got married?" Max asked her.

"And divorced, unfortunately," she answered.

"I'm sorry to hear that. How long ago?"

"Well, I married Derek right after you and me split. We were young. He was a stock boy at the supermarket by campus, and he didn't make a lot of money. So, I dropped out of school and got a job at a bank as a teller. Then Zach was born. Derek couldn't handle the responsibility. He left, got in with a bad crowd, shot a deli clerk, and now he's serving a life sentence. I filed for divorce as soon as I could afford a lawyer. It's been twelve years, now. Just me and Zach."

"Wow! That's quite a story," Max said in amazement. "What do you do now?"

"I'm teaching fourth grade," she replied.

"I always had a feeling you'd be a great teacher. And how old are you, Zach?"

"Twelve," he mumbled.

"Almost Bar Mitzvah age, huh?" Max asked Roxy.

"Yeah, this summer. We don't really go to temple or anything. But I never miss a night of Chanukah, right Zach?"

"Right," Zach answered with a big smile.

"Why'd you keep Derek's name, Rox?" Max asked.

"I didn't want to confuse Zach," she answered.

"Well, I think you should change it back. Put this Derek guy behind you. It's been long enough."

"But what about Zach? He'd still be Miller."

"We can change his name to 'Fidelis,' too. Right, Jack?"

Armstrong, in the lead of the group, turned to face them but continued forward by pacing backwards. "I think we could arrange that, Mr. . . . ."

"You see," Max interjected. "We'll get to work on it right away."

"You can't just do that, Max," Roxy protested. "You need to go before a judge or something, don't you?"

They reached the front door, and Jack held it open for all of them. As they entered the house, Max whispered in Roxy's ear, "I can arrange it. I can arrange anything, now."

With a puzzled look, Roxy responded, "Okay."

CHAPTER 10

"Three trucks, Bobby," Bam Bam greeted Dalton as he exited his car in his driveway. Three trailers were parked in the street in front of Dalton's house. "Can you fuckin' believe it? These skinheads stashed three fuckin' truckloads of guns, rockets all sorts of other shit. There's even a mini-tank in that one over there," he said as he pointed to the first trailer.

"A tank?" Dalton asked sounding impressed.

"Yeah, getting' it in the trailer was a bitch," Bam Bam told him.

Boots and the Aryan got out of the car and went straight into the house. Dalton noticed the Peach talking to three men outside the cab of the first truck. "Who's Peach talking to?" he asked.

"That's my brother-in-law, Vick DeCosta, and two of his buddy's from work. Don't worry, Bobby. They're in the union. They know better than to ask any questions."

"Good. Tell them to leave the trailers and get out of here. Then meet us inside. We gotta go over our next move." Dalton let out a lion-sized roar. "Then, I'm gettin' some sleep."

"No problem, Bobby. I'll be in with Peach in a few minutes."

Dalton went into his house through the garage entrance, pressing the button to close the garage door behind him. The entrance placed him in his storage room, which doubled as his trophy room. Rather than idols of brass and wood sealed in his trophy cases, he had warrior helmets from different eras on one wall and an assortment of weapons on the other. One case contained spears, bows and arrows, while another protected a sword display. A third case contained a collage of implements; there was a mace, Chinese throwing stars and several daggers. The display in the final case was comprised of handguns and a musket from the American colonial period.

With his gun weighing heavy in his shoulder harness, Dalton removed it and placed it in a drawer beneath the gun display. From the storage room, he went through the hallway into his den. The Aryan and Boots waited for him on the beige leather couch in front of his sixty-four inch plasma television that hung on the wall. A matching recliner sat next to the couch, and Dalton collapsed into it. "Oh, that feels good," he noted as he nestled in. He turned his head to look out the window into his backyard. The house was situated on three acres of land. His backyard had rolling hills and sporadic trees. There was an Olympic-sized in-ground pool, as well.

"Where's Bam Bam and Peach?" Boots asked.

"They're coming," Dalton replied. On cue, the doorbell rang. "That would be them. I'm too tired to move. Hey, Aryan motherfucker, go get the door."

"C'mon, man," the Aryan answered. "I'm not your slave." A clicking sound followed.

"Go let them in or your brains are gonna stain Bobby's couch," Boots explained as he pressed the barrel of his gun to the back of the Aryan's head.

"You guys can't keep treating me like this," he protested as he got up and answered the door.

* * *

Refreshed from his shower, Dalton stood in his trophy room examining his automatic rifle. He made sure the chamber was clear. Raising the gun to his eye, he checked the alignment of the scope. Finally, he took several magazine cartridges from the drawer in the wall display and stuffed them in the pockets of his camouflage vest. He looked around as if to take a visual inventory, shut the light, and exited into the garage.

The cold air in the garage was almost as strong as the sunlight that broke the darkness as the automatic garage door opened. The reflection of sunlight from the three white trailers in front of the house magnified its effect. The hum of his SUV's engine provided a soothing break to the neighborhood's silence. The crisp winter wind bit at his face as he approached the car, in which the four men from his new posse waited in warmth.

Dalton joined them. He handed his gun to Boots, who sat up front with him. The ride to the base was silent. The excitement was gone from their mood. This particular mission was their most important of all: Recruiting military experience was vital to Dalton's plan for Max's army.

The guardhouse to the base was unmanned, although the gate was locked. Dalton parked the car at the gate and the five men got out, four of whom had guns drawn. Dalton led the group onto the grounds through a gap between the electronic arm that blocked traffic and the guardhouse.

His eyes scanned the rooftops of the building: The barracks and mess hall were clear. As he turned his head to the left he saw movement atop the chapel. Two gunshots broke the silence as the slugs landed in the dirt about three feet in front of him. Clearly, they were a sniper's warning.

The four-man support team dove for cover. Dalton put his gun above this head and walked further into the center of the base's quad. The public address system came to life, "Attention! Attention! You are trespassing on property of the United States Army. If you do not leave immediately, you will be shot."

Dalton remained still. He proceeded to announce himself, "P.F.C. Robert Dalton reporting for duty. I am looking for my commanding officer, Lieutenant John Sharpe."

Silence followed. Dalton was relieved that the voice was American. His breath became shorter in the cold air and a tear streaked from his left eye as the wind blew from the west. The door to the administrative building opened and two fully armed soldiers approach with their M-16 rifles pointed squarely at Dalton's chest. He stood perfectly still keeping his arms and weapon raised above his head.

"Don't move!" he heard from behind. From his peripheral vision he could tell that more soldiers were approaching from the flanks.

"Don't shoot! We surrender!" the Aryan shouted.

"Listen to them, Aryan," Dalton cautioned. "Just do as they say. We are all on the same side."

"Drop your weapons, all of you," one of the soldiers ordered. The five intruders complied. The soldiers took out plastic ties and bound their captives' hands behind their backs as though taking prisoners in Baghdad. A black soldier of gigantic stature kept his rifle aimed directly on Dalton while the rest of the platoon brought the remaining four prisoners forward. Dalton noticed from the bars on his sleeve that the soldier was a lieutenant.

"Let's go, Loo," a shorter, but equally brawny Latino sergeant said. "We gotta get out of sight."

"Right, Gonzo," the lieutenant replied. "Bring their car over to the garage, Delfino," he ordered one of his soldiers. "The rest of you, take the prisoners to the colonel and report back to your posts."

"Yes, sir!" was the collective response.

The soldiers marched the men into the mess hall, and lined them up, still bound, with their backs to the buffet counter. Two of the soldiers kept their guns pointed at the prisoners at all times.

"Attention!" the gargantuan lieutenant ordered. The entire company stood at attention as their commanding officer entered the room. Roughly six feet tall, he walked with purpose. He lacked the middle-age potbelly most men his age displayed. His full head of silver hair was closely cropped to the pale skin of his scalp. Standard military-issued aviator's sunglasses hid his blue eyes.

"At ease," the officer ordered. He marched directly over to the prisoners, eyeing them up and down and surveying their respective characteristics. When he came to Dalton, he squinted into his eyes. "Dalton?"

"Sir, yes, sir!" Dalton responded.

"It's been a long time, soldier," the officer added. "I admit I remember the name, but your face doesn't ring any bells. Maybe it's the age."

"Sir, I . . ." Dalton began.

"You will only speak when spoken to for now, prisoner," the officer explained. "I am Colonel John Sharpe. If you are Dalton, you would be able to tell me how this happened," he said as he pointed to a scar that ran along his right cheekbone.

"Sir, you were grazed by a bullet in the jungle outside of Quy Noh'n. We were ambushed that night; half of our platoon was wiped out. Even though you were hit, sir, you still managed to carry three of our men back to the extraction point. You should have received a commendation - hell, the Purple Heart - but Colonel Harmon . . ."

"That's enough, Dalton," he interrupted. He patted

Dalton on the shoulder shaking his head as he played out the rest of the memory in his head. "What brings you here, Dalton? You do know that we are technically 'outlaws' right now, right?"

"Yes, sir," Dalton answered. "But so are we," he said as he motioned to the others with his head.

"Right," Sharpe noted. "Chatty, release the prisoners."

The lieutenant took out his knife and cut the plastic restraints from each of the prisoners' wrists. Though freed, the soldiers still did not return their weapons.

"Thank you, sir," Dalton acknowledged. "We are here on behalf of the President, Colonel."

Puzzled, Sharpe angrily retorted, "The President is dead, Dalton. Haven't you been watching the news?"

"Yes, sir, I saw what happened last night. But the enemy missed someone."

"Who?" Sharpe asked.

"Max Noble, sir."

"The freshman Congressman? He can't be President! First off, he's not old enough. Secondly, he's not in the chain of succession. Our Constitution doesn't allow it."

Impressed by Sharpe's knowledge, Dalton countered, "With all due respect, sir, in these times, the Constitution is open to the interpretation of the courts. And last night, Judge Arthur Vineri administered the oath of office for the President to Maxwell Noble. He is our new Commander-in-Chief," he announced to the soldiers proudly.

A murmur swirled among the soldiers. "Attention!" Sharpe ordered bringing a hush to the room. "How could a federal judge ignore the law of the land like that?"

"He's a patriot just like you and me. He knows that the President's power may not be completely legitimate, but he also knows that Noble is the last elected member of the federal government. Since we can't just have an election tomorrow to pick a new President, especially with the enemy in control of our military, he's the only one who can make any claim." He paused as Sharpe looked away to ponder Dalton's reasoning. "Colonel, we came here today to ask you to lead our rebellion against the enemy. Regardless of who occupies the presidency, will you serve?"

Sharpe took a step back. He had been passed over so many times. First, it was the Purple Heart. On numerous occasions, it was a higher rank. A widower with no children, Sharpe constantly searched for a purpose. Now, opportunity had presented itself. "I would like to speak with the President about this," he told Dalton.

"We can take you to him right now," Dalton assured him.

"Lieutenant Chatham and Sergeant Gonzalez will join me," Sharpe explained as he looked at the lieutenant and the sergeant Dalton recognized from outside. The two officers stepped forward. "Dalton, I would like you to meet Lieutenant Leon Chatham and Sergeant Raul Gonzalez.

"Nice to meet you, Lieutenant," Dalton answered as he offered a handshake. The lieutenant shook his hand and nodded.

"Chatty doesn't say much. Only talks when he's working," Sharpe explained.

"And what's your job, Lieutenant?" Dalton asked.

"Communications Officer," the lieutenant responded.

Laughing, Sharpe added, "We call him Chatty for that reason. Ironic, isn't it?" Chatty remained stoic at the comment.

Sharpe continued, "And this is Sergeant Gonzalez."

"Nice to meet you, too, Sergeant," Dalton welcomed as the two shook hands.

"It's always good to meet a patriot willing to lay his life on the line for our nation," the sergeant confirmed.

"Gonzo is our drill instructor, and a martial arts specialist," Sharpe explained. "I suggest you refrain from upsetting him."

"Duly noted," Dalton said with a nod of understanding.

"And who might your friends be, Dalton?" Sharpe inquired.

"These three are the President's private security detail," he said as he pointed to the three Italian-Americans. "That's Boots. That's Bam Bam. And the fat one is the Peach." The Peach leered at Dalton, angry with him for choosing the distinguishing adjective. "And this guy is . . . shit, I forgot your name."

"Hicks, Timmy Hicks," the Aryan said.

"Right," Dalton acknowledged. "We found him at a rally for the Aryan Brotherhood last night, so we've just been calling him 'Aryan.' It just stuck." Chatty and Gonzo stared at him with steely eyes. The Aryan looked down at the floor, clearly afraid of them. "I say he's a traitor, but the President pardoned him and put him on his own security detail."

"If I'm not mistaken, isn't the President a Jew?" Sharpe asked.

"He is indeed," Dalton confirmed. "And a better man than me, that's for sure."

"I must admit, I am very curious to meet him."

* * *

The *minyan*, a prayer group of ten men, broke as soon as Max finished saying *kaddish*, the mourner's prayer.

Shortly after the men left Max's basement they collected their things and went home. Armstrong left a few hours earlier to spend some time with his own family. He was comfortable that Max would be well cared for in Roxy's hands; although, he caught her off guard when he asked her if she and Zach would stay with him for a few days until things returned to "normal." Roxy happily accepted.

After putting Zach to bed in the guest bedroom, Roxy returned to the sofa where she and Max sat for nearly two hours, talking the entire time about the diverging paths their lives had taken over the course of the years since their last encounter.

"I wish I could afford to go for my Master's," she told Max. "It's hard being a single mom."

"From what I can see, you're a great mom," Max offered.

"Thanks. I don't know. Maybe I just wonder what my life would have been like if I made different choices all those years ago. Maybe I would have been the one to go into politics," she teased.

"I never really thought I was going to run," Max tried to explain.

"Why not?"

"Well, I really did it as a favor to Jack. He wants to be nominated chairman of the D.N.C., but he had to show the big wigs down in D.C. that he knew how to get someone elected."

"Ah, so you're a guinea pig. Should I get you a wheel?"

"I like to think of myself as a lab experiment that's percolating . . . you know, just waiting to erupt!" Max began to show his excitement, flailing his arms in the air.

Roxy laughed so loud she had to cover her mouth so as not to wake Zach. "I guess that makes Jack the mad scientist, huh?"

"Something like that."

"And Bob?"

"That's easy! He's Igor."

Roxy laughed again. "Well, I think they did a great job putting you together, Frankenstein."

"Thanks, Rox. I just hope I don't scare the villagers," he joked. His mood suddenly turned serious. "There's something I have to tell you, Rox."

"What's that?" she asked with baited breath expecting another one-liner.

"They swore me in as President last night."

"Yeah, okay. May I shake your hand Mr. President?" she asked sarcastically.

Max extended his right hand, grabbed hers, and said in a deep baritone, "Yes, you may."

Roxy's eyes grew wider as she realized he was not kidding. "Holy shit! You're serious!"

"I am. And I have lots to do if we're going to take this country back from those bastards."

"Max, are you ready for this? I mean, you don't have a clue what you're doing. No offense."

He knew she was right. He also knew she picked up on the one thing he could not hide from her: He had no idea where to start. Even though he was the one with the power, he needed Dalton and Armstrong to give him direction. He sat next to her on the couch, reclining his head so that he was staring at the ceiling.

"Don't think about work, Max," Roxy told him. "Take some time tonight to relax. Even with everything, you are still entitled to some 'you' time," she explained as she poked him in the sternum.

He looked at her and wondered how he ever let her get away. Her presence calmed him. It was a refreshing change from Valerie's constant demands that riled him. It was only one day since he buried his wife; guilt crept into his head but his heart repelled it.

Suddenly, their attention was drawn from their banter to the headlights visible through sheer curtains in the bay windows slowly stopping in front of the house. "C'mon," Max complained, "It's eleven o'clock. Don't people know that we stopped taking guests three hours ago?"

He reached over the back of the sofa and moved the curtain aside. From the silhouettes he could make out, he could tell that Dalton was among the visitors. "This may be a business call, Rox."

"Who is it?"

He pointed out the window to try to show Roxy who was who. "That's Bob; I could spot him anywhere. The Aryan kid is next to him. And that one is that Boots guy. Which means that the other two must be Bam Bam and the Peach. I don't know who the other three are."

"Should I wake Zach?"

"Nah, let him sleep. We'll go downstairs and talk. I'll try to keep Bob quiet."

"Okay, I'm gonna put up some coffee for you guys though."

"You're the best, Rox."

They left the sofa for their next destinations: Max went to the front door to greet the newcomers, while Roxy went to the kitchen to brew her promised elixir. Max opened the door before Dalton had the opportunity to ring the bell.

"Shh!" Max cautioned Dalton as the entourage approached, his breath visible in the winter night. "I've got a house guest who is already sleeping?"

"A house guest?" Dalton challenged loudly. "We're in

the middle of an invasion and you've got a fuckin' house guest?! Get your priorities straight! I raised you better than that!"

"His priorities are just fine, Bob," Roxy confirmed from the kitchen.

"A woman?" Dalton asked in a state of shock. "A fuckin' woman? *That's* your houseguest? Max, you're wife's body is barely cold, you're the leader of the free – or not so free, anymore – world, and you want me to shut up so you can get laid?"

Hearing Dalton's assumptions caused Roxy to fly to Max's defense before he had the opportunity to plead his own case. "Bob Dalton! Do you really think I am *that* kind of woman? I've known Max just as long as you, and I came here to make sure he was keeping it together!"

A puzzled Dalton stared at her trying to place the face. Finally, it came to him. "Roxy? Roxy Fidelis?"

"The one and only," she replied raising her hands to the sky as she smiled wryly.

"Wow! I haven't seen you since you guys dated in college."

"That's right. Now, if you don't mind, keep your voices down so my son doesn't wake up."

"Son?" Dalton asked, his mouth agape.

"Yeah," Max answered. "Now come in before you all freeze."

"I'll bring the coffee down when it's ready, Max," Roxy assured him.

The men entered and followed Max to his basement, where Dalton proceeded with the interrogation. "Where the hell did she come from?" he asked.

"Just showed up this morning," Max answered. "She's gonna stay with me for a couple of days. Maybe longer, if I'm lucky."

"Well, as long as she's around you, she's gonna need protection. Her son, too. Boots, you guys keep your eyes on her and the kid at all times, got it?"

"Got it, Bobby," Boots replied. Bam Bam and the Peach nodded in agreement.

"Good," Dalton confirmed. He took off his coat and collected the others', as well; he threw them on a table off to the side. "Now, Mr. President, I would like to introduce you to Colonel John Sharpe."

"Hi," Max said as he offered to shake Sharpe's hand. Sharpe, Chatty and Gonzo saluted Max simultaneously. Max stood still not knowing what to do. "Oh," he said when he realized the protocol, and he offered a weak salute back. The soldiers remained at attention and said nothing. "Um, cat's got your tongue, Colonel?"

"Sir, no, sir," Sharpe responded, annoyed that he was answering to someone half his age who did not know anything about military protocol. He considered the lack of knowledge a symptom of society's disrespect, in general, for the sacrifice of military families; nonetheless, he honored the only military protocol he knew, and he respected the Presidency regardless of who occupied the office.

"You have to put them 'at ease,' Max," Dalton explained.

"Oh, right," Max responded, embarrassed. "At ease, men," he ordered in a false baritone. "Colonel, please sit."

"Thank you, Mr. President," Sharpe said as the men all sat on the brown leather couches surrounding a rectangular, antique, oak coffee table. "As Mr. Dalton explained, I am Colonel John Sharpe, Base Commander, Mitchel Field. This is Lieutenant Leon Chatham, Communications Officer, and Sergeant Raul Gonzalez, Drill Instructor. Requesting permission for the three of us to speak freely, sir."

"Sure," Max permitted.

"*Granted*," Dalton half-heartedly coughed through his hand.

"Right," Max acknowledged. "Sorry, men. Permission granted."

"Thank you, sir," Sharpe began. "Mr. President, Mr. Dalton has brought us up to speed as to last night's events. I believe we should keep all of that information classified."

"Alright," Max concurred.

Sharpe continued, "Sir, if we are to retake our nation, it is going to take a coordinated effort. We believe we can raise a volunteer militia, but we will still be significantly outnumbered. Surprise is our only chance at victory."

"What do you have in mind, Colonel?" Max asked.

"To be honest, sir, I don't know. It will take some time to plan. We will need reconnaissance, recruitment and training. Since the enemy has complete control of our satellites, this mission must be completely underground – literally. If they identify a single aspect of our plan, they will swoop in and crush us. The enemy has proven that it is not stupid, and we are not afforded the luxury of underestimation."

"Given the proper intelligence, can you coordinate our attack?"

"With information and time, Mr. President," Sharpe paused. "Absolutely. You see, Mr. President, the enemy has opened with the King's Gambit."

Puzzled, Max asked, "The King's Gambit?"

"Yes, sir," Sharpe confirmed. He directed their attention to the chess board that was set up on the coffee table. Pointing to the pieces, he explained, "It's a chess term for an opening strategy, actually, in which the two center pawns take control of the center of the board early, but leave the king vulnerable. Let's assume the white pieces represent the enemy since they made the first move," he explained. He moved the white pawn in front of the white king forward two spaces. "Our actions over the last twenty-four hours have been undetected and are harmless as far as the enemy is concerned," he said as he moved the black pawn in front of the black king forward one space. "The enemy will continue to establish his positioning," he continued, moving the white pawn in front of the white queen up one space so that it protected its brother white pawn. "However, if we can manage to obtain information about the enemy's strategic positioning, we can strike quickly and accurately, forcing him into mistakes that will leave him exposed and on the defensive," he said, moving the right-side black bishop into the open black square that left the black bishop staring directly at the white king. "That would put him in check on the third move," he explained pointing to the board. "He would be forced into making a series of rash decisions to counter our resistance.

"Now, he could use his other pawns or more powerful back line pieces to thwart our attack," Sharpe went on, moving the white pawn in front of the left-side bishop forward one square to block the black bishop. He then moved the black bishop back one square along the line from which it came. "Remember, his strategy was to take complete control of the board from the onset. But if you look, he has left many of his pieces vulnerable. Thus, he has unwittingly diminished his chance at victory and this will lead to his ultimate defeat."

Max looked at the men's faces. Dalton and his entourage wore blank stares, evidently concerned only with their directive—his protection. The soldiers displayed only their discipline and stoicism. "What happens if he uses those more powerful pieces to counter attack?" Max asked, advancing the white bishop next to the white queen two spaces so that it threatened the pestering black bishop.

"There is sacrifice in every war, sir," Sharpe answered as he used the black bishop to take the white bishop, and then replaced the black bishop on the square with the white pawn that had sat dormant in front of the white bishop adjacent to the white king.

"But you said that this would thwart the enemy's strategy of taking control of the center of the board. Does it, Colonel?" Max challenged. "I mean, he has his pieces set out in the center and all we have left to counter is one pawn. We're out maneuvered!"

Sharpe smirked. Max's ability to analyze the board was beginning to impress him. Taking the black pawn in front of the black queen from its original position, Sharpe moved it forward two spaces, where it challenged the leading white pawn and was protected by the black pawn he advanced on his initial move. "Are we, Mr. President?"

"It sounds like you have thought about this already," Max said.

"Just analyzing the situation, sir," Sharpe replied.

"What's his next move?" Max asked.

"Well, he has several options, but none that are immediately threatening," Sharpe explained. "He'd most likely resist the urge to take our lead pawn; doing so would mean relinquishing control of the center position. Not to mention that it would provide an opportunity for us to bring out our queen early in the game. His more likely choice will be to bring out a knight to reinforce his established positions," he said moving the white knight on the right-side of the board up and over so that it came to rest on the white square two rows ahead of the remaining white bishop. "We would respond in kind," he pressed, moving the right-side black knight into the mirroring position.

"And from there?" Max asked curiously.

"Please remember, sir," Sharpe pleaded, "the enemy is a megalomaniac concerned with maintaining control. From his vantage point, he reaches victory by attacking from the middle." Sharpe took the lead white pawn and advanced it one square so that it threatened the black knight. "We, in turn, must be prepared at all times to run, but maintain our attack in the process." He took the endangered black knight and moved it to safety on the white square in the fourth row of the rightmost column. "Satisfied that he is in control, the enemy seeks to attack," he said moving the rightmost white pawn forward one square. "With no direct threat, we will quietly castle, keeping our king – that's you, Mr. President – safely guarded by the rook," he continued by swapping the black king with the rightmost black rook two squares each. The "rocade," or "castle," as the move is more commonly called, was Sharpe's favorite; it allowed him to protect the king and place the oft-forgotten rook on the offensive simultaneously.

"Don't be so quick to consider me the king in need of protecting," Max cautioned. "I intend to fight in this war."

"We'll see about that, Maxie," Dalton interjected.

"Nevertheless, Mr. President," Sharpe continued. "The enemy will then aggressively pursue the black knight," he said, advancing the last of the unmoved right-side pawns two squares to threaten the black knight. "The knight responds aggressively," he said moving the black knight down to rows and one column to the left, "so that it 'forks' the enemy into a decision: Which would he rather lose? His bishop or his rook?"

"That's a tough one," Max replied.

"True, and we'll be satisfied with either," Sharpe

granted. "But having already lost one bishop, I am guessing he would choose to sacrifice the rook," he explained and moved the remaining white bishop to the white square in between the white rook and the black knight. "We then sacrifice our brave knight for his rook, which will be of greater advantage to us." He then swapped the black knight with the white rook on the corner square, and immediately replaced the black knight with the white bishop. "We will then move out another piece to attack," he said while advancing the remaining black knight two rows forward and one column left. "From here, the enemy will become angry, for he will have lost an important piece that he expected to play a highly important role. He will hastily move to take a piece, any piece, to feel as if he has an advantage." Moving the white pawn that he used to block the bishop's check on the third move forward one square, Sharpe threatened the lead black pawn. "We must use his aggression to our advantage, so we will humor him." Sharpe removed the threatening white pawn with the lead black pawn.

"I don't know, Colonel," Max resisted. "There are so many variables here. Any one different move changes the entire outcome of the game."

"Without question, Mr. President," Sharpe conceded. "But look at the board now. The enemy's initial intent was to control the center of the board. In the process, we have positioned ourselves better to control play in the middle, and we have exposed his back line tremendously. They're entirely out of position with no foreseeable plan of attack; it's chaos back there! We, on the other hand, have the better positioning and have the ability to develop our attack. I can't tell you how this will end; only God can see that. But, I can tell you this: It will take time and patience, and a little divine intervention, but we are still better positioned to ultimately prevail. All we have to do is make the appropriate decisions."

Max considered the impressive display of Sharpe's analytical skills closely. He sat quietly for a moment scanning the facial expressions of the company. None was telling. His eyes squinted as they met Sharpe's, which were locked in a hopeful gaze; he could tell that the colonel's apprehension toward him was thawing, albeit not entirely. Each realized that the chess tutorial was nothing more than test to feel each other out. Satisfied that he could work with the colonel, Max finally stood and extended his hand to Sharpe. "Very well, then. The soldiers of this army will take their orders from you, *General* Sharpe," Max instructed, emphasizing the promotion in Sharpe's rank.

Chatty and Gonzo looked at each other and smiled as they rose with Sharpe; they were obviously thrilled that their commanding officer finally received the recognition they knew he deserved. Sharpe embraced Max's hand with his own; although, he hid his excitement as they engaged in a firm and vigorous handshake. "Thank you, Mr. President," was his stoic response.

PART II

Confronting the Demons

CHAPTER 11

Even the thaw that accompanied the warmer spring weather could not melt Sultan's grip on the nation. To the contrary, his weeks in power brought a rapid cultural change that resembled Taliban-ruled Afghanistan. Men were forced to grow beards, while women were required to wear *burkahs* in public.

Communication networks were wiped out; Sultan's troops destroyed all wireless relay towers and land-based cable connections. Direct satellite uplinks, if available, were the only links Americans had to the outside world; SBN was the only network still broadcasting the news. Sultan's men maintained contact through the military's communication networks.

Transportation was also limited. Mass transit systems were run by Sultan's troops, which were a skeleton crew at best, in urban areas and non-existent in the suburbs and rural parts of the country. Driving a car anywhere became impractical since the price of gasoline soared to over ten dollars per gallon with a supply that resembled a trickle. That, combined with the limited availability to work centers and communications, created economic conditions worse than the Great Depression.

Sultan's men oversaw all major corporations and schools. Prayers were mandatory five times each day. Only men were permitted to work and only boys were permitted to attend school; the curfews in effect required them to return immediately home when their day was over. Sultan had men in the Pentagon monitoring every neighborhood in the country with a geothermal satellite.

There was a natural resistance to the changes. Unlike American riot police who used tear gas and rubber bullets to control unruly mobs, Sultan's troops used live ammunition. Night after night those with access to SBN watched Sultan's men broadcast images of their comrades unleashing rounds randomly into the crowds of gathered protesters. Occasionally, armed protesters would return fire, even killing some of their invaders. However, their lack of organization hampered their efforts; often those protesters bearing arms were the ones killed first. After a few weeks, the protests ceased. Resistance proved futile. The United States truly had become the Islamic Republic of America, as Sultan promised.

Most, if not all, Muslim-Americans were not pleased by the changes. They had grown accustomed to their freedom; many were prospering businesspeople. Sultan's new society destroyed their lives in the same manner. Although they were often granted privileges by Sultan's men, such as being placed at the head of the lines for both food and the trains, they also lived in constant fear of reprisals from their neighbors.

Hakim "Hank" Youseff was one of the adversely affected Muslim-Americans. The son of Egyptian immigrants, Hank was born in New York City. His first job as a delivery boy for a deli supplemented his father's income as a taxi driver. He graduated high school and moved out to Long Island to begin working at a convenience store owned by his friend's uncle to support his family; a college education was not an option for him. He married at the age of twenty-three, and he and his wife had five children, three boys and two girls, ages four to fourteen. He still worked at the convenience store; only now, he owned it.

However, being unable to receive shipments of food to restock his shelves, the health of his business was failing. In order to pay his mortgage, Hank had to beg for pennies at his local mosque. In his life, he had never felt such shame within his community. He resolved to correct that feeling.

Hank once met a man in his store who knew people. He never forgot this man's name: If someone needed something, Bob Dalton was the man to speak to. Although they were not close friends, by the time Hank's fifth child was born, Dalton was close enough to Hank's family to make certain that his wife received a bouquet of flowers in her hospital room.

Despite their friendship, Dalton was wary of Hank's motive when he approached him about setting up a resistance against Sultan's men. Dalton understood Hank's plight, but it was possible that he was a spy. Dalton told Hank nothing about Max and General Sharpe's plan. But he also realized that if he could be trusted, he could be a very useful ally. Dalton assigned the Peach to tail Hank for three weeks.

Dalton was surprised to see that the Peach took copious notes about Hank's behavior. "I didn't think you knew how to write," he teased. In addition to notes about Hank, the Peach had records about everyone Hank came in contact with. They were all family men, Muslims born in America, and were not enjoying the same freedoms they did before Sultan's arrival. Most importantly, they all publicly aired their grievances about Sultan's regime, and they all expressed their desire to eliminate him. The Peach's summation: Hank and his peers could be trusted.

Dalton arranged a meeting at his house between Hank, his peers and General Sharpe. Sharpe arrived first with Chatty and Gonzo in tow; all three wore plain clothes and had grown in their beards to blend into Sultan's new society. When the five Muslim men arrived, Bam Bam searched each of them for weapons while Sharpe scanned them from head to toe with curiosity.

"They're clean," Bam Bam reported. Sharpe nodded

and the men took their seats around Dalton's dining room table.

Sharpe cleared his throat. "Bob has explained to me that you are as unhappy with the new order in Washington as we are. Is that accurate?"

The men all nodded as Hank spoke up, "I speak for all of us when I say, 'Yes, it is.'"

"Then I will cut to the chase Mr. Youseff," Sharpe said as he leaned forward. "Are you men prepared to die for the United States of America, to protect and defend its Constitution and laws, if need be?"

"Without question," Hank declared. "Our oppressors have shamed Islam. We study the Koran every day. Nothing in it states that Allah wants Muslims to kill non-Muslims in Jihad. Not only have they killed innocent people, but also these men are ruining the lives of hard working Muslims who have prospered in America. I vote in every election! I pay my taxes on time every year! I do these things so that my right to worship Allah as I choose will remain intact! More importantly, I respect the rights of others not to. Jihad is not a war, as these men claim. Jihad is a struggle to accept Allah into your heart. That is why the Koran speaks of Muslims waging Jihad. Not to convert infidels, but to strengthen the beliefs of faithful Muslims whenever they may wane. As far as we are concerned, this Sultan and his men are the infidels, not the American people."

Sharpe sat silently for a moment. "Mr. Youseff, you and your friends can be of great assistance to our cause. We need men who can get close to the enemy, and who the enemy feels that they can trust. We need to learn as much as we can about their operations so that we may identify and exploit their weaknesses."

"You want us to spy on them?" Hank asked.

"Not just spy, Mr. Youseff. I would like you to

infiltrate their operation. Your work will determine the level of our success. You would be serving as our special reconnaissance team."

Hank and his friends looked at each other. They spoke in Arabic briefly. "We accept. We are all eager to help, General."

"Excellent. Go home to your families. We will meet back here tonight at twenty-three hundred hours for your first briefing."

"Very well, General," Hank replied. The Muslim men shook hands with Sharpe. They looked Chatty square in the eyes, and he nodded at each of them as they left. Bam Bam closed the front door behind them.

"Status reports," Sharpe ordered.

"Word has spread throughout Long Island," Chatty reported. "About one thousand men with military experience volunteered. The rest of the troops are young men between the ages of fifteen and twenty-two. In all, we have approximately ten thousand men."

"We will begin training at the local high schools in their neighborhoods at night," Gonzo explained. "Sultan's men report to several mosques miles away from any school grounds. We assume that these mosques have been adopted as their barracks. Each school will raise its own company of troops. I intend to visit a different school each night to make sure that the veterans who are leading the training are on schedule."

"Discipline is the first order of business at basic training," Sharpe ordered. "General physical fitness is the second. Use calisthenics to accomplish both. Combat training and weapons instruction are going to be more challenging to teach given the conditions. I am loath to waste live ammunition, but most of these boys have probably never picked up a rifle before."

"Wait a minute, General," Dalton chimed in. "I have

an idea." He disappeared for three and a half minutes. When he returned, he brandished a rifle that mirrored the M-16 assault rifles that would be issued to the troops. He raised it at Chatty, whose eyes bulged in fear.

Chatty managed to duck just a second before Dalton pulled the trigger. He heard three shots hit the wall behind him. "Are you out of your fuckin' mind, Dalton?" he excitedly demanded to know.

"Interesting," Sharpe responded. Chatty, stunned by Sharpe's calm, looked at the wall behind him to see yellow paint splattered in three places and dripping down the wall.

"I know a guy who owns a paintball course out in the woods in Suffolk County," Dalton explained. "My team won his Capture-the-Flag league last year."

"And those guns, what's the recoil like?" Sharpe asked.

"Same as the real thing, General," Dalton answered. "Wouldn't be any fun without it," he continued with a large grin.

"Can your friend arrange to set up combat training exercises for ten thousand men?" Gonzo inquired.

"Seeing as how he's already enlisted with us, you can probably coax him with a higher rank," Dalton explained.

"Set it up, Gonzo," Sharpe ordered.

"Sir, yes, Sir," Gonzo replied. "Permission to speak freely, Sir," he requested.

"Go ahead," Sharpe replied.

"What of our President, Sir," he asked. "The veteran troops often ask who is leading the insurrection."

"I know it's an issue. For now, just tell them that the President is, 'A fine patriot, whose identity we must keep secret for his protection,'" Sharpe explained. Gonzo understood that Sharpe had just provided the answer to be given every time that question was asked. "That should keep them quiet until you are able to train him."

"With all due respect, sir, I will not be able to train the troops and the President at the same time," Gonzo warned. "Is it essential that we take him into battle?"

"He's goin' into battle, Sergeant," Dalton insisted. "If you don't want to train him, I will. I raised him and mentored him all of his life. I've got a military background. He'll be ready to lead by the time I get through with him."

"Are you sure you can get him battle-ready?" Sharpe asked.

"When I get through with him, he'll be more dangerous than a green beret!"

"Alright, then, Dalton," Sharpe replied. "He's all yours."

* * *

General Rogers paced behind the chairs of Sultan's men who were monitoring the activity on the ground picked up by the military's geothermal satellite. It sat in geosynchronous orbit constantly monitoring the entire contiguous portion of the nation. During the Cold War, its primary purpose was to monitor the shorelines for potential encroachments by Soviet nuclear submarines. After the events of September 11, 2001, the CIA and FBI began to use it to monitor activity within the nation itself. Never did Rogers expect it to be used like this. Nor did he expect to be the one using it in this manner.

To Rogers, General Harmon was a brilliant man and a patriot; if Harmon said that it was best to allow Sultan to control the Pentagon for now, Rogers trusted his judgment. Even when the other American officers questioned Harmon behind closed doors, Rogers assuaged them to trust their general.

Harmon and Sultan stood at the rail of the balcony overlooking the pit of computers and monitors in the belly of the Hub. Large plasma screens hung on the wall in the front of the room. The geothermal fingerprints of the cities under Sultan's control appeared on those screens, while the men in the pit monitored the other areas of the nation.

One of the men in the pit spoke up. "Sir, I have some unusual activity appearing on Long Island," he reported. Rogers walked over to the monitor and leaned down to get a closer look at his screen. It showed the yellow and red thermal signatures of about five hundred people doing calisthenics in rows of ten with about ten people on the outside of the formation.

"Where is it?" Harmon asked from the balcony above.

"Looks like they're on a football field, Sir," Rogers replied pointing to the outline of the goal posts appearing through the thermal signatures.

"Sultan, this could be an attempt to organize," Harmon said.

"Excuse me, sir, but it could just be some coaches holding tryouts for a football league," Rogers proffered.

"True, but it is after curfew. That makes it suspicious," Harmon countered. "Keep monitoring it, General."

"Yes, Sir," Rogers acknowledged. He turned back to the monitor, and did a double take in Harmon's direction. He saw Harmon walk over to Sultan and whisper something in Sultan's ear. Suspiciously, he tried as hard as he could to eavesdrop on the conversation.

"If it continues, I will strengthen our defenses in New York," he heard Sultan say. "If there is one city we cannot afford to lose, it is that one. To lose it would give European nations access to aid an insurrection." Rogers listened for Harmon's response, but it was intelligible.

* * *

Max's training began in a classroom setting at his home. After breakfast with Roxy, Max received private tutoring in the complete works of Voltaire, Machiavelli and Payne, among others, from Armstrong. Dalton added a translation of the ancient Chinese text, *The Art of War*, for "light" reading, too. Armstrong assigned Max different readings each night, and quizzed him on them each morning. Following the quizzes, Armstrong and Max would discuss the essential teachings of each passage. Zach, being kept home from school for Max's protection, would sit in on the sessions, as well; occasionally, he would add some insight to the conversation from the previous day's lesson, which he had apparently absorbed like a sponge. What Max did not know was that Dalton authorized these sessions as a distraction until he was ready to begin Max's military training. Although he would never admit that the knowledge contained in these works was more important than a weapon in any battle, he recognized that these sessions were entirely necessary in Max's metamorphosis.

The knolls and wooded areas in Dalton's backyard were transformed from a scenic view to an obstacle course. Boots and the Aryan spent days setting up the obstructions. Old tires were set in two parallel lines. They erected a twelve-foot wall with random handgrips for scaling, installed a set of monkey bars, and placed large pyramids made of plywood in the dales. Though the craftsmanship was suspect, Dalton knew that it would serve its training purpose.

The exercise would be man-on-man Capture-the-Flag. Dalton would stand by the pool overlooking the yard from the plateau on which the house sat. Max, armed only with a three-foot dowel one-quarter of an inch thick to simulate his sword (since he did not yet know how to use it), would begin at the bottom of the yard and have to ascend the slope to claim the flag Dalton staked at his own side. More importantly, Max would have to do it without being hit by the paintballs Dalton would be firing at him. It was the best method Dalton could conjure to teach Max how to survive in the heat of battle.

Dalton set the booby traps in the woods himself: There was a tripwire that caused a net to drop from above with weights at its edges making escape impossible; a ditch was covered with a sheer camouflage sheet that would give way as soon as it was stepped upon; and the most sadistic of his snares was a tranquilizer gun that was activated by a foot pedal covered by the underbrush. Dalton hoped that Max would find each one, especially the tranquilizer; one way or another, he would learn to expect the unexpected.

Max's first attempt was over before it began. He thought the woods would provide the necessary cover from the paintballs. He darted into the woods hastily, gaining speed as he ran. That Dalton might have set traps never occurred to him. He was making great progress, and he had Dalton in his sights when, to his surprise, the ground gave out underneath him. He found himself in a hole in the ground eight feet deep with only a sheer camouflage sheet next to him. He heard Dalton's laugh. "Forgot to tell you about that one, Maxie," he called.

"Thanks, Bob. How about getting me out of here," Max called. There was no answer. Max sat in the ditch for the remainder of the day. Finally, a rope was thrown down to him.

"Bobby wants to know if you learned your lesson," Boots explained.

Max grabbed the rope and climbed out of the ditch. "And what lesson would that be?" he asked.

"Don't know. You'll have to ask him. I can't figure that fuckin' guy out."

When he finally reached the house, Max confronted

Dalton. "Bobby, what the hell are you doing? Why did you leave me out there all damn day? We're wasting time, you know!"

"Well, if you didn't fall in the fuckin' ditch, we wouldn't have wasted all day."

"What kind of shit is that? How was I supposed to know there was ditch? You hid it under a camouflage sheet!"

Dalton was enraged by Max's insolence. "Guess what, Max. Your enemies aren't gonna tell you where they hid a landmine or a trip wire. Or worse, where they have snipers planted. You better to learn to open your fuckin' eyes. Until you learn that lesson, you only get one shot each day. If you're so upset about what's goin' on out there in the world and you wanna do somethin' about it, you better learn that lesson fast. I'm not lettin' you go into battle until you get that flag from me. Is that clear?"

A dejected Max hung his head before answering, "Yes, sir." He never saw Dalton's hand, and he was shocked when it slapped him across the face knocking him to the ground.

"Don't you ever put your head down!" Dalton commanded. "Do you hear me?"

Angered, Max got up and charged at Dalton knocking him over the back of the sofa in his den. "Who the fuck do you think you are?" he demanded mid-lunge.

Both men rebounded from their fall with their fists raised. "C'mon, Maxie. Throw a punch. I dare ya," Dalton coaxed.

Max threw a right hook. Unfortunately for him, Dalton dodged the punch and countered with an uppercut that knocked Max into the wall, breaking the glass on the picture frame behind him. He felt the warm blood ooze from his nose. His eyes fluttered and closed as he slumped down to the ground.

When he woke, the Aryan was cleaning the blood from his chin. "How you feelin', Ali?" Dalton asked him.

Max saw that Boots, Bam Bam and the Peach were in the room. None of them would look at him. "Fuck you," Max responded.

"Max, listen to me. You got that fight in you. That's good. But you have to learn when and how to use it."

"Bobby, don't you ever fuckin' hit me again. That's an order, got it?"

"Let's go outside and talk," Dalton said as he offered Max a hand up. He was aware of the embarrassment Max was feeling in front of his own bodyguards. Max accepted the offer.

"Max, no one knows you like I do. Until you prove to them that you can beat me, they will question your ability to lead them."

Max had no response. In fact, he did not say a word for the rest of the evening. Dalton explained to Max's entourage that Max was woozy; Boots was designated to drive Max home. Dalton's words echoed in Max's head for the entire ride. Boots broke the silence. "Don't let him get to you like that."

Max looked at him; his thoughts dwelt on the challenge Dalton had issued. He thought to himself: *What is it going to take? He's bigger. He's more experienced. He anticipates my every move.* Making sure not to ignore Boots, he said, "I know."

"I'm just sayin', he's a ball buster," Boots clarified. Max stared out the window. He was relieved to see that they were pulling up to his house.

As the car pulled into the driveway he said, "Thanks, Boots." Once the car stopped Max exited, but before closing the door, he continued, "Listen, Boots, tell the guys that I'm not gonna lose to him anymore."

"Sure thing," Boots replied. Max could detect that he was being polite, not sincere. He held his head up and entered his house through the garage.

Inside, Roxy was waiting for him. "What happened to you?" she asked upon seeing the dried blood on his face.

"I had a fight with Bob."

"What?!"

"I had a fight with Bob. He thinks he's teaching me some sort of lesson. First he left me in a ditch all day, and then he laced into me when I asked him about it. And then he fuckin' hit me! I just lost it and started fighting with him."

"Who won?"

"What does it matter? It's over. We're still friends. He says that I won't be ready until I can beat him."

"So you're gonna fight him every day?"

"No, he wants me to win at Capture-the-Flag. I have to get this flag from him while he's shooting paintballs at me. If I get hit, I lose. But he set traps in the course. I fell in a ditch today, and he left me there all day. It's just a waste of time. I guess I got frustrated."

"Max, I've known you and Bob for a long time. He loves you like a son. Trust him. He's obviously doing this for a reason. You're gonna be a better man for this."

Roxy caressed Max's hair. They stared into each other's eyes. Then their lips locked taking each other's breath away. It was as if they had last kissed that morning, not thirteen years prior.

"Roxy, I love you," he said when they broke from their embrace.

She smiled. "I love you, too."

CHAPTER 12

"Come," Sultan answered to the knock at the door. Harmon and Rogers entered the office once belonging to Harmon; Sultan was its new occupant. "Ah, General Harmon. What is the report on these gatherings sighted on Long Island?"

"Well, Sultan, we cannot be certain," Harmon explained. "General Rogers believes that the activities are benign."

"Benign, General Rogers?" Sultan inquired.

"That's correct," Rogers reported. "The behavior has been the same every night for the last three weeks. It simply looks like boys doing exercises. We have not detected any formal military training, and no gunfire that would signify weapons training has been reported by your men in the area. Therefore, we believe that this is most likely an unauthorized athletic activity."

"I see," Sultan responded while stroking his graying beard. "General Harmon, do you agree?"

"The analysis seems logical," Harmon replied. "Still, I would say that a risk of attack exists, albeit minimal."

"What course of action would you recommend, General Harmon?"

"Well, Long Island is just that: an island. Your men are in control of the bridges and tunnels. Reinforcements at the East River crossings will prevent a land assault. The only other viable threat would be to cross the river by boat. A larger naval presence in the river should deter that attempt."

"Very well, General. Tell my men to double the guard at the bridges and tunnels, and send three destroyers and three submarines into the East River."

"Right away, Sultan. You will be able to focus your attention on monitoring the rest of the country that way. No need to waste more time on this anomaly."

As Harmon and Rogers turned to leave, Sultan gave one more order. "Oh, and General, send a nuclear warhead to Emir."

"I'm sorry," Harmon stunningly asked. "Did you say a *nuclear* warhead?"

"Yes, nuclear. Just in case they find a back door."

"Are you sure that's entirely necessary? What if he activates it against your wishes?" Rogers questioned.

"Emir would not do that," Sultan instinctively insisted before pausing to digest the question. "But you raise a valid point. Allah will guide his hands, but I should keep them tied together. Send him the warhead, but do not supply him with the activation code. Tell him that if we need to use the bomb, we will give him the code at that time."

"It will be done, Sultan," Harmon assured. Neither Harmon nor Rogers wore their concern well. They rushed to the elevator maintaining complete silence along the way. Once inside with the doors closed they felt secure within the metallic box to speak about Sultan's final order.

Rogers broke the silence. "We're not really going to give his lunatic brother a nuclear bomb, are we, General?"

"I'm afraid we have to. He is still in control, and we must accept that for now."

"General, with all due respect, it's April now, and we've been saying that for three months. When are *we* going to answer the call of duty? We can take him out at any moment. What exactly are we waiting for?"

"Patience is a virtue, Chet. Trust me. *That* is an order."

"Yes, Sir." The elevator door opened and the generals resumed their silence.

* * *

After the ditch incident, Max determined that attacking Dalton from the open side of the hill would prove more successful. He felt that the plywood pyramids would provide the necessary cover to protect him from Dalton's paint pellets. For three weeks Dalton proved him wrong on a daily basis. The welts on his body reminded him that he should avoid getting hit at all costs; had it been live fire, he was a dead man.

Today would be different. General Sharpe was coming to the house to hold a strategy session. That was Sharpe's way of saying that he would be checking in on Max's progress. Although he had the power in theory, Max heeded Dalton's warning fully realizing that he had to prove himself a capable leader before he would be allowed to exercise it. Max knew very little about Sharpe, but from what he could glean from their brief encounters he surmised that Sharpe had little patience for civilians meddling in military affairs. Whether Sharpe considered him a civilian was still questionable; therefore, the only way to gain Sharpe's complete trust would be to perform in this pseudo-military setting.

Max sat at the base of the hill where he drew a map of the course on a piece of notebook paper. His repeated failures in the open field persuaded Max that attempting his assault through the woods was a strategy worth revisiting. Clearly, it must have been a weakness if Dalton went through great lengths to set booby traps, he thought. In blue ink, he placed a circle in the woods where he fell into the ditch and triangles that signified the plywood pyramids; however, in red ink, he put dots in between his stick-figure trees that signified the woods to mark the most probable locations of other snares in his estimation. Dalton's plan was actually working: Max was beginning to learn how to develop strategy; he was expecting the unexpected.

Sharpe arrived with his usually entourage, which included Chatty and Gonzo. Hank was summoned for this meeting, as well. Dalton would sit in, of course; as the host he could not be denied access to his own dining room. Max, on the other hand, was not invited. Dalton explained that there was no need to concern Max until viable options were ready to be presented to him for his decision. Max knew that the excuse was cover for Sharpe's untrusting nature. Despite voicing his disagreement to Dalton, the meeting went on without him.

"Regular reports," Sharpe insisted.

"The men are ready for combat training," Gonzo reported. "The captains have all reported that their companies are disciplined. They've also reported that there is a sense of monotony seeping in. We need to move on to keep up morale, sir."

"Dalton, is your man ready to begin weapons training?" Sharpe asked.

"Just say the word, General," Dalton replied. "I've also reached out to my neighbor, Sensei Jimmy Takinawa, founder of the Rising Sun Dojo franchise. He's agreed to lend us his senseis to train the men for hand-to-hand combat."

"Will that suffice, Major Gonzalez?" Sharpe asked. He always felt it important to listen to his officers.

"It should boost morale, sir," Gonzo replied. "I'll alert the captains."

"Very well," Sharpe responded. "Mr. Dalton, coordinate Sensei Takinawa's participation with Major

Gonzalez." Dalton nodded affirmatively. "Lieutenant Youseff, what can you tell us about the enemy's operations?"

"General," Hank began, "we have infiltrated Sultan's army as you have asked. They believe that we have joined their cause, and they treat us as one of their own. The enemy has a very loosely based chain of command. The brother of Sultan is a man named Emir. He is the caliph responsible for the New York metropolitan area. He broadcasts orders over the radio, and whoever deciphers the coded messages first is the leader for that operation."

"You say he is broadcasting?" Chatty interrupted.

"Yes, that is correct," Hank replied. "There is a radio frequency that the men keep on at all times. His orders are disguised as *fatwas*, or religious edicts. They are really coded messages."

"General," Chatty inserted, "all telecommunications we are aware of have been shut down. If he is broadcasting, he has to have a central location with the capacity to reach the entire metropolitan area. And we need to find this frequency to start deciphering these messages."

"Good thinking, Colonel Chatham," Sharpe agreed. "Where is the best place to broadcast?"

"The highest point in the area," Chatty answered. "In New York, there is only one place I can think of: The Empire State Building."

Sharpe's eyes narrowed as he rubbed his bearded chin in deep thought. "Well, then, I supposed that our mission is to take control of the building. Anything else, Lieutenant?"

"Yes, sir," Hank answered. "Rumors of a planned attack have spread, sir. The enemy is suspicious. They have doubled their guard at the bridges and the tunnels, and ordered additional naval patrols."

"It's gonna be hard to get an army into Manhattan

without using the bridges and tunnels," Dalton offered. The military council was less than pleased with his statement of the obvious. He responded to their scowls, "What? It ain't gonna be easy. I'm just sayin'."

"There is one other way into Manhattan from Long Island, Mr. Dalton," Sharpe countered. "The Long Island Railroad runs into Penn Station. We can steal some trains from the central yard in the middle of the night, take them into Penn, and then attack our strategic targets through the subway tunnels."

"There is a problem with that plan, sir," Hank said. "Control of the subway system has been turned over to a gang warlord."

"Gang warlord?" Sharpe questioned.

"Yes, sir," Hank affirmed.

"What kind of gang?" Chatty asked.

"I don't know, Colonel," Hank replied.

"We need more intelligence about this warlord, Lieutenant," Sharpe stated. "Can you and your men get close to him?"

"No, sir," Hank answered. "The warlord avoids contact with anyone he does not feel he can trust. Whatever deal he has struck with the enemy, it appears as though a part of it is for the enemy to ignore their underground activities."

"General, if I may," Chatty offered, "allow me to do some undercover recon. My cousin was a Blood. He was killed in a drive-by shooting when I was fourteen. As a matter of fact, he's the reason I joined the army when I turned eighteen. I understand the gang mentality, sir. Let me go undercover."

Sharpe was uneasy about the idea of sending his second in command on a reconnaissance mission involving noted criminals. "That's an awful risk, Colonel."

"I'll get closer than any of you will," Chatty said. "They are less likely to question what a black man is doing there than any of you."

"They might not question me either, as a Latino, sir," Gonzo offered.

The conundrum was clear to Sharpe. He could not risk losing his top two men if their identities were discovered. At the same time, he could think of no other men better suited for the task. He sat in a state consternation for several minutes. The silence in the room was deafening. Finally, he said, "Major, can any of your captains oversee the remainder of the troops' training in your absence?"

"Captain Williams was special ops in Operation Desert Storm, sir," Gonzo confirmed.

"Special ops, huh?" Sharpe questioned. "He wouldn't happen to be black, would he?"

"He is, sir," Gonzo replied.

"That settles it, then," Sharpe decreed. "Colonel Chatham and Captain Williams will gather intelligence about this warlord, and provide us with a plan of attack. Sorry, Major Gonzalez, but you are too important to the training operations to risk you in a recon mission."

"Understood, sir," Gonzo answered.

"I will notify Captain Williams to discuss logistics," Chatty asserted.

Sharpe was satisfied. "Very well. Lieutenant, see to it that Colonel Chatham and Captain Williams get access to the trains when they need it."

"Yes, sir," Hank replied. "I will move them to the front of the lines myself."

"Is there anything else?" Sharpe asked. The table replied in the negative. "Good. Mr. Dalton, let's see how far along you've managed to bring the President."

Max saw the men file out of the house at the top of the hill. He knew that his opportunity to impress had arrived. Dalton picked up his paintball gun, and waved down to Max to signal that he should begin his attempt. Max waved back and immediately darted into the woods.

"He's trying the woods this time," Dalton noted. "This should be interesting."

Max carefully stepped around the sheer camouflage sheet covering the ditch this time. Having safely passed it, he looked at his map and noted that the most likely chance for success was the path about ten degrees to his left. He started on his way, and came to rest at a tree after about thirty yards. Safe again. His map told him to cut back to the right for five yards, and then continue forward through the heavy underbrush for about fifty yards. Following his own hand-drawn guide, he entered the brush.

A snap sounded when Max took his first step. He felt something under his foot, and he assumed it was a branch. However, he did not expect the biting pain in his buttocks that ensued a split second later; the pain riveted his body. Slowly he felt himself become weak.

"What was that?" Sharpe asked Dalton.

"That," Dalton answered with a sense of disappointment, "was the President failing without me firing a shot." Max stumbled out of the woods waving his arms in the air. Once visible to the gallery, he collapsed on his front. The yellow feather of the tranquilizer dart pointed into the air from his buttocks.

"You shot the President with a tranquilizer gun, Dalton?" Sharpe asked in an astonished tone.

Dalton grinned widely. "Technically, General, he shot himself."

"When he wakes up tell him I want him to start training with Sensei Takinawa," Sharpe ordered. "Don't waste my time with this damn game of yours until the sensei says he's ready to perform." His disappointment in Max was turning rage; his patience for the civilian trainee was waning. "Colonel, Major, let's go. We have important work to do."

* * *

The sunlight burned Max's corneas as he opened his eyes. His temples ached as if someone had placed his head in a vise. He tried to stand up, but the soreness in his left buttock made the sudden movement painful. He had been lying on a lounge chair by the pool; he managed to pull himself to the nearby patio table where he was able to lean on his right side, which alleviated the pain.

"Well, well," Dalton bellowed from the section of the patio behind Max. "Looks like Sleeping Beauty decided to rejoin us."

"What happened?" Max asked, sounding as if he had been on a drinking binge for hours.

Dalton slowly approached the table so that he could look Max in the eye. "You thought you could outsmart me by cuttin' through the woods, but you didn't watch where you were walking, did ya? You hit the foot pedal I set up to this." Dalton, grinning widely, held out his hand in which laid the yellow-feathered tranquilizer dart.

Max shook his head. "You're a sick fuck, Bob."

"Hey, you always did prefer to learn the hard way. Maybe now you'll finally realize that you gotta keep your eyes open at all times. You're going off to war! This is no joke! We're raising an army here that's gonna follow your lead. If you trip, they trip. You have to be able to see three and four steps ahead, at a minimum."

"You know something, Bob," Max seethed, "I ran a successful business before running for Congress. I know how to think and strategize, but you and Sharpe won't let me in on your damned strategy sessions. I know how to lead! What I need to learn, and what I've not learned from you, is how to fight!"

The grin dimmed from Dalton's face. He knew the truth had been spoken: He was failing as Max's teacher. He hated failure. It burned him to his core. Normally, fury would rush to his aid to turn failure into success. But he knew that in this situation, fighting with Max would accomplish nothing. He mumbled, "You're right. I've taught you everything you've needed to know in life, but I haven't been able to teach you that. General Sharpe knows it, too."

"What?" Max asked.

"Sharpe knows it, too," Dalton repeated. "Jimmy!" he yelled toward the obstacle course. "Jimmy, he's awake!"

"What are you doing?" Max inquired nervously. A short Asian man approached the pool. He wore a tight black tee shirt that accentuated his muscle tone; Max was convinced that there was not an ounce of fat on this man's body. His hair was salt-and-peppered, but had more pepper than salt.

Clean-shaven, he looked younger than a man in his forties, but Jimmy Takinawa grew more recognizable as he approached. He was Max's neighbor as a child. A few years older than Max, Jimmy looked after him like a little brother. He supported *Intensity* by advertising for his Rising Sun Dojo franchise when he knew that the magazine's target audience was women aged eighteen to thirty-five. (It also cost him a fortune to design an entire marketing campaign with ads promoting the martial arts as self-defense for young women.) During Max's Congressional campaign, Jimmy donated ten thousand dollars to support the cause.

"Jimmy?" Max asked. "What's he doing here?"

"Sharpe ordered him here," Dalton explained.

"Jimmy's senseis will be training the troops in hand-to-hand combat."

"That's great," Max said.

"Yeah. But he's also here to teach you what I can't." Max sensed the shame in Dalton's tone.

"Why, Bob? I didn't mean what I said before. I was just blowing off some steam."

"Don't sweat it, Maxie. Sharpe ordered it, too. I'm gonna stay out of the way on this one. But remember," Dalton said as he poked his finger in Max's chest, "you're not ready to lead until I say so."

"Maxie, it's great to see you again," Jimmy said exuberantly as he gave Max a hug.

"Thanks, Jimmy. It's great to see you, too."

"I only wish it was under better circumstances. Bobby tells me what you're up against. It's my job, here, to teach you . . . ."

"I know," Max interrupted. "You're here to teach me how to fight."

"No," Jimmy told him adamantly. "You will learn how to defend yourself and how to balance your duties. If I do my job properly, you will never be in a fight. Do you understand me?"

"I guess so," Max answered.

"Either you do or you don't," Jimmy demanded in a serious tone.

"I do, Jimmy."

"Good," Jimmy acknowledged. "But I am no longer 'Jimmy,' to you. From this point forward you will call me 'Sensei.' Is that clear?"

"Yeah," Max said haphazardly.

"Answer him like you mean it," Dalton scolded.

Max looked at both men in awe. The gravity of the situation suddenly hit him. In a bold voice he answered, "Yes, Sensei."

CHAPTER 13

No longer responsible for Max's training and having set up the paintball combat training for the troops, Dalton found himself grasping for ways to contribute to the cause. Unfortunately for Boots, Bam Bam, the Peach and the Aryan, that meant spending time on projects he devised on a whim; Dalton was a master of projecting his own misery onto others. He charged Boots with the task of taking a complete inventory of the arsenal that still sat on the trucks in front of his house; Bam Bam was assigned sniper duty from the roof of the house to defend against a potential attack; and the Peach and the Aryan patrolled the neighborhood in shifts for enemy scout teams. The banality of these projects frustrated them to no end.

Occasionally, Dalton would set up an archery target and teach Zach how to use a bow and arrow. He started the boy at a distance of ten yards from the target. After several tries where he could not figure out how to hold the weapon, Zach hit the red center of the target. "Impressive," Dalton told him. Eventually, they made the exercise part of the daily routine. Zach had impeccable aim; archery seemed a natural talent. His accuracy improved with practice, and Dalton encouraged him to begin shooting from greater distances. Zach enjoyed the drill; it gave him a sense of purpose and belonging. Although he never admitted to it, Dalton enjoyed coaching the lad, too.

During the evenings, Dalton focused on Max's equipment. He refinished the cherry wood handle of the sword Max received from Judge Vineri. He also sharpened and polished it. If, indeed, it was once George

Washington's sword, it now looked like it. To Dalton, the sword was dead technology. He believed that Max needed, at least, to have a gun. He was, after all, from the school of thought that one can never have enough weapons to protect oneself. However, he also recognized that Max, like an ancient king, would not head into battle without armor, so he altered his best bulletproof Kevlar vest to fit Max's proportions.

All the while, Max continued his combat training with Takinawa. The technique was a combination of tae kwon do and judo, a unique scheme Takinawa invented. Max began by learning the different *katahs* associated with each belt level. He was a quick study. In a few short weeks, Max had worked his way up to a second-degree brown belt. He was not a master by any means, but he had learned how to fight. Max sparred with a different sensei every day, and occasionally, he would spar with Takinawa himself. "Focus," Takinawa would repeatedly tell him. "Your world will come into balance when you are able to focus on the task at hand." The senseis were obviously more advanced fighters, and it was clear, even to Max, that they were taking it easy on him. Dalton fumed; he believed that the only way to train was for Max to face real hand-to-hand combat. Takinawa won the debate by explaining that sparring would build Max's confidence.

The sparring mat was set up on the patio in between the pool and the makeshift archery range (the target, of course, standing away from the mat so as not to create a threat to anyone from an errant shot). As Max would spar, Zach would practice. There was something about hearing the repeated whizzing sound of the arrows that Max found relaxing. And the thud following each as the arrow pierced the target bolstered Max's a sense of pride, as if a cosmic connection existed between his success and the boy's.

Sharpe appeared each day to inspect Max's progress. While pleased, he was less than impressed. In the privacy of Dalton's den, he expressed his opinion to Dalton; he believed that allowing Max to fight was too great a risk. "Presidents should stick to politics and leave warfare to generals," he said.

He was beginning to convince Dalton that he was right. But Dalton was not one to give in easily. "Don't lump them all together, General. Several presidents were generals before they turned to politics. Washington, Jackson, Grant and Eisenhower; you can't question their warfare credentials."

"Yes, Bob. But they were battle-tested before taking office. This President has never seen battle. He's never watched a man die. How can we follow him into battle knowing that he's never killed a man?"

Dalton angrily retorted, "With all due respect, General, I have never questioned your military standing. And I have been with you to see countless men die in the jungles of 'Nam. But, I don't remember you taking credit for any kills over there. Unless you killed men while assigned to base administration duty, can you honestly tell me that *you* have killed a man?"

Sharpe glanced out the den window at Max's sparring session. He watched as Max blocked a punch from his attacker, grabbed his arm, and flipped him over his shoulder and onto the mat. "No, Bob. No, I can't," Sharpe answered quietly.

* * *

Hank was the first to arrive for the strategy session. His report was to be the focus of the meeting: He and his men had devised the perfect plan for commandeering the trains Sharpe wanted for the attack. He had arranged for his team to guard the rail yards on the Sunday before what would normally be Memorial Day. The trains were to be shut down on weekends anyway, so they would have all day to access the Long Island Rail Road's breaker system and prepare the trains for the assault. It would require five trains with ten cars each to get the entire strike force into Manhattan. His team's mission that day would be the key to the troops' success; as the guards, they were in position to explain any "irregularities" that may be picked up by Sultan's monitors back at the Pentagon. If questioned, they would report that everything was normal, and that there must be some computer error. It would be a weak excuse, but it would be sufficient to buy them enough time to load the troops and launch the assault.

Chatty and Williams were next arriving. Williams was slightly shorter than Chatty although just as stocky. He had some grey hairs on his scalp and his beard that were noticeable against the contrast of his dark hair and skin, but he looked young enough to pose as an elder gang member. The two had been undercover for weeks, and this was their first contact with anyone since they began their mission weeks before. In fact, the last of the group to see them was Hank, who literally pushed people aside on the train platforms to ensure that they would be able to board and get into the city. They wore matching outfits: Skin-tight red t-shirts, black leather vests with the word, "Demons," embroidered in gold thread across the shoulders on the back of the vest, and black leather pants.

Dalton returned to the house with Sharpe and Gonzo. Shortly after, Armstrong appeared; Sharpe invited him to observe the strategy session as Max's proxy. The men gathered around the dining room table and were about to begin discussing the business at hand when Max barged in.

"General, I hope you don't mind if I sit in," Max announced as he pulled out a chair at the table and sat down.

Sharpe steamed. Although outranked by the President,

he considered Max's intrusion an act of insubordination. "Mr. President," he began, "with all due respect, the time for our attack is quickly approaching. Don't you think your time would be better spent preparing yourself for the operation, rather than interfering with our planning?"

"Interfering?" Max asked with a tone that spoke volumes to the insult. "General, you are here for your expertise, but make no mistake about it – *I* have final say over all plans, military or otherwise. Is that clear?"

Every man at the table was astonished by Max's assertion of his authority. Even Dalton was impressed. The general was clearly upset by this public admonition. "Yes, Mr. President. That is understood. In fact, it has never been a question. My question reflected only my concern that you should be ready for battle."

"I am ready, General," Max assured him.

"With all due respect, Mr. President, I have not heard that from anyone who has been observing your training," the General fired back.

Max knew that he would not be able to lead this group, or any group for that matter, until he proved himself on the field. "Very well, General. Bobby, get your paintball gun. You'll see how ready I am."

"Mr. President," Sharpe objected, "watching you get shot with paintballs is a monumental waste of time!"

"Maybe so, General, but that's also an order," Max countered. "Now, if you'll all please accompany Bob to the patio, I will signal you from the bottom of the hill when I am ready to begin. I'll meet you at the top of the hill once I've captured the flag."

The group did as instructed. They were joined by Takinawa and Max's security team, who were already seated at the table on the patio talking about nothing specifically important. "Bobby," Sharpe called as Dalton prepared his paintball gun, "do us all a favor and make this quick. We have more important things to do."

"Not to worry, General," Dalton assured him, "he still hasn't figured my course out."

"Well, if he doesn't do it this time, this'll be the last of his orders I ever obey," Sharpe warned. Armstrong grimaced at the words, but said nothing. He knew that Max could ill afford to lose control of Sharpe and his commanders.

Standing at the bottom of the hill, Max pulled his hand-drawn map from his pocket. He had added an arrow since his last attempt at the course to demark the location of the tranquilizer gun. He waved to Dalton, who acknowledged by bellowing, "You're on, Maxie!" He immediately began firing paint balls at Max. They exploded all around Max's feet, and he reacted by dashing into the woods for cover. The sound of the firing gun ceased.

Max hid behind a tree and caught his breath. Once ready, he started on the path he had outlined on his map. He sidestepped the camouflage ditch again. When he reached the thick brush that previously hid the trigger to the tranquilizer gun, he paused. He looked to his right and saw the gun. Dalton reloaded it, but he did not move it. Max picked up the gun, adjusted the shoulder strap attached to it, and placed it over his head so that it dangled at his side. This was the furthest he ever came to the flagpole, and he realized that he still was not close. Surely, he surmised, there would be another trap. He proceeded with the utmost caution; each step, each movement was carefully calculated.

He reached a clearing in the woods safely. He could see the patio ahead. Dalton stood in front of the flagpole scanning the woods through the gun's eyepiece. Relieved that the woods were still providing sufficient cover, Max ducked behind a tree and looked around. Then, he saw it. A thick rope hung in the midst of the branches. He followed it, only to find that it was attached to a net that hung above the clearing. He smirked.

"Bobby, I'm growing impatient," Sharpe announced. "Let's cut through the bullshit here."

"Maxie, where the hell are you?" Dalton called out. "Don't make me come in there only to find you in that damned ditch again!"

"I'm fine, Bobby," Max's voice sounded from the woods. "But if you want to find out where I am, you're gonna have to come in here and find me!"

Dalton was shocked at the response. He looked at Sharpe, who cautioned, "Be careful, Bobby. Remember 'Nam."

"Don't worry, General," Dalton replied. "Unlike 'Nam, I set the traps in these woods." He walked down the hill and entered the woods at the clearing. "Max! Max!" he called.

The sound of the tree branches rustling drew his attention. As he turned to look at the cause of the disturbance all he could see was Max swinging at him from the rope that held the net above the clearing. Before he could raise his gun in defense, Max struck him over the head with the dowel he carried in place of his sword. The blow rendered Dalton unconscious.

Max dropped from the rope and picked up the paintball gun. He moved into the clearing but maintained his cover amongst the trees. The men in the gallery on patio stood abreast behind the flagpole. Max raised the paintball gun and took aim. Paintballs exploded as they hit each of the men directly in chest with the exception of Sharpe. After a pause in the shooting, the general was struck with the yellow-feathered tranquilizer dart on his left shoulder. Surprised by the sting, Sharpe looked at his men before collapsing from the drug's effect.

Max appeared from the woods, the tranquilizer gun

dangling from his shoulder and the paintball gun raised with one hand and the dowel in the other. He marched straight for the flagpole maintaining his aim on the conscious men with the paintball gun. As he approached, he said, "Now, under the rules of this exercise, you're all dead already. Don't make me shoot you again." The men all backed away from the flagpole as Max arrived. He untied the rope on the pole, lowered the flag, unhooked it, and placed it over his shoulders. He smiled and said to his paintball victims, "When Bobby and the general wake up bring them into the dining room so we can begin this strategy session. They're wasting my time." He placed the gun on the ground and walked into the house.

"What just happened here?" Armstrong asked.

"The President just showed us why he's in charge," Chatty answered while wiping the paint from his leather vest. No one disagreed.

* * *

Sharpe's head throbbed from the tranquilizer and he was still groggy, but he was well enough to convene the meeting. Dalton sat in a corner listening with an ice pack on his head. Hank presented his proposal for transporting the troops into Manhattan. Gonzo reported that the troops were ready and awaiting orders for the attack. Sharpe only nodded giving his tacit approval of both reports.

Chatty began the report of his and Williams' covert operation. "The subways are unusable. They have been flooded and taken over by a gang called, 'The Demons.'"

"Actually," Williams added, "the Demons are made up of all the gangs that used to run New York. There's Bloods, Crips, Latin Kings; you name one, they're Demons now."

"That's right," Chatty continued. "Their leader,

Hades, united them. He's a crafty brother who speaks perfect English. He doesn't utter a word of slang, which makes me believe he is educated, and not a gang member himself. He made an off-the-cuff remark about 'his teaching days' at one point, but that was about all he let on about his past life. We've managed to get close to him. I am his second-in-command, and he has me going by my new gang name, 'Cerberus.'"

"And he calls me 'Charon,'" Williams added. "I'm driving his personal boat through the tunnels. He's also got these three personal bodyguards that no one, not even the colonel or me, wants to upset. The first is a brother bigger than the colonel here," he said pointing to Chatty. "He wears a pirate's eye patch over his left eye, so Hades has everyone callin' him 'Cyclops.'"

"The second bodyguard is a woman," Chatty explained. "And she is a vicious fighter. She has long, thick dreadlocks, and beautiful blue eyes. A simple stare usually freezes men in their tracks before she lands her fatal blow. Hades calls her 'Medusa.'"

"His last bodyguard is called, 'Typhon,'" Williams said. "He can swallow fire and spit it up to fifty feet. It's awesome when he does it."

"What's with all these Greek names?" Armstrong asked.

"Mr. Armstrong," Sharpe spoke weakly, "I remind you that you are here to observe only."

Max rolled his eyes. "No, he's onto something," he said. "You said that you think this guy is educated, right, Colonel?"

"Just a guess, sir," Chatty answered.

"Okay," Max continued. "Let's say he is. He speaks well, and he seems to have a penchant for Greek mythology. Now, call me crazy, but I think I know who this guy is."

"And how is that, Kreskin?" Dalton asked sarcastically.

"We ran an article in *Intensity* about three years ago," Max explained. "It was about a professor at Columbia University who was the son of a Black Panther. He was fired by the university for preaching at a rally that African-Americans should get their hands on all the guns in the country and take control of it by force."

"No wonder he's hooked up with Sultan's forces," Armstrong commented drawing the ire of Sharpe's stare.

"Wait, there's more," Max persisted. "He was a professor of Greco-Roman literature, and his name was Hayworth Davis Edwards. His initials are H, D, E – Hades."

The room was silent. Max was two-for-two on this day having bested the obstacle course and now significantly contributing to the strategy session. Sharpe, himself, was impressed. "You seem to know more about Hades than any man here, Mr. President," Sharpe confidently stated. "What do you suggest we do about it?"

"Well," Max said after a brief pause. "Hades is not a true threat to us. More than anything, he just seeks an expanded role for African-Americans in governmental affairs. If I can talk to him, offer him a position in my cabinet, we can buy his loyalty."

"Talking to him will be easier said than done, sir," Chatty cautioned. "Hades and his bodyguards rarely leave their lair at Grand Central Station, which he calls 'Tartarus,' but the Long Island Rail Road will deposit you and the troops at Penn Station, where Captain Williams and I will be waiting for you. But travel to Grand Central by subway is no longer possible because the Demons keep the drainage shafts shut so that the tracks flood. It is impossible for the trains to run, and as Captain Williams explained, the Demons are forced to navigate the subway system by boat. It wasn't the best plan on their part, though. The water shorted out the electricity. There are no lights; each station is lit by barrels of fire and torches. The heat and moisture have given rise to a terrible mold problem, which I don't think they realize, because they all have terrible, hacking coughs."

"But you can get me to Hades by boat, right?" Max asked Williams.

Chatty looked at Williams, and then answered, "Of course, sir. The only boat that is permitted to navigate the tunnels without being questioned by the Demons is Hades' boat, and Captain Williams is the boat's captain. But the boat only holds about five people."

"Good," Max responded. "General, when you plan the logistics of the attack, bear this in mind: I will go ahead of the troops, rendezvous with Chatty, and meet with Hades."

"Sir, that is a risky proposition," Sharpe objected. He did not see any need for additional risks, especially one that left the President exposed.

"I am aware, General," Max replied. "But it is also an order."

* * *

Max asked Takinawa to join him in a sparring session once the meeting ended. They began with simple hand-to-hand combat and progressed to fighting with dowels to simulate swordplay. The wooden rods made a clacking sound each time they struck each other. The longer they sparred, the faster and louder the sounds grew.

Dalton joined them on the patio after a while to observe Max's fighting technique. He was impressed with what he saw, but he was not entirely convinced that it would be sufficient. When Max and Takinawa agreed to rest for a few minutes, Dalton decided to seize the opportunity to discuss his feelings with Max. "Max, can I talk to you for a minute?"

"Of course, Bobby," Max replied as he walked over to the patio bench where Dalton was perched. "What's up?"

"I'm gonna be blunt, Maxie. I don't think you should confront this Hades guy."

"I can handle it, Bobby. I mean I beat you today, right?"

"Yeah, and it's not really him I'm concerned about. It's his bodyguards. If you have to confront them, then shit. Let's put it this way, I don't think I would be able to take on the three of them. Do you really think you're ready?"

"Yeah, Bobby, I do think I'm ready," Max said indignantly. "Why don't you?"

"To be honest with you it's because I don't think you have what it takes to face someone who is actually trying to kill you. Look around Max. I've been shooting paintballs at you. Jimmy's been taking it easy on you and you know it. If you have to face these bodyguards, I don't think you'll know what to do first."

"What about my bodyguards? Don't they count for anything?"

"Trust me, Max. If you want to get close to this guy, they won't be allowed anywhere near you. You'll be completely on your own."

"So what am I supposed to do, Bob? Sit back and let things happen around me?"

"When it comes to military operations, that's the best idea you've had yet. Let Sharpe handle this guy."

"Absolutely not! I believe that there's a political solution here. I won't give up on negotiations. A confrontation is the last thing I want."

"That's the fuckin' problem, Max!" Dalton chastised. It was clear that his anger was getting the better of him. Max's stubborn insistence on diplomacy was frustrating Dalton's ability to communicate his point. "You think this is a game? Your enemies don't want to talk to you. They want to fuckin' kill you! If you're too naïve to realize that, then I made a huge fuckin' mistake by believing in you." He stood, enraged, and stormed into the house.

"Fuck you, Bob," Max yelled as Dalton left.

"You okay, Max?" Takinawa asked.

"Yea, Jimmy," he replied. "I'll be fine, thanks. We're done here for tonight. I'm just gonna stay and clear my head." Max turned and watched the sunset in the distance.

Takinawa patted Max on the shoulder and told him, "You got it, Max. I'll see you tomorrow." With that, he left Max in solitude to ponder the challenges ahead.

Max stared at the sunset. It was a thing of beauty like the sunsets that appear on postcards from exotic places. He thought of Roxy and how he wished she were standing next to him to see it with her. Unlike Dalton, she would support him. She would tell him that he could defeat anyone based on his courage alone. She would convince him that it would all somehow be alright. While he did not need her to carry on with his mission, he wanted someone to share in this peaceful, joyous moment with him. A small token of sanity in this new insane world would go a long way toward convincing him that laying his life on the line was worthwhile.

Dalton was wrong. It was not fear that Max needed to defeat those who wanted to kill him; it was love. Love would be his driving motivator. Love would carry him to victory. And not just any love. Unconditional love. The love he got from Roxy, and not the love he could get from politics. Only she was close enough to him to make a difference in his life. Everyone else, including Dalton, was merely a distraction from his cause: Defeating Sultan so that he could live out his years in peace with Roxy at his side.

"Max," Dalton hollered from behind Max, "catch!" Max turned and caught his sword mid-air. He looked at the handle and took notice of its shiny handle.

"Thanks, Bob," Max said. Max unsheathed the sword and was amazed at how the setting sun reflected off of the newly sharpened and polished blade. "You polished it for me. You shouldn't have."

Dalton held one of his swords from his collection in his left hand. He reached for the grip with his right hand and unsheathed his sword. He slowly approached Max with the sword, his hands shaking as he pointed it at Max. "They won't have a chance to kill you," Dalton said, his voice quivering as tears welled up in his eyes.

"Bobby, what's gotten into you?" Dalton lunged at Max, who quickly moved out of the way. "Are you out of your fuckin' mind?"

"You'd better defend yourself, Maxie. I won't let anyone else have the satisfaction of killing you!" Dalton chopped the sword down, and again Max was forced to dodge a potentially lethal strike.

Max was confused; he did not understand why Dalton was attacking him. But he realized that Dalton was serious. He raised his sword and offered, "Bobby, come to your senses. You don't want to hurt me, and I don't want to hurt you. Put your sword down and let's talk like men."

Dalton inched closer. The blade of his sword was only inches from Max's. "There's nothing to talk about. You've never been in battle. You don't know what it's like to smell the breath of a man who wants to kill you. Well, you're about to find out! You're term in office is over. This whole idea was a mistake. And there's only one way to stop it!" Dalton swung his sword again, but this time Max countered by striking the blade with his own.

"Bobby, chill the fuck out! I don't want to hurt you!"

Dalton ignored Max's plea.

The clang of metal on metal echoed. "What's goin' on down there?" Bam Bam asked from his assigned post on the roof of the house. There was no response. Only the repeated clanging of the blades as Max and Dalton continued their clash.

Dalton swung horizontally at Max's head. Max ducked and threw out his leg in a roundhouse kick that tripped Dalton causing him to fall on his back. Max popped up and swung his sword down as if to slice Dalton in half. Dalton saw it coming and rolled out of the way. When he stood and regained his balance, he caught Max off guard and punched him in the face causing blood to run from the fresh cut on his cheek.

The punch forced Max backwards. As he stumbled, Dalton swung his sword three times; first, to Max's left, then to Max's right, and finally, directly down at him. Max dodged the first two, and managed to recover in time to catch the third blow with his own blade. They remained locked in close quarter staring into each other's eyes. Fierce anger was visible to Max in Dalton's eyes. And while Dalton expected to see fear in Max's, he saw nothing more than a determination not to lose. What he did not see was the knee that Max kicked into his stomach.

Dalton's strength left his sword, and Max was able to push Dalton two steps backwards. Max followed with a jab to the face that drew blood from Dalton's nose. He allowed Dalton to regain his stature. They raised their swords at each other again. Max said, "You won't beat me, Bob. And neither will they. Now, can we end this?"

Dalton did not reply. Instead, he charged at Max.

Max sidestepped the charge, and turned to see Dalton stop sharply as he realized that he missed Max and swung his sword wildly at Max's head again. Max dropped to a knee and spun entirely around on it, swinging his sword as his body turned around to face Dalton. He was surprised at the little amount of resistance his blade received from the flesh of Dalton's abdomen.

Dalton dropped his sword and grabbed his midsection as he fell forward landing on Max. Max managed to catch Dalton and turn him onto his back. Blood covered both of them. He held Dalton's head in his lap and looked at the wound to determine its seriousness. Max was not a doctor, but the fact that he could see Dalton's entrails told him that the next moments would be Dalton's last.

"Oh, shit! Bobby, I'm so sorry!" Max began to cry.

Dalton reached down to the wound. As he felt his own intestine he tried to laugh but could only cough out blood. Catching his breath, he said, "Maxie, it's okay. I didn't think you had it in you."

"Oh, Bobby. I didn't mean to . . . ."

"Bullshit!" Dalton interrupted as he coughed out more blood. "You had to! Now, Maxie, listen to me."

Max nodded. "Anything, Bobby."

"Now, you are ready. Don't let these fucks beat you. Any of them. You're the only one who can save our country, Max. Our country! That's what it's about. Promise me, something, Max."

"Anything you want, Bobby."

"Victory, Max. Promise me victory even if it means your own life."

"Victory, Bobby. I promise. Victory."

"Good. Good." Dalton coughed out some more blood as blood continued to ooze from his massive wound. Boots, Bam Bam, the Peach and the Aryan came running to the patio.

"Bobby," Boots shouted, "what the fuck happened?"

Dalton kept his eyes focused on Max's. "It's cold, Maxie. It's . . . so . . . cold." His voice trailed off as his last breath escaped.

Max cried. He closed Dalton's eyes, and hugged his carcass rocking back and forth repeatedly crying, "No! No!"

CHAPTER 14

In what was once the souvenir shop of the observatory of the Empire State Building, Emir watched as his soldiers connected the nuclear warhead Sultan had sent to them to a detonation device. The view from the observatory was awe-inspiring. From there, Emir could see out to the horizon for miles in every direction. It served as an ideal headquarters and observation tower, and doubled as the perfect minaret in his new Islamic nation.

The warhead itself had an encryption code that was required to activate it. Emir's instructions were to contact Sultan for that code only in the event of an attack on New York. In the meantime, Emir kept the remote detonator for the non-nuclear portion of the bomb on his person at all times.

"Brother Emir," one of the soldiers called in Arabic. "The Great Sheik wishes to speak you," he said referring to Sultan by using the nickname given to him by his followers.

"Very well," Emir answered turning his attention away from the sunset that cast light over the Hudson River to the west. He sat at his desk with his computer and web cam so that he could speak to his brother face to face. When Sultan's face appeared on his screen he greeted him, "As-salaamu aleikum, my brother."

"Wa aleikum salaam, Emir," Sultan replied. "What news do you have?"

"N-N-N-Nothing of consequence. Our guards have been doubled at th-th-th-the bridges and tunnels, as ordered, and our men are patrolling the waters surrounding Manhattan and Long Island. Nothing unusual has been re-re-reported."

"And what of the subways?"

"We have enlisted those who suffered under American f-f-f-reedom to guard and protect the tunnels."

"At what price?"

"They ask only that we allow them to live as they ch-ch-ch-choose in their underground domain."

"They did not ask for money? What about food and water?"

"Well, brother, we do s-s-s-supply them. But I do not consider that a p-p-p-price."

"They cost money, Emir! And any outsider that would help us for anything other than the love of Allah cannot be trusted. Their loyalty can be bought and sold, and they can turn on you on a whim."

"D-d-d-do not lecture me, br-br-br-brother!" Emir protested, his stutter worsening from fear of reprisal. "While you s-s-s-sit in an office secluded from the w-w-w-world, I am up here m-m-m-making sure that your p-p-p-precious city does not fall! Allah guides me and my men, not you!"

Emir's passionate rebuke was nothing new to Sultan. As far as he was concerned it was nothing more than sibling rivalry. "I occupy this secluded office because someone must make sure there are enough funds to pay for unauthorized promises. Now, if you are done lecturing me, you may return to whatever is was you were doing."

Emir conceded the point. "Th-th-th-thank you, brother. I will k-k-k-keep you updated as to our circumstances." He did not miss the opportunity to prove that he was hard at work for the cause, either. "And thank you for the b-b-b-bomb, brother. I have just finished installing the d-d-d-detonator," he said as he waved the remote in front of the web cam.

"Good. Very good. Now, let us hope you are right, and I will not need to give you the code to activate it." Abruptly, Emir's screen went black.

* * *

The plywood pyramids that dotted Dalton's obstacle course provided the kindling for his pyre. Boots and the Aryan spent the entire day breaking down the structures to prepare Dalton's final bed, which was built on the patio several feet from where he died. Bam Bam and the Peach drew on their experience with corpses from their days as Don Vito's hit men to prepare Dalton's body for a makeshift wake.

The gathering of those paying their respects included Don Vito, Tommy Corvalo, Elizabeth Magnuson, Bill Worthington, Judge and Mrs. Vineri, and the paramilitary crew with whom Dalton spent his final days. Dalton traded his Christian beliefs for his patriotic conviction; it seemed appropriate to all that Sharpe lead the funeral service. It was not the full-fledged military funeral Dalton would have wanted. The circumstances still called for a low profile when it came to any sort of military operations. Armstrong gave a fitting eulogy that elicited laughs from those assembled. He made sure to highlight Dalton's trademark cigar, his conservative views, and of course, his coarse manner.

Max did not speak. He did not cry, either. Roxy stood at his right side holding his hand, while Zach took a place in front of him; Max kept his left hand on Zach's shoulder throughout the service.

Hank, Chatty and Gonzo were given the honor of lighting the pyre when the ceremony was over. As the flames engulfed Dalton's massive carcass, Max stoically watched and clutched Roxy's hand tighter. She knew he had something to say, but this was neither the time nor the place.

Most of the guests retired to the house. Those remaining gathered in small groups and began to talk amongst themselves. Sharpe, Chatty, Hank and Gonzo huddled several feet from the fire, and kept watch to make certain that it burned properly. They said nothing but shared the same thought: Would they be able to trust their commander in chief, a man who inexplicably killed the one most responsible for putting him in the position? To their right, Boots, Bam Bam and the Peach surrounded Don Vito. The don explained that, "Things in the neighborhood were good." However, it did not hide the men's wonderings about whether there was still someone worth protecting. Armstrong assembled with Judge Vineri and Bill Worthington by the glass door to the house where they reminisced about their now-departed friend. The Aryan remained by himself, his eyes fixated on the fire. He thought of the bonfire on the night his life changed, then of Dalton knocking him unconscious, and finally of how merciless Dalton was in arguing why he should be put to death. Max remained alone, having sent Roxy inside with Zach. He felt the insecurity around him.

Max ambled to the Aryan and softly asked, "Gonna miss him?"

"Why should I?" he retorted. "He wanted me to die because he thought I would hurt you."

"If Bob Dalton wanted you dead, you wouldn't be here today," Max answered loudly. All side conversations ceased, and every man on the patio turned toward Max. "It's true," he continued aware of his audience. "If he wanted me dead, I wouldn't be here today either. No, Bobby wanted you and me to live. Deep down, he believed in you – in us." Max made eye contact with each man on the patio. "In all of us."

"Yesterday," Max explained, "he had a crazed look in his eyes. It was one I had never seen before in any man. There was rage combined with fright. Almost as if he knew he had lived out his purpose. He wasn't trying to kill me, he was killing himself." Tears filled Max's eyes and nary was a word spoken. For several minutes all that was audible was the sound of the fire crackling around Dalton's body.

Eventually, Max composed himself. "General Sharpe," He called.

"Yes, Sir," Sharpe answered.

"General, we shall reconvene here at oh-nine-hundred for our final strategy session. I expect that Mr. Dalton's ashes will be waiting for me. Understood?"

"Yes, Mr. President," Sharpe sincerely answered, trying to contain a smirk. It was one of relief; finally, Max had come to exhibit the compassion and confidence he believed necessary of a president.

As the night wore on, the fire began to die. Dalton's body had disappeared. Ashes were all that was left of the pyre. On Sharpe's orders, Gonzo collected the ashes and placed them in a gunpowder satchel.

Boots drove Max, Roxy and Zach back to Max's house. Zach went to sleep as soon as the car began to move. No one spoke in the car as not to wake him. When they arrived at the house, Roxy hurried inside as Max began to carry Zach inside. "You need a hand?" Boots asked.

"No, thanks, I got him," Max replied. "Go home and get some sleep. Big day tomorrow."

"I know, oh-nine-hundred," Boots assured.

"Good. See you then." Max brought Zach into the house where Roxy waited as Boots drove away. Once inside, he and Roxy put Zach to bed. After changing out of their suits from the funeral and into something more comfortable, they sat on the living room sofa. Max let out a deep sigh.

"Tell me about it," Roxy said. "Are you holding up okay?"

"Yeah, I'm fine."

"Don't keep it inside, Max. Let it out. He was like a father to you."

Max shook his head from side to side. "No, he was more than that. He was my best friend." Tears slowly began to stream down his face. "I'm gonna miss him, Rox. For the first time, I've lost someone I care about. And it hurts."

"I know," she consoled. "But he'll always be with you."

"It doesn't help that I killed him," Max confessed. "I didn't want to. It was an accident."

"I thought you said that he wanted you to kill him?"

Max, vexed, looked at her asking, "How did you know that? You weren't out on the patio when I said that."

Roxy put her arms around Max's shoulders and looked into his eyes, "You can't hide anything from me, Max. I know you too well."

"Oh, really?" he joked.

"No, I was listening to you speak to make sure you were doing alright."

"You don't have to do that, Rox."

Perturbed, she said, "Yes, I do, Max. You see, with Bobby gone, I am your new best friend."

"You sure are, Rox," he told her as he leaned over and kissed her more sincerely than he ever had before. "I love you. You know that, right?"

"Of course, Max. I love you, too." She kissed him

again and then paused. "And Bobby loved you, too."

"I know."

"Good. Now, can you do me and him a favor?"

"What's that?"

"Send this Sultan guy home so we can get married and live our lives in peace."

Her words emboldened him. "Definitely," he responded. They kissed passionately this time, and made love until dawn.

CHAPTER 15

The meeting began promptly at nine in the morning. Unlike other strategy sessions, this one was somber. Sharpe sat at the head of Dalton's dining room table and ran the meeting in a monotone business-like manner. Max sat in the chair normally occupied by Dalton, yet said nothing. There was no bickering. No wise remarks. No jokes.

The plan was set. Sharpe gave each man his orders. Hank and his men were charged with securing the rail yard on the Sunday of what would normally be Memorial Day weekend. Bam Bam would arrange with his brother-in-law to have the trailers holding the weapons delivered at sunset. Max, Boots, Bam Bam, the Peach and the Aryan were to meet at the rail yard at that time to use the ASV (which Sharpe explained was the military's acronym for "Armored Support Vehicle"), or the "mini-tank," as Bam Bam called it, to enter Penn Station; the tires were to be removed so that the gas-powered vehicle could travel on the tracks without powering up the rail system in order to avoid detection by Sultan's monitors. It would also give Max six hours to negotiate with Hades before Sharpe and Gonzo arrived with the rest of the troops. Chatty and Williams, in their Demon disguises, would wait in Penn Station for their arrival in order to lead them to Hades. Once Max convinced Hades to join the cause, they would meet up with the troops and launch the attack on Manhattan from the subways below ground, invading without detection. The plan hinged on Max's success, which made Sharpe nervous. Only this time Sharpe hid his feelings.

There being no questions, the men concluded the meeting. It was the last time they would meet like this until the rendezvous at the rail yard. One by one they filed out of Dalton's house and returned to their regular routines. Sharpe handed Max the gunpowder satchel with Dalton's ashes before he left. "Do what you must with him, Mr. President," he said. "He wants it that way."

Max accepted the sack and said, "Thank you, General." He remained at the house after the rest of the men left. The house had particular significance to him. It was the house in which Dalton raised him. It was his childhood safe haven. In a way, he felt responsible for the dark and lifelessness he would leave behind. He walked through each room. As he did, he could see the ghosts of the younger versions of Dalton and himself in scenes from his past. The bathroom he used as a boy showed him the first time Dalton taught him how to use a razor to shave. In the kitchen, the argument they had when he was a high school senior over his curfew played out. The den was filled with the Christmas tree Dalton decorated and the Chanukah menorah that Max lit with candles burning on the fireplace mantle; Dalton insisted that Max honor his heritage. Finally, Dalton stood in his trophy room polishing the bayonet on a Civil War era musket. When the ghost faded, Max saw his sword that killed Dalton in the corner; he forgot that he put it there when they cleaned the house for the funeral. He picked it up and began to weep. After a few loud sobs, he hugged the gunpowder satchel and then composed himself. On the floor, he saw a black vest with a patch containing his last name sewed above the left breast. "Bobby, you shouldn't have," he said. He looked around the room at all of Dalton's weapons. "This is what you were preparing for, Bobby. The time has come."

He loaded all of Dalton's weapons into the trunk of his car. Included in the collection were the bow and the arrows that Dalton had shown Zach how to use. "Bobby,

I promise that I'll make sure he's the sharpest shot in the army," he said as he placed them in the back seat of the car. When he finished loading the car, he went back into the house and took one last look around the empty trophy room. He saluted and said, "To victory, Bobby. To victory." He shut the light and closed the door, leaving his childhood home for the last time.

* * *

The Hebrew lunar-based calendar often dictates that the Jewish observance of the Passover festival coincide with the Christian observance of Easter, a logical overlap considering that Christ's Last Supper itself was a Passover *Seder*. This year was one such year. Unlike previous years, there were no Easter parades, egg hunts or bonnets; the newly imposed Islamic laws prohibited the observance of non-Islamic holidays. The Christian population obeyed, fearing the bloody consequences for which Sultan's regime showed a propensity. However, the Jewish population observed the Passover festival in secret. Hiding their faith was a skill almost innate to the Jews given the centuries of persecution by various oppressors. Whether it was the Babylonians, the Greeks, the Spanish, the Cossacks or the Nazis, Jews have always found ways to express their faith and keep to their traditions. Sultan would not suppress them, either. Roxy made certain of that.

Although she was not overly religious, Roxy insisted that Max change their dishes for Passover to dishes that had not been used throughout the year, a traditional Jewish custom. She felt it was an important part of Zach's development to learn his heritage. Max resisted at first, but after a little prodding from Roxy, he agreed. "I'm doing it for Zach," he told her.

That was weeks ago, before Max fell into Dalton's ditch. With all of the constant training, he neglected to put the Passover dishes in the attic despite Roxy's repeated requests. The assault on Manhattan was two weeks away, and Max took advantage of the time by spending it with Roxy and Zach. Since he no longer had an excuse, he carried the box with the Passover dishes up to his attic.

Boxes were stacked everywhere. There was no order to their arrangement. Max gently placed the box of dishes on the floor in the corner of the attic by the small window. As he turned to leave, a copy of *Intensity* in one of the boxes caught his eye. Valerie graced the cover wearing only a black bra and black panties and petting a polar bear cub. He recognized the issue instantly. The cover story was about Valerie's newfound cause to save the polar bears. It was his worst selling issue ever. He reached into the box and fished out the magazine. He leafed through it, and came across a column written by one of his editors that stood out in his memory:

Racial Anger Is 'Unbecoming'

By David Saunders, Editor

Columbia University has come under fire for firing a professor for 'behavior unbecoming the university.' Professor Hayworth Davis Edwards, the son of the former Black Panther leader Byron Edwards, spoke at a rally organized by the Columbia Students for African Revolution on March 4th. The professor of Greco-Roman literature delivered the keynote speech that drew substantial criticism from most of Columbia's student body after he said, 'African-Americans were forced to come to this hemisphere by white Europeans with guns. Times have surely changed, and the tide has turned. Now, we have the guns. Rather than turn them on each other, killing brothers like game in the streets, African-Americans need to rise up and take this country for our own prosperity.'

Does Professor Edwards have a point? Are the sins committed by the nation's founders to be repaid with the blood of their descendants? The State of Israel was created out of the world's outrage toward the Nazis' sins. Surely,

Professor Edwards cannot mean to liken the plight of African-Americans to that of the Jews of Hitler's Germany.

'Jim Crow,' Edwards told *Intensity*, 'was the mere continuation of slavery. African-Americans see the inequality between white and black in this nation and they are politically powerless to stop it. Revolutions are often bloody.'

But what if African-Americans had a greater say in the affairs of the nation? Would Professor Edwards change his tune then? 'Ask me again when that day comes,' he responded when *Intensity* posed that question to him.

It cannot be overlooked that Professor Edwards is, essentially, promoting treason, which is a crime punishable by death. For that reason, we here at *Intensity* cannot see any reason to disagree with Columbia's action. Columbia can call it 'behavior unbecoming the university,' if it chooses, but the reality is that by taking away Professor Edwards' platform for hate speech, Columbia has protected the lives of Americans, both black *and* white.

At the bottom of the article there was a photograph

of Edwards taken at the rally. His skin was as black as the night and rage erupted from the whites of his eyes. Max knew that Dalton was right about him. *This guy is a very dangerous man*, Max thought to himself. Max rolled the magazine into a cone and placed it in the back pocket of his jeans before heading back down the stairs to find Roxy.

A robust aroma emanated from the kitchen. Roxy was preparing dinner; it was a Cantonese chicken recipe. She knew that these days before the attack were precious. After the victory, Max would not have time to have family dinners with Zach and her, and she accepted that fact. That was the best-case scenario. She did not allow the thoughts that accompanied the worst-case scenario to linger in her mind. *The mission will succeed*, she thought. *It has to.*

Max approached her from behind while she was peeling a potato over the sink. He placed his hands over her eyes and said, "Guess who." Seated at the kitchen table reading Harper Lee's, *To Kill a Mockingbird*, Zach giggled at Max's prank.

"Um," Roxy played along, "Zach." Zach laughed loudly from his seat.

"Nope," Max said. "Guess again."

"The boogie man," she teased, again drawing a raucous laugh from her son.

"How'd you know?" Max joshed as he removed his hands from her eyes.

"The sweaty palms gave it away," she snidely answered, wiping her forehead with the back of her wrist before kissing Max on the lips.

Max turned to Zach and said, "Really nice, isn't she?" Zach laughed again. The entire exchange was a glimpse of a normal family moment that he secretly cherished for years.

Roxy noticed the rolled up magazine in Max's back pocket. "What's this?" she asked as she pulled it from his pocket and unrolled it so that Valerie's half-naked picture stared her in the face. She looked at Max stunned.

"It's not what you're thinking," Max explained.

"How do you know what I'm thinking?" she quipped.

"C'mon, Rox. There's an article in there about this Hades guy."

"Do you miss her?"

"What?" Max was taken aback by the question.

"Do you miss her?" Roxy repeated holding up the magazine pointing at Valerie's picture.

"I don't even think about her anymore. That was a lifetime ago."

"It was only a few months ago, Max. Don't lie to me!"

"A lot has happened since then, Rox. It was a blessing in disguise. My marriage was a prison. That bullet liberated me. I'm a new man. And I couldn't be happier that you're back in my life. Both of you. You're all I have, especially now that Bob is gone. You're my family. You're my only family. She's a distant memory."

Roxy hugged him tightly. "I'm sorry, Max. It's just that I'm worried."

"About what?" he wondered aloud.

"Well, you're the President of the United States. What if you forget about Zach and me once you're back in power?"

"Don't be ridiculous, Rox."

"No, seriously," she demanded. "What if you get so busy trying to win this war and rebuilding the country that you don't have time for us? I don't think we can handle that type of life, you know?"

Max finally understood. She could not bear the thought of losing him to the way he had to live his life. Life, he decided, is a series of choices packed into a limited amount of time; he could not be all places at all times, especially given his new career, but he could make a choice to spend just enough time where it mattered most.

For better or for worse, he still had his life in front of him. No Ku Klux Klan wannabe or Islamic fundamentalist had managed to take it from him. That was the message Dalton was trying to teach him: As long as there are choices to be made, life goes on. Dalton made his final choice before he gave Max the sword. Dalton chose to give his own life in order to make Max understand that the most difficult choice he would ever be confronted with would be to take away that same freedom from another man. Max learned the hard way that the freedom to choose how to live one's life is more important than life itself. With that in mind he promised Roxy, "There will always be time for you two. I want you and Zach to be with me every step of the way once we set up the new government in New York. Okay?"

"You promise?" she asked with a tear streaming down her cheek.

"I promise," he answered.

"Okay, then," she accepted as she kissed him and hugged him even tighter than before.

"Good," Max replied. "Then let me give Zach his surprise."

"Surprise?" Zach asked excitedly.

"Yeah, surprise?" Roxy asked with a puzzled look.

"Yes, his surprise," Max told them. "Zach, meet me in the back yard."

"Max, what did you do?" Roxy asked.

"You'll see," was his only answer as he walked down

to the garage where his car awaited. He opened the back car doors and reached in to take out the bow and arrows he gathered at Dalton's house. With the bow slung over his shoulder and the arrows in one hand, Max grabbed the seat cushion from an old couch that sat next to his workbench in the corner of the garage, and some rope, a paintbrush and a can of white paint from the shelf above it.

Zach waited eagerly for Max in the back yard. It was not quite as spacious as Dalton's, but it was vast enough to allow Zach room for target practice. When Max joined him in the yard, he put the bow and arrows down at Zach's feet and walked over to a wide oak tree about fifty yards away onto which he fastened the couch cushion with the rope. He opened the paint can, dipped in the brush and painted a dot with a circle around it on the cushion. "Okay, Zach, you know what to do," he shouted.

"It's too far away," Zach complained.

"Nonsense," Max assured him as he walked back toward him. "Take a shot."

Zach raised the bow and took aim. He pulled back on the bowstring as hard as he could and squinted with one eye focused on the white dot on the cushion. As soon as he felt comfortable, he released the arrow. It took off well, but the projectile fell about ten yards shy of its target. Zach did not wear his discouragement well. "It's too far, I told you," he repeated to Max.

Max kneeled down to look Zach square in the eyes. "That's okay, Zach. We're going to work on this every day. Once you build up your muscles, you'll be able to hit that target with no problem. Practice is all it takes. I know you can do it."

"Thanks, Max," Zach said. "Hey, Max, did you really mean what you said about us being your family?"

"I did. Is that alright?"

Zach hugged him without saying a word. When he let go he asked Max, "Can I tell people you're my dad?"

Max froze for a moment because he did not know how to respond. Then he thought about the choices associated with his answer. *Life is a series of choices*, he thought. Finally, he said, "I'd like that." He put Zach over his shoulders and began to spin around. Zach squealed with laughter.

Roxy witnessed everything from the open kitchen window. She began to sob hysterically, but these were tears of joy. For a brief moment, she enjoyed the stability in her life.

CHAPTER 16

True to the adage, April's showers brought May's flowers. The trees were in full bloom, and the colors of different species of flora accentuated the brush that was horribly overgrown on the sides of the highways; highway maintenance was just one of the thousands of municipal tasks that evaporated under Sultan's regime. Max made a mental note of the work to be done as the car sped east to the rail yard.

Boots was driving with Bam Bam in the front passenger's seat. Max was sitting in the back between the Peach and the Aryan with the former to his left and the latter to his right. As the sun began to set, Max began to think about the long night ahead of them.

"Vick and the boys should be there soon," Bam Bam said. "I told them to unload the mini-tank first. Then they're gonna take the tires off and roll it on to the tracks."

"How do they do that?" Max asked. He was merely curious, but not genuinely interested in the answer.

"If I know Vick," Bam Bam explained, "they'll probably use a couple of two-by-fours to get it on there. He's pretty good like that."

"Guy, you're lucky that your wife got the brains in the DeCosta family," the Peach interjected. "Vick's as smart as a fuckin' carrot."

"Granted, he's no fuckin' Einstein," Bam Bam conceded, "but he's good at figurin' this kind of shit out."

"It doesn't matter as long as it's ready to go by

midnight," Max told them. "Boots, are you sure you'll be able to drive it?"

"Yeah, no sweat," Boots assured them. "I checked it out already. It's like driving a monster truck. And I've always wanted to drive one of those bad boys."

"Yeah, those things are sick," the Aryan commented.

"What about you?" Max asked the Aryan. "Are you ready?"

"Hells yeah," he answered. "You're finally gonna give me a gun and a chance to kill these sandniggers. I been waitin' for this since nine eleven."

"Just don't get any funny ideas about shootin' us," the Peach warned him. "Especially the President. Coppice?"

"Yeah, I got ya," the Aryan replied. "You ain't got nothin' to worry about. I'm on your side now. I promise you, Mr. President, they're gonna have to kill me before they can get to you." The sincere look in his eyes gave Max comfort that his words were not empty.

"So, what's the deal with this Hades guy?" Boots asked. "We're just gonna drive into Penn, hop out and tell him to join the fight, which, oh yeah, starts in an hour?" Bam Bam and the Peach laughed at the sarcasm.

"Not quite," answered Max. "Chatty and Williams will be waiting for us when we pull in. Then they'll be taking us as 'prisoners' to meet Hades."

"That dumb fuck bought the whole undercover thing, huh?" Bam Bam asked.

"Big time," Max responded. "Chatty's been saying all the right things to all of the Demons. They like him so much that Hades was forced to name him second in command. He could overthrow Hades, if he wanted to."

"So why doesn't he?" the Peach asked.

"We told him not to," Max said. "We don't want to

blow our cover. Everything in our plan hinges on the six hours we'll have to negotiate with Hades. All we need is for his Demons to join our cause. Ideally, Chatty won't have to reveal his true identity to them at all. And that's a huge advantage that we need to gain their trust."

"And what if it doesn't go according to plan?" the Aryan inquired.

"We'll be taking matters into our own hands," Max answered.

* * *

Dusk covered the rail yard. The sky to the east began to show stars, while the red sun was slowly swallowed by the western horizon. Gnats arose from their slumber looking to feed in the hot and humid conditions. Though a nuisance, Vick brushed them away with ease. His workers complained more. They took exception to the pests who were attracted by the scent of their sweat; moving the ASV onto the tracks had to come at a price.

The car arrived at the rail yard as the last bit of the sun disappeared in the distance. Hank's men opened the gates to allow it to enter, and then hurriedly closed them once the car was safely within the grounds. The car pulled around in front of the trucks carrying the arsenal. Once parked, the doors opened and Max's entourage exited. Max followed closely behind, making sure to grab his sword and a black gym bag from the trunk before joining the others.

"You did it, ya son of a bitch!" Bam Bam yelled to Vick. Max looked at the tracks where he saw the ASV was perched. It faced west, and the tires were removed so that it would be able to ride the tracks.

"Whad'ya expect?" Vick hollered back as he approached the car. "Wasn't easy ya know. Had to build a ramp from the scraps of track in the warehouse just to get it up there."

"Your country owes you its gratitude," Max told him. He extended his arm to shake Vick's hand. As they embraced, Max said, "Thank you."

"Yeah, no sweat," he answered as he wiped his brow.

Bam Bam was much warmer, hugging Vick and kissing him on both cheeks. "How long did it take you guys?" he asked.

"We been here all day," Vick told him. "Hey, Joey, you know I don't usually ask questions, but how am I gonna pay these guys on this one?" he asked pointing to his crew.

"Um . . ." Bam Bam thought out loud. His verbal response mimicked the answer, or lack thereof, in his mind.

"You'll each get five thousand dollars for your work here today," Max declared. The crewmen's eyes widened. Five thousand dollars for one day's work was a fortune even when times were good.

"When?" Vick asked.

"Tomorrow," Max falsely assured him.

"With all due respect, Mr. President," Vick began, "what if there is no tomorrow? I mean, we gotta eat."

"I understand, Mr. DeCosta. I promise you that the sun will rise in the morning on a new nation," Max vowed.

"That sounds good and all but . . ." Vick said skeptically before he was interrupted.

"He said 'tomorrow,'" Bam Bam explained to Vick sternly.

"Right, tomorrow," Vick acknowledged as he skulked back to his crew.

Hank approached from the breaker house to the east

of the ASV. Two of his companions followed. "Welcome, Mr. President," he said when he arrived.

"Thank you, Lieutenant," he responded. "Is everything ready?"

"Yes and no, sir," he answered. "The ASV is gassed up and ready to go. But we can't start lining up the trains until we turn on the electricity in the tracks."

"When's that gonna be?" Boots asked.

"About an hour after you leave," Hank explained. "We can't risk electrifying the system until you are safely out of the tank. The trains are electric and their systems need the voltage the rails provide. Your vehicle has a battery for its electrical systems, and its engines run on diesel gasoline. If we turn it on while you are on the tracks, the overload of electricity will probably cause it to explode. An hour should be enough time for you to go thirty-eight miles. Once you arrive safely, the tank is no longer a concern."

"Good thinking," Boots replied.

The Peach said, "I ain't no genius, but what happens once we get to Penn and you turn the tracks on?"

"As soon as the electricity hits the vehicle," Hank began, "it will be horrific. Once you arrive, get as far away from the vehicle as possible."

"One hour before we go 'Boom,'" the Peach said. "Everybody got that?" he asked the crew while making eye contact with Max. They each shook their heads affirmatively.

"Is that gonna fuck up the plan?" Boots asked Max.

"No," Max answered. "We'll have to use it to our advantage. If anything, the explosion will scare the Demons. But it will also give Chatty a reason to bring us before Hades. My assumption is that word will spread of the event quickly, and all of the Demons will be excited to see Hades' response. With them out of the way, our trains will be free to enter Penn undetected."

"But we don't know how Hades will respond," the Aryan added.

"It seems that he has a flair for the dramatic," Max said. "Whatever his response, you can bet all of the Demons will want to see it."

"How dramatic are we talkin' here?" Bam Bam asked.

"You guys better hit the trucks and grab some guns," Max replied.

"What about you?" Bam Bam wondered aloud.

"I have you," Max joked. They all chuckled at his response, and headed to the trucks uneasy with it. Unsheathing his sword, Max mumbled, "and this."

"Mr. President," Hank said, "maybe you should send a scout team for this job. I mean, why does it have to be you?"

"Lieutenant, in my brief lifetime I have learned one thing: If you need something done right, you better do it yourself," Max said as he held the blade of his sword to Hank's eye for effect. "Now, is there a place I can prepare?"

"Yes, sir. Right this way." Hank led Max into the breaker house. A meal was waiting for him on a small card table flanked by two folding chairs in the room that formerly served as a break room for railroad employees. It was not extraordinary; it was merely a piece of chicken and some mixed vegetables.

"A last supper?" Max asked in jest.

"A warrior needs all of his strength for battle," Hank answered. "It's very good. My wife made it for you."

"What about the other guys?"

"We have for them, too. But judging by the size of the portions, the fat man may still be hungry." Max bellowed a laugh. Hank could not help but join in.

Max ate the meal, but the anticipation was filling his stomach more than the food. In a few short hours he would reveal his presence to the world. No longer a secret, he would become a target. Changes loomed large on the horizon. He hated change. Lately, there had just been too much of it. *Choices*, he reminded himself. *Life is a series of choices. I chose this life. It did not choose me.*

When he finished the meal, Max put his empty plate in the sink. He took the gym bag with him to the bathroom. A small window allowed some moonlight to illuminate the room enough for him to locate the light switch. There, he changed his clothes from his jeans and his white tee shirt to a pair of black cargo pants and a black tee shirt he pulled from the bag. Once dressed, he took the Kevlar vest Dalton prepared for him from the bag. He slipped it over his head and fastened the straps around his torso. Lastly, he put on his belt and affixed his sword so that it hung at his left side, and he pulled a nine millimeter handgun from the bag as well as several bullet clips. He loaded the gun in its holster at the right side of his belt, and fastened the bullet clips to his belt. Pulling the gunpowder satchel with Dalton's ashes from the gym bag, Max tied the pouch on his belt next to the gun. "You're gonna get to fight this one with me, Bobby," he said aloud.

The mirror showed his reflection, but he did not recognize it. Max Noble, the magazine publisher turned meager Congressman, did not stand before him. This new persona was more empowering and rancorous. On this night, he was not a politician. He was a soldier about to enter battle.

Max could not bring himself to leave just yet. Instead, he turned out the light and stared at his reflection in the darkened room. Even with the moonlight, he was nothing more than a silhouette. A flash of light entered the window and Max heard a car pull up to the rail yard gates. He heard the gates open and when the engine was silenced he heard, "Good evening, General." It was one of Hank's men greeting Sharpe. Time was no longer a luxury. His mission would commence shortly. He picked up his bag and made his way to greet Sharpe.

Gonzo drove Sharpe to the yard. The two were being briefed by Hank as to the details of the trains' departures. Hank pointed to the trains and then to the tracks; Gonzo's eyes followed Hank's fingers. "It will take about two hours to load the trains," Hank explained. "When you arrive at Penn Station, tracks thirteen through twenty-one will be available for your arrival. The train conductors have been briefed and are aware of which track they must use."

"How long will it take to arm and brief the men, Major?" Sharpe asked.

"Arming them will take a couple of hours, sir. We will brief the unit commanders while the weapons are distributed to the men."

Sharpe began to mumble, "Two hours to arm, two hours to load, and an hour to get there." If time was money, they were very poor. "We need to have everyone here by midnight, at the latest."

"Not to worry, General," Gonzo assured him. "The buses are being loaded at their respective depots at twenty-two hundred. They will be here with time to spare."

"Good," Sharpe replied. "I only hope that we don't walk into an ambush once we get there."

"You won't, General," Max said. His presence startled the officers. With all of their calculating and planning, Max was able to hide in the shadows and approach undetected. "We know what we have to do," he said referring to his team's plan to secure the underground tunnels. "I am curious about one thing, though."

"What is that, Mr. President?" Sharpe asked.

"Once we rendezvous with the Demons on our side, what's the plan?"

"Major," Sharpe deferred. "Please brief the President."

"Yes, sir," Gonzo replied. He rolled out a map of Manhattan on the hood of the car. Since the moonlight provided very little illumination, he pulled a flashlight from his shirt pocket and held it about eighteen inches above the map. Certain areas were circled in black, others in blue, and the area around Thirty-fourth Street and Fifth Avenue in red. He explained, "The blue areas represent the electrical substations. They are being lightly guarded, and so smaller units should be able to capture and destroy them."

"Destroy?" Max interrupted.

"Yes, sir," Gonzo replied. "Basic urban warfare requires that we eliminate the electrical supply to put the enemy at a disadvantage."

"Maybe it's the politician in me, Major, but how long will it take to restore the electricity to the city after the assault?" Max asked.

"That depends on the amount of damage each substation sustains in battle, sir."

"Well, let's try to keep that to a bare minimum, then," Max said half-jokingly.

"Duly noted," Sharpe interjected.

"The areas in black," Gonzo continued, "represent the more heavily fortified areas. This one is their barracks," he noted while pointing at a mosque. "Our intelligence tells us that they have doubled the fortification at the tunnels and the bridges. If we cannot capture or kill them at these locations, we will at least be able to drive them off of the island. Then our men will be the ones fortifying the ingress and egress to the city."

"And this one?" Max asked while pointing to the

large red circle in the center of the map.

"That, sir, is the Empire State Building. It is the most heavily guarded; our intel tells us that there are ten men on each floor."

"So how do you plan on taking that position, Major? Isn't that checkmate, General?" Max snidely asked.

"Indeed, Mr. President," Sharpe answered. "There are two parts of the plan that hinge on your success: Overthrowing Hades to gain access to the underground tunnels, and capturing the Empire State Building."

"*My* success?" Max asked.

"Yes, sir," Gonzo replied. "We are outmanned ten to one. Our forces are needed in numbers in the blue and black areas. Only a small team will be able to gain access to the Empire State Building."

"How small are we talking here?" Max asked.

"You'll have your crew," Sharpe answered.

"That's it?" Max sought to confirm.

"Yes, sir," Sharpe obliged. "Lieutenant Youseff and his men will get you into the building. They'll lead you to the elevator banks that will take you to Emir on the observatory deck."

"General, has the lieutenant explained what will happen to the ASV as soon as he electrifies the tracks?" Max asked as he patted Hank on the back.

"No, sir, it must have slipped his mind," Sharpe told him.

"Boom," Max said making an expanding motion with his hands. "Now, don't you think that they're gonna hear that in the Empire State Building if it blows up in Penn Station a few blocks away?"

"I would think so, sir," Gonzo interjected. "But we don't have to worry about it."

"Why not, Major?" Sharpe demanded.

"According to Colonel Chatham, Emir's men stay away from the underground. That's part of their deal with Hades. For all they know, it will be part of some infighting among the Demons. What will be more important, and what is more concerning, for you is to get to Emir before the substations are destroyed."

"And how exactly is that going to happen?" Max asked.

"With all due respect, Mr. President," Hank interjected, "when we come to that, don't ask questions and just do what you are told."

Max was uncomfortable with the answer. However, he remembered everything he read at Armstrong's behest. In all of the volumes about leadership and management styles, he remembered a common thread: In order to gain others' trust, you must first be willing to trust others. "Very well, Lieutenant," he told Hank. "I trust you have this figured out."

"Of course, Mr. President," Hank assured him.

* * *

"That's the last one," Gonzo said as he pointed to the yellow school bus entering the rail yard. Max and his entourage stood with Sharpe, Gonzo and Hank outside of the breaker house observing as the troops arrived. The last bus parked, and its passengers disembarked and lined up in perfect rows. They were boys, not men; most of them barely had a reason to shave. Yet they stood at attention ready to give their lives for the promise of freedom. The unit joined the others.

In all, ten thousand relatively untested soldiers were awaiting orders. Not one of them spoke. Max could see fear in their eyes. While they were too young for war, this was a fight to defend their homes. He knew that they would have to understand the difference if they would be able to use that fear to their advantage. "They look scared," he said to Sharpe.

"They probably are," Sharpe retorted. "Only the unit commanders have seen battle before. They have no idea what lies in store. Even if they manage to stay alive, combat changes a man. You see things that you only imagined. Take corpses, for example. It's harmless when you see a dead guy on the television or in a movie, but the first time you see a dead person . . . it can make you sick. Only in battle, there is no time to get sick. You have to keep moving or else you're sure to be killed yourself. That's the fear you sense: The possibility that they won't be coming home."

"How do we make them unafraid?" Max asked Sharpe.

"Well, Mr. President," Sharpe answered with a smirk, "as Commander-in-Chief, part of your job is to instill morale in the troops."

"What should I say?" Max wondered aloud.

"Whatever comes natural," Gonzo offered.

Max asked for a megaphone. Hank sent one of his men into the breaker house, and he returned a few moments later with the device. Grabbing the shoulder strap and slinging the megaphone over his head and shoulder, Max walked to one of the trucks, climbed up the side of the cab and ultimately perched himself atop the roof of the trailer. The soldiers' attention turned to him and a hush fell upon the army's underlying murmur. Just to be certain that he had their complete attention, he pressed the button on the bullhorn that sounded a short blast of its siren. When it stopped, he switched to the microphone. Of the politician's skills he learned from Armstrong, oration was one that he was never taught; it was an innate ability, and one that Judge Vineri had promised him would be readily available when needed, almost as if it were a gift granted from above.

"Gentlemen," he began, "my name is Max Noble. I am your President and Commander-in-Chief." As he gazed out among the crowd, he saw the unit commanders, most of whom were veterans, salute him, and as they did so, the infantry followed. He offered his salute back to them, and continued, "For five months we have been living in our founding fathers' worst nightmare. Our freedom has been revoked, and the very essence of their vision for an American nation is being extinguished by a tyrant.

"This is not a time to place blame. How it has come to this is irrelevant. While the fire that burns for freedom is dying, it is not dead yet. It is alive in each of us. You must feel the warmth of freedom inside of yourself as you prepare for battle today. I realize that most of you have never experienced anything like what is about to ensue. You are not alone, for I have not experienced it either. You have every right to be afraid. But do not let the cold that accompanies that fear to chill you. When the hair rises on the back of your neck and your heart starts to race, think of the way your life was at this time last year. Think of your friends and family. You are fighting for their freedom even more than your own.

"It is fitting that tomorrow is Memorial Day. Think about it for a moment. In a few short hours, it will be the day for honoring the memory of those who gave their lives to protect our freedom. Now, we have the opportunity to repay them for their sacrifice. We cannot allow for them to have died in vain! Collectively, we are a young and untested army. This much is true. But more importantly, we were once free men, and tomorrow we will be free men again! I will ask of you men all that has been asked of those who have given their lives defending our freedom. Do not stop fighting until victory is declared. Our mission is vital to the survival of our nation and our freedom. If we fail, the United States of America shall exist no more. I will not have that happen on my watch, gentlemen! I promise you this: I am prepared to fight until my death for my family and freedom, as well as yours. We are brothers in arms. I ask only that you grant me the same fortitude, and promise me that if I fall in battle and you do not, you will carry our flag on to victory. That is the sacrifice that the Continental Army made during the Revolutionary War; it is the same sacrifice that the Union Army made during the Civil War; and it is the same sacrifice that delivered victories in both World Wars.

"Courage is having the knowledge that you should choose life over death, and yet remaining willing to choose death to save the lives of others. You have all exhibited that you have the necessary courage by merely your presence here; for you have shown that you want to be free to live your lives as you see fit, rather than to waste your lives under the auspices of a tyrant's rule. You know that, and you are willing to die for it. Indeed, that is courage.

"So, my brave brothers, I ask: Are you prepared to fight for your freedom?"

"Sir, yes, sir!" the army responded in unison.

"Then victory will be ours," Max continued. "General Sharpe, are we prepared for launch?"

"Sir, yes, sir!" Sharpe shouted loudly enough for the army to hear.

"To victory, gentlemen!" Max announced to the soldiers' raucous cheer. He dismounted the truck and made his way to the ASV where Boots, Bam Bam, the Peach and the Aryan awaited each with a handgun holstered at his side and an automatic assault rifle in hand. The army cleared a path for him, and each soldier stood at attention saluting him as he walked by. He had their full admiration and respect, which is exactly what he knew he needed.

Sharpe joined him on his walk, taking the megaphone from him. "Nicely done, Mr. President," he said.

"Thank you, General," he answered. Max and his entourage entered the ASV one-by-one, Max being the last. Once he was in, he looked at out Sharpe and said, "See you on the other side, General."

"Indeed," Sharpe answered. "Give 'em hell, Mr. President," he said as he closed the door. He pounded twice on the side of the door, and Boots started the engine and began to drive down the track to Penn Station.

Sharpe stared at the ASV as it headed into the dark horizon. Gonzo and Hank fell in behind him.

"Sir, are you okay?" Gonzo asked.

"Perfectly fine, Major," Sharpe answered. "How are we looking, Lieutenant?" he asked Hank.

"Fifty-nine minutes until we flip the switch in the breaker house, General," Hank replied.

"Then it begins," Sharpe commented. He turned to the army, which remained at attention awaiting orders. Speaking into the bullhorn, he ordered, "Unit commanders fall out and meet Major Gonzalez and me in the breaker house for mission briefing. The rest of you men may remain at ease."

CHAPTER 17

"Do us all a favor," the Peach said as he stroked the straggly blonde hair on his chin, "let us shave this shit off as part of the festivities when this is all done."

The company laughed. The beards were not a big hit with the men to begin with, but their hatred of them had grown as the temperatures rose and they began to itch in the heat. "Gladly," Max assured them while scratching his chin hair.

Room was sparse in the fuselage of the ASV. The vehicle was not intended for long distance travel, and comfort was not atop the list of the defense department's specifications for its design. Unlike the luxury sedans to which Max had grown accustomed, the ASV was not quiet; in addition to the roar of the engine, every clang and screech of the metal wheels on the steel track was audible.

"How much longer 'til we get there?" the Aryan asked.

"About ten minutes," Boots answered.

Max asked the more important follow-up question: "How much longer 'til they turn the power on?"

"About fifteen minutes," Bam Bam answered.

"Oh good," the Peach added sarcastically. "I wouldn't want to cut it close or nothin'."

"Relax, Peach, it could be the other way around," Max reminded him.

"Yeah, listen to him, ya dumb bastard," Bam Bam

insisted.

They entered the tunnel that ran under the East River. The increase in pressure caused their ears to pop. Ten minutes passed quickly, although it felt like an eternity to them. As they passed through the tunnel and into Penn Station, they could see the train platforms ahead. Boots slowed the vehicle, which came to a halt next to the platform marked "Track 16." They disembarked, weapons in hand, and looked around. Not seeing anyone, Max said, "C'mon, let's go find Chatty before this thing blows." The men followed Max's lead up the nearest staircase to the main concourse.

* * *

"It's oh-one hundred, sir," Gonzo said.

"Very well, Major," Sharpe answered. Turning to Hank, he said, "Light up the rails, Lieutenant. The time is upon us."

"Yes, sir," Hank replied. After briefing the unit commanders Sharpe gathered Hank's men in the kitchen of the breaker house to go over the plan of attack for the Empire State Building. They had just finished discussing the logistics when Gonzo looked at his watch. With Sharpe having given the order, Hank took his men to the upstairs level of the breaker house where the controls to the railroad's electrical system were housed.

After a few minutes of turning knobs and flipping switches, the generators began to churn and hum. Then the signal lights came alive. Hank returned to the kitchen to report. "Status, Lieutenant?" Sharpe asked.

"We're live, sir," Hank told him.

"Thank you, Lieutenant. Have the engineers align the trains for boarding. Major, tell the unit commanders to begin arming the troops."

* * *

"Psssst! Over here," Chatty called. He had been waiting for Max to arrive at the rendezvous point for nearly half an hour. His black leather Demon outfit hid him well in the shadows of the main concourse, which was one level up from the tracks. What had once been the bright central hub of the commuter rail system was now another dark and neglected cavern occupied by new, unwanted tenants.

"Sorry we took so long," Max began to explain.

"There's no time, sir," Chatty interrupted. "Give me your weapons, quickly," he urged. Max and his team complied. Chatty had a gym bag with him, and he placed the guns in it, except for one handgun from which he removed the magazine containing the bullets and made sure the chamber was empty. He picked up the bag with his left hand and kept the gun in his right. Checking his watch, he said, "Not a word. Wait for it."

Puzzled, the men did as they were told. Although obedience was not part of their nature, they knew that too much time had been spent planning this moment. None of them was prepared to risk compromising the mission, so they each did as instructed.

Without warning, a large explosion rocked the station. The ground shook as the thunderous roar of the detonation extended upward from the tracks below. Fire and smoke quickly poured into the concourse from the staircase that the team used to ascend from the tracks. The men dove for cover. When the dust settled, they heard voices approaching.

Chatty was the first to rise as a horde of Demons neared. When they were within earshot he pointed the empty gun at Max and his team, which was still prone on the ground. "Don't move!" he ordered.

"Who are they, Cerberus?" one of the Demons called.

"That's a good question," Chatty shouted back answering to the name given him by Hades. "Who are you?" Chatty demanded as he approached Max.

Max and the entourage slowly rose to their feet. Looking at each of their soot-covered faces, he nodded and said, "I am Max Noble, President of the United States."

Laughter broke out among the Demons. "This mother fucker must be crazy, Cerberus," one of them shouted.

"There ain't no more United States," another called.

"And I'll be a damned if you think some cracker looking down the barrel of a gun is gonna tell me what to do," the first one retorted.

"Silence," Chatty yelled to the Demons. They immediately complied. It was clear that they respected him and would honor his every command. Looking at Max again he said, "What are you doing here? What was that explosion about? Did Emir send you? Your presence here is a violation of his pact with Lord Hades."

"Who is Lord Hades?" Max asked. With the Demons as an audience, he had to further authenticate Chatty's cover so as not to rouse any suspicion.

The Demons laughed again. "Shit, this mother fucker is so dumb, he don't even know who the great Lord Hades is!" one of them exclaimed.

"I said, 'Silence!'" Chatty sternly reminded the Demons. Again they immediately ceased their antics. "Gather the others," he said to them. "Meet us in Tartarus. I will bring these intruders before Lord Hades. He can decide what their fates will be. Spread the word that Lord Hades will be doling out justice."

The Demons began to howl and holler as Chatty gathered the men and marched them to the subway platform for the number "one" train. The turnstiles had been removed in what seemed like a violent manner judging by the twisted metal hinges where their stanchions were once fastened to the floor. Fires were burning in the metallic garbage receptacles that lined the platform. Water filled what were once the subway tracks nearly entirely up to the platform's edge.

Demons lined the platform; their faces were covered in soot from the continually burning fires, and they wheezed and coughed, presumably from the mold that was visibly growing on the walls of the warm, dank environment. They kept their distance from Chatty and his captives. "Where are you going, Cerberus?" one of the Demons asked.

"To Tartarus to bring these intruders before Lord Hades," he replied. A boat approached from the south and slowed as it approached Chatty. Williams, also donning his Demon uniform, stood in the rear with a long oar in his hand that he used to propel the vessel. "Good to see you, Charon," Chatty greeted Williams.

"Likewise, Cerberus," Williams said. "What is our destination?" he asked as he and Chatty helped their secret comrades onto the boat.

"Tartarus," Chatty answered.

"Splendid," Williams said. They cast off and Williams began to paddle. The Demons on the platform began to shout and curse as the boat passed them. Chatty was stoically perched at the bow and kept the unloaded gun pointed at the passengers. As soon as the light from the platform dimmed and they were clearly out of range to be heard, Williams asked, "You alright, Mr. President?"

"Fine, Captain. How about yourself?" Max replied.

"Feeling great, sir," he answered. "Now, listen up boys," he continued addressing the rest of the team. "When we get to the platform at forty-second street, we're gonna hop out and head over to the Shuttle platform to get to Grand Central. Got it?"

"Why do we have to do that?" the Peach asked.

"'Cause the Demons are gonna see us, and they think you're our prisoners," Chatty answered.

"Is there another boat there?" Bam Bam asked.

"Of course," Williams explained.

"Listen, guys, not another word," Max said. "You never know who may be listening." They realized that he was right, and continued silently in the dark until they reached the Times Square-Forty-Second Street Station platform, where the fires raged and more Demons awaited their arrival to get a look at the men who dared to invade Lord Hades' domain.

"Y'all gonna die, bitches," one of the Demons told them. "Lord Hades is not feeling merciful today!" he assured them as he caused a loud outburst of laughter from the crowd.

Though the Demons taunted, they did not impede the group in any way. They reached the Shuttle platform and loaded into the awaiting boat. As the boat made its way from Times Square to Grand Central Station through the dark tunnel, Max sat in the silence and pondered how he was about to either claim his first great victory or suffer a horrendous death. The only thing he knew for certain was that the choice was his.

* * *

"General Rogers," Norton called across the upper level of the Hub, "we're detecting a spike in the electrical grid in New York."

"How so?" Rogers queried.

"It seems that the rail road generators on Long Island have been activated," Norton explained.

"I see," Rogers reacted. "Who is on duty there today?"

"We're checking with Sultan's men, sir. They are handling the daily ground operations in the area," Norton said.

One of Sultan's men entered the room and reported to Norton, "Mujahadeen Hakim Youseff has been charged with guarding the rail road today, sir."

"Very well," Rogers interjected. "Get me Youseff on the phone."

Norton walked to a computer terminal in the lower section of the room. There, he located the phone number for the breaker house where Hank was stationed. He picked up the phone adjacent to the console; he dialed, and after three rings Hank answered, "Yes, sir."

Norton flipped a switch on the console and said, "Mujahadeen Youseff, I have General Chet Rogers on the line. We have detected an electrical spike coming from the rail road."

"Status report at once, Youseff," Rogers demanded.

"All systems normal, General Rogers," Hank explained. "I will have my men check the area immediately for any trespassers, sir."

"We await your report, Youseff. You have ten minutes to investigate," Rogers ordered.

"Yes, sir," Hank answered.

* * *

Hank hung up the phone in the kitchen of the breaker house. "We have ten minutes to investigate the electrical spike before they call back, General."

"Are the trains loaded, Major?" Sharpe asked. He needed all information available to make a decision. The call from the Pentagon was expected, but it came earlier than he had initially anticipated.

"Not yet, sir," Gonzo explained. "Three are loaded with another seven in position."

"Get them loaded immediately, Major. On the double! We have to get out of here now!"

"But we're two hours ahead of schedule, sir," Gonzo pleaded. "Is that enough time for the President to secure the landing zone?"

"Probably not, Major. But we can't stay here much longer without blowing our cover." Sharpe turned his attention to Hank and ordered, "When they call back buy as much time as you can, Lieutenant. I don't care what you have to tell them."

"Understood, sir," Hank answered.

"Good. Major, are those teamsters still here?" Sharpe asked referring to Vick DeCosta and his men.

"I believe so, sir," Gonzo answered.

"Bring them in here, quickly. We need a favor."

* * *

"Kids playing by the tracks?" Harmon questioned as he and Rogers spoke in the confines of his office. "I don't buy it, General Rogers."

"I know, sir," Rogers agreed. "Kids couldn't cause a spike like that. That's the report we got from this Youseff, though. Do you think they caused a malfunction in our systems, sir?"

"It's possible, I suppose," Harmon replied. "Have it checked out anyway. How many men does Emir have in the Long Island brigade?"

"About one thousand, sir."

"Good. Call Emir and tell him to deploy the entire brigade to the rail yard. Tell him we have detected some suspicious activity."

"Yes, sir," Rogers responded.

"In the meantime, I will consult Sultan to see if he thinks we should give the nuclear codes to Emir."

"Sir? Is that necessary? I mean, with all due respect, we should be protecting New York, not threatening it."

Harmon became cross. "I am drawing tired of your second-guessing me, General. If it happens again, I will demote you for insubordination, and you'll be guarding a food silo in West Virginia. No questions asked. Is that clear?"

"Crystal, sir," a dejected Rogers replied.

* * *

"All trains ready for departure, General," Gonzo reported through the walkie-talkie. "We are 'go' on your order, sir."

"We've left no trace, right Lieutenant?" Sharpe asked Hank who sat next to him in the first car of the lead train.

"That's correct, sir," Hank assured him.

Sharpe took his walkie-talkie and declared, "We're 'go,' Major."

"Roger, General," Gonzo confirmed.

The trains pulled out of the yard and began their trek into the bowels of New York City. As they left, Sharpe looked out of his window and saluted to a man with a cane in a white suit with a white hat. The man in the suit returned the gesture.

* * *

Chatty led Max and the company into the great hall that was once Grand Central Station. The aquamarine ceiling still had the constellations of the Zodiac painted upon it, but the American flag that once hung from it had been destroyed. Only the tattered remnants of the flag remained; they were partially charred. Chatty carried the gym bag with the weapons, while Williams followed the company, whose hands were placed on their heads like prisoners.

Demons filled the hall, cheering as Chatty paraded the prisoners in from the underpass by the East Balcony and lined them up shoulder-to-shoulder just in front of the West Balcony. Fires raged all around providing light to the lair; Tartarus was not a friendly environment to Max and his companions. The Demons' cheering grew louder as four figures descended the staircase onto the West Balcony. The first was a gargantuan black man who wore a patch over his right eye; the second a black woman with long dreadlocks; the third a short Latino man who carried a bottle of clear liquid on his belt; and finally, a red and black robed man whose face was hidden by the robe's silk black hood.

The hooded man raised his hands and the Demons became immediately silent. "Who dares to enter the underworld uninvited?" the hooded man asked.

Max stepped forward and declared, "I do."

"And who might you be?"

"I am Max Noble, President of the United States," Max answered. "I presume that you are the one that the Demons call 'Hades.'"

"Indeed, I am," Hades said as he removed his hood, exposing his dark skin and shaved head. "Welcome to Tartarus, my home. Surely, Mr. Noble, you will mind your manners while you are here. You will, of course, excuse me for refusing to recognize your title. Your precious United States of America no longer exist. Down here, I am the law." The Demons cheered loudly.

Hades raised his hand again, and the cheering ceased. "But of course," Max assured him diplomatically. However, he refused to accept Hades' lack of respect, and instead returned the sentiment. "Tell me, Professor Edwards, why have you aligned yourself with those who seek to destroy my country?"

Hades laughed aloud. "So, you know who I am. Well then, I presume you also know how I feel about your beloved country. How it oppressed my people at every given opportunity. How it caused generations of African-Americans to wallow in poverty while the white man grew richer on my people's backs. And, let us not forget how when I chose to mobilize my people, your country failed to protect my precious right to do so. Persecuted me, they did!"

"I remember your story differently, Edwards," Max interrupted.

"Hades!" the robed lord corrected.

"I beg your pardon, Hades," Max responded. "You see I remember that you advocated for the violent demise of the American government, and that you encouraged African-Americans to partake in a treasonous insurrection that would have brought them death not freedom."

Hades was visibly uncomfortable with Max's interpretation of his beliefs. "Are you not doing the same?" he asked. Max could sense that Hades was onto him. "I presume you are here to plead for my assistance. I am sorry to disappoint my dear child, but once a soul is brought before me, forever does it remain under my command. My legions will not join you." Concern became visible on Max's face. "And now, your souls belong to me, as well." The Demons roared with approval of Hades' decision.

"Very well, Hades. You have signed your death certificate," Max challenged.

"Sir," the Aryan called in a voice louder than a whisper. "You're gonna get us all killed!"

"Trust me," Max answered him.

"Are you threatening me?" Hades asked with a hint of annoyance in his voice.

"I challenge you to a battle to the death, just between you and me. If I win, your Demons will join my men and our fight to reclaim the city. If you win, you may keep my men to add to your minions."

A murmur spread among the crowd. "Are you fuckin' crazy?" Boots asked Max. "We're not gonna be barter for you with this fuckin' guy."

"Relax, Boots," Max calmed. "I know what I'm doing."

"Silence!" Hades declared to the Demons. "I accept your challenge, Mr. Noble. But you will not fight me. You will fight my three proxies, Cyclops, Medusa and Typhon." The roar from the Demons was immense, and caused a vibration throughout the hall.

"That was not the challenge," Max protested.

"True," Hades responded. "But those are the only terms under which I will allow you to fight for your precious freedom. So, my dear child, do you accept?"

Max looked at his friends. He saw fear in their eyes. It was the same fear he saw in the younger troops' eyes in the rail yard. He turned back to Hades, and called, "Allow me a sword and we have a deal."

Hades briefly pondered the request. "So be it," he declared. He extended his arm toward the balcony staircase, and Cyclops led the trio down toward the main floor, followed by Medusa and Typhon, where the Demons had cleared the area surrounding Max. Williams led the rest of Max's company to the side leaving Max standing alone as his three assailants approached. Chatty pulled Max's sword from the gym bag, unsheathed it, and handed it to Max before retiring to the West Balcony to stand at Hades' side.

Cyclops raised his hands, clenched in tight fists, toward the ceiling and roared. The crowd mimicked him. Medusa made an acrobatic entrance onto the floor performing several handsprings; her dreadlocks flailed in the air as her body flipped. Again, the Demons cheered. Typhon descended the staircase and took a swig from the bottle attached to his belt. He pulled a lighter from his pocket and sparked a flame. Spitting the liquid through the flame, a stream of fire raced toward Max stopping only feet in front of him. Again the crowd exploded.

Max raised his sword and assumed a defensive position. His sessions with Takinawa raced through his mind. He knew that he could not make the first move, so he held his pose. His stoic posture masked his trepidation. *Where will the first strike come from?* he thought. *The giant? No, he is only muscle. The fire-breather? No, he is only effective when he has time to attack. It will be the woman. She is agile and ferocious.*

Max's eyes locked with Medusa's. He kept his focus on her, but was mindful of Cyclops' and Typhon's positions as well. His instinct was correct; Medusa charged at him with a hellish yell and a continuous thrust of roundhouse kicks aimed at his head. Max dodged her kicks and swung his sword upwards as she neared slicing through three of the dreadlocks on the right side of her head, which flew through the air and landed on the floor. The Demon crowd gasped, for Medusa had never before been touched in battle.

Max regained his balance and fronted her. But before he could reposition himself to front all three attackers, two enormous arms were wrapped around his chest squeezing the air from his lungs. His sword fell to the floor as Cyclops lifted him off the floor and threw him across the room like a rag doll. His limp body slid across the marble floor. When he came to a stop, he lifted his head only to see fire coming straight for him.

He rolled quickly to the side as the fire from Typhon's mouth charred the floor where he laid only a split second before. This time, he had the opportunity to compose himself. With his sword lying across the room, he had no other choice than to engage in pugilism. He assumed a stance and began one of the *katahs* Takinawa taught him. Medusa attacked again, but Max was able to block her kicks and punches. He was also able to land a punch of his own squarely to her sternum which drove her backwards and causing her to stumble and fall to her back.

Cyclops followed Medusa with a charge at Max. Eyeing his sword, Max dove through Cyclops' legs intentionally using his momentum to slide across the floor to his weapon. He felt the heat from another of Typhon's fire streams at his heels, but the flames did not touch him. He grabbed his sword and leaped to his feet as Cyclops charged again. Max wielded his sword with ease, and lopped off Cyclops' right arm. The crowd was stunned as the mammoth man dropped to his knees. Max seized the opportunity to finish his enemy and thrust his sword into Cyclops' skull through his good eye. After the strike, he removed his sword and Cyclops' giant carcass collapsed at his feet.

Typhon and Medusa looked at each other in shock. Their trio's lethal talents had conquered all unscathed until now. Rage took control of Medusa who launched another barrage of kicks and punches at Max. With Typhon's fire streams being spewed toward him incessantly, Max blocked Medusa's punches with his forearms before slashing at her with his sword; this time, he cut off two of the dreadlocks on the left side of her head. She howled to express her ire. Blinded by her thirst for revenge, she never saw Max's punch, which landed between her eyes and knocked her backwards into Typhon. Her momentum carried her ally to the floor with her.

The sound of glass shattering ensued, and Typhon's

lighter flew out of his hand and landed at Max's feet. He picked up the lighter, and sparked a fire. Max approached his prone opponents marching at a determined pace. As he neared them, he threw the lighter on the ground. It immediately ignited the puddle that was once the contents of Typhon's hip flask. Medusa managed to scurry away with only several singed dreadlocks.

Her associate was not as lucky; the flames completely engulfed Typhon. His shrieks of pain were high-pitched. The Demons in the crowd watched in horror as Typhon burned to his death before their eyes. When he finally collapsed to the ground, they turned their attention to Medusa, hollering "Kill him!" repeatedly, in hopes that she would send the intruder to his death. She was energized by the crowd's support. Smiling at Max, she laughed out loud and launched her most fervent attack yet. Her kicks were fast and furious; her punches landed and stung Max with venom he never felt in any of his sparring sessions with Takinawa. She paused when she had exhausted herself, and Max, bloodied at the nose and near his left eye from her beating, began his own assault. His punch knocked her backwards, and he used the opportunity to reset himself in a defensive position.

Medusa began another series of leaping roundhouse kicks. As she approached Max, he was able to dodge them again, and to strike with his sword; this time, he swung in a downward thrust. His blow decapitated her in midair. A hush fell over the Demons as they watched the body of Hades' final protector fall to the floor; her head rolled in the direction of her former master.

"Fuck, yeah!" the Peach yelled breaking the silence.

* * *

"I have no intention of giving him the codes, General," Sultan scolded Harmon in the privacy of his office. "I appreciate your concern for our cause, but I know my brother better than you. He is, how do you say, trigger-happy? We cannot afford to destroy New York City under any circumstance. Annihilating it completely would cause all of the world's markets to collapse, even in the Middle East where my accounts are hidden. I do not like to lose money. Do you, General?"

Harmon was puzzled. "So, it's all about money, now? Then why give him the warhead, at all?" Harmon demanded to know.

"General, it has always been about money and power. You Americans spread your capitalism to the world and declared that since you had the most, you were the ones in charge. Why do you think oil is priced on the dollar? Now, I have the power. And I will not part with it easily. My brother is not me. He has power only through me. Your idea of giving him a warhead only strengthens his standing with my men. And more importantly, it further endears him to me."

"You used me? You rat son of a bitch!"

Sultan pulled his gun from its holster on his belt and pointed it directly at Harmon. "Don't get any funny ideas, General. I am still firmly in control."

Harmon controlled his temper and composed himself. "Of course you are, Sultan. But tell me again, how did you get that control?"

* * *

The trains pulled into Penn Station, which was still filled with the smoke from the exploded ASV. The troops unloaded and the unit commanders led them up the platform stairwells. They gathered on the main concourse where Sharpe and Gonzo, having been the first to disembark, waited for them. The general raised his fist next to his head to signal to the unit commanders that he wanted absolute quiet. The ensuing silence was deafening.

"Major, form a scout team," Sharpe said. "We need to find the President."

"General," Hank called, "these halls are empty. The only time the Demons abandon their posts is when Hades calls them to assemble in Grand Central Station."

"If we bring the army above ground now we'll lose the advantage of surprise," Sharpe explained. "I'm open to suggestions."

"We could wait it out, sir," Gonzo offered. "We're just ahead of schedule."

"I have a better idea, sir," Hank said.

* * *

Max sheathed his sword and slowly approached the West Balcony where Hades seethed over the deaths of his protectors. Bleeding, but none the worse for wear, Max strode with confidence. He looked at his team and winked. They smiled, and Boots even gave a slight fist-pump as if to say, "Congratulations!" As Max neared the balcony, the Demons followed. The space around him grew smaller, and soon he was again reunited with his team looking up at Hades.

Max reached down and picked up Medusa's head. He presented it to Hades as a peace offering. "I believe we had a deal, Professor Edwards," he said refusing to recognize that the man had any authority left. "Order your men to report for assignment in my army."

"They will do no such thing!" Hades proclaimed. The crowd of Demons cheered in defiance of Max's demand.

"Hey, you agreed," the Peach protested. The Demons responded by pointing their guns at him; not a single one was unarmed. "I'm just sayin'," the Peach said as he accepted that, at this point, the balance of his life rested clearly in Max's ability to negotiate their way out of the existing predicament.

"What my colleague is trying to explain, Professor," Max interrupted, "is that your men would be better off serving me. I am a man of my word, unlike you. The Demons will find mercy and freedom in my army, and once we win back our country all freedoms previously enjoyed by all Americans will be restored." The Demons began to nod. Suddenly, Hades' dictatorial style of leadership did not seem so appealing to them.

While the Demons were paying attention to Max and Hades' exchange, no one noticed that Chatty had slipped a magazine clip from his vest pocket and loaded into his gun. With the tension rising in the room and Max's men still unarmed, he would certainly need some protection.

"I've heard these promises before, Mr. Noble," Hades replied. "It was, oh, every year around election time, I believe. Freedom! Ha! What do you know of it? My people were oppressed for nearly four hundred years in this country! Do not be fooled, my Demons. In Mr. Noble's vision, you are nothing more than pawns to do his bidding."

"Remember where you came from!" Max insisted as he faced the thousands of Demons standing behind him. "Months ago, you lived free lives above ground. Your children could play on the playgrounds. You were permitted to see the light of day. Do you really wish to spend the rest of your lives below ground serving a man who sends others to do his dirty work, and then reneges on his promises?" This time the Demons shook their heads negatively to answer Max's question. Again, he was winning over the crowd. "Who among you will join me?"

"None of them will!" Hades commanded.

"I will," Chatty announced.

"Cerberus?" Hades asked in a state of shock as he turned to Chatty. "How could you betray me? I gave you power beyond what you could have possibly attained in the upper world. This is how you repay me?"

"Actually, Hades, my name before I met you was Leon Chatham, and I was a colonel in President Noble's army." A great murmur spread throughout the crowd of Demons. "Now, Hades, your reign is over. You pledged the Demons to the President. He defeated your guardians who you cowardly sent to fight in your stead. If you do not give the order for them to join our fight, I will." Chatty raised his gun and aimed directly at Hades.

"Are you challenging my authority?" Hades asked. "I think not," he said. He began to reach to his side. Chatty, knowing that Hades was so distrusting that he would never be unarmed, pulled the trigger of his gun. Bang! The bullet hit Hades directly between the eyes; Chatty could see blood spew out of the back of Hades head. The bullet's momentum snapped Hades' head back and his weight forced his dead body to tip over the balcony railing. The corpse landed at Max's feet, and a ruckus began among the Demons.

Suddenly, machine gun fire erupted from the outskirts of the crowd. "Nobody move!" was the order that came from a voice in the back. It was a familiar voice to Max and his soldiers. The crowd parted as a man walked directly toward Max.

"General!" Max excitedly exclaimed as Sharpe marched to him, coming to a halt and saluting.

* * *

The sun began to rise over the rail yard as Sultan's soldiers approached the gate. The yard was empty except for a man with a cane in a white suit and a white hat.

"You there," the head mujahadeen cried, "identify yourself."

"I love watching the sun rise over here," the man

said. "It's dawn on a brand new day. The air is fresh." He wafted the air to his nostrils. "And it was so quiet you could hear a pin drop. Then you boys showed up. "

"Do not move!" the mujahadeen ordered as he cocked his machine gun.

"Okay, okay," the man replied putting his hands in the air. "But I should warn you that you're not the first guy who pointed a gun at my back."

"Show yourself!"

"Well, make up your mind. Should I move or not?" he asked as he slowly turned to reveal his face. Don Vito looked into the mujahadeen's eyes.

"What are you doing here?"

"I already told you, I love watching the sun rise over here."

"We have reports that there were some spikes in the electricity."

"What? Spikes in the electricity? I wouldn't know nothin' about that."

"You cannot be trusted! Come over here at once. You are under arrest."

"Me? You can't trust me?" Don Vito said noting that he was insulted. "You're the ones who pointed your guns at my back, and you can't trust me? I've done nothing to you."

"True, but this is an unauthorized area, you are here, and we have reports of . . . . "

"I know, reports of a spike in the electricity," Don Vito interrupted. "You sound like a freakin' robot that's got a skip or somethin'. Come here. There ain't no electricity spike here. I told you, I just love to watch the sun rise from here. Come here, seriously," he said as he waved the leader to him.

The leader approached slowly keeping his gun aimed at the don's chest the entire time. When he reached him, he asked, "What is over here?"

"You see these tracks," the don explained, "there's three of them, right? Two for the choo-choo trains to ride on and one to carry the electricity."

"I know how the trains work, wise ass!"

"Don't get fresh! It's rude. I'm just trying to explain to you that if you touch the third rail when there's electricity running through it, you'll get roasted like a marshmallow. But when there's no electricity running through it, it's just another piece of metal."

"Yes, all of this I know. What is your point?"

"Touch it. You'll be fine. Go on. You'll see."

"You touch it, and we'll see who the marshmallow is. After all, you are wearing the white suit."

"You want me to touch it? Okay, fine. You'll see, I'll be just fine." Don Vito knelt down and reached his hand over the third rail. He slowly lowered it, but before he could touch it, Bang! A shot rang out catching the mujahadeen in the kneecap. The soldier fell down, and in his effort to break his fall, he slammed his hand onto the third rail.

Electricity pulsed through his body. It singed his hair and blackened his skin. He cried in pain for less than a minute before life left his body.

All the while, Don Vito's men surrounded Sultan's brigade and opened fire. It was the perfect ambush. Those few mujahadeen that were able to escape the slaughter were immediately met by Takinawa and his senseis, who were able to quickly disarm and subdue them. The fight lasted less than three minutes; the surviving mujahadeen were rounded up and chained together.

Don Vito walked over to Takinawa. "Nicely done,

Sensei," he said extending a handshake to him.

"Thank you, Don," Takinawa replied as he gripped the don's hand and shook it firmly. "Not too bad yourself. Now what do we do?"

"You should probably go home, and watch the news to see if it was worth it. In the meantime, my boys want to have some fun with these bastards, and my guess is that it won't be pretty."

* * *

"I'm glad we got here early," Sharpe told Max as he looked around the great hall. The Demons were silent but tense; the slightest distraction would have upset the herd.

"You're a couple of hours ahead of schedule, sir," Chatty noted. "Is Operation King Kong still green lighted?"

"Absolutely, Colonel Chatham," Sharpe assured. "Glad to see your men are ready," he said referring to the Demons.

"They are, sir. Right boys?" he asked the Demons.

"What you want us to do, Cerb- I mean, Colonel?" one of the Demons asked.

"We'll split you up and assign you to companies with the rest of the men," Sharpe said while pointing to the troops who stood at attention in their units surrounding the Demons.

"We only answer to the colonel," the Demon insisted.

"Then listen to this order, Demons," Chatty announced. "You will be assigned to the companies in this room. Each company has a unit commander. You will do what your unit commander tells you to do, or else you will answer to me. Our mission today is to retake the City of New York. This is going to be gang warfare at its meanest, its ugliest. You will guide your units through the subway tunnels to your respective targets. And then you will unleash hell on your enemy. Am I clear, Demons?"

The Demons cheered and hollered. Gonzo and Chatty began talking about the Demons' unit assignments. Meanwhile, Sharpe pulled Max and his crew to the side. "Are you alright, Mr. President? I mean you look like hell."

"I'm fine, General," Max assured him. "Thanks. It was a little scrimmage."

"It was awesome, General," Boots said. "He would have made Bobby proud today."

"Really?" Sharpe asked. "Well, I am just glad that you are in one piece," he said hiding his admiration of Max's triumph.

"Why are you here so early, General?" Max asked.

"Well, the funny thing is, Mr. President," Sharpe began, "is that the phone rang, and wouldn't you know it, but it was the Pentagon."

"The Pentagon?" Bam Bam asked. "Are they onto us?"

Sharpe smiled. "They were. But we called in a favor from an old friend of yours. We won't have to worry about being followed. Since we had extra time at Penn, Lieutenant Youseff led his men to the subway's drainage controls. Once they figured out how to drain the subway tracks, we marched our asses here as quickly as we could."

"That's a relief," Max said. "An impressive adaptation to the plan, General."

"Thank you, sir. I have spent a lifetime in the army, you know."

"What's our mission, General," the Peach wondered.

"I'm glad you asked, Mr. DeMartino," Sharpe said. It was the first time that anyone addressed the Peach so formally. "Lieutenant, please help me brief the covert ops team."

Hank came over to the general with a duffel bag over his shoulder. He placed the bag at Sharpe's feet and pulled five white robes from the bag. He handed one robe each to Max, Boots, Bam Bam, the Peach and the Aryan. "Put these on," he said. He reached back into the bag and pulled from it five *kefiyahs*, the headwear made famous by Palestinian leader Yassir Arafat. "And these," he said.

"Do we have to?" the Aryan asked, only half-jokingly.

"Absolutely," Hank affirmed. "My men and I will escort you to the elevator bank that will take you up to the observatory where Emir is. The rest is up to you."

"That's it?" Boots asked. "That's the big plan? Shouldn't we have some more details?"

"That *is* it, Boots," Max confirmed. "It's time." Max told Sharpe, "General, we're 'go' on your signal."

CHAPTER 18

The infrared images on the main screen at the Hub showed a group of men standing with their hands over their heads while other men stood facing them with guns in their hands. The train rails at the rail yard of the Long Island Rail Road blazed a bright red on the screen from the heat of the electricity that pulsed through them. Every few minutes, Rogers would shake his head in disgust as one of the captive men would be called forward from the rest of his peers so that the men standing with guns could use him for target practice. Sultan paced in the back of the room and yelled occasionally at his men in Arabic. Harmon stood next to Rogers quietly distancing himself from Sultan.

"General," Rogers said quietly to Harmon so as not to rouse Sultan's men, "this has to stop! Look at what those savages are doing! When are you going to say something to Sultan about the conduct of his soldiers?"

"Open your eyes, Rogers," Harmon whispered back. "Something is wrong. His men haven't been able to contact their guard at the rail yard. Sultan is hoping that your analysis is correct, and that those doing the shooting are his men. At the same time, he is growing increasingly worried that those are his men being shot."

"What do you think?" Rogers inquired.

"Tough to say," Harmon answered. "But the longer Sultan stews, the more nervous I get. We may be a few short hours away from a major catastrophe."

"I thought you told me that he wouldn't let his

brother use that nuke on New York."

"That was before there was any doubt about his grip on the situation."

"General," Sultan called from across the room, "get my brother on the phone at once!"

"Yes, Sultan," Harmon replied. Turning to Rogers, he softly said, "A major catastrophe, General."

* * *

"The unit commanders are leading their troops to their respective targets as we speak, General," Gonzo explained to Sharpe; the general set up a central command station on the West Balcony from which Hades reigned. Gonzo's map, with the blue, black and red circles, was secured to the balcony wall with masking tape.

"I hope we didn't make a mistake by mixing those thugs in with our men," Sharpe said.

"They'll be fine, sir," Chatty countered. "The Demons understand the concepts of honor and loyalty. They no longer respect what Hades' stood for because he was not prepared to honor his word. That, and that alone, won the president their loyalty. Max Noble may have given them the direction they need."

"Lost souls," Sharpe mumbled before turning back to the map. "Major, get regular reports on the radio. Green light when all units are in position." Like a chess master, Sharpe preferred to establish his positioning before his first strike.

"All units, all units," Gonzo called over the walkie-talkie, "this is Home. E.T. phones Home when he's ready," he ordered using code so that unwanted listeners would not be able to undermine the attack. "The Home light is currently red. Repeat, Home light red."

* * *

Emir stepped out on the balcony of the observatory to survey the crown jewel of his brother's new empire. There were no clouds in the sky to block the glaring sun light that turned the eastern side of Manhattan orange while the buildings cast their shadows over the west side of the island. The wind whistled in his ear as it whipped through his hair. Only the ringing phone on his desk called his attention away from the serenity.

He pushed the red button for the speakerphone, and turned on the monitor to his computer. Sultan appeared before him. "As-salaamu aleikum, my brother," Emir said.

"Wa aleikum salaam," Sultan answered. "We have a problem, my brother. Something is afoot at the rail yard on Long Island. Are you certain that you have secured the trains?"

"Absolutely, I've told you that I made a d-d-d-deal with the gang leader to g-g-g-guard them. There is no way to enter the city. My m-m-m-men have everything above ground covered, and his h-h-h-have the tunnels below the streets."

"Report anything out of the ordinary at once. I may ask you to activate that nuclear warhead after all."

"W-W-W-Why not just give the c-c-c-code to me now, brother? Do you not trust me?"

"I trust you more than anyone. Right now, I don't trust myself."

Emir nodded. "Anything out of the ordinary. Absolutely, my brother. You will be the f-f-f-first to know."

* * *

The covert operations team strolled casually into the sunrise along Thirty-Third Street toward the Empire State Building; dressed in the traditional Muslim garb worn by Sultan's soldiers with their faces hidden by the *kefiyahs*, they were unrecognizable to their passing enemies on the street. Not a word was spoken by any of the men. Max could not believe that the city was as eerily silent as it was. Then again, he realized, he had not been to the city – or anywhere else besides Long Island, for that matter – since Sultan arrived. *Focus,* he heard Takinawa's voice in his mind. *Your world will come into balance when you are able to focus on the task at hand.* Max did all he could to heed Takinawa's advice as they approached the skyscraper.

Hank led the team into the building through the service entrance on Thirty-Third Street. He made some small talk in Arabic with the sentry as the rest of the team walked passed him unquestioned. Once they were inside, Hank cut his conversation short and caught up to them. He tugged gently on Max's right sleeve and pulled him toward the elevators; the rest of the team followed.

The sign above the elevators read, "OBSERVATORY." Hank gathered the team in closely to him. "Take this up to sixty-eight. When you get there, transfer to the elevator across the way and press the button for eighty-four. That will put onto the Observatory level. From there, you're on your own."

"Thanks, Hank," Max said as he placed his hand on Hank's shoulder. "You're a great friend. We couldn't have gotten here without you."

"It has been my honor, sir," Hank replied. "Now, please, go. You have a job to do. I look forward to seeing you at the rendezvous."

* * *

"That was the last one, General," Gonzo reported. Tension grew tight in the grand hall. Chatty and Gonzo locked eyes; Sharpe had his back to them. The seconds it took for him to answer seemed like years.

"We're green, Major," was all Sharpe replied.

Gonzo pressed the talk button on his walkie-talkie

and spread the word: "All units, all units. The Home light is green. Repeat, Home light green."

* * *

Smoke rose in the east. Emir grabbed binoculars from his desk. Through the enhanced optics he focused on the large gray pillar. He could see at its base a building was burning. Which building it was he could not determine. Sultan's orders were clear, and while a building on fire was not entirely out of the ordinary in a four hundred year-old city, the mere sight of it made him nervous.

He scurried around the observation area moving from the eastern view to the northern view. Raising the binoculars to his eyes again he scanned the horizon as best he could. A sudden flash caused him to flinch. A faint rumble like thunder was audible. That two buildings were now ablaze was certainly out of the ordinary. The echoes of repeated gunfire were increasing.

The western view made matters worse as buildings burned there as well; the southern view provided more of the same. Emir knew that it was time for him to call his brother. He ran inside to his desk and made the call. Within moments, Sultan appeared on his computer screen.

"What is it, my brother?" Sultan asked.

Emir struggled to catch his breath. "There are . . . there are s-s-s-several b-b-b-buildings on f-f-f-ire," he said; his stutter was worsening from his excitement. "And I th-th-th-think I am h-h-h-hearing g-g-g-gunfire." As he reported to Sultan, he could hear voices calling his radio speaking Arabic in a panic.

"Gunfire?" Sultan retorted. "I've heard enough. I want you to activate the warhead. Our Man says that the nuclear material will not detonate unless you have entered the code. He also says it takes about fifteen minutes for the device to warm up, and then you can enter the code."

"G-g-g-give me the c-c-c-code," Emir demanded. Between the conversation with his brother and the radio voices, Emir did not hear the ping of the elevator that arrived at the floor.

Five men stepped off the elevator into the foyer. To their left, they could see the windowed walls of the observatory. They could hear Emir screaming, "The c-c-c-code! I n-n-n-need it n-n-n-now!"

They peered around the corner of the foyer and saw Emir working away at his computer. Retreating into the foyer, they removed their robes and *kefiyahs* revealing their weapons. Max nodded to Bam Bam, who promptly knelt and aimed his automatic rifle around the corner of the foyer wall at Emir. Bam Bam pulled the trigger and Emir's desk was quickly sprayed with bullets. They missed their intended target, but sparks flew as they destroyed the computer equipment on Emir's desk.

Emir dove for cover. As he hid, Max, with his sword drawn, and his team, also brandishing their guns, slowly approached the desk where he was last seen. Shots were fired at Max, but missed. "Look out!" the Aryan warned as he tackled Max to the ground. Boots, Bam Bam and the Peach all opened fire in the direction of the desk, but gunshots from their enemy continued. It became clear that they lost track of him, and that they were now the ones standing in the midst of open ground.

As the exchange of gunfire persisted with only short breaks for the men to reload, Max pushed the Aryan off of him. The two remained prone on the floor; Max quickly noticed blood on his shirt. He did not feel pain anywhere. *Must be a flesh wound,* he thought to himself. Then he saw the puddle of blood growing underneath the Aryan's body. His eyes were open, and his chest continued to expand and contract; he was still alive.

Max grabbed the Aryan by the collar of his shirt and pulled him into the hallway of the elevator bank. He was careful not to stand entirely so that he kept himself a small target for the barrage of errant bullets that were whizzing by them.

Suddenly, the gunfire ceased from the enemy; Boots approached the desk to look for Emir's corpse. "He's not here," Max heard Boots yell.

"Come out you little fuck!" the Peach taunted. "You're dead one way or another!"

Max returned his attention to the Aryan. "Where are you hit?" he asked.

"Mr. President," the Aryan weakly replied, "it has been an honor to serve you."

"Don't talk like that," Max ordered. "You're not going to die."

The Aryan pulled down the neck of his shirt to expose two bullet holes in his chest to Max. "My time is now," he said as he coughed blood onto the floor. "Bobby wanted you to kill me because he thought I would hurt you, but you let me live. I hope I made you proud, Mr. President." He coughed more blood, and Max saw the life disappear from his eyes.

Max hung his head momentarily out of respect for the Aryan, his fallen comrade. He placed his hand over the corpse's eyes and closed its eyelids. "Indeed you did, Timothy Hicks," he said aloud while composing himself. Unlike Valerie's death, which in actuality did not affect him, or Dalton's death, which saddened him, the Aryan's death enraged him. Max took a deep breath and stood, sword in hand. He marched into the foyer. "Show yourself Emir, you coward!" he demanded.

There was no response. Boots, Bam Bam and the Peach were investigating the scene. "Nothing here," Bam Bam said from Emir's desk.

"Same here," Boots said from the observatory platform just behind it.

"Behind you!" the Peach warned Max. He wanted to shoot, but he could not get a good shot off with Max in the way.

Max heeded the warning and was able to raise his sword to thwart Emir's attempt to strike him with a metal rod. They traded attempts to strike at one another, and when it became clear that this fight was now just between the two of them, they stepped back from each other and each took a defensive posture.

"Your reign is over, Emir," Max informed his foe. "Surrender now, and I will spare your life."

"I d-d-don't know who you are, or who you th-th-think you are," Emir countered, "but it is not my r-r-r-reign you should be w-w-w-worried about. In a few moments, we will all be d-d-d-dead. And then my brother, the great and mighty Sultan, will p-p-p-punish your countrymen. Infidels! Your insolence will not be t-t-t-tolerated! Your allies will learn to f-f-f-fear him, too!"

"Don't be so quick to think that your presence here is permanent," Max answered as he wielded his sword toward Emir. Again they traded several strikes, each blocking the other's attempts; sparks accompanied the clangs of the metal as they battled.

"Do you really th-th-th-think you can stop us?" Emir taunted. "Your p-p-p-president was b-b-b-blind, and Our Man was able to outsmart him. N-N-N-Now you have no l-l-l-leader to stop us," he said. He pulled a knife from a sheath hidden behind his back, and attacked Max with both it and the metal rod. Max was able to repel the strikes from the rod, but Emir landed one strike across Max's lower left bicep that caused his left arm to go limp.

Max cringed with pain. He spun counter-clockwise

to avoid Emir's next attempt, and with a downward strike using his good arm, his sword severed Emir's left leg just below the knee. The Arab fell to the ground and unleashed a deafening scream. As Emir floundered on the floor of the observatory foyer Max ambled next to him. "I am the leader. And as I told you before, your reign is over!" he declared as he raised his sword with his good arm.

"Do it!" Boots encouraged even though encouragement was not needed. Max decapitated Sultan's brother with a single blow.

Max grabbed a knapsack, rattled with bullet holes, from Emir's desk and dumped its contents on the floor; there was nothing of value in it until Max picked up Emir's head and stuffed it into the bag.

"What's that for?" Bam Bam asked. "A keepsake?"

"No, we'll need proof that he's dead," Max answered.

"Uh, guys," the Peach interrupted, "I think you better come look at this." They walked over to where he was standing and saw exactly where it was that Emir had disappeared to prior to attacking Max: The timer on the bomb casing was running backwards with just over two minutes to spare.

"Oh, shit!" Boots yelled. "Did he start the nuke?" he asked as he pointed to the nuclear hazard sticker on the side panel of the devise.

"I don't think so," Bam Bam said as he pointed to a digital panel screen just above a keypad below the sticker. "It's blinking as if it's waiting for someone to enter the code."

"Well, we're not gonna wait here to find out," Max told them. "This way!" he ordered as they ran toward the door below a sign marked, "STAIRS." There were eighty-four flights for them to run down. Encumbered only by their respective weapons, and Max by the knapsack with Emir's head, as well, they were able to run down to the sixty-something-eth floor before they heard the explosion and felt the heat and vibration from the blast.

* * *

The battles raged in the streets of Manhattan. The American boys fought with purpose. They followed the protocols that the veterans taught them. No man was left behind, and their advances on Emir's men's positions were furious.

They attacked the power plants; their destruction shut down all electrical systems on the island. Their attacks on the bridges and tunnels caught Emir's men by surprise, for their defense was prepared for an attack from the outer boroughs, not from within Manhattan itself. Most of Emir's men were killed in the onslaught. Those who survived were quick to surrender; although, a few managed to escape southward by boat. Word of each victory spread quickly among the troops through their walkie-talkies. Finally, once it was announced that Home was declaring victory, the American gunfire transformed to a signal of celebration.

The celebrations in Midtown ceased when the Empire State Building erupted. The Americans, awed, watched the twenty-story radio spire collapse at its base and slam into the staggered façade of the landmark on its way to the ground.

The vibration from the crashing spire could be felt throughout the city; it was reminiscent of the collapse of the Twin Towers. In the grand hall of Grand Central Station, Gonzo was puzzled. "What the fuck was that?" was all he could ask.

"I don't know," Sharpe replied. "I just hope the President is alright."

The Battle of the Bridges

CHAPTER 19

The constant beeping of the monitors in the hospital room roused Max from his slumber. The fluorescent lighting made it a struggle for him to open his eyes. When he finally was able to focus he quickly noted his surroundings. He was lying in a bed with an intravenous line inserted into his right arm; his left arm was in a sling, and now that he thought about it, his lower bicep was radiating great pain. A clear tube hung over his ears and pumped oxygen directly into his nose. He lifted his right hand toward his forehead and felt the damp gauze that was covering some sort of wound that caused a searing jolt of pain to run through his system when he furrowed his brow. His throat was parched, and his speech was slow to come to him. He remembered the intense heat; he remembered the loud explosion; but what he could not recall was how he arrived at his current location in this condition.

A woman walked into the room wearing maroon scrubs. She was a large black woman with a heavy Jamaican accent. "Well, look here who decided to join us," she said. "Everyone's gonna be glad to see you awake." She handed Max a cup of water and some pills. "Take this," she said.

Max did as instructed, and with his throat properly lubricated, he asked, "Where am I?"

"You're at Tisch," she replied, referring to New York University's hospital. Max was impressed; it was one of the best medical facilities in the country, and conveniently located on the corner of Thirty-fourth Street and First Avenue, only several blocks from the Empire State

Building.

"How did I get here?"

"Your chubby friend carried you in. The one with a big mouth and that ugly-ass patchwork beard." The nurse began to check Max's vital signs and write them on his medical chart.

"Oh, you mean the Peach," he said.

"I don't care what you be calling him, but he's a huge pain in my big black ass, that's for sure. Kept on complainin' about a broken wrist when you is lying here with a broken head and limp arm."

"Yeah, that's the Peach alright. Was he alone?" Max asked wondering if she knew he was the President.

"No, he came in with two other fellas. They were also complaining about some pain, but those two were real men. One has a broken leg and the other a separated shoulder, but they were more worried about you than themselves."

"Please tell them that I'm glad to hear that they are alright," Max pleaded as she finished writing on his chart and replaced it on the hook on the foot of the bed.

"You'll be able to tell 'em yourself," she said. "Your wife is here with your son. They can't wait to see you." Max knew she meant Roxy and Zach. "And that general has been asking me about your condition every half hour since you been here. Another pain in my big black ass."

"Don't worry, I'll give him someone else to bother for you Miss . . ."

"Carter," she completed his sentence. "Tasha Carter."

"Well Miss Carter, I don't think I can thank you enough for all of your kind care and attention."

"Get better and get out of my hospital, Mr. President," she said with a smile. Max was comforted that she knew who he was; more importantly, this woman who he never met could not have been happier to see him awake. She left the door open as she left the room. She winked at Max from the hallway. "Doctor Patel," she called down the hallway. "He's awake and alert."

There was a great ruckus in the hallway. Roxy burst into the room with Zach in tow. "Oh, thank God you're okay, Max!" she exclaimed as she gave him a large hug.

"Ow!" Max yelled as she caught his left arm with her hug. "Careful, honey. I feel like I just fought a war."

"You look like it, too," she joked. "I'm just so glad to see you." She kissed him gently on the lips; careful of Max's condition, she did not want to hurt him further.

"Love you, too, honey," Max told her. He looked at his right side and saw Zach examining the intravenous tube in his arm. Max rubbed Zach's head messing up his hair in the process. "Did you miss me, little man?"

Zach nodded affirmatively. "What happened to you?" was all he asked.

"I got into a couple of fights," Max explained.

"I wanna be just like you when I grow up," Zach told him.

"Zach!" Roxy scolded. "Fighting is a bad thing!"

"You know, Rox, I'm gonna be a little busier now. It might not be a bad idea for him to spend some time around me," Max offered. "A boy his age needs a good male influence."

Frowning, Roxy asked, "Do I get to spend more time around you?" Max did not answer right away. "I told you that Zach and I are a packaged deal."

"A former teacher would make a good Secretary of Education," Max thought aloud.

"I was thinking more along the lines of First Lady,"

she insisted.

"I don't know. What do you think, Jack?" Max asked Armstrong who was standing in the doorway.

"Sounds good to me," Armstrong said. He walked over to Max's bedside and gave Max a pat on his right shoulder. "Glad to see you're still in one piece, buddy."

"Glad to see you, too Jack," Max told him. "You ready for the hard part? You know, we have to govern this place now."

"I've been waiting my whole life to say this," Armstrong began. "I serve at the pleasure of the President."

"Good," Max said. "We'll start tomorrow. I need a good night's sleep."

"Great," Armstrong affirmed, "but don't pass out on us just yet. There's a whole bunch of people here to see you right now."

"Oh, yeah? Who else is here?" Max wondered.

"C'mon in everyone," Armstrong hollered toward the hall. The anxious crowd rushed in, each offering congratulatory sentiments to Max:

Judge Vineri led the group. "Fine job, Mr. President! I told you that sword would change you forever."

Don Vito followed closely. "My boys tell me you're pretty good in a fight. When this is over, you should come work for me. I pay better," he said.

Takinawa ensued. "Looks like my lessons paid off. I heard you took on Hades' three henchmen at once. By the end of all this, I may be calling you, 'Master!'" he joked.

Boots, Bam Bam and the Peach were the next ones to enter. Boots' right arm was in a sling; Bam Bam hobbled in on crutches with a cast on his left leg that came up to his knee; and the Peach had a cast on his wrist.

"I owe the three of you my life," Max told his compatriots with a tear in his eye. They looked at each other, humbled.

With his chest puffed out, Boots said, "No, we owe ours to you. You led us into the thick of the battle. You saved our lives by takin' on Hades' guys. And you got us out of there before the bomb went off. It was an honor for us just to be there with you today. Saving your life was a privilege."

"Just knowin' that someday I'm gonna be able to tell my grandkids that I fought at Max Noble's side," Bam Bam said as he choked up, "I couldn't be prouder."

"Fuck that!" the Peach said. "I carried your sorry ass down fifty flights of fuckin' stairs that were on fire! And all I get to show for it is a fuckin' cast on my wrist? Where's the pride in that?"

"Oh, shut up, Peach!" Bam Bam said. He would have hit him if he was more confident in his ability to stand on his crutches. "It's not always about you! We all went down those same stairs, me with a busted leg and Boots with his shoulder outta whack!"

"No," Max said, "today it is about you, Peach. And you, Boots. And, of course, you, Bam Bam. It's about all of us, together. We made it out of there alive because we looked out for each other." He paused and looked around the room. "I'm lucky to have you guys as my friends. But we lost the Aryan today, too. So, let's take a moment to remember Timmy Hicks. When I met him, he was considered an enemy. But he quickly showed that he was nothing more than a confused young man. In the end, he saved my life. We were lucky to have him as our friend, too."

The room was silent for a moment. Max looked around the room as they all bowed their heads. Suddenly, he disrupted the serenity, "What happened to the knapsack?"

"We, uh, . . .," Boots began, trying to think of how to explain its whereabouts without revealing its contents to the rest of the people in the room.

"My boys got it down in the morgue for ya," Don Vito announced, apparently already aware that it held a human head. "They put it in a cooler and stuck it in the fridge so it wouldn't spoil."

"What was in there, Max?" Armstrong asked.

"Just some perishables," the Don answered before Max had the chance. It was clear that Don Vito had mastered the art of providing elusive answers to mask his actions; many a federal agent lost sleep pouring over transcripts of wire taps where Don Vito said just enough to give an order to one of his Capos without giving the FBI any conclusive or useable evidence.

"Just perishables," Max confirmed.

An Indian doctor burst into the room in blue scrubs and a white lab coat. "There are too many people in this room for me to concentrate." He walked to the foot of Max's bed and picked up Max's chart. After quickly perusing Nurse Carter's notes, he said, "Well, Mr. President, you're going to be just fine. Your CT scan was negative, and that bump on your head will heal in no time. Your arm is a different story. The tendon at the base of your left bicep was severed. That's why you can't curl your arm. We can repair it surgically, but I would imagine that you will be in no condition to take part in any sort of physical activity for six to eight weeks after the operation. You can expect another six to eight weeks of rehab after that."

"Don't worry, Mr. President," Boots assured, "we're on the shelf, too."

"When can I get out of here?" Max asked Doctor Patel.

"I want to keep you overnight for observation," the doctor explained. "We'll discharge you first thing in the morning, and schedule an appointment for your surgery in about two weeks."

"Sounds good," Max said.

"What's so good about me losing my best soldier for four months?" a voice boomed. It was Sharpe, who could not contain his smile. It was the first complement he ever gave Max, and the respect was well-received.

"We did alright, huh, General?" Max asked.

"Sir," Sharpe replied, "in all of my years of military service, I have never seen such an ass-whoopin' as we saw today. We estimate that we were facing one hundred thousand enemy troops today, most of who surrendered when their commander, Emir, failed to respond to their calls on the radio. We've confirmed about three thousand dead, mostly from the initial blasts in our strikes, and the rest retreated to the ocean and were last seen on Coast Guard ships heading south. We presume they fled to either Philadelphia or Washington to await Sultan's orders."

"And what of our men, General?" Max asked. He knew that as Commander in Chief, he would have to accept losses, as well.

Sharpe's voice became grave. "We lost four hundred and thirty-seven, with another five hundred or so wounded. Only several of the wounded are critical, sir."

"They will not have died in vain," Max sadly decreed. "What's our next step, General?"

"Well," Sharpe began, "Lieutenant Youseff is overseeing the imprisonment and interrogation of Sultan's troops. Major Gonzalez is fortifying our defensive positions. Colonel Chatham has been in contact with the head of SBN. He believes we will be able to restore full communications to the country by the morning. He also thinks he can use the SBN server to upload a virus in the Pentagon's server to disable the Defense Department's network. This will give us the intelligence advantage, but it may take a day or so for him to upload the virus."

"I didn't realize that Chatty was that computer savvy," Max said, astonished.

"He's been my communications officer for eight years, sir," Sharpe confirmed. "He doesn't talk much to people, but he knows how to talk to computers."

"Great," Max said. "Is that all?"

"For now, Sir," Sharpe acknowledged.

"Well, it's been great to see all of you," Max said, "but if you don't mind, I would like to get some sleep."

"Absolutely, Mr. President," Sharpe said on their behalf.

"Jack," Max called as the guests began to leave, "could you, Roxy and Judge Vineri wait here for a moment."

"Certainly," Armstrong said.

"I'm in no rush, Mr. President," the judge answered.

Doctor Patel, being the last of the non-requested visitors and recognizing the inference that Max wanted privacy, closed the door behind him.

"What is it, Max?" Roxy asked.

"Judge Vineri, will you marry Roxy and me right now?" Max asked. "Jack is our witness." Max saw Zach was elated by the thought. "And Zach, too."

"Technically, you need a license issued by the state to do that," the judge replied.

"And technically, you have to be thirty-five to be the president, but we seemed to have been able to bend that rule a little," Max retorted.

"Touché, Mr. President," the Judge conceded. It was neither the intimate ceremony nor the extravagant reception she dreamed of, but Roxy could not have been happier about marrying Max at his bedside in the hospital.

* * *

A great scream emanated from Sultan's office. It was followed by the thunderous crash of the desk he flipped over. Although his top aides, who were meeting with him behind closed doors, spoke Arabic, the conversation was carried out in English; it was a relief to Harmon, who stationed himself outside of the door to eavesdrop in hopes of getting a glimpse into Sultan's state of mind.

"What do you mean we have lost communication with New York?" Sultan interrogated.

"We have been unable to receive any signal with any of our people in New York," one of the aides replied.

"Where is my brother?" Sultan wanted to know.

"We cannot say," an aide answered. "We have reports from Philadelphia that some of our troops fled to the city after an attack, but we have not yet spoken with any of them. It may be a decoy."

"Emir said that there was gunfire," Sultan recalled. "It must be true. Get Our Man in here immediately. If we have, indeed, lost New York, we need to rework our strategy. We cannot afford to lose our other cities. It is time to institute more control. Arrest every man between the ages of eighteen and fifty! We cannot risk further insurrection. And, Allah, please do not allow me to be merciful if they have harmed my brother!"

"Sultan," the aide asked, "if we have lost New York, why not just blow it up with a nuclear bomb? That would take care of our enemies there."

Sultan abruptly slapped his aide across the face. "Idiot! Do you really think that it is that simple? I don't think that our brothers back in the Middle East would appreciate us if we had to call them to explain that their money disappeared because their banks are headquartered in New York. Or that their diplomats – who, in some cases, are the princes and family members of the emirates – were suddenly wiped out because we could not maintain our positions in New York." The aides began to cower in fear of their leader.

"Forgive me, Sultan," the denigrated aide begged.

"Bring me the cowards who fled to Philadelphia so that I may punish their cowardice," Sultan said. "And then, I will decide whether to forgive you or punish your idiocy, as well."

* * *

Max was in no condition to consummate his marriage; however, that did not prevent him from spending time with Roxy. He told her all about his adventures during the previous twenty-four hours. She cringed in horror when he explained how Typhon burned to death in front of him, and became nauseous when he described how he decapitated Medusa. For that reason, he did not tell her that he decapitated Emir, too. She became teary-eyed when he told her how the Aryan gave his life to protect him, and she cried on his chest when he told her that the most important part of his day was when she said, "I do."

Roxy decided that it was getting late, and told Max that she was taking Zach back home for the night. He understood, and they agreed to talk in the morning once Chatty had reestablished the communications links. He asked her to send Armstrong and Judge Vineri in to see him before she left.

"You wanted to speak to us?" Armstrong asked.

"Yeah," Max said. "You two are my wisest advisors. Sharpe is a military man, but it doesn't look like I am going to be fighting again anytime soon," he said pointing to his left arm. "That means that my focus must shift to the politics of the situation."

"Ah," Armstrong sighed, "now you're talking about my area of expertise."

"Exactly, Jack," Max agreed. "That's why I need you to be my Chief of Staff. Tomorrow, I want you to contact as many governors as you can and tell them what happened here today. Assure them that we will liberate them from Sultan's regime. There can be no dissention among them, Jack. We need them all on our side."

"I'm impressed, Mr. President," the judge said.

"Jack made me read all those books about political philosophy," Max explained. "Now it's time to use that knowledge."

"Well done, sir," Armstrong said. "I'm glad you listened to me and actually read the books. I thought for sure that you were caught up in Bobby's philosophy."

"Ha!" Max laughed. "Bobby didn't have a political philosophy! He was a punch-first-and-ask-questions-later type. His idea of philosophy was the chicken versus the egg."

"True," Armstrong agreed. "Will that be all, sir?"

"I think so," Max said. "Now, go figure out what you're gonna say to the governors."

"Yes, sir," Armstrong obeyed. He left Judge Vineri in the room with Max.

"With all due respect, sir," the judge began, "I am not sure how helpful I can be in the political arena. Even though I'm a Catholic, I'm not really a popular figure in the red states."

"I know that, Your Honor. That's why I don't want you to have anything to do with the American body politic."

"I don't think I follow, Mr. President."

"You're highly educated, rational, and most

importantly, diplomatic. That makes you a perfect candidate for Secretary of State."

"Secretary of State, huh? Interesting."

"Very interesting, I think," Max explained. "We need to reestablish ties with the leaders of the free world. For the first time in a long time, we need their help. We need military and economic support. I need you to get it for us. Can it be done?"

"Well, I would think that the Europeans would be willing to help," the judge surmised. "I'm not too sure about the Russians and the Chinese. But I'll do what I can."

"That's all I can ask, Your Honor."

"It will be my pleasure, Mr. President. Will that be all?"

"Actually, no. There is one more thing. I have to be honest with you, Your Honor."

"About what, Mr. President?"

"I killed four people today and, by the end, felt no remorse. It's the same empty feeling I had when my father died from a heart attack in front of my eyes."

"It's natural for adrenaline to kick in during stressful situations."

"This was more than adrenaline. My dad's life never meant much to me because he was such a son of a bitch. He ruined the Noble name, and I've spent my entire lifetime trying to restore it. His death was a relief. But I didn't know these people today. They were my enemies, and I guess you could say that it was self-defense in each instance, but their lives were meaningless to me. I don't like feeling this . . . this soulless."

"Mr. President, with all due respect, why are you telling me this?"

"I trust your advice, Your Honor. You're a religious man, and you know about matters of the soul. I don't feel like myself anymore. I used to care about people. Life was precious to me. Now, life itself means very little to me. It's eating away at me. How do I get back to being the person I was?"

There was a brief pause while the judge scratched his head. "Religion doesn't offer answers, Mr. President. It can only act as a guide. According to the Bible, murder is a sin. However, in our legal system, we look to a person's mental state to determine if the act of killing someone rose to a level of murder. We use a 'depraved indifference' standard to make that judgment. If you show no mercy, if you fail to value human life when yours is not at risk, then I would say you are nothing more than a soulless murderer. However, you spared the life of the Hicks boy. That show of mercy should be seen as an act of adding to your soul. Take great value from that. As long as you continue to show mercy, you will retain what soul you have left."

"But beware," the judge continued. "If you fail to show mercy, it would surely cause you greater suffering than you feel right now and it would almost certainly take whatever soul you have left into the deepest depths of hell."

"I'm Jewish," Max pointed out. "We don't believe in hell."

"Hmmm," the judge pondered how to communicate his point. When it came to him, he said, "General William Tecumseh Sherman marched the Union army to the sea during the Civil War. He destroyed everything in his path, including the entire city of Atlanta. His most famous quote was, 'War is hell.' Now, I never served in the military, and I don't know what it's like to fight in a war, but I would imagine that war *is* hell.

"So," the judge continued, "if war is hell then peace

must be heaven. Regardless of your religious beliefs in heaven and hell, you're sort of in a personal purgatory right now, Mr. President. Your position requires that you fight this war, which is pulling your soul toward hell. At the same time, you are longing for peace, which is the pull you feel in the opposite direction." The judge gestured with his hands to accentuate the pulling effect. "Unfortunately, this is the product of the choices you have made, or were forced to make."

Max shook his head and sighed. "It's not fair."

"No one ever said that life was fair, Mr. President. Peace comes to all of us in time, and often we have no control over when or where it will come. If you began your descent into hell when your father died, it would follow that your ascent to heaven must somehow be related to your father or your family."

"My family? I don't follow. Roxy?"

"Time, Mr. President. Give it time and you will understand."

CHAPTER 20

The blood that dripped into the sink basin swirled amorphously in the soapy water. Despite having trimmed his beard with a scissor, Max could not help but nick his face as he shaved the remaining hair. The razor blade pulled at the facial hair with each stroke causing a painful sensation. He did not care. Finally, after months of hiding, Max was prepared to reveal his true identity to the world. It did not matter that Sultan still controlled most of the country; Max had his fiefdom and that he stole it from Sultan's own brother bolstered his confidence. Momentum was changing, and Max knew it.

He emerged, clean shaven, from his hospital room to cheers from the hospital employees. He waved with his right arm; his left arm remained in a sling. He proceeded down the hall to the elevator, which he took down to the first floor administration area so that he could formally receive his hospital discharge. The people on the first floor applauded him, as well. Boots, Bam Bam and the Peach, who were all formally discharged the night before, waited for Max in the waiting room. Max saw them as he made his way to the administration desk, and he rubbed his shaved chin while smiling at his three bearded bodyguards. "Finally, I can get rid of this ridiculous fuckin' thing," the Peach said referring to his patchwork facial hair.

After signing several releases and consents, Max left the hospital with the three remaining members of his entourage. They got into a parked sedan in front of the hospital. Boots was relegated to the back seat as his separated shoulder made it impossible for him to turn a steering wheel. Bam Bam joined him in the back seat; he could not drive with his foot in a cast. The Peach, with a cast on his wrist, struggled to place the cooler from the morgue in the trunk of the car; being the most able of the foursome, he became the new chauffeur.

As the car left the hospital, Max asked the first thing that came to his mind, "Where to now?"

"The SBN Centre," Boots said referring to the monstrous office, hotel and condominium building that doubled as SBN's international headquarters. It was the center of communication for the largest satellite television network in the world. "Sharpe's set up shop there for you."

"What kind of shop?" Max wondered.

"You know," Bam Bam said, "he got you an office so now you can be presidential and all that good shit."

"A place to bang your interns," the Peach added.

"You're a fuckin' moron," Bam Bam chastised. "If you weren't drivin' I'd smack ya right now!"

"Well, I am drivin' ya fuckin' gimp!" the Peach retorted. His remark drew Bam Bam's ire, who reacted by smacking the Peach on the back of the head. "Oh, that's it! You're fuckin' dead!" the Peach announced. He let go of the steering wheel and turned to try and smack Bam Bam with his cast.

"Hey!" Max scolded as he grabbed the steering wheel with his good hand to hold the car steady. "Keep your hands on the wheel, you idiot! We didn't just survive a battle to die in a car accident because you can't behave like a human being!"

"Right," a dejected Peach acknowledged as he returned to his driving position. "Sorry about that. But he hit me first!"

"How old are you?" Boots asked. "Four?"

"Very funny," Peach said.

"Some things never change," Max commented. An awkward silence followed, and the four men looked at each other and could not help but burst out in laughter at the truth of the statement when they considered the silliness of what had just happened among them. "That's good. It's healthy," Max said.

The car pulled into the valet driveway at the SBN Centre. A throng of photographers and reporters stood practically beating each other to get the first pictures and quotes from Max Noble, the leader of the revolution that restored a free press to the United States. Boots and Bam Bam got out of the car while the Peach drove into the parking garage. Their injuries did not prevent them from escorting Max into the building. "Congressman Noble! Congressman Noble! Over here!" the reporters cried. Max waved and smiled and walked into the building through the entrance where Sharpe, Armstrong and Judge Vineri were waiting.

"Why are they calling me 'Congressman,' Jack?" Max asked as he shook Armstrong's hand.

"We haven't been able to issue a press release yet," Armstrong told him. "Don't worry about it. We'll fill you in on everything when we get upstairs." Max saluted Sharpe and greeted the Judge. The three proceeded to the elevator bank and took the first car up to the seventh floor.

After the door closed, Armstrong said, "Roxy and Zach are already up in the Penthouse apartment waiting for you."

Max was impressed. "The Penthouse, huh?"

"They've been there since the general called and said that we secured the city. You'll be living there until this whole thing is over. Your bodyguards are heading up there to make sure everything is in order."

The elevator came to a halt on the seventh floor and

there was a dim "ping" as the door opened. "Welcome to your West Wing, Mr. President," Sharpe announced as they stepped off the elevator. "We've made arrangements with the owner of SBN so that you will have full and complete access to all of its worldwide communications and technologies. In return, SBN wanted the exclusive press rights to you."

"Press rights?" Max asked. "I didn't know there was such a thing."

"We've agreed that you will grant exclusive access to SBN for interviews," Armstrong explained.

"What about the press downstairs?" Max wondered.

"They can get you to answer questions on your way in and out of the building, but the sit-down, one-on-one stuff is exclusive to SBN," Armstrong clarified.

"I see," Max said.

"Good," Sharpe said. "This way, then." He led them into the large conference room where Hank, Gonzo and Chatty sat at the long table. There was also a short balding man with thick glasses, a tall thin woman with blonde hair and red-rimmed glasses, and a rather portly older gentleman who sat at the head of the table smoking a cigar. All those present stood and applauded Max's entrance.

"Thank you, thank you," Max said. "Please be seated. Who are these people?" he asked referring to the newcomers to his meetings.

"Thad Morris, the Third," the large gentleman said. Max knew of Morris; he was the controlling stockholder of the largest worldwide multimedia conglomerate, Communication Technology Solutions, which was the parent company of SBN. It was also the parent company of CTS Publications, publisher of most of *Intensity*'s competitors. "This is Susan Teller, my best reporter who will be covering your every move, and this is your new speechwriter, David Bard."

"Hello," Susan said as she smiled and waved.

"Hi," Bard said softly.

"Hello," Max answered. "Nice to meet all of you."

"Well, Noble, I don't know that I will say the same just yet," Morris continued. "I have yet to meet a Noble that I like. I hated your father with a passion. He was such a prick. Certainly, he ruined your family name. My magazine sales finally picked up after he died, and then you came along and scooped up my profits."

"Then why help me now?" Max asked.

"Because I haven't been able to sell a single magazine in six months! There's plenty of money to be made now that I can publish and broadcast again. And since you're such a celebrity now, you can consider exclusivity as payback for years of lost profits."

"I don't have a problem with the exclusivity arrangement, Morris," Max began, "but why the speechwriter?"

"To make sure you say the right things, my dear boy."

"Morris, let me make something perfectly clear," Max said sternly. "Don't ever refer to me as 'boy,' again. You will address me as 'Mr. President,' or 'Sir.' Is that clear?"

"You're kidding, right?"

"Chatty," Max said.

Chatty stood and walked over to Morris. He bent down and stared him in the eye, their faces not more than a quarter of an inch from each other. "I would listen to him if I were you," Chatty suggested as Morris began to perspire. It became clear that Morris could only talk a good game.

"Is that clear, Morris?" Max asked again.

"Crystal," Morris answered as he cowered away from Chatty in his chair.

"Crystal, what?" Chatty asked in a deep baritone.

"Crystal, sir! Crystal, sir!" Morris excitedly declared.

"That's more like it," Max said. "Now, Morris, I hope you, Ms. Teller and Mr. Bard will understand that I have work to do that does not involve them."

"The press needs access to the President in order to report accurately," Susan said, insulted that she was being asked to leave.

"And you'll get it, Ms. Teller," Armstrong answered on behalf of Max; he was taking to his role as Chief of Staff like a fish in water. "But for now, cabinet meetings are off limits to the press. I will brief you afterwards so that you can - what was the phrase? - 'report accurately.'"

Susan closed her notebook and left in a huff. Bard quietly followed. Morris paused to protest before leaving, "You could be a little nicer to my people, Jack."

"I could be, Thad," Armstrong retorted. "But I won't be when we have business to attend to." Morris nodded and closed the door behind him.

"Well, now that we've straightened that out," Max said, "how about some reports. Let's start with you, Secretary Vineri." The title did not sound right to Max; he would always be the Judge in Max's eyes.

"Very well, Mr. President," the Judge began. "To be blunt, the world is a mess. Iran has tried to make a power play in the Middle East. Israel is taking a beating, but the Germans and the Russians have come to her aid."

"The Germans and the Russians?" Max asked astonished.

"Yes," the Judge confirmed. "The Germans feel compelled to support Israel as penance for the Nazis' crimes, and the Russians were brought in by their expatriates who immigrated to Israel. There's a question as to how much the Russian mob is involved. Most believe that they've told President Kharanov that they'll have him killed if he doesn't support their comrades in the Holy Land. Of course, when the war is over, Israel will have a domestic organized crime problem. But for now, she'll take whatever help she can get.

"At any rate," he continued, "the British and the French have sent troops to Iraq, Egypt, Lebanon and Jordan to bolster and support their militaries so that the Iranians don't get any funny ideas about exerting their influence elsewhere. Fortunately, the strategy has been working, and the Palestinians and the Syrians are waiting to see what happens to the Iranians before joining the fray. They don't want to end up on the wrong side of a war with Israel, like they did in 1967 and 1973, especially since the Europeans have already chosen Israel's side. Although, suicide bombings inside Israel are almost a daily occurrence, and the Iranian-backed Hezbollah and Hamas are the usual suspects.

"In addition to the Middle East, the British and the Australians are also helping the Pakistanis and the Indians battle extremists along the Afghan-Pakistani border."

"The Indians are supporting the Pakistanis?" Max asked, again astonished.

"That's correct, sir," the Judge answered. "The way the Indians see it, if the Pakistanis lose control to the extremists, India faces an unpredictable nuclear threat. Common enemies often bring rivals together. The two nations have agreed to put aside their differences over Kashmir until the war is over.

"The Chinese are not engaging anyone, but have at least kept the North Koreans in check. Bottom line, Mr. President, is that Asia is an absolute mess. Africa is not much better, as several of the African governments are defending against military coups."

"There are wars on three continents, that involve nations from five of them," Max commented.

"Actually," the Judge added, "there is a war raging in South America, as well. The Venezuelans are attempting to spread their socialist message to its neighbors, and the Colombians have taken exception. The drug kingpins are protecting their own respective territories; basically, South America has been turned into a free-for-all. So, at the moment, the entire world is at war."

"World War Three, huh?" Gonzo asked.

"It seems that way, Major," the Judge responded.

An eerie silence fell until Max broke it. "Where does all of this leave us, Mr. Secretary?" he asked.

"The British have offered two thousand troops to help defend territory under purely American control. The Canadians have also offered supplies for the military effort. They are waiting for a formal invitation from the new American president."

"Two thousand. That's it?" Sharpe asked.

"I'm afraid so, General," the Judge answered. "Her majesty's army is stretched mighty thin at the moment."

"What about the French?" Armstrong asked.

"The French haven't been able to protect their *own* interests since Napoleon," Sharpe critiqued. "They would be useless even if they came to our aid. At least the Canadians are offering supplies."

"Well, then, General," Max interrupted, "what's your plan?"

"In one word, sir," Sharpe said, "Philadelphia."

"What about Philadelphia, General?" Armstrong asked.

"The enemy has shown that it will not fight without orders from its leader," Sharpe explained. "Their leader is in

Washington, D.C. Therefore, we must get to Washington and kill the leader."

"So that would be 'checkmate,'" Max asked.

"That's correct, Mr. President," Sharpe confirmed. "But in order to get to Washington, we must first go through Philadelphia."

"How do we know that?" Armstrong asked.

"We have interrogated the prisoners of war, sir," Hank offered. "They told us that the men who fled our attack were going to Philadelphia to join their brethren there. They also confirmed that Sultan definitely got help from the inside. He has full trust in someone he refers to as, 'Our Man.' We were also able to extract from them the positions of the enemy's forces in Boston."

"Which brings us to our next problem," Gonzo interrupted. "We liberated close to seventy-five hundred police officers from Rikers, which is where we are now keeping our prisoners. They immediately enlisted, voluntarily. That brings our total force to almost twenty thousand. We will be significantly outnumbered in Philadelphia, and we do not have the means to transport that many men. It also means that there won't be any troops left to protect New York from an attack by the enemy's troops, except for the two thousand British soldiers. When we captured New York, we had the element of surprise and a method of transportation. We are simply not equipped for this battle."

Discouraged, Max asked, "Is there any good news?"

"Some, sir," Chatty said. "SBN has given me access to its satellite network. I am designing a computer virus to upload into the Pentagon's server. It will take out the DOD's network, instantly neutralizing the enemy's ability to monitor our actions through geothermal technology. It will also take out their communications entirely, and most importantly, it will eliminate the enemy's ability to launch our nuclear warheads."

"How long until the virus is ready to be uploaded, Colonel?" Sharpe asked.

"Anywhere between seventy-two and ninety-six hours, sir," Chatty answered.

"Okay, boys, here's the deal," Max decreed. "Later today, I will go on the air and announce my presidency to the world. I will invite all foreign aid in my speech. Otherwise, we don't make a move until that virus is uploaded. Any questions?"

The military men looked at each other and shook their heads negatively. "Good," Max said. "Now, turning our attention to domestic matters, Jack, what were you able to find out?"

"I spoke with thirty-eight of the fifty governors, and have left messages for the other twelve," Armstrong reported. "They are leery of your presidency, but they are all relieved that there is some sort of federal government to take the pressure off of them. Each governor agreed to send a representative so that we have an ad hoc council to vote on matters concerning the nation as a whole. They understand that such a council is for show only; they don't expect it to enact any actual legislation."

"They were all on board, really?" Max asked.

"Pretty much," Armstrong assured him. "Only Governor Thomas of Illinois resisted. At one point he used the word 'usurper' to describe you. But in the end, he went along with it."

"Why would he feel that way?" Max wondered. "What did I ever do to him?" Although he never met the governor, Max knew that Martin Thomas, an African-American hothead from Chicago who had mastered machine politics, was making preparations for a presidential run prior to the State of the Union speech.

"Well," Armstrong explained, "he was expected to be the frontrunner for the Democratic presidential nomination next year. You're sitting in his chair, so to speak."

"Do you see him as a threat to me?"

"He could undermine your authority," Armstrong answered. "I think we should keep him close to us."

"Terrific," Max lamented. "Now I have a political rival. How am I supposed to fight both Thomas and Sultan at the same time?"

"No one said that being president was easy," the Judge offered.

* * *

Morris and Bard hovered over the newscast's production team in the engineer's booth. Bard paced as he reread the speech he wrote for Max repeatedly; the president snatched it out of his hands without even looking at it. "Just stick to the script," Bard implored over and over hoping that his inaudible instruction would somehow reach the orator.

The newscast's director flipped a switch and said, "Cue intro," as the screen in the center of the console went from black to an American flag background. "Cue music," he said as a blasting overture began. The words, "Special Report," flashed across the screen. "Cue Suzie," he said.

Susan, wearing a blue pinstriped suit with an American flag lapel pin and her usual red-rimmed glasses, appeared on the screen standing in front of the rubble from the Empire State Building that remained on Thirty-fourth Street; fortunately, it was only the antenna, some nonstructural bricks and lots of glass. "Ladies and gentlemen of the United States of America," she began as her name appeared at the bottom of the screen. "This is a special report brought to you exclusively by SBN News. Two days ago, an American militia led by former Congressman Max Noble of Long Island, who was spared from his own death at President Cole's State of the Union speech in January because he was mourning the loss of his wife, has conquered Sultan's army in the City of New York, and is reestablishing a government for the United States of America. The battle was quick, as the attack clearly caught the city's occupying regime off guard. We are told that Mr. Noble, himself, was involved in the battle, and that he killed the enemy leader who was stationed at what was once the Empire State Building, which erupted in a massive explosion at the end of the battle. You can see the rubble of the building behind me here on Thirty-fourth Street, and while the majority of the structure still stands, we are told that the explosion destroyed most of the top floors and, for the moment, has rendered the building unsafe. City building inspectors will be working throughout the coming days to determine the extent of the damage suffered here and throughout the city.

"While several hundred American lives were lost in the battle," she continued, "enemy casualties are reported to be in the thousands. Celebratory gunfire filled the streets. Men are shaving their beards and women are insisting that they will return to work, as New York is once again free. Here now to describe the situation in his own words is Max Noble."

The screen froze on Susan for several seconds. "Cut to camera two," the director said in the booth. Max appeared presidential, wearing a solid navy blue suit with an American flag lapel pin, a light blue shirt and a red tie, and sitting at a desk in front of a bookcase flanked by two American flags; he was not wearing the sling on his left arm, which dangled lifelessly at his side, to minimize the impression that he might be weakened, but the bandage over his head wound remained. Bard became obviously nervous as he tightly hugged his draft of Max's speech; he mouthed the words as Max spoke them.

"Friends of liberty," Max started, "greetings. For several months it has seemed as if the torch of freedom was extinguished. While it is true that the flame dimmed, it did not die. It burned brightly in the hearts of our countrymen, who joined me in taking the first step in returning liberty to our nation.

"For those of you who do not know me, my name is Max Noble. Only three weeks into my service as a United States Congressman, my wife, Valerie Mintz, who many of you may remember from her career in the fashion industry, was taken from me in a botched assassination attempt. President Cole granted me permission to skip the State of the Union address, and so I was not present in Washington on that dark evening. This Sultan fellow either did not consider me a threat to his regime, or was unaware of my survival entirely. Whichever the case may be, my friends, the mission to restore the United States of America to its former glory has chosen me as its leader, and I will not fail. Therefore, it is with great pride that I announce that I have accepted the challenge that confronted me to serve as the Commander in Chief of this nation's armed forces. It is an honor for me to serve as the President of the United States, and I promise you that I shall serve until the earlier of the first election after our victory or my death.

"The strength of my resolve is evident by our sound victory in reclaiming the City of New York. We were outnumbered ten to one, and yet we conquered completely both above and below the streets. Our forces are led by a man of incredible military genius, General John Sharpe. It is only a matter of time before our liberating forces arrive in your city to combat the enemy. Until then, I ask only for your patience.

"In the meantime, I am asking that the governors of each state send a representative to New York to partake in an assembly that will reshape our nation. I would also like to extend a formal invitation to our allies abroad for any aid, military or otherwise, that they may be able to provide. I understand that most of the world is at war. But any contributions to the American cause that can be made will be paid back by future American generations tenfold.

"We will not stop fighting until we have achieved complete victory. I promise you, America, that the flags behind me will fly in your neighborhoods once again."

Bard continued to mimic Max's words in the control booth.

"May freedom reign supreme," Max said.

"That was beautiful!" Bard cried. "I didn't realize how much of a natural he is! Perfect! No coaching necessary! Absolutely perfect!"

"And one more thing," Max added.

"One more thing?" Bard questioned. "I didn't write anything else!"

Max reached underneath his desk with his right arm. "Know this, Sultan," he said. "Your fate will be the same as your brother's." He pulled Emir's head from the cooler, and placed the decomposing skull on the desk. A collective groan erupted in the booth as the grotesque image of the head appeared on the screen; the eyes had rolled back so that only their whites were visible, and streams of congealed blood decorated Emir's upper lip just under the nose.

"Cut back to Suzie!" the director demanded.

The image of Max and Emir's head was immediately replaced by that of Susan standing in front of the rubble. "There you have it, ladies and gentlemen. Max Noble, the President of the United States, in his own words. I am Susan Teller with SBN News."

"And . . . cut," the director ordered. The image on the screen faded to black.

"Beautiful," Morris said to the production crew. "Loop it so that it runs every fifteen minutes."

"Sir, I just want you to know that I did not write that last part," Bard whined. "My speech stopped with 'May freedom reign supreme.'"

"Don't worry about it, David," Morris said as he stuck a new cigar in his mouth. He could think only of the advertising revenue and the intellectual property value of the footage. "That clip is going to make us a fortune."

* * *

A commotion erupted on the floor of the Hub as the image of Max standing over Emir's head remained frozen on the center screen. Though he missed the live broadcast, Sultan viewed its third repetition on SBN only a short while after. His anger was so great that he pulled his pistol from its holster and shot two of his own men dead in order to release his aggression. "In my office, immediately, General!" he ordered Harmon.

The two retired to Sultan's office for nearly half an hour. The American soldiers tried to contain their sense of pride. Some of Sultan's men noticed their wry smiles and took exception. A fight broke out amongst them, and Rogers was quick to break it up and restore calm to the room before Harmon and Sultan returned.

Upon emerging from the meeting, Harmon handed Rogers a piece of paper with numbers and letters written in what appeared to be a random manner. "General, launch a nuclear warhead at these coordinates immediately," he said pointing to the top numbers and letters. "The code is right here," he indicated as he pointed to the lower line of numbers and letters.

"Sir, these coordinates are on our own soil," Rogers

noted.

"That's correct, General. Sultan wants revenge against the new president for his brother's death."

Rogers turned red and bit his lip. Reluctantly, he walked over to the computer console and programmed the coordinates and the code. "Missile ready for launch on your signal," he said to Harmon.

"How long until impact?" Sultan asked.

"Approximately fifteen minutes from launch," Rogers answered.

"Launch now," Sultan ordered. "And get me the SBN News center in ten minutes. I want to speak to Mr. Noble."

Rogers fulfilled the order.

* * *

"There's a call coming in for you, Mr. President," Chatty said on the floor of the SBN newsroom. "It's from the Pentagon."

"Put it on the big screen," Max said. He quickly removed the sling from his left arm, which he put back on after his speech, so that the enemy would not know of his injury.

Sultan appeared on the large center screen. "Mr. Noble, how nice to meet you," he said.

"Have you come to offer terms of your surrender?" Max asked.

"Not quite," he responded. "I've come to express to you that I am extremely disappointed that you could not follow directions. I warned you that there would be dire consequences if my men were attacked. But you did not believe me. And to make it worse, you killed my brother – my one and only baby brother!"

"Don't preach to me, Sultan! You're nothing more

than a murderous criminal. It's only a matter of time before your regime falls!"

"I look forward to meeting you in person. It will be such an honor to be the only man in history to kill two presidents of the United States."

"Surrender now and I'll spare your life."

"Oh, Mr. Noble, don't be a fool. You control one city compared to my entire country. You don't scare me."

"Tell me how you feel when the blade of my sword is at your throat."

"Tell me how you feel after you see this!" The screen cut away from Sultan and an image of the skyline of the city of Chicago appeared. "What you are looking at is the live video image from a Department of Homeland Security camera looking at Lake Michigan. The camera's primary use is to scan the water for unusual boating activities that may be linked to what you people consider 'terror activities.' You will notice the city of Chicago in the background."

"I'm familiar with the image."

"Good. Then watch this image with me for the next thirty seconds." There was silence as the image remained on the screen. Suddenly, a bright light could be seen in the upper left corner of the picture. It was moving quickly and getting larger as it neared the city.

"You son of a bitch!" Max cried. The moving light ducked behind some of the buildings and a bright flash followed. A mushroom cloud began to rise as the buildings in the picture crumbled instantaneously. Suddenly, the screen cut to black and white "snow."

"Consider us even, Mr. Noble," Sultan dryly said.

"You son of a bitch!" Max cried again.

"You have twenty-four hours to notify me of your intent to surrender. When you do, we will make arrangements for your public hanging. Good-bye, Mr. Noble." The screen went black.

"Connection lost," Chatty said. The room was silent. Every man and woman present was mortified by what they had just witnessed. Chicago had become only the third city in history to be destroyed by a nuclear device; that it was the third time it was an American device made the loss even more difficult to bear.

Millions of lives were extinguished in an instant. Max began to feel dizzy from the guilt that each death was his fault. He collapsed into the nearest chair and looked at the ground with his head resting in his right hand.

"Mr. President," Sharpe whispered.

With tears in his eyes, Max stood up. "I want that virus uploaded in twelve hours, Colonel. No excuses!" He abruptly made his way to the elevators.

"Twelve hours," Chatty confirmed. "Consider it done, sir!"

CHAPTER 21

Max stormed off the elevator into the penthouse apartment's living room. The view of Central Park was spectacular, but unnoticed. Boots, Bam Bam and the Peach, however, were taking it in while sitting at the dining room table on the other side of the couch playing poker. "What's up, boss?" Boots asked.

"Nothing," Max tersely replied. "Where's Roxy?"

"In the bedroom with Zach watching TV," Bam Bam answered pointing to the closed bedroom door. "You okay, sir?" Max ignored the question and marched into the bedroom slamming the door behind him.

"SBN News has just learned that Sultan has launched a nuclear missile and annihilated what only moments ago was the City of Chicago, Illinois," Susan's voice emanated from the plasma television that hung on the wall. "The death toll is currently unknown, but it is estimated that it stands in the millions, as no survivors are expected." The image of the missile striking the city and its mushroom cloud appeared on the screen.

Roxy looked at Max in horror; she could not bring herself to words.

"Is that real?" Zach asked.

"Turn it off!" Max demanded of Roxy.

"Oh my God, Max!" Roxy exclaimed. "How . . ."

"Turn it off, I said!" he interrupted. Before she could react, he grabbed a small sculpture from the credenza beneath the television and began pummeling the screen with it. Sparks and glass flew with every blow, and the smoke from damaged appliance set off the smoke detector in the room. Max screamed as he continued to pound away at the destroyed television.

The Peach barged in with his gun in hand. Max dropped the sculpture and collapsed to the floor. "Holy shit, boss!" the Peach exclaimed.

"Peach!" Roxy scolded. "What did I tell you about that mouth?"

"Right, I forgot," the Peach admitted as he put his gun away. "Not in front of the kid, Mrs. N. Sorry."

"I'm not a kid!" Zach protested. Max raised an eyebrow. He was actually feeling better now that he released his frustration.

"What are you then?" the Peach asked.

"I'm almost thirteen," Zach explained. "That means I'm almost a man!"

The Peach, not knowing how to respond, could only offer, "No problem, Little Man."

"Thank you," Zach said. Max was impressed at the sudden change in the boy's demeanor.

"He's been practicing for his Bar Mitzvah," Roxy explained.

"He's right," Max said. "He is almost a man. And he needs to learn about what it's like to be a man. I'm not going to be around forever at this rate, and he has to learn how to take care of you."

"Max!" Roxy screamed. "Don't say things like that!"

"Yeah, boss," said Boots who snuck into the room with Bam Bam in tow. "We got your back. Nobody's gonna touch you."

"That lunatic wants me to surrender in twenty-four hours or he's going to wipe out another city," Max said pointing to the remains of the television. "And he's going to publicly hang me if I do."

"You can't just give up, Max" Roxy said. "Look at everything that's happened in the last three days. That's all because of you."

"Sharpe could have done it without me," a self-deprecating Max said.

"Sir," Bam Bam interjected, "no, he couldn't. I like the general, don't get me wrong, but ain't none of us could have taken down Hades' three thugs."

"Yeah, and as much as the three of us tried to kill Emir, it was you who got him, boss," Boots added. "Don't sell yourself short. You're the one everyone's looking up to now. Not Bobby. Not Sharpe. Everyone's pullin' for you in this fight."

"Yeah, Dad, you can do it," Zach said. "No one can stop you."

"I'm just a man, Zach," Max explained. "Let this be your first lesson for your Bar Mitzvah. Being a man is hard. You have to remember that you can get hurt, too, and that the people you love are counting on you, so you have to be careful."

"I won't let anybody hurt you," Zach said as he leapt off the bed and hugged Max. "And like Uncle Bam Bam said, they got your back."

"Ha!" the Peach laughed. "He called you 'Uncle Bam Bam,'" he said to his colleague.

"You're all my uncles," Zach said.

"Thanks, kid," Boots said.

"Ahem," the Peach cleared his throat to correct him. "It's Little Man, now."

"You see, Max," Roxy said, "You talk about being a man and making choices for your family. Well, your family is all here, in this room right now. We love you. And we're all ready to do whatever we have to do to make sure that you keep going. I'd love for us to have a normal life. It would be great to be married to a magazine publisher, and live in a big house in the suburbs, and watch Zach grow up and go off to college. And we can have that life soon. But first you have to set things right. And that starts by setting things right in here," she said as she set her hand on his sternum. "Being a man means that you care for others first, especially the ones you love. What does your heart want you to do at this very moment?"

Max looked around the room. He saw his wife. He saw his adopted son. He saw the closest thing he would ever have to brothers. After thinking about what he truly wanted for a moment, he announced his choice. "I want that house. I want to grow old with you. I choose that life. And I'll do whatever it takes to get it."

* * *

Sultan summoned Harmon to meet with his top aides in his office. Harmon recognized the blue folder on the desk as a Department of Defense personnel file. Whose it was Harmon could not see. He wondered if Sultan was becoming suspicious of him; the Arab's behavior was erratic and entirely unpredictable now that his brother was gone. Paranoia is sometimes a soldier's best friend.

"General," Sultan began. "Join us. We were just discussing how to prepare for Mr. Noble's hanging."

"Noble himself is not the threat, you know," Harmon offered relieved that he was not the topic of conversation.

"I am aware, General. He is merely a figurehead. That is why I will insist that John Sharpe surrender with him," Sultan said pointing to the personnel file. "Tell me, General, why does Mr. Noble call him 'General,' when his file states that he is only a colonel?"

"I honestly don't know," was Harmon's only reply.

Sultan opened the file and began to peruse its pages. "It seems, General, that you know this Sharpe fellow well."

"I served with him, if that's what you're asking."

"Yes, I see that you were his commanding officer in Vietnam. But tell me, General, how come every time he came up for promotion above the rank of colonel did you urge your superiors to deny him of the rank?"

"Sharpe is a man of keen intellect. He is a strategist, not a soldier."

"It would seem to me, General, that your military would have benefited from promoting a strategist, no?"

"The United States armed forces require that its soldiers be led by soldiers. In this country, we let the politicians do the planning and strategizing."

"Yes, and a fine job of that they did indeed. So, if Sharpe is a strategist, what would his next move be assuming he refuses to surrender?"

"Well, he thinks of war as if it is a game of chess."

"Chess?"

"Yes, I used to play with him in 'Nam. He likes to set up his pieces for a forward advance. He doesn't believe in backdoor attacks. I must admit that his backdoor approach in New York was out of character for him. At any rate, he wouldn't try the same strategy a second time. That leaves him with one option only: He has to head south to Washington to attain checkmate."

"Would he abandon New York, then?"

"Unlikely. He'd want to leave some troops behind to guard it. But his army is considerably smaller than yours, and is probably ill-equipped to fight on two fronts."

"Two fronts? What are you suggesting?"

"I'm an American military officer, Sultan. To suggest an attack on my countrymen would be treason. Nonetheless, it would seem to me that in his effort to get to Washington, he would first have to go through Philadelphia." Harmon pulled a map from the shelf to illustrate his point. "If you were looking to prevent such a move, you would take out the infrastructure between New York and Philly. While he's running around the swamps of New Jersey trying to figure out how to get to his target, you can sack New York with half of your forces from Boston. In the meantime, you can bolster your troops in Philadelphia with half of your troops from Washington. By fighting on two fronts, you'll have wiped out his entire army before he gets anywhere near Washington."

"Checkmate?"

"Checkmate," Harmon confirmed and placed a large "X" over Philadelphia on the map with a black magic marker. A sudden knock on the open door behind him caused him to jump a bit.

"Pardon the interruption, Sultan," Rogers said. "I was wondering if I might have a word in private with General Harmon."

"I do not see why I should permit such a request," Sultan said. "Anything that must be said to the general can be addressed to me, as well."

"With all due respect, Sultan, it is a United States military personnel matter," Rogers explained. "It's more bureaucracy than anything else. You see, it's my son's birthday, and I would like to celebrate it with him. I am required to get my commanding officer's signature before taking any leave. The forms are in the Secretary of Defense's office"

"He's right, Sultan," Harmon confirmed. "It's a standard procedure. Would forty-eight hours be sufficient, General Rogers?"

"Amply, Sir," Rogers replied.

"I do not see the need for you to follow the rules of a defunct military, General," Sultan said.

Harmon sensed Sultan's paranoia heightening. "Soldiers are trained to follow the rules, Sultan," he said. "As I said before, the United States armed forces require that its soldiers be led by soldiers. I would suggest that you institute a similar procedure for your own troops. It helps to keep order."

"Very well," Sultan acquiesced. "You may have twenty-four hours' leave for your son's birthday, General Rogers. General Harmon, go sign his silly form."

"Thank you, Sultan," Rogers said. He and Harmon left Sultan and made their way to the Secretary of Defense's office. The office was soundproof; Harmon knew that Rogers wanted to discuss something more sensitive than having him sign a leave form. It was also locked with a retinal scanning mechanism. Because Rogers was previously assigned to the Secretary's staff, his retinal scan was the only one that would open the door. He placed his eye next to the scanner, and a small light quickly read his retina and compared it to its stored computer images. The lock opened, and the generals entered the office.

Inside, stood every American officer under Harmon's command. "What is this?" Harmon asked.

"You didn't tell him?" General Norton asked Rogers.

"It was too risky to discuss it on the way here," Rogers defended.

"Discuss what?" Harmon sternly demanded.

"Sir, we've decided that after this morning's events, the time has come for us to act," Rogers explained. "We have been patient as you ordered, but we can't sit around and watch this guy kill Americans."

"I appreciate your enthusiasm to play hero, General,

but you can drop the Captain America routine with me," Harmon quipped. "Sultan's unstable. If we make a move on him now, he's liable to nuke every city in North America." Harmon was right: Paranoia was his best defense. He could not have his authority questioned. "We remain patient, and you will not act until I give the order. Is that understood?"

"I was afraid you'd say that," Rogers said. "Norton," he called.

Norton, who had been holding the office's fire extinguisher in his hand the entire time, hit Harmon over the head with it rendering him immediately unconscious. Had Harmon been less paranoid about the topic of discussion he might have noticed it in Norton's hand. The men acted quickly to bind and gag Harmon; they tied him to a chair and placed him outside the Secretary's office.

Safely locked inside the office, Rogers looked at the officers; they were following his lead now. He walked over to one of the Secretary's bookcases and pulled out the top portion of *The Great Escape* by Paul Brickhill. The bookcase sunk into the wall and then slid to the left leaving a cold, dark opening. "Follow me," Rogers ordered.

* * *

Max emerged from the elevator onto the floor of the SBN newsroom. People were too preoccupied with their own responsibilities to even notice that he entered the room. The first to spot him was Armstrong, who grabbed his pad and ran over to Max. "Max, where the hell have you been?"

"I had to clear my head for a moment," Max told him.

"Well, I'm about to fill it up again for you. The mayor called. She wants to know who's going to pay for the clean-up of the mess we made."

"Tell her to send me the bill," Max quipped.

"Alright," Armstrong said as he made a note on his pad. "And Governor Thomas has called six times in the last two hours. He's hotter than hell right now, and said to, quote, 'Get that mother fucker,' that's you, 'on the phone so he can tear him,' again, that's you, 'a new asshole so he,' again, you, 'can shit out whatever he,' you again, 'has for brains.'"

"Jack Armstrong," one of the SBN pages called, "Governor Thomas on extension one four two for you."

"I got it," Max said as he picked up the nearest phone and pressed the extension. "The next time you call me 'shit for brains,' Thomas, I hope you'll realize that I am trying to prevent a repeat of what happened this morning."

"How dare you?!" Thomas' voice echoed through the phone. "How could you let millions of my constituents die like that? Oh, that's right! It's because they are the people who elected *me*, not you!"

"This isn't personal between us, Thomas. I don't see you making any effort to stop Sultan. Until you do, stay out of the way!"

"You have no authority to act as President, Noble," Thomas bellowed. "You were never in the chain of succession, and you're too young, to boot! Your inexperience is what caused this morning's tragedy!"

"You may be right on both counts, but right now I have twenty hours to figure out how to prevent it from happening to more American citizens. So do me a favor and call back tomorrow, Governor."

Thomas seethed on the other end of the phone. "Don't you hang up on me or else I'll . . . ." Max did not let him finish the sentence before hanging up.

"Anything else, Jack?" Max asked with a grin on his

face. He enjoyed the conversation.

"No, I'm all set," Armstrong said. "Gotta go call the mayor and get that bill for you. Nicely done, Mr. President."

"Mr. President," Sharpe called from a computer terminal at the front of the room where Chatty was sitting plugging away at the keyboard. "Mr. President, over here. You've got to see this."

Max strolled leisurely toward the terminal. "What is it, General?"

"Colonel Chatham finished writing the code but can't figure out the upload mechanism without first establishing an IP connection," Sharpe said slowly trying to make sure he got the terminology correct. "Right?"

"Not exactly, Sir, but you get an 'A' for effort," Chatty joked.

"Okay," Max said. "What the hell does that mean?"

"It means that the virus is written and ready to go," Chatty explained, "but if I try to upload it through the Pentagon's firewall, they'll be able to find the source code and erase it in a day or two, which will give them all the capabilities they currently have."

"How can we avoid that?" Sharpe asked. He had no patience for the technical jargon.

"It will take me at least thirty-six hours to write enough code to hide the source. If we had a direct connection with them I wouldn't have to go in through the firewall. They'd never know where to look to deactivate the virus code."

"Well, we can't just call them up and chat so that you can upload the virus, Colonel," Sharpe said.

"Yes, we can," Max differed. "Sultan wants me to call him to offer my surrender in twenty hours."

"That's perfect, Mr. President," Chatty confirmed.

"How is that perfect?" Sharpe asked clearly confused.

"The Pentagon's call before came in over the Web, not a traditional phone line. It's called Voice-Over-Internet-Protocol. The two servers are talking to each other. I can upload the virus during the call, and they won't have a clue as to where the source code is!"

"How long does the connection have to be?" Max asked.

"Thirty seconds or so," Chatty answered. "A minute tops."

"I don't know if I can stand talking to that scumbag for that long," Max said.

"Do it for the love of your country, Mr. President," Sharpe encouraged.

I'm doing this for Roxy, Zach and me, Max thought. "Anything for my country," he said.

CHAPTER 22

"There is a call coming in, Sultan," one of the aides called from the floor of the Hub.

"Put it on the screen," Sultan commanded as he assumed his position in his chair much like a king on a throne. Max appeared on the screen, seated in much the same manner. "How nice of you to call, Mr. Noble. Fifteen minutes before the deadline. Too bad, I was preparing to eliminate another one of your precious cities."

"Sorry to ruin the party," Max quipped.

"Let's discuss the terms of your surrender, shall we?"

"Once you tell me your terms, I will decide whether or not to accept them."

Sultan paused, annoyed that Max was not yet begging for mercy. "Fair enough, Mr. Noble. But I do suggest that you remember that if you do not surrender more of your fellow citizens will perish."

"So you've said," Max said.

"Very well then," Sultan began. "I will send a legion of my men to New York. Upon their arrival, your men will hand control of your positions over to them. Your men will then be jailed for their treachery. You will make a speech to your people declaring your official surrender, and you and Colonel Sharpe will be taken into custody. In three days' time, you will both be hanged in Times Square."

"I'm a general, Sultan, not a colonel," Sharpe said as he moved into the picture.

Sultan reached over to the desk nearest his seat and picked up the blue personnel folder. "Not according to your file, Colonel," Sultan taunted as he waved Sharpe's file at the camera. "No reported kills, Colonel? I can see why your government did not feel you were worthy of the rank of General. You're no soldier!"

"Why you…" Sharpe started before Max interrupted.

"Allow me, General," Max said, emphasizing Sharpe's rank. Max looked at Chatty who nodded affirmatively to him. "Sultan, I take exception to your very presence here. You're like a cockroach – you show up uninvited, scare people into a frenzy, and don't understand that, in the end, we are still bigger than you, and we will ultimately crush you. And for what?"

"The next words out of your mouth had better be 'I accept,' or else you can say good-bye to St. Louis!" the insulted Arab decreed.

"Your terms are hereby rejected, Sultan," Max defied.

"Very well, Mr. Noble. Have it your way." Sultan called to his men in Arabic. "Let's see how long your own people allow you to stay in power after they see that you have caused the annihilation of two cities in one day!"

The image of Max began to blur. One by one, the screens in the Pentagon's operations center went black. First, it was the geothermal imaging satellite. Next was the map of the Pacific Coast of the United States, followed by the maps of the Midwest, and then the Atlantic Coast. When the image of the American nuclear silos disappeared, panic spread among Sultan's men.

"What is going on?" Sultan asked in Arabic.

"We seem to have lost access to the server, Sultan," one of the aides replied in his native tongue. "All systems are shutting down. The nuclear missiles are off line, and the silos are sealing themselves. We've also lost the satellite transmissions."

"What?!" Sultan cried. "Get them back! Get them all back!"

"We can't," the aide responded. "The entire network is non-responsive."

"What have you done, Noble?" Sultan demanded to know, returning the conversation to English. Max's image was frozen, but the audio remained intact.

"What do you mean, 'What have I done?'" Max snidely replied.

"Get me back online!" Sultan scathed to no one in particular and yet everyone simultaneously.

"I don't know how," the aide responded in English. Sultan, having no further patience for the aide's incompetence, pulled his gun from his holster and shot the aide in the chest.

Upon hearing the gunshot, Max asked, "Having trouble with your computers, Sultan?"

"You're a dead man, Noble! Do you hear me? Dead!"

"I don't think so, Sultan," Max said confidently. "The next time you and I talk, it will be face-to-face. And the next words I hear from you will be your plea for mercy just before your surrender." Max ended the transmission; his frozen image disappeared from the screen, replaced only by a picture of Mount Rushmore, in which the four sculpted images of Presidents Washington, Jefferson, Lincoln and Teddy Roosevelt were laughing. Chatty thought the barb to be humorous, and so included it in the virus code.

Sultan seethed. While he never expected that he would implement his plan perfectly, he did not have a contingency for this scenario. How Max Noble eluded his death was not of concern to him; however, that Max raised an army and managed to neutralize him stirred great rage within. Now, denied access to the American military's spy satellites and nuclear arsenal, he knew that his power had been diminished. Fear of reprisals was no longer a weapon. His hold on his newfound power would only last as long as his men could corral the masses.

His men could see the anger radiating from within. They kept their distance knowing full well that Sultan would not hesitate to kill them if he felt so fancied. The tide was turning, and they could sense it. Internal dissension was inevitable; only they knew that it would not be tolerated. Their fates rested entirely in the hands of the most unstable man in the world, and they knew that if he could not torment the Americans, he would resort to tormenting those around to him. Such is the behavior of a mass murderer.

"Sultan, come quickly!" a younger one of his men called in Arabic as he ran into the Hub.

"Now what is it?" Sultan wanted to know.

"It is the American general," the young aide replied. "He has been bound and gagged!"

"Take me to him, at once!" Sultan instructed less than enthused that something else had gone awry. The aide led Sultan to the corridor leading to the Secretary of Defense's office. There, still bound to the chair and gagged, sat Harmon; he was trying to say something to Sultan's men who had their guns pointed at him but the gag made it impossible for him to speak.

"At ease!" Sultan ordered his men. He rushed over to the general and loosened the gag so that Harmon could speak. "Who did this to you?"

"Rogers and my men, Sultan," Harmon replied. "They ambushed me. The whole thing about his kid's birthday was a set-up."

"Where are your men now?"

"I don't know. They hit me over the head, and the

next thing I remember was waking up in this chair."

Sultan checked Harmon's skull. He could see the dried blood in Harmon's hair where Norton hit him with the fire extinguisher. Sultan touched it. "Ow!" Harmon reacted. "Watch it!"

"My apologies," Sultan offered. It was clear that the injury was not a fake. He pulled a knife from its sheath on his belt and cut the ropes off of Harmon's wrists and ankles before helping the general to his feet.

"Thank you," Harmon cordially replied.

"Alert all posts to be on the lookout for the Americans," Sultan ordered in English to the two mujahadeen that were watching Harmon. "They cannot have gotten far, and I want them alive!"

"What will you do to them once you catch them?" Harmon asked.

"We have lost all computer access," Sultan explained. "Without computers access, I no longer have access to the satellite images. More importantly, I no longer have access to the nuclear arsenal. Your men are the only ones who can fix the computers. Once we find them, they will give me back that access. Then, and only then, they will be killed for their treachery."

"It would seem that you are losing your grip, Sultan," Harmon noted.

Unappreciative of the comment, Sultan pulled his gun from its holster again and placed the barrel between Harmon's eyes. He cocked the hammer, but did not pull the trigger. "Make no mistake, General. I am still firmly in control."

* * *

Susan graced the small television screen in the Penthouse kitchen Roxy was watching as she prepared dinner for her family. "This is Susan Teller, SBN News," she began. "America can sleep easier tonight. SBN has learned that Sultan no longer has the capability to launch nuclear weapons. President Noble's Press Secretary, David Bard, issued a statement a short while ago that reads:

> Through the diligent efforts of the American military under General Sharpe's command, the enemy can no longer use the nuclear weapons that once protected this great nation to harm us. While we continue to mourn those lost in Chicago, we are thankful for those who helped prevent similar tragedies from occurring in other American cities. President Noble reaffirms to all Americans his commitment to defeat the occupying force, and to restore our great nation to its glory. He urges all Americans to join him in resisting our oppressors, but to use caution in so doing.

"While President Noble's next move remains unclear, what is clear is that he has no intention of backing down. The President has said that this fight has only just begun, and given the events of the past four days, he means it. I'm Susan Teller, SBN News."

Roxy put down the knife she was using to peel some carrots. She looked into the living room where Max was teaching Zach one of the prayers for his upcoming bar mitzvah. "I'm proud of you, Max," she said softly, not intending for Max to hear.

"What was that, Rox?" Max said.

"Nothing," she replied as she returned to peeling carrots. "Nothing at all."

CHAPTER 23

Global warming brought the dog days of summer earlier than expected. The temperature on Independence Day, which would normally be in the low eighty-degree Fahrenheit range, nearly reached one hundred degrees. Without having to fear the threat of a reprisal from Sultan, fireworks displays were seen across the country; none were as spectacular as those in New York, which SBN broadcast to the entire world to a customarily patriotic American musical accompaniment. The trees were in full bloom, and New York's Central Park never looked greener. Roxy loved the view from the apartment's terrace, although the oppressive heat kept her indoors for much of the summer. Max, on the other hand, insisted on spending as much time outdoors as possible; being cooped up inside the SBN Newsroom every day and not being allowed to leave the building for security purposes nearly drove him mad. While Armstrong and Judge Vineri took to their jobs (the air conditioned offices made it a pleasure for them to spend all day on the phones overseeing the country's day-to-day domestic and foreign operations), Max's only desire was to spend as much time with his new family as possible. He made decisions when he had to, but he trusted his advisors to handle the ministerial tasks.

His surgery considered a success, Max no longer wore the sling on his left arm. He tried to use the arm as often as possible, but the muscles atrophied; his schedule did not allow for the considerable physical therapy that was needed. In what free time he did have, Max often practiced the *katahs* he learned from Takinawa. The meditation soothed him and kept his fighting skills honed.

While Roxy insisted that Max help prepare Zach for his bar mitzvah, Max insisted that Zach spend time outdoors, as well. He set up the archery target on the terrace so that Zach could practice with his bow and arrows as a study break from the bar mitzvah lessons. The boy's muscles were beginning to develop, and his strength became obvious as he hit the target each time more vigorously; the repetitive sound of each arrow cutting through the air relaxed Max. Zach's improved accuracy impressed even Sharpe, who would deliver nightly reports of each day's military developments; although, there had not been much to report in recent weeks. "Hell of a marksman, young man," Sharpe would tell him. "You're ready to be one of my soldiers, I'd say." Zach always thanked him demurely and politely.

To Roxy's relief, Zach's bar mitzvah arrived. She planned all she could under the circumstances: Rabbi Schonberg, who brought one of the Torahs from his temple, officiated a small ceremony on the terrace. While quaint, it was everything she dreamed it would be for her only son. The beauty of Central Park in the background as Zach read his *haftorah* brought tears to her eyes. Afterwards, a small reception in the apartment followed. Max played the role of a proud father, and his speech made Roxy cry again. He waxed poetic about watching the boy develop his own work ethic and personality, even mentioning how Zach's countless hours of archery practice led his friends to ask for the "Archer," when they called the apartment. Zach and his friends laughed. It was a brief moment of normalcy in an aberrant world.

Max was able to enjoy the ceremony and the first hour of the reception before being called into a meeting in the SBN Newsroom. It was a brief meeting, as his daily briefings generally were, with his regular advisors, Judge Vineri, Armstrong and Sharpe. Judge Vineri, who elected to keep his beard although it was no longer necessary because he felt it made him appear distinguished, announced that he secured an additional one thousand troops from France to aid the British in defending New York; Sharpe was pleasantly surprised. Armstrong informed the group that the governors' representatives for forty-nine of the fifty states had arrived, and that the ad hoc council's first session would begin on Monday morning at nine o'clock. "The missing fiftieth representative had not been named yet by Governor Thomas," he explained. "However, Thomas promised me that the State of Illinois would be in attendance at the start of the session."

"That's odd, no?" Max inquired.

"It certainly is, Mr. President," Armstrong confirmed. "Let's make sure to keep our ears close to the ground on this one. Thomas is a wily politician. We can't trust him. Ergo, we can't trust his representative, either."

"Agreed," Max acknowledged.

Armstrong continued with his report. The regional economy was gaining steam as people began to return to work in New York; nationally, Sultan's grip was squeezing Americans for every dollar they had. "Conditions are approaching lows not seen since the Great Depression," he warned.

"What's our strategy?" Max asked. In truth, he did not have one and was relying on Armstrong to provide an answer.

"Our strategy for what?" was the antithesis of what Max wanted to hear, yet it was the response Armstrong proffered.

"C'mon, Jack," Max prodded. "You know that the economy is going to be one of the first things we're pressed about by the council. We need a plan of some sort."

"People need to go back to work," Armstrong said. "That's what'll stimulate the economy. But there won't be any jobs for them while Sultan remains in control."

Max turned to Sharpe. "I guess that makes you our economic strategy, General. How soon can we expect to win this thing and get people back to work?"

"Thanks for the added pressure, Mr. President," Sharpe quipped. "The British are scheduled to arrive on Monday, and the Canadian supplies are scheduled to be delivered in a matter of days; Major Gonzalez is stationed in Kingston ready to receive them. Colonel Chatham and I will be leading our men from New York on Wednesday. The major and his attachment will rendezvous with us once he has the supplies at Washington's Crossing on the Delaware River."

Max nodded as if he agreed, so Sharpe continued, "From there, we will commence our attack on Philadelphia from the east. The first position will prove the toughest," he said pointing to a map of the Philadelphia area hanging on the wall behind him. "We must take the Ben Franklin Bridge, and judging by the enemy's strategy here in New York, it will be heavily guarded. We will contact you once we have taken the bridge. I would say that we will be in a position to begin the siege on Philadelphia in about two weeks, depending on when the supplies arrive. I am leaving Lieutenant Youseff and his men behind as a liaison between you and the British . . ."

"Don't forget the French," the Judge interjected.

"And the French," Sharpe snidely continued. "My suggestion, Mr. President, is that you leave the logistics to the British commander, but have the lieutenant make it clear that you are calling the shots."

"Will the British and French troops be enough to defend the entire city from a possible attack?" Armstrong asked.

"They will have to do, Jack," Max answered. "The general is going to need every man available to take

Philadelphia."

* * *

The SBN Newsroom was abuzz. The forty-nine expected representatives were escorted to the general assembly auditorium on the premises; it would serve as the council's de facto chambers. But because no one expected Governor Thomas, himself, to arrive as the fiftieth representative, a sense of impending tumult began to brew in the auditorium.

Max entirely ignored the ruckus, and Thomas, for that matter. Instead, he was liaising with Colonel Malcolm Barrington, the commander of, as he put it, "Her majesty's bravest soldiers who have been ordered to assist our American allies." Barrington was a lifetime military man with a complete understanding of modern urban warfare and respect for the chain of command; he found Max's request that he take his orders from Hank insulting. "I am to take orders only from you, Mr. President. Luftenants," he said using the British pronunciation for Hank's rank, "are inferior in rank to colonels, Mr. President. It is the equivalent of my directing you to take orders from me."

"That's fair, Colonel Barrington," Max acknowledged. "But often times I may be tied up in meetings with members of our new council. Therefore, it will be easier for you to communicate with Lieutenant Youseff when you require direction. I assure you, Colonel, that any order you receive from him originates from me. Isn't that right, Lieutenant?"

"Sir, that is absolutely correct, sir," Hank said to assure Barrington that there was no misunderstanding as to the chain of command.

"Very well, Mr. President," Barrington conceded. "My men and I serve at your leisure. To where should we report?"

"Lieutenant Youseff will take you to the briefing room," Max explained. "He will show you the map of the city that outlines our current positions. I trust your judgment and expertise as to where you will want to position your men."

"Thank you for your confidence, Mr. President," Barrington said as he saluted Max with an upward, open-palm motion. Max saluted with a downward motion, the American equivalent to the British salute. Hank led Barrington to a conference room in the SBN Newsroom where the maps of the city were strewn across the table.

Max exited his office to make his way toward the auditorium for the inaugural session of the council. As he approached the elevator, Armstrong hurriedly approached him, grabbed Max at his weakened left bicep and dragged him back into his office shutting the door behind them. "What the hell, Jack?"

"He's here," Armstrong said.

"He? Who?"

"Thomas! Thomas is here! He's representing Illinois himself!" Armstrong exclaimed.

Max could tell that he was beginning to hyperventilate. "Okay, relax. I mean, c'mon Jack! Calm down! What's the big deal? So, he's here. So, what?"

"Don't you get it, Max? This guy's a pro. He spent three terms in the House, and four more years in the Senate before winning the governorship. He knows parliamentary procedure better than anyone in that room, and he's got it out for you! He'll make you look foolish, and then where will that leave us?"

Max straightened his tie using the reflection of himself in his window as a mirror. "Don't worry, Jack. It's gonna take more than a little parley-pro to get rid of me," he said with a grin.

"Wait!" Armstrong yelled as Max left the office and headed toward the elevator.

Max ignored him at first. As he boarded the elevator, he yelled back to Armstrong pointing to the television screen monitoring the auditorium, "Watch this!"

Max disembarked from the elevator only to find Bard waiting for him. "Sir, thank goodness you're here," the little man said as he handed some papers to Max. "Here's your speech."

Taking the papers from Bard in stride, Max made his way into the auditorium. Most of the representatives rose and applauded; Thomas was not one of them.

Back in the SBN Newsroom, Armstrong watched as Susan detailed the entrance for the viewers. "And President Noble has now entered the chamber," she said. "We expect that this session of the council will be more of a formality, as the body is not expected to vote on any matters of substance today. We will report back with a full analysis of the council's meeting today later in your program. For now, as President Noble prepares to take the podium, this is Susan Teller, SBN News."

Max took his place at the podium that was placed in front of an oversized American flag; the room had been altered so that the stage resembled the front of the chamber in the House of Representatives. He tapped the microphone, and after hearing that it was working, he began, "Distinguished representatives of the United States of America." The applause finally subsided and quieted as he continued. "It is with great sorrow that we convene here today to act in the stead of our slain predecessors. And yet, it is with great pride that we will act as a result of the will of the American people to be resilient. Our fellow citizens do not tolerate the oppression of inalienable rights, such as the rights to life, liberty and the pursuit of happiness." The chamber gave him a standing ovation. "They have been taken away from us by an enemy who will stop at nothing to oppress us. In the wake of the Chicago holocaust, I wish to thank Governor Thomas for representing his constituents personally, as they will certainly not be let down." The body gave the governor a standing ovation.

Puzzled, Thomas rose and nodded to acknowledge the honorable mention.

Max continued, "Fortunately, we have disabled the enemy's ability to strike Americans in such a cowardly manner. As we speak, our forces are preparing for the next confrontation with the enemy." Another ovation followed. "We have proven here in New York that we can be successful. And we know that we must be successful in all of our campaigns. For that, let us thank General John Sharpe and his men for all of their sacrifices and efforts." The room stood again and applauded Sharpe, who was seated on the stage to Max's left.

Max finished his opening remarks and called the roll state by state, ending with himself as the Chair and the tie-breaking fifty-first vote. Once he formally established that all fifty representatives were present, he sought to move into the first order of business. "We now move into the report of General Sharpe as to the military's operation," he said as Sharpe replaced Max at the podium.

"Point of order!" Thomas hollered to the chamber.

Max returned to the podium to address the issue; Sharpe remained patiently. "The chair recognizes Governor Thomas of Illinois," Max said.

"I move to break with the agenda and to move into New Business where we must elect a leader of this council," Thomas said. Murmurs followed.

"This country has a leader, Governor," Sharpe defiantly spoke into the microphone. "His name is President Noble."

Max covered the microphone and told Sharpe, "I

can handle this, General." Removing his hand, he said, "Thank you, General Sharpe. Governor Thomas, your motion is premature, and not recognized at this time."

The chamber began to boo. "This is a democracy, where we elect our leaders," one representative cried.

"Put it to a vote!" another pleaded.

"Very well," Max conceded.

In the SBN Newsroom, Armstrong hung his head and mumbled, "We're in deep shit, now."

"Is there a second to Governor Thomas' motion?" Max asked.

Most of the room responded, "Second."

"The chair recognizes the distinguished lady from Oregon," he said. "All in favor?" Max asked.

They responded with a resounding, "Aye."

"All opposed?"

There were several, "Nay," responses, but it was overwhelmingly clear that the "Ayes," prevailed.

"The 'Ayes,' have it. We are now in New Business. Are there any nominations for the position of the Chair of this council?" Several hands were raised. "The chair recognizes the distinguished gentleman from New York."

Donald Hack, the Speaker of the New York State Assembly, rose and said, "I nominate Max Noble." Applause ensued.

"Thank you, Mr. Hack," Max said. "Is there a second?"

Several representatives called, "Second."

"The chair recognizes and thanks the distinguished gentleman from Mississippi," Max said. "Are there any other nominations?" Walter Straight, the representative from Indiana raised his hand. "The chair recognizes the distinguished gentleman from Indiana."

"I nominate Martin Thomas," Straight said.

"Is there a second?" Max asked.

Again, there were several voices that called, "Second."

"The chair recognizes the distinguished lady from Missouri," Max noted. "Are there any other nominations?" Silence ensued. "Very well, nominations are hereby closed. Governor Thomas and I are the nominees to serve as Chair of this council. Governor Thomas, the podium is all yours."

Thomas approached the podium and readjusted the microphone. "Ladies and gentlemen, I have been involved in American politics for decades. I have seen this nation go through wars both at home, such as the Civil Rights Movement, and abroad, such as Vietnam and Iraq. And never in all my years have I seen a leader as callous as Mr. Noble. His inexperience is the direct cause of the Chicago holocaust, a tragedy that obviously weighs heavily on my heart. We cannot afford another gaffe. Now, everybody here appreciates what you've done for us, but we just can't risk the chance that you might let it happen again. So, I urge each of you to vote for me. I will never allow your states to suffer the way mine has. Thank you."

Max replaced Thomas at the podium. "Thank you, Governor Thomas. And now, for my remarks," he said before Sharpe tugged on his sleeve and nodded. "I defer to General Sharpe." A murmur followed.

Sharpe took the microphone. "Ladies and gentlemen, please allow me to take a few minutes to tell you about President Max Noble. When I met him, I was extremely skeptical that this young man would be up to the challenge of leading this country. I have watched him for the last six months go from an insecure widower to a confident hero. That's right, ladies and gentlemen. Max Noble is a hero. He, alone, made it possible for us to reclaim New York. He, alone, conquered Sultan's brother. And yes, he, alone, confronted Sultan just prior to the Chicago incident. Leaders are not always right, and they must live with the consequences of their actions and decisions. I know that President Noble has felt horrible about Chicago. I know that he does not bask in our victories for they came at a great cost for Americans. And I know that my men respect him more than anyone for what he has done for our country. I know all of this, ladies and gentlemen, because I have had the opportunity to know Max Noble. Before you vote, you should do the same. Thank you."

"Agreed!" a representative cried. Others mumbled in agreement.

"Motion to table the vote for two weeks to allow us to get to know the candidates," Jim Parker of Virginia said.

"Know the candidates?" Thomas protested. "Jim, you've known me for twenty-three years. How much longer do you need?"

"It's only fair, Martin," Parker answered.

"Very well," Max said. "There is a motion to table the vote for two weeks. Is there a second?"

"Second!" the representatives cried in unison.

"All in favor?" Max asked.

They responded with a resounding, "Aye."

"All opposed?"

"Nay," Thomas said.

"Motion passes," Max announced. "The vote for Chair of the council will be held in two weeks."

"Shit!" Martin exclaimed as he made his way back to his seat.

"Now, we shall move into our military report to be given by General Sharpe," Max said.

The television coverage cut away from Sharpe as

he took the podium. Susan appeared in her red glasses. "Ladies and gentlemen, there you have it. Illinois Governor Martin Thomas is challenging Max Noble's presidency. General Sharpe has made it clear where the hearts of his soldiers stand. Now it is a question of where do the hearts of the American politicians stand. We'll find out in two weeks. This is Susan Teller, SBN News."

In the Newsroom, Armstrong shook his head. He looked at Judge Vineri, who had been watching the coverage with him. "Well, at least Sharpe bought him two weeks."

"He's gonna have to win Philly before that vote if Max has any chance of staying in power," the Judge said.

"Even that may not be enough."

* * *

Two days uneventfully passed after Thomas threw down his gauntlet. At Armstrong's request, Roxy began to fill Max's social calendar with dinner plans with small groups of the representatives so that they could get to better know him. The conversation at the first two dinners was nearly identical: Max told his life story, and the representatives hung onto every word. After the second dinner, Max asked Armstrong if there was any other way. *Another one of these, and I may puke*, he thought.

Max greeted Armstrong at his office the following morning, "How many more of these bullshit 'wine 'em and dine 'em' dinners do I have to do, Jack?"

"Good morning to you, too," Armstrong snapped back. "I've got you with five representatives at each dinner. There are fifty of them – counting Thomas, who you don't need to break bread with – and you've already met ten of them. That leaves you with eight more dinners so you can charm the remaining thirty-nine."

"Then you can expect eight more miserable morning

meetings," Max replied. "What's going on today?"

"Sharpe is setting out for Philadelphia with the army this afternoon," Armstrong reported. "He'd like you to see them off before they go." Max nodded that he would do so. "In the meantime, Hank and Barrington are monitoring the city's security posts, and the Judge says that the French troops are en route."

"Anything else I need to know about?" Max asked, confident that there was not.

"Yes, there's a man in your office waiting to talk to you."

"A man? Who is he?" Max asked as he craned his neck to look into his office. Max saw the back of a man seated at the chair in front of his desk. His hair was grey, and he exhibited a bald spot on the back of his head typical of a middle-aged man.

"His name is Arnold. Bill Arnold."

"Bill Arnold? Is that his real name?"

"Yep. Driver's license says he's William Arnold from Macon, Georgia. I didn't have time to take fingerprints for you. All he had with him was his wallet and a briefcase filled with money."

"Money? For what?"

"Don't know that either. He said he was here to return it to you, and that he would only speak to you privately."

"Do you think he's dangerous?"

"Not for a war hero like you," Armstrong said sarcastically. "Your Italian boys frisked him. He wasn't hiding any weapons, and he seems harmless enough."

"Right," Max acknowledged. He left Armstrong and walked into his office, shutting the door behind him so that he and Arnold could speak privately. "Mr. Arnold, is it?"

"Yes," Arnold excitedly replied with a southern drawl. "Yes, Mr. President. Bill Arnold. It's certainly nice to meet you."

"Likewise, Mr. Arnold," Max said as he scanned his guest to gauge his background. His gray suit was worn and slightly tattered; *he must be of humble means*, Max thought. He wore a white shirt that was desperately in need of collar stays, and his red polka-dotted tie screamed of a conservative nature. "Where are you from?"

"Macon, Georgia. Drove all the way up here just to see you, sir."

"Did you, now? And what for?"

"It's about my son, sir." Arnold's face became grim. "You see, he used to work for the government, sir."

"I see. It must be difficult for him. We haven't exactly been keeping a steady payroll, if you know what I mean."

"I know, sir," Arnold acknowledged as a tear came to his eye. "My son, Ben, used to be a Secret Service agent."

"That's a very honorable job. I'm sure we can find a space for him here since he's got experience. Let me just call . . . ."

"Ben's dead, Mr. President," Arnold interrupted. "He hung himself two months after that monster took over our country," he sobbed uncontrollably.

"I'm sorry to hear that, Mr. Arnold," Max consoled as Arnold waved his hand at Max.

"You probably shouldn't be, Mr. President. He left this note, and I think . . .," Arnold paused to compose himself. "I drove all the way up here for you to read it," he said. He reached into his jacket pocket and pulled out a crumpled piece of paper. Max took the sheet and struggled to read its sloppy handwriting:

Dear Pa,

I'm so sorry that it has come to this. I let my country down. I let my friends down. And I let you and Mama down, too. I can't bear the guilt anymore, and I can only think of one way to escape. I hope that Jesus can help me bury the pain when I meet him.

I did something awful, Pa. A man approached me in October of last year. He told me that he needed me to get him some information about the State of the Union. He said that he'd pay me $250,000 for it. I told him that I should report him to my supervisor. But he told me that he worked for the CIA, and that my supervisor was in on his plan. He said that if I didn't go along, they would kill me!

Then I thought about it, and I figured you and Mama could sure use that money to pay off the bank so they don't come and take your house. They can't take the house, Pa! That's our home!

So, I gave that man what he wanted. I told him where he could get into the Capitol during the State of the Union. I told him which doors would be left unguarded. I told him who would be sitting where, and how to get to them. Everything is my fault! I didn't think this guy would actually do what he did.

I did it for the money, Pa. I took the money, and buried it in a briefcase in the backyard of the house at Christmas. It's behind the myrtle tree with the tire-swing. Dig it up and give it to the bank. Don't let them take the house from you and Mama. I love you guys. I'm sorry, but this is the only way.

Love,

Ben

Max was taken aback by the letter. "How old was Ben?" he asked.

"Would have been twenty-nine next month," Arnold replied. "I found the money, Mr. President. Bank says that they're gonna take my house next week. But this is blood money, Mr. President. My wife and I . . . we can't keep it." He placed the briefcase on Max's desk and opened it for Max to see the hundred-dollar bills.

"Where will you live then?"

"Don't know. We don't have much money. I own a stationary store in Macon, but with the economy as bad as it is, I'm gonna have to sell that, too. I'm hopin' some of the folks from church can take us in, but things ain't too good for them, neither."

Max leaned back in his chair. *What's the right thing to do?* he thought. He stared out the window pondering the question. *Dalton would shoot Arnold on the spot for being the father of a traitor. Judge Vineri would open an investigation, and then tell the world. Roxy . . . Roxy would tell this man that she wished she could help. Screw it! We don't need the money! Let him keep his house and have some dignity. His son is gone, now. He was the real traitor here. Let this man go with peace of mind.* "Well, Mr. Arnold, I think you should keep the money."

"I'm sorry, sir? Did you say to keep the money?" Arnold asked, astonished.

"Yep. Surprised?"

"Very much so, Mr. President. I mean, I heard you was a Jew, and you know this is a lot of money. I thought for sure you would tell me to hand it over."

Max, upset by the stereotype, explained, "Mr. Arnold, divisive beliefs are what got us into this mess. We thought that good people look and act one way, and that bad people look and act another. The truth is, there is good and bad in all of us, and ultimately, we will only be judged by what we do, not what we are."

"But this is blood money, sir. How can we possibly keep it?"

"You and your wife need this money more than I do. Your son committed treason out of his love for you. And his guilt forced him to take his own life. That is punishment enough for any parent. So, take the money. Burn the letter. You and your wife should enjoy what days you have left. No one knows about this, and it would not help matters if anyone found out. All we know from the letter is that our enemy conspired with someone who claimed he worked for the CIA. I'll have my people look into that. You brought that to me, and for that information, consider the money in the briefcase as payment for it."

"I . . . I don't know what to say, Mr. President. My wife and I couldn't possibly do anything to repay you for this."

"Continue to be good people. Help me return America to what it once was before the greed and corruption ruined it. That will be repayment enough. Can you handle that?"

"As Jesus Christ is my Lord and savior," Arnold declared.

"Now, go home and give your wife a hug. She probably needs it."

"Thank you, Mr. President," Arnold said as he stood and shook Max's hand. He took the suitcase containing the money, walked out of the office teary-eyed, and made his way toward the elevator. He paused when he passed Armstrong to say, "He's a good man."

"I agree," Armstrong concurred.

CHAPTER 24

The noon sun beat down upon the former site of the World Trade Center. Renamed "Ground Zero," because the rubble left from the destruction of the Twin Towers on September 11, 2001, resembled the aftermath of a bomb-testing site, Sharpe felt that it was necessary to remind his troops that this war was not initiated in January when Sultan usurped the government; but rather, it began on that day when three thousand innocent civilians were murdered by terrorists who misguidedly believed that it was the will of their god, Allah, that they were to fly commercial airliners into the buildings to kill non-Muslims. Judge Vineri once casually suggested to Sharpe that the four airplanes that were hijacked that day - two that crashed in New York, one in Washington, DC, and one in Pennsylvania - were akin to the Four Horsemen of the Apocalypse described in the Book of the Revelation of St. John. Sharpe paid the comment no mind publicly; he argued that an ancient text could not actually prophesize the events of the future. But privately, he accepted the notion that if that day was the Rapture, then he was leading the Sons of Light in the Battle of Armageddon. Of course, that meant that Sultan was the Beast, and only the second coming of Jesus Christ, himself, could conquer him. Sharpe knew that he was not the man charged with the task. That responsibility, rightly or wrongly, would be Max's burden to bear; he was a humble and peaceful man who believed in the innate good of mankind when Sharpe first met him. But Sharpe was left to wonder if Max's transformation from politico to warrior was corrupting his soul. Only time would tell, he believed, and judgment was better reserved for the totality of Max's actions. History would record them appropriately, and it was too early for Sharpe to label him either the Christ or the Antichrist. Nonetheless, Ground Zero was a bold reminder of the horrific atrocities of that clear September day when the world was reminded that evil exists in the hearts of men. It was hallowed ground, and an inspiration to his Sons of Light that this next battle was one they could not afford to lose.

Max's car, chauffeured by Boots, pulled up to the entrance that was heavily guarded by British soldiers. Boots honked the horn and cursed at the reporters who were blocking the gate. SBN had cornered the market on Max, and its competitors clamored for any contact they could get. Governor Thomas was a mainstay on their airwaves, but he was nothing more than a talking head compared to Max; he had no real power, and could do nothing more than criticize his opponent by responding to the comments Max made the day prior. Max, on the other hand, was dictating the terms of the debate. Morris backed his horse early and hated to lose; it was impossible to turn on SBN without seeing Max's face. Bard carefully scripted every word Max uttered, and Susan, who was the most attractive of the media's television reporters, was the perfect "eye candy" for Max's interviews. His popularity soared among the American people, although it was suspect among the representatives on the council. Sponsors were flocking to SBN, and the other networks figured that their only way to survive in the troubled economy was to seize on every opportunity to put Max's picture in their broadcasts; live shots were better than stills. A live shot of Max meeting with his army brass before the military force set out for its next battle was widely viewed as gold.

Boots had no patience for the media. His job was to get Max to his meeting with Sharpe. He watched as the British troops struggled to keep the press away from the car. Finally, he rolled down his window and yelled, "I'll give you three minutes if you back off and let us in!" His words worked like magic, and the path that led into the complex through the gate was cleared. He rolled up his window and drove through to the construction trailer that Sharpe adopted as his temporary office to plan the assault.

"You know, I'm not supposed to give them any interviews, Boots," Max complained.

"Yeah, I know. But it got them to move the fuck out of the way, didn't it?"

"I guess so."

"Besides, all I said was that *I* would give 'em three minutes," Boots said. "You go do what you gotta do. I'll go have some fun with 'em."

"Ha!" Max laughed. He loved the plan. "What are you going to tell them for three minutes?"

Boots reached into his glove compartment and pulled out a copy of *The Little Engine That Could.* "My wife's been houndin' me to read this to my kids every night. So, I figure I can go practice for three minutes," he said as the car came to a halt by the trailer. Both he and Max got out of the car. Boots straightened his tie, put on his sunglass and began to stroll back toward the gate.

"Have fun," Max said with a smile as he exited the car and walked into the trailer. While Boots was occupying, and generally annoying, the members of the press, Max quickly realized that he had intruded on Sharpe's officer briefing.

"Ah, Mr. President, you've come to see us off," Sharpe announced.

"Of course, General," Max confidently replied secretly hiding his own surprise. He only stopped by because Armstrong told him that Sharpe requested his presence. He was not aware that Sharpe had anything planned for him.

"Excellent, sir," the general said. "We were just briefing our unit commanders as to the plan of attack." He pointed to a map of New Jersey on the wall of the trailer. Tracking the route that was highlighted on the map in red ink with a pointer, he explained, "We'll be leaving through the Holland Tunnel, through Jersey City to Route 22, then to Route 202, to Route 31, and then to Route 579 into Washington Crossing State Park. The total trip is sixty-nine miles, and we'll be making it on foot. We'll be leaving here with supplies for ten days. Marching at three miles per hour for ten hours per day, we should reach Washington Crossing on the third day."

"Excuse me, sir," one of the unit commanders interrupted, "but why are we setting out on foot, and why all of the back roads?"

"Fair questions," Sharpe responded. "Our enemy is most likely expecting this assault. Major Gonzalez led a scout team that discovered that the major highways between here and Philadelphia have been bombed and are impassible. However, the enemy left the back roads intact. They are also better covered with foliage, so we will be able to take cover in the woods if we hear bombers overhead. If we were to take a caravan of trucks or busses, we would become an obvious target." The unit commanders nodded in agreement with Sharpe's logic.

"Once we reach Washington Crossing," Sharpe continued, "we will rendezvous with Major Gonzalez and his unit, which is currently in Kingston awaiting a delivery of supplies from our friends in Canada. We'll rest there for a few days, and then launch in rafts from Washington Crossing down the Delaware River at night. We will proceed down the river approximately thirty-five miles to the Back Channel piers in Camden, New Jersey. From there, we will proceed into Philadelphia over the

Ben Franklin Bridge. The bridge, gentlemen, is the key to the attack," he cautioned. "We expect that it will be heavily guarded, and any failure on our part, there, will surely lead to defeat. We'll reconvene before we launch from Washington Crossing to brief you on the strategy for taking the bridge. Any questions?"

An eerie silence reigned as the men digested the plan of attack. The looks on the unit commanders faces were grave. It was a long physical journey to make before the assault was to begin, and most of them were concerned that their men would not be up to the task. Sharpe shared the concern, but would not admit it. Their previous success was planned months in advance; not a detail was left to chance in the New York campaign. Now, they were being asked to march and paddle their way to Philadelphia with no tactic for taking the one strategic point that was critical to victory. Max could sense that morale was low.

"Alright, then go prepare your companies," Sharpe ordered. "We move out at thirteen hundred hours." The unit commanders filed out of the trailer, leaving Max and Sharpe secluded.

"General, how comfortable are you with this plan?" Max asked while pointing to Sharpe's mapped route; he was wary not to overstep his bounds.

"Honestly, Sir?"

"Yes, honestly."

"Not very. We're going to take on heavy casualties at the bridge. There's no avoiding it."

"Can we take the bridge at all?"

"It would be much easier if we had a force to distract the enemy's troops at the bridge."

Max pondered the scenario. "Then why not send a portion of your men into the city through another route?"

"I can't risk weakening our attack force at the bridge,"

Sharpe explained.

Max was having difficulty accepting that failure was an option being discussed. He knew that if Sharpe could not reclaim Philadelphia, then Thomas would surely convince the council that new leadership was needed. He tried to flex his left arm, but he could not; it dangled like a languid worm. The rigors of battle would be stronger this time, and he knew that he was in no condition to join the troops for the campaign. *There has to be a contingency plan*, he thought. *Sharpe would not dare enter battle without one.* "Hypothetically," he said, "if you had that other force, what would be your plan?"

"Well," Sharpe said as he thought of a response. He picked up a blue magic marker from the desk, and turned to the map on the wall. "Hypothetically," he stressed, "I would bring the force through the Holland Tunnel to Route 139, and then to Route 7," he demonstrated as he highlighted the new route in blue ink. "From 7, I would go to Route 508, to Route 21, straight to U.S. Route 1. Then just follow Route 1 into Pennsylvania, crossing the Delaware River here," he drew an "X" as he tapped the marker on the map while continuing, "at Calhoun Street. Then take that to U.S. Route 13, which would put me in the heart of Philadelphia, where I could launch an attack on City Hall from South Penn Square. With that distraction, I could have one force take City Hall, and then the rest of the troops would be able to enter the city at the Franklin Bridge. Victory would be within our grasp."

Max smiled, but said nothing. He was reveling in Sharpe's genius. He let out a soft chuckle.

"What is it?" Sharpe asked.

"Let's go, General. I want to address the men before you leave at thirteen hundred."

Sharpe, puzzled, asked, "But what is so funny?"

"Nothing," Max answered. "I want you to call me as soon as you and the men dock at Camden. That is an order, General. Am I clear?"

"Absolutely, Sir," Sharpe confirmed with a salute. "But why?"

"I don't report to you, General. You report to me."

* * *

"Thank you for taking the time to have lunch with me, Jack," Roxy said as she showed Armstrong into the dining room. The table was set for three, but the bread crumbs on one of the plates told Armstrong that their third had already eaten.

"I'm sure it was good," he said pointing at the used plate.

Embarrassed, Roxy explained, "Zach couldn't wait. Peanut butter and jelly is his favorite. He keeps going out there to shoot that damned bow and arrow." She craned her neck toward the terrace. Armstrong's eyes followed the motion through the glass terrace door to find Zach pulling the bowstring and aiming his arrow at the target. Almost simultaneous to Zach's release, the sound of the arrow piercing the target could be heard through the door; it was like seeing a thunderbolt.

"He seems to be good at it."

"That's all he does these days, Jack. Max says it's his way of blowing off steam, and that it's just a phase. He's thirteen, now. Shouldn't he be blowing off steam with girls?"

"In all fairness to the boy, Roxy, it's not his fault. We can't risk his security by letting him out into the world. Max is right. It's just a phase. When all this is over, he'll be a regular Casanova. Don't worry."

"I know. It's just frustrating that we can't live normal

lives."

Armstrong nodded as he took his seat at the table; he neatly placed the napkin in his lap exhibiting perfect manners. Roxy retired to the kitchen to retrieve the lasagna tray from the oven. "Is that what this lunch is all about?" he asked.

Roxy was unsure of the answer herself. More than anything, she was lonely and wanted someone to talk with. Max was working long hours, and while he was honoring his pledge to be attentive to his family, he spent most of his time mentoring Zach; Roxy was beginning to feel unappreciated, but she was unsure how to tell Max. Armstrong would know. "Sort of," she said as she brought the lasagna tray to the table. She cut a square with spatula and served Armstrong. After taking a piece for herself, she continued, "How is Max doing?"

"He's okay," Armstrong assured her. "This thing with Thomas is getting to him." He ate a forkful of the lasagna. "Wow! This is delicious!"

"Thank you," Roxy coyly replied. "I wouldn't know, you know?"

"You wouldn't know what?" Armstrong asked as he chewed his food. His uncharacteristic rudeness caught her by surprise.

"About this Thomas thing. Max doesn't really talk to me about it."

"He probably figures that it would upset you. He'll tell you when he's ready."

"Will he, Jack? You know him. He can bottle up his true feelings better than anyone. Look at his marriage to Valerie. Did he ever complain about how miserable he was?"

Armstrong searched his memory. "You have a point."

"I need to get him to talk to me. I need him to know

that I am here for him."

"I don't know what you want me to say, Roxy. He's his own man."

"Cut the bullshit with me, Jack," she crossly demanded. "He's what you and Bob made him! And since Bob is dead, that means only you know how to get through to him."

Armstrong put down his fork and wiped his mouth with the napkin. "I'm a political advisor, Roxy, not a marriage counselor. What I do know about him is that he can be as cold-hearted as his father, and as stubborn and short-tempered as Bob. Put it together, and you never know what will set him off." He could see a tear well up in Roxy's eye. "But he can also be as kind and gentle as any man alive. That is his saving grace." He stood and began to make his way toward the front door, leaving the rest of his lunch uneaten on the plate, when he turned and said, "Just be honest with him. Tell him how you feel and take whatever reaction comes your way. But remember that no matter what he says, he loves you and will do anything for you."

"Are you sure?"

Armstrong took a brief moment and thought about the proper answer. "He never looked at Valerie the way he looks at you."

* * *

"We are told that President Noble has finished his address to the troops," Susan explained to the SBN audience in her trademark red glasses. Among the viewers were Sultan and his men, Harmon included. "It is clear that there is a military operation underway, but no one, not even the troops are talking about it."

The image on the main screen in the Hub cut from the beautiful Susan Teller to a scruffy, unshaven man with a machine gun hanging from a strap over his shoulder as he marched with his comrades. "We're taking this fight to the enemy, Ma'am," he said. "We don't know where or when it will be, but Americans can rest assured that every man in this army is ready."

"General Sharpe hasn't told you about the mission? Isn't that unusual?" Susan asked him, walking quickly to keep up with the troops' pace.

"A little," he answered honestly. "But we have full faith in the general and the President. They've proven that they know what we have to do. It's up to us soldiers to execute."

"What did the President say to the troops?"

A tear came to the soldier's eye. "He reminded us what we're fighting for."

Susan compassionately asked, "What is that?"

"Everything that the people who died here at Ground Zero lost out on," he answered. "It was the most beautiful and inspiring speech I ever heard. I speak for all of the men when I say that we are ready to do America proud."

The screen image cut back to Susan. "There you have it, ladies and gentlemen. America's bravest are off to fight again. General Sharpe led them from New York a few short hours ago. To where, is anyone's guess. Reporting live from Ground Zero, I'm Susan Teller, SBN News."

The screen image cut back to the SBN anchor desk. Sultan pushed a button, and the screen went entirely black. "So, they are going to attack again," he said.

"It would seem that way," Harmon retorted.

"Do you still believe that they will attack Philadelphia, General?" Sultan nervously asked.

"Indeed," Harmon replied. "It is the only logical choice. And Sharpe is a conventional thinker."

Sultan stroked his beard for a moment. He thought of the plan Harmon suggested weeks earlier in his office. "Alert our men in Philadelphia that they will be the target of an attack. Then order half of our Boston battalion to head to New York. We will crush their attack and take back what is ours."

"You do not have the intelligence you once did," Harmon cautioned. "You would be wiser to focus the effort on Philadelphia. Once you have fended off the attack you can advance on New York with your Philadelphia troops from the south, and then reinforce them with the Boston troops from the east. Given the change in circumstances, fighting on two fronts at the same time, now, is too great a risk."

"Not for my men, General. They are Allah's warriors. He will protect them."

"If you are wrong, if he doesn't and Philadelphia falls, Washington will be next. Sharpe will have the momentum, and he will gain troops, food and supplies from a victory."

"So be it, General. My orders stand."

CHAPTER 25

The council meetings nauseated Max to the point where he had almost decided to stop attending them. He could only bear so much mudslinging, and despite his ballooning popularity among the American people, the undecided council members were slowly beginning to intimate that they were leaning toward casting their votes for Thomas. The charges levied against him could not be further from the truth, and were clearly crafted by a political veteran whose successes were defined by personally humiliating his opponents; Thomas' fingerprints were all over them. The claim that Max intentionally allowed Sultan to destroy Chicago to eliminate Thomas as his competition particularly irked him. While he could have silenced the debate through filibusters and other parliamentary stalling tactics, he chose instead to let Thomas wage his war of words. Armstrong and Bard were holed up in Armstrong's office hard at work on Max's responses for several days. He knew that he would have his chance to strike back, and patience was his strategy. Thomas would have the opportunity to make all the claims in the world, and Max would dismiss each one of them before stating his own case. That way, Thomas would not be able to react. Indeed, he fathomed, patience would pay off. In the meantime, he could only tolerate the tripe and hope that the damage Thomas did to him with the undecided council members would not be irreversible.

It had been three days since Sharpe left New York with the army. Max was anxiously awaiting his call from Camden to say that the attack on Philadelphia was imminent. However, he kept that to himself as he sat through another painful council meeting. When it finally ended by a majority vote to take a recess for the day, Max made his way up to Armstrong's office to check on his and Bard's progress. He heard the two of them arguing through the door; sleep deprivation made both Armstrong and Bard irritable.

"How's it going?" Max asked as he barged in without knocking.

"He wants you to draw a comparison between what happened to Chicago and the events of September eleventh!" Armstrong exclaimed in outrage. "Thomas is hammering you on the Chicago incident! We can't even mention it, or else we are playing into his hands!"

"I told you, the President is a New Yorker who survived nine-eleven," Bard countered. "Thomas was nowhere near New York when it happened. It makes the case that the President is more experienced than Thomas to deal with the aftermath."

"No, it doesn't!" Armstrong shouted. "It makes the case that this vote is all about Chicago, and that's exactly what Thomas wants!"

"If I may," Max interjected. "Why don't we just stick with the recapturing of New York and leave Chicago out of it?"

"Ha! I told you!" Armstrong gloated.

"Fine! Three days' work down the drain, and for what?" Bard cried. "If you don't like what I have to say, then write your goddamned speech yourself!"

"I heard that, Bard!" Morris announced from his office next door; the walls were apparently paper-thin. "Quit on him and you can find yourself a new job!"

"Damn it!" Bard said as he sulked in his chair.

"Sorry, sir. I was just letting off some steam!" he cried so that Morris would know he had no intention of actually leaving.

"David, it's been a long couple of days," Max said. "Why don't you go home for the night and start fresh in the morning?"

"That sounds like a good idea," Bard concurred. "My wife is beginning to forget what I look like."

"So is mine," Max said.

"More than you know," Armstrong added.

"What does that mean?" Max asked.

Armstrong, realizing that he should not have said anything at all, answered, "Nothing. Nothing. You should just talk to her sooner rather than later, that's all."

"Okay, I will first chance I get," Max promised.

"Well, gentlemen, I'll see you both in the morning," Bard said as he left the room closing the office door behind him.

"Good night," Max and Armstrong offered simultaneously.

"I'm getting killed in those meetings, Jack," Max said softly when Bard was safely out of earshot. "Am I in trouble, or what?"

"It's not looking good," Armstrong offered. "We need Sharpe to deliver Philadelphia quickly."

"It's not looking good," Max retorted. The sarcasm drew a wince from Armstrong.

Suddenly, there was knock on the door. "Come in," Armstrong called.

It was Barrington. He saluted Max as he walked in, and remained frozen in the pose until Max returned the honor. "We have a developing situation, Mr. President," he announced.

"What is it?" Max asked.

"Luftenant Youseff led a scout team to Hartford, Connecticut," Barrington reported, again using the British pronunciation of Hank's rank to Max's chagrin, "and has reported a mass migration of the enemy's soldiers heading west. We assume that they are on their way here."

"Mass migration?" Armstrong asked.

"Yes, Mr. Armstrong," the British colonel said. "It seems that as many as fifty thousand men are heading this way."

"Fifty thousand?!" Max asked, astonished. "Where did they come from?"

"Somewhere in the east, sir," Barrington replied. "I would assume Boston, as the enemy has a garrison there. Although," the colonel admitted, "we cannot rule out the possibility that the enemy dispatched them from a southerly city in an effort to hide their attack."

"Can we hold them off?" Max asked.

"We will defend strategic positions," Barrington explained. "Specifically, we will do everything we can to defend the bridges in northern Manhattan. But, truthfully sir, we are greatly outnumbered. I cannot say for how long we will be able to maintain our control on the situation."

"Very well," Max resigned. "Do your best, Colonel. That is all that I can ask." Turning to Armstrong, he said, "Well, Jack, it looks like we've got bigger problems than Thomas once again."

* * *

Rain pelted Sharpe from above as he stood atop a hill overlooking the Delaware River. Violent thunderstorms were causing flooding from Toronto to Washington, making certain main roads impassable; the river's rapids raged from the resulting runoff. It took just over three days to reach Washington's Crossing State Park, and Sharpe's men were thoroughly exhausted. They set up tents in which to camp; they would need at least two days to recover from their trek. That much was irrelevant, as Gonzo had not yet arrived with the supplies from the Canadians, which included the rafts. Fortunately, he called to report that the delivery was being delayed by the inclement weather and not for any other reason.

His gaze fixed on the cresting river and his mind mesmerized by the sound of the large rain drops impacting the saturated ground, Sharpe thought of the task ahead. Casualties would be heavy, and the thought of young men, boys in some cases, perishing from his orders chilled him more than the continuous rain. Preserving freedom is the central theme of every American military cause in history; some, like the Revolutionary War, the Civil War and the World Wars, were worthwhile. Others, like the Korean War, the Vietnam War and the Iraq War, were not. He could not believe that it was mere coincidence that the wars formally declared by Congress and supported by the American people led to overwhelming victory, while those imposed upon the people by zealous presidents led to humiliation and paralysis for the nation. This war was different. It was thrust upon the people; it was declared neither by Congress nor a president. While the cause was enjoying widespread support since the victory in New York that support did not translate into very many more troops weapons or other basic supplies the military needed. Sharpe knew that victory would require men from all over the country to join the cause; his battalion from Long Island could not do it alone. Victory at Philadelphia would provide a rallying cry, and would allow them to recruit more men to the cause. Secretly, he was beginning to doubt that victory was possible. Casualties would be heavy, and young boys and men would surely die under his command. Not even the sudden cessation of the rain and the rays of sun that broke through the clouds could remove that chill from his body.

So lost in thought was he that he did not hear Chatty approach from behind. "General, the men have set up camp and await orders," the colonel said.

"Tell them to relax for a couple of days," Sharpe said keeping his gaze fixed on the river. The roar of the rapids had a soothing melody. "Major Gonzalez was delayed by the storms. We move out when he arrives. In the meantime, tell them to enjoy the serenity of this place," he said, turning to Chatty while holding his arms out to the sides so that they pointed to the river and the open fields in the park.

"Perhaps they could use some recreational games tomorrow to keep their morale high, sir?" Chatty suggested.

Sharpe glanced at the bottom of the hill where the troops had set their tents. Some of the younger men were horsing around and mud-sliding. Their laughter echoed in his ears. "Perhaps," the general agreed.

* * *

Thomas stormed into the SBN Newsroom with several council members in tow. Among them were Walter Straight of Indiana, who was Thomas' nominator and greatest supporter; Christine Davenport of Iowa, another staunch Thomas supporter; and Jim Parker of Virginia, who up until this moment was believed to have been undecided between the candidates. "Noble!" Thomas called. "Noble, where the hell are you?"

Armstrong emerged from his office and immediately confronted the Illinois governor and his entourage. "This area is restricted, Governor. What can I do for you?"

"Where is he, Jack?" Thomas demanded. "I have a bone to pick with him."

"That's been apparent since you got here," Armstrong

retorted. "Why don't you pick it with me for right now, and I'll have him get back to you as soon as his schedule clears up?"

"I told you that he'd send his lapdog to do his dirty work," Straight chided. Armstrong's face turned red as his blood pressure rose, and he bit his lip. "What's the matter, Jack? Are the realities of your job getting to you?" Straight pressed.

"The only part of this job that I can't stand is dealing with trailer trash like you, Walter," Armstrong blasted.

"There's a reason we never elected you to be the DNC Chairman, Jack," Straight began. "You take everything too personally."

"That's enough, Walter," Thomas interjected. "Why did he cancel this morning's council meeting, Jack? Is he afraid that he's going to lose the vote?"

"He's dealing with a problem right now, Governor," Armstrong explained. "It's not going to be resolved easily."

"Jack, if there's a problem, don't we have a right to know about it?" Parker asked. "After all, we represent the American people."

"It's not that simple, Jim," Armstrong pleaded. "This problem is currently classified. When the President feels that it is time to declassify the information, you'll be fully briefed."

"That's a bunch of hooey!" Davenport challenged. "Tell that coward that if he doesn't answer to the council within the next thirty minutes, then I'm calling the question!" she declared, employing the parliamentary terminology that would end the debate over the candidates and move the proceedings to a vote.

Max appeared from the doorway of Armstrong's office flexing his weakened left arm; the bags under his eyes were dark and puffy. He looked as if he aged twenty years. "We're about to be attacked," he said.

At first, Thomas and his people froze. They had not counted on Max's presence, and had only intended to create a scene as a means of forcing Max to reconvene the council. The news he gave them was entirely unexpected. "I thought you said that New York had been secured," Thomas challenged. "If you were up to the challenge of being President, you would have been prepared for this."

Remembering all of the books on leadership that Armstrong made him read, Max sensed a weakness in his opponent. He realized that Thomas could not offer any solution to the problem at hand; Thomas' only strategy, as it had been all along, was to lash out at Max in hopes that he could create personal gains. Thomas embodied the antithesis of every leadership quality Max read about. The opportunity to eliminate him as a threat had to be seized. "Fifty thousand of the enemy's troops are on their way here, and all we have to defend this city are two thousand British troops. No one has heard from General Sharpe since he left for our next offensive campaign. And now – now! – you're going to stand there and lecture me?" "We represent the American people, and we . . ." Parker started.

"Have a right to know what's going on," Max finished his sentence. "I know. I get it. I really do. But, Jim, you have got to understand that while we're wasting our time on this debate over my qualifications our enemy is preparing our slaughter. Our top priority has to be fortifying the city, not debating who should lead a government that will be irrelevant if the city falls to the enemy again."

"I don't believe a word of this," Davenport announced. "You're just trying to scare us into putting this vote off for as long as you can," she charged. "If this is really going to happen, why haven't you evacuated us? Isn't our safety just as important as yours?"

She struck a nerve, and Max could no longer contain

his rage. "Listen to yourself! You're ready to skip town!" he chastised. "Who's the coward now?" He approached Thomas so that their faces were inches apart, and looked him directly in the eyes. His stare was practically lethal; if he could get this close to Sultan, the war would be over. "You want this job? You can have it when I'm dead, and only then, if someone else lets you. For now, it's mine and I'm not lettin' go! You want a council meeting today? Fine! Let's have a meeting today. Jack, tell all the council members that we're meeting at noon." His eyes never left Thomas'. "And make sure they know that this meeting will break with the agenda. No debate today. Instead, I'll be briefing them about the upcoming battle that we're about to face. And I promise you this," he said shaking his head at Thomas, "I'll be here to fight, that's for sure – no matter where you and your cowardly crew may be, Governor."

Thomas backed away from Max. Less than confidently, he said, "Noon, it is, then. We'll be there."

"Reporting to the council is the right thing to do, that's all," Parker commented. He joined Thomas, Straight and Davenport as they left the SBN Newsroom. They got onto the elevator, and as the door closed, everyone present in the SBN Newsroom who witnessed the exchange applauded and stood to pay homage to their President.

"That was a thing of beauty, Mr. President," Armstrong offered.

"Thanks, Jack," Max replied. "Now we need a speech on two hours' notice. Has anyone seen Bard?"

* * *

Bard was running through the hall clutching a stack of papers to his chest when the intern accidentally knocked into him causing the papers to fly everywhere as Bard tumbled to the floor. His glasses atilt, Bard scowled at the young man but said nothing. He hurriedly gathered the papers, without taking a moment to place them in any discernable order, and continued his sprint to the engineer's booth. His entrance was unnoticed as it was lost in the commotion. "Jack! Jack! Where's Jack?" Bard timidly asked; no one answered. Finally, he spotted Armstrong against the side wall, hidden by Morris' obese profile. "Jack, I have the pages you asked for," he said offering Armstrong the stack of crumpled papers.

"I hope you gave the President cleaner copies," Morris said pointing to the wrinkled pages.

"Of course, Mr. Morris," Bard assured him. "These are for Jack to follow along. Sorry about the condition. I had a slight misstep in the hall."

"There's no page numbers here, David," Armstrong complained flipping through the pages. He tried to match the sentences from page to page to determine their sequence. "They're completely out of order."

"We're on in ten seconds people!" the director called. The room grew silent as he counted down. "A-a-a-and, cue camera one . . . now!"

Susan appeared on the screen at the news desk in her signature red-rimmed glasses. "Good afternoon," she began. "This is Susan Teller with an exclusive SBN News special report. After cancelling this morning's council session, as SBN reported earlier, President Noble suddenly reconvened the council only moments ago. Unlike the council sessions we have recently been covering, today's session will break from the agenda. There will be no debate about the impending vote to determine if President Noble or Governor Thomas should lead the nation through these trying times. Instead, we are told that the President will be addressing the council about an emergency situation." She touched her finger to the earpiece in her right ear. "I have just been informed that the President has taken the podium. We now join the council session for his remarks."

The screen cut to the auditorium where the council convened. Max stood behind the podium in a blue suit with a light blue shirt and his favorite red and white-striped tie. The make-up caked on his face hid the lines that had formed from the stress of his job; it also hid the black, puffy bags under his eyes. His hair was molded perfectly to his scalp, which was no surprise considering the enormous amount of hairspray the cosmetics crew used to prepare him for the speech. He looked handsome and charming. He looked presidential.

When the tepid applause subsided, Max began, "Thank you. Thank you. It's not often that we, as individuals, have an opportunity to reflect on how we arrived at our positions in life. Some people are fortunate, and have the means to follow in the footsteps of family members who came before them. Some people are less fortunate, and are forced to struggle merely to maintain their existence. I can admit that I was a fortunate son. My father was a media mogul. The world was to be my oyster.

"But my father rejected me. Instead of allowing me to follow in his footsteps, he forced me to struggle. I hated him for it. In the end, I became a media mogul, too, but in my own right. And although I should have been thankful that I arrived at the same position, every day I looked in the mirror to ask myself, 'Was it worth the struggle to follow in my father's footsteps?' My answer was, 'No, it was not.' I looked around and saw people who needed someone to fight for them. And I knew that I had a duty to use my position to fight on their behalf. So, I ran for Congress to fight for others. Sadly, I never got the opportunity to fight for them in Congress. And now, I stand before you today fighting for our country's survival.

"You see, there comes a time, ladies and gentlemen, when we must ask ourselves, 'What is it that we are fighting for?' The freedoms that we once enjoyed are worth fighting for. For that, I am willing to lay my life on the line. No other man or woman in this room has taken up arms against Sultan as I have. Yet, at least one of you suggests that I am not qualified to lead this country. Well, in a matter of days – if not hours – we will find out who is better qualified to lead this nation. You see, our enemy is sending troops this way to attempt to recapture this city."

The crowd gasped in unison and a murmur broke out.

"But that won't happen! Americans will not allow it! Now, I will lead all those who are willing to fight here in New York. I urge Americans all across the land to ask yourselves, 'What is it that you are willing to fight for?' I am fighting for you. But are you willing to fight for me? If the answer is, 'Yes,' then I have no doubt that we will be victorious. Our belief in our right to freedom and self-governance is greater than any belief our enemy possesses. Together, we must rise up! The time has come for the American people to answer the call. It is time to take the fight to the enemy! We can no longer sit idly by! Join me in the fight for our freedom!"

Applause filled the room.

"Ladies and gentlemen, I called you here today to tell you that this may well be our last stand. Before that happens, let us unite and end this debate as to our leadership now. Let us call the question. And so I ask, is there such a motion on the floor?"

"Motion!" Hack shouted.

"The chair recognizes the distinguished gentleman from New York," Max announced. "Is there a second?"

"Second!" Davenport called.

"The chair recognizes the distinguished gentlewoman from Iowa," Max said. "We are now in a vote for the chairmanship of this council. I will call the roll, and you must answer either, 'Noble,' 'Thomas,' or 'Abstain.' A majority of the votes is required to declare a winner."

Susan's voice cut in over the picture of the auditorium chamber as Max read the roll. "There you have it, ladies and gentlemen. President Noble has thrown down the political gauntlet. In a matter of moments, we will know if it will spell the end of his political career. Of course, we cannot overlook the fact that despite the outcome of this vote, he called upon Americans to lay their lives on the line the way he has his. Will it be enough to stop the impending attack on New York? Will it be enough to conquer Sultan and his invaders? Only time will tell, but for now we will see if this ad hoc council of Americans supports this war by choosing to retain President Noble as its chairman, or if it seeks a different solution under the leadership of Governor Thomas."

Max continued to call the roll. After he said each state's name into the microphone, its representative publicly announced for whom he or she was voting. Parker was asked to keep the official tally. After he called Wyoming, Max asked, "Mr. Parker, what is the final tally?"

Parker cleared his throat. "Abstain, five. Thomas, ten. Noble, thirty-five."

CHAPTER 26

Sultan paced on the floor of the Hub. His men were nervously awaiting his orders. SBN continued its coverage of the council vote on the main screen; Susan was interviewing several talking heads about what Max's victory would mean for the country. Each time she said, "President Noble," Sultan grew more cross. The mere mention of Max's name reminded him of Emir. He could not quell his need to avenge his brother's death, and his men were beginning to secretly wonder if it was clouding his judgment.

Harmon observed the room from the top of the stairs. His eyes fixated on Sultan, sweeping back and forth with his movements. He, too, was wary of Sultan's motives, not because he cared what they were, but rather because Max had issued a call to arms, which would undoubtedly intensify the war and test Sultan's resolve. If it wavered, Harmon knew that the Americans would rake him over the coals for answers into Sultan's whereabouts. The presumption, of course, was that Sultan would allow him to live.

Indeed, the game was changing, and although Harmon was confident that Sultan positioned his pieces well, any misstep could cause the defense to collapse and provide Sharpe an opportunity on which to capitalize. While Sultan may have dismissed Sharpe as a fool, Harmon knew that to do so was dangerous. Sharpe was worthy of the rank of general; the only reason he had been denied it was Harmon's doing. The wounds from Vietnam never healed.

Sultan stopped pacing and paused for a moment, staring down his men and instilling fear into them, before calling to Harmon to ask, "Why does he try to defy me, General?"

Harmon did not hesitate. "He feels a duty to serve, Sultan, as if it is his responsibility to protect the American citizens."

"They praise him for it, don't they?" Sultan asked.

"Most definitely," Harmon confirmed. "He's a national hero."

"Hero?" Sultan asked, perturbed. "That man murders my brother, and they call him a hero? I bomb their infrastructure, and they call him a hero? We must unleash the wrath of Allah upon them, and then we'll see how much of a hero he is!"

"Be careful, Sultan," Harmon cautioned. "You're losing your focus. You have him with his back to the wall. This little speech wasn't about some council's vote. It was a desperate cry for help. Somehow he found out about the Boston troops heading to New York, and with Sharpe on his way to Philadelphia, Noble is stuck in New York without any protection. He is as vulnerable now as he ever will be. Your opportunity to strike will never be greater."

Sultan nodded in agreement, but wondered, "What about this cry? Will they hear it in other cities and feel compelled to help?"

"They may," Harmon conceded. "But if you trained your men properly, they will be able to withstand a minor resistance from a few zealous Americans. Violence will engulf the country, and they will quickly relent. It will be exactly what happened in Iraq, only now you are playing the role of the occupiers."

Sultan grinned from ear to ear. He turned to his men and ordered in Arabic, "We take back New York tomorrow at sunrise! Send word to our men!"

* * *

Even several hours in the strong sun could not dry the ground completely. Sharpe's men were covered in mud from head to toe. Some were the victims of tackles in one of the many football games that were ongoing; others partook in games of "ultimate Frisbee;" and some were competing to determine the best mud slider. Their laughter soothed Sharpe in this time of war. He had almost forgotten how important recreational time was for the company's morale.

"General!" Chatty called as he and Williams ran over from the sidelines of one of the football games. "General," he panted, "I've been scanning all known frequencies for enemy signals, and I just came across this." He held up a pocket-sized tape recorder and pushed the "Play" button. A faint voice could be heard through the heavy static; it was speaking in Arabic.

"What's he saying?" Sharpe asked.

"It says, 'Red Crescent! Red Crescent!'" Williams said drawing on his experience in special operations in Iraq where he learned Arabic. "Allah has revealed his will to Sultan . . . Avenge Emir . . . Take Noble alive . . . Our Man says to go at dawn . . . ."

Sharpe was stunned. He knew that his current mission had its risks; however, he had hoped that it would draw attention away from New York and Max. It was apparent that he failed in that regard. "We need to warn the President," he said. "Get word to Colonel Barrington immediately that the attack will come at dawn."

"Yes, sir," Chatty answered.

"Where is Major Gonzalez?" Sharpe asked.

"Last he reported he was about an hour away," Williams said. "He should be here shortly."

"Tell the men that fun time is over," Sharpe ordered.

"I want them all to rest for the remainder of the day. Tell them to nap if they can. They are to report to the river at dusk." He looked down at the men in the field. Their faces were perfectly blackened from the mud. "Make sure they do not wash up. They're perfectly camouflaged for a nighttime operation."

* * *

Zach had been practicing his archery on the balcony for nearly an hour. It was his only escape from the argument Roxy and Max were carrying on in the apartment. The more they argued, the greater the intensity of the speed of his arrows. His aim was becoming nearly perfect, and he repeatedly hit the center of the target. When he finished firing the arrows, he pulled them from the target and repeated the exercise robotically.

Boots, Bam Bam and the Peach joined him on the terrace; they knew it was not their place to intervene on Max's behalf in this case. They sat around the patio table playing cards. They tried to focus on the sound of Zach's arrows cutting through the high-rise air instead of the muffled shouts that were seeping through the glass doors to the apartment. From what they could gather, this fight was about how Roxy felt like Max was ignoring her; she wanted him to do his job, but also be an attentive husband. He admitted he was having difficulty balancing the two responsibilities. The argument spiraled out of control from there.

Zach grew angrier as the argument drew on. When he finished his latest round of arrows, he finally asked, "Why are they fighting like that?" The question was posed to any of them that would answer.

Awkwardly, the three men looked at each other. Bam Bam was the oldest and was married the longest, but he did not have any children, and so he was unsure how to answer the youth. The Peach had never been in a meaningful relationship, and was equally unqualified to answer. Boots, who was happily married and the father of two young boys, nodded to his colleagues to affirm that he would answer the question. He said to Zach, "Sometimes married people have to fight like that so that they remember how much they really love each other."

"But she's yelling at him like she hates him, right now," Zach said confused.

"That's nothing," Bam Bam said. "You should hear my wife yell at me when she gets mad. You'd think that the neighbors would have called the cops on her by now."

"Yeah," Boots added, "and my wife can yell at me pretty loudly, too."

"Then why did you marry them?" Zach asked Boots and Bam Bam.

"Love is a funny thing," Boots explained. "Even though our wives fight with us, they do it because they love us. If we were ever in trouble, they would be the first ones there to help us and protect us."

"What about you, Peach?" Zach questioned.

"I can handle myself," the Peach answered defiantly. "You don't always need a woman to nag you like that."

"Don't listen to him, Little Man," Bam Bam urged. "He's just bitter because he can't find a girl to suck his dick on a regular basis!"

"Ahem!" Boots interrupted.

"Oh, don't give me that shit, Boots!" Bam Bam protested. "The kid's a teenager now. He's old enough to hear about girls suckin' dick!"

"For the record," the Peach commented, "I get plenty of girls to suck my dick!"

"Yeah, but you can't find one to do it every night!" Bam Bam argued.

"Why would a girl do that?" Zach wondered.

"Okay," Boots said. "I think that's a question for you to ask your father."

"You mean Max?" Zach asked.

"Yeah," Boots confirmed. The conversation was suddenly interrupted by the ring of his cell phone. He answered the call. "Yeah, go ahead," he said into the phone. "Hold on." He sprang up and ran into the apartment. He ignored Max and Roxy, who were continuing the argument in the bedroom, and headed for the front door, which he opened. Armstrong and Barrington were standing in the hallway with harried looks on their faces.

"Where is he?" Armstrong asked.

"In the bedroom," Boots said. The two guests entered the apartment and followed the sounds of Max's shouting. Armstrong knocked on the door, and without waiting for an answer pushed it open.

Max was in mid-sentence when they walked in. "I've told you fourteen times already that I'm doing the best I can!" he yelled at his wife. Noticing the intrusion, he shouted at Armstrong, "What is it?!"

"Sorry to interrupt, Mr. President," Armstrong apologized. "Roxy, I'm sorry we had to intrude."

"It's fine," Roxy said in a huff. "I'm used to getting treated like a second class citizen to you guys."

"I promise you, this concerns you, too," Armstrong offered in an attempt to ease her pain.

"Whatever," she responded wiping tears from her face.

"What is it, Jack," Max calmly asked.

"We've received a message from a . . . Captain Williams," Barrington reported after checking his notes.

"Williams?" Max questioned. "Is everything alright?

Where's General Sharpe?"

"They've intercepted an enemy communiqué," Barrington explained. "The enemy intends to invade this city at dawn. They have orders to capture you alive."

"What about my family?" Max asked looking at Roxy with concern.

"They are in grave danger," the colonel replied. "General Sharpe is launching his attack at dusk. He should be in position to begin his assault on Philadelphia by morning."

Max sat on the bed. His shoulders slumped as he placed his head in his hands. "Is that all?" he asked.

"No, sir," Barrington answered.

Max looked at him hoping that he was kidding. "What else, then?"

"The weather forecast shows a hurricane has formed in the middle of the Atlantic," Armstrong said. "It is heading straight for Philadelphia and should make landfall as a category three or four storm."

"When?" Max asked.

"It formed quite suddenly, sir," Barrington added. "No one saw it coming until about an hour ago, and it's moving rather rapidly."

"When will it make landfall, Colonel?" Max sternly asked.

"At approximately seven hundred hours tomorrow, sir," Barrington answered.

"Does Sharpe know?" Max queried.

"No," Armstrong said. "He doesn't. And we can't get word to him without risking revealing his position."

Max looked at Roxy. His stomach was churning and she could see the pain caused by acid reflux on his face. He didn't say anything. "Do what you have to do," she said with an air of disgust. "We'll finish this discussion later."

"Thank you," Max said feeling slightly relieved that she understood. "I love you."

"I love you, too," she said.

Max looked passed Armstrong and Barrington at Boots. "Can you guys fight?" he asked.

"Honestly?" Boots asked.

"Yeah, honestly," Max said.

"Not really. Maybe Peach can, but Bam Bam is still on crutches and I can't lift my shoulder yet. Docs say we're about three weeks away from being fully recovered."

Max shook his head. He understood. His own left arm was practically useless. He could flex it, but he had difficult gripping things with his left hand without pain. Nonetheless, duty called him. "Very well. I want you three to take Roxy and Zach back to the house on Long Island immediately. They must be kept safe and alive, no matter what." He turned his attention to Barrington. "I'll meet you and your men at the toll plaza to the Triboro Bridge at four hundred hours," he ordered, using the bridge's original name; he was not yet in the habit of using its new moniker, the "Robert F. Kennedy Bridge."

"Yes, sir," Barrington said.

"We'll start packing," Roxy said.

"Rox," Max said softly. "I promise you that we'll finish this discussion."

She approached Max and bent down to him as she kissed his lips lovingly. "I know we will," she said.

* * *

Max went to bed at nine o'clock that night since he set his alarm clock for three o'clock in the morning so that he could meet Barrington an hour later. He tossed and turned in his bed all night long. He was able to fall asleep in small increments, but the day's images flashed through his mind causing him to wake up in a cold sweat. Each time he woke, he sorted through his memory. First, he thought of the elation of confronting and defeating Thomas. Then, he thought of how he went to share the sentiment with Roxy, but how the conversation turned on him quickly. There was the conversation with Armstrong and Barrington about the attack, and then there was the hasty good-bye as his guardians took Roxy and Zach back to his house. Finally, there was the view of the satellite image of Hurricane George, which was churning so powerfully in the midst of the Atlantic Ocean that it had a perfectly formed eye and counter-clockwise rotation. A SBN staffer, who was working the satellite controls so that Max could view the image, commented at the time, "It's becoming so perfect that it could bring the wrath of God wherever it hits."

The staffer's comment, more than anything from the day's events, resonated with Max. As he lay in solitude in his bed in the perfectly quiet apartment, he thought repeatedly about why God would get involved at this point. At midnight, after getting a combined half hour of sleep in the previous three hours, he walked to the window after he woke in his latest cold sweat. "Why would you unleash your wrath on us when we are fighting to free your children?" he cried aloud looking out the window at the nighttime sky. "Whose side are you on, anyway? I hope it's ours. But know this: If you are against me, you aren't going to get me without a fight! Your children, especially my wife and her son, deserve to live in freedom. And I will do *anything* to make sure that they can. Do you hear me? ANYTHING! I'll give you my life so that they can live if I have to!"

There was, of course, no response. No sign appeared; there was not a bright light, or a deep voice, or even a bird to fly by to signify that his plea had not fallen upon deaf ears. Disgusted, Max made his way back into bed and was able to fall asleep until his alarm clock sounded.

Upon waking, he brewed a cup of coffee and quickly scrambled some eggs. He inhaled them like a vacuum. After his rushed breakfast, he showered. Feeling awake, despite the dark night's sky still hiding the day, he dressed, donning the uniform Dalton made for him, including the gun powder satchel containing Dalton's ashes. "Here we go again, Bobby," he commented as he tied it to his belt. He grabbed his sword from its place in his closet, pulled it from its sheath to examine the blade, and once satisfied that it was battle-ready, made his way to the elevator. The time for battle arrived.

The elevator opened and Armstrong was standing in it waiting for Max. Surprised, Max asked, "What are you doing here?"

"You didn't think I was going to send you off to battle without making sure we had everything in place in case the worst should happen, did you?"

"I should have known better old friend."

Armstrong pressed the button for the main floor. "You should have. Your car is waiting for you outside. Barrington's men will take you to him at the bridge. I've contacted Judge Vineri in France to inform him of what's about to happen. I told him that if anything happens to you, he's the new President."

"What did he say about that?"

"He asked that you try not to die," Armstrong deadpanned. "He also asked me to remind you that you should be merciful."

"Of course, he did."

"Now, the council members have been evacuated, and Boots called in to tell us that they got Roxy and Zach home safely. Don Vito and his best men are helping to guard the place. Jimmy also offered the senseis' services."

"I hope you accepted all of their help," Max said.

"Of course we did, Mr. President," Armstrong said as the elevator door opened. They arrived at the ground floor. "They are better protected than you, I'm afraid."

"Thanks, Jack, for everything. You've been a great friend."

"As have you, Mr. President. Now, go kick some ass! I'm not in the mood to plan your funeral just yet," Armstrong said with a smile. "Oh, and by the way, SBN is reporting that there's rioting across the country and Sultan's troops are having difficulty containing the chaos. Looks like your pep talk worked."

Max shook Armstrong's hand. He turned to the three British soldiers standing by the lobby's main door. They saluted him, and he returned the gesture. "Right this way, Mr. President," one of the soldiers said as he led Max to the armored car awaiting him. He boarded the vehicle with the soldiers, and they drove away to rendezvous with Barrington.

* * *

Rafting through the Delaware River proved to be more of an excursion than Sharpe anticipated. The river was swollen and the rapids vicious. Sharpe's raft, in which he was joined by his top commanders including Chatty, Gonzo and Williams, led the way. Many men had difficulty remaining in their rafts; most that fell out were picked up by their comrades in other rafts, but some found themselves left to fend off the rushing waters sans rafts and gear. While Sharpe hoped that they would make it to the river's banks safely, he knew that there must have been some men who were injured from their falls, either from the river's rocky bed or stray tree limbs of decent size that were occasionally carried by the waters, and were not capable of surviving.

By the time they reached the piers at Camden and disembarked onto dry land they were exhausted. It was near dawn, only there were thick clouds covering what should have been a bright sunrise. The wind swirled and howled. Sharpe could barely believe how ferociously the wind whipped through his men, chilling their wet clothes. He expected a tough fight from the enemy's troops, but he did not count on having to fight the elements, too.

"Were you able to reach the President?" Sharpe shouted to Chatty above the howling wind.

"No, sir," Chatty said back. "We can't get a strong enough signal in this weather."

"What are our orders, sir?" Gonzo asked.

The time had come for Sharpe to decide. His commander-in-chief ordered him to report when he reached Camden, but the elements would not allow for it. If he waited for the weather to cooperate, he would risk having his opponent discover their presence. He looked to the clouds in the east and saw that there was a storm approaching. After weighing his options, he decided that the weather was the great equalizer he needed to take the Ben Franklin Bridge. "Prepare your men, Major," he said. "We're going to take that bridge."

"But, sir, shouldn't we wait for the weather to pass?" Gonzo questioned.

"No, Major, we shouldn't," was all Sharpe replied.

* * *

Barrington stationed armored tanks to blockade egress on the bridges leading over the East and Harlem Rivers into northern Manhattan. Each tank had a full complement of artillery shells, and the British colonel supplemented the make-shift barricades with his soldiers. While most were positioned to defend their respective bridge by using the tanks as cover, others took to the heights of the stanchions to act as snipers. Barrington even considered placing guard boats in the Harlem River to protect the bases of the bridges' stanchions. He ultimately determined that to do so would be a waste of his precious manpower, as it was unlikely the enemy would attack the support structures that would collapse the bridges if destroyed; the bridges had to remain intact and structurally sound if the enemy was to utilize them. It was a clever defense, and the only question that remained was how long it could hold.

The sun rose in the east to reveal the enemy caravan approaching in the distance. In the back of a motionless, topless jeep behind the wall of tanks and well out of danger for the time being, Barrington stood and handed Max his pair of binoculars so that he could assess the situation for himself. Max stood at the colonel's side and stared at the approaching horde. Fifty thousand men, all on foot, approached the Triboro Bridge. There was no sign of any portions of the group detaching to head for the other bridges. "Do you think we've spread the defense too thin, Colonel?" Max asked.

"It may appear that way, at first, Mr. President," Barrington answered. "But I assure you that once they face resistance here, they will dissolve into smaller units and attempt to utilize the other bridges. It is at that point that we will realize the benefits of whatever advantage we have."

"Do we have enough men here to repel their attack?" Max wondered aloud.

"We have more than double the number at the other bridges," Barrington confirmed. "Relax, Mr. President, I am descendant from a long line of great military generals. I am not the first of my line to fight here for king and country."

"Oh, yeah," Max said, impressed. "Who was, and

what war was that?"

"The conflict in the colonies, of course," Barrington said with a wry smile. "Perhaps you've heard of General William Howe?"

"Perhaps," Max said, which was a tacit admission at best.

"My mother's maiden name was Howe, and she was his great-great-great-great granddaughter. He defeated your General Washington in the Battle of New York."

It was a barb that only a descendent of British hierarchy would dare make, disparaging George Washington on his own soil. Nonetheless, Max could not afford to distract the colonel with petty squabbling. "Well, let's just hope that you can channel that victorious spirit today," he said semi-sarcastically.

"Indeed, Sir," Barrington replied. He missed the sarcasm, and relished in the instant credentials his familial line brought. He was impressed that Max respected the honor.

A roar exploded from the attacking throng of Sultan's fighters as they yelled in Arabic. They began to run at the ramp leading up to the bridge, chanting mantras the entire way. They fired their guns in the air as they approached.

Barrington grabbed the portable radio from the jeep's console. He spoke into the mouthpiece, "For queen and country, chaps! Triboro tank commanders, fire at will at enemy threat when in range! Repeat: fire at will at enemy threat when in range!"

Sultan's men continued their charge gaining speed and momentum as they neared. Some began firing their weapons on the run; the bullets flew errantly, with some hitting the tanks merely to clang off the metal armor, and others whizzing by, randomly missing everything and everyone. The tanks opened fire with their artillery shells. Several large explosions threw hundreds of maimed attackers flailing through the air. The British soldiers opened fire on their opponents, too. The front lines of Sultan's soldiers fell almost immediately. From the middle of the pack, soldiers screamed frantically, and the bearded army began to retreat. The tanks fired again, and the second round of explosions sent hundreds more of Sultan's soldiers hurtling to their deaths. The survivors regrouped out of the tanks' firing range, and several smaller groups began to break away; as Barrington predicted, they would head for the other bridges.

"Cease fire! Cease fire!" Barrington called over the radio. He looked out at the corpses and maimed bodies strewn across the bridge. "Well done, chaps! Prepare for a second wave, Triboro! Outer bridges, fire at will when the enemy is in range!"

"Very impressive, Colonel," Max offered.

"Thank you, sir," Barrington acknowledged. "But I doubt that they will attempt the direct approach again." The thunderous sound of waves crashing against the base of the bridge stanchions nearly drowned out the sound of Barrington's voice; Hurricane George was churning the waters. Max could not help but wonder about how the storm surge was affecting Sharpe and the attack on Philadelphia.

* * *

The wind's velocity grew, and Sharpe's men began to have difficulty keeping their feet on the ground. If an unexpected gust grabbed them, they were tossed about like rag dolls. The roofs of the warehouses that surrounded the piers were becoming unfastened, and pieces of rippled aluminum and other random lightweight objects like bicycles and boat oars swirled through the air at high speeds. Several men were struck by the unexpected projectiles, some of which became lodged in their bodies like shrapnel. The waves from the storm surge began to pound the bridge stanchions ferociously.

"Tell the men to take cover in that warehouse," Sharpe yelled to his officers over the deafening winds as he pointed to the building closest to the bridge. They nodded affirmatively and began directing their units to the structure. The men ran, fighting the wind and dodging the obstacles it carried, into the warehouse thankful for the little shelter it offered.

"All here, sir," Gonzo reported after catching his breath from his own run. "Now what?"

Sharpe swallowed hard; he, too, was not in prime physical condition as his age was beginning to show. Once he was able to return his heart and breathing rates to a normal level, he said, "We can't wait for this to pass, or else we'll lose whatever advantage the storm gives us."

"With all due respect, sir," Chatty began, "what advantage is that? Right now, it's kicking our ass!"

"Only because we did not anticipate it, Colonel," Sharpe chastised. "But the enemy did not anticipate it, either. I guarantee you that they are not guarding the bridge closely right now, which means that *this* is the moment to strike."

"What do you suggest?" Williams ask.

Sharpe thought for a moment, formulating his plan from scratch. "What supplies do we have?"

"Each man has his M-16 assault rifle, a backpack with additional ammunition, a knife and twelve feet of nylon rope," Gonzo explained.

"Rope?" Sharpe asked. "Good. Have the men tie the ropes around their waists and to the waists of another so that they form groups of ten. Each group's heaviest man will use his rope to anchor to the bridge's lattice work. We'll send them out one at a time so that they can tie their group to a fixed location. Then, the next group will use the anchored groups to help pull them closer to the Philadelphia side of the bridge so they can anchor to it, and so on. When the storm subsides, we'll cut the ropes and be able to charge into the city."

"Won't we meet resistance on the other side of the bridge?" Chatty asked.

"Most definitely," Sharpe responded. "But it will be better than meeting resistance on the bridge itself after the enemy has had the opportunity to reestablish its defensive positions."

"The men are physically drained," one of the unit commanders protested. "They can't sit through a major storm like this on a bridge – which is made of metal and will be a prime candidate to be hit by lightning! This is insane!"

"I beg your pardon, Captain!" Sharpe admonished. "These are your orders, and if you or your men ignore them, I will have you arrested on the spot and you will stand before the President for court martial when he arrives!"

A murmur broke out among the men. They were told that this mission would be carried on without Max's presence, and the mere mention that he was going to be there inspired. "The President is coming?" one of the unit commanders asked.

"Is he bringing reinforcements?" another inquired.

Sharpe had not intended for the suggestion of Max's arrival to have any effect, let alone be an inspiration. Nonetheless, if that was what it took to motivate them, he was not about to risk mutiny. "Yes, gentlemen, the President is leading a second wave of men later today. We must take this bridge by the time he gets here. Prepare to move out!" It mattered little that he lied. If they were victorious, Max would join them in Philadelphia and he would explain to the men that although the President was late, he arrived as promised. If they were not able to take the city, the cause would be lost along with their lives; Max's whereabouts would then be irrelevant.

* * *

Another explosion rocked the Bronx side of the Triboro Bridge. Similar explosions at the other bridges were both visible and audible. Sultan's army was suicidal and relentless. They sent wave after wave of men toward the tanks and barricades. With each advance, the British tanks unloaded their artillery at the attackers. In all, nearly twenty thousand of Sultan's men martyred themselves for Sultan's cause. Thirty thousand remained, but for Barrington the heavy casualties were meaningless. The artillery shells were almost depleted, and it was only a matter of time before Barrington would be forced to consider surrender. He hoped that the enemy would permit it.

"We can only hold off a few more waves, Mr. President," Barrington explained. "I suggest that you evacuate."

"Not on your life, Colonel," Max said indignantly. "How many more rounds do you have?"

"Three shells per tank, sir."

"Use them wisely, Colonel."

Barrington nodded. "Make your shots count, men," he said over the radio. "We don't have a lot of them."

Another wave of Sultan's men advanced only to be met with another round of shelling. The British troops opened fire with their rifles as well. They were determined to take out as many of their assailants as possible. Bodies fell as men screamed. In the enemy's eyes, death was more honorable than life.

"Maintain radio silence," Barrington ordered over the airwaves. "Retreat after firing your final rounds."

Static scratched through the radio followed by a faint, inaudible voice. "I thought I said to maintain radio silence," Barrington said. The static came through again. "Identify yourself, bogie!" he ordered.

"Loo . . . kim . . . seff . . . sir," the voice said.

"Who is this?" the British colonel questioned, frustrated.

Max snatched the radio from Barrington's hand. "Hank? Is that you?" he asked.

"Yes . . . dent . . .," the voice said through the static.

"I didn't copy," Max said. "Hank, is that you?"

"Yes, sir, Mr. President," Hank said. "Our E.T.A. is ten minutes. Hold on, sir."

"E.T.A.?" Barrington asked Max.

"Who are you with?" Max asked over the radio.

"Some new friends, sir," Hank replied. "Just hold the bridges for ten minutes. I promise you, Mr. President, we'll be there."

Turning to Barrington, Max asked, "Can we last for ten minutes?"

"It will be difficult, but we'll try."

Max spoke into the radio. "Listen up, men! This is the President of the United States. You have fought brilliantly today, and we are indebted to you. Now, I need you to fight harder for a little longer. Our friends are on the way. Hold the bridges at all costs."

Barrington took the radio from Max. "Give no ground, men," he ordered. "These bridges are ours."

The enemy sent another wave, and the British troops repelled them with the last of their artillery shells. "That's all we have, Colonel," one of the tank commanders reported.

"Hold your ground!" Barrington answered.

Sultan's men prepared for another advance when an explosion rocked not their front lines, but their rear ones. They were utterly confused, and began to scatter. There was nowhere for them to run. Those who ran toward the bridges were gunned down by the British troops. Those who tried to retreat were killed by the oncoming caravan of cars and trucks with license plates from each of the New England States; they carried Han army. The vehicles in the caravan drove haphazardly through the throng of Arabs. Hank and his men were leaning out the windows of the lead truck with their guns firing randomly into the fleeing troops. Within minutes, the enemy threat was entirely eliminated. British and American casualties were minimal.

The car carrying Barrington and Max approached the caravan. Hank and several men jumped from the lead truck and ran to greet the car. "I told you we'd make it, Mr. President," Hank said.

"I'm glad you did," Max said. "And who are our friends?"

A redheaded man with a thin beard reached out his hand. "Sean Ryan," he said as Max shook his hand.

"Nice to meet you, Mr. Ryan," Max said. "Your country owes you its gratitude."

"Ha!" Ryan laughed. "Get this! The fuckin' President callin' me 'Mr. Ryan!' Now, that's wicked funny!"

"Would you prefer I call you, 'Sean?'"

"No, sir. It's just that we're nothin' more than a bunch of Southies from Boston. Sister Mary Margaret used to call me 'Mr. Ryan,' in the third grade. Otherwise, everyone usually calls me, 'Shithead!'"

"Where are you manners, Shithead?" one of Ryan's comrades, who had blonde hair that was unkempt, asked. "We want to meet the President, too."

"Sorry about that, fuck face," Ryan said. "Mr. President, this is Pat Connelly. That over there is John Murphy," he said pointing to the man who drove the truck, and then, while pointing to a scrawny boy who did not appear a day over the age of sixteen, "and that's his kid brother, Scottie."

"Nice to meet all of you," Max said. "How did you get here?"

"We drove," Scottie said.

"He knows that, you douche!" the elder Murphy admonished.

"Hey! Morons! Let me do the talkin', okay?" Ryan pleaded. "Mr. President, we were hangin' around one day when we saw that half of those Arab bastards just left town. So, since there was half as many, we figured that we'd pick a fight."

"Southies love a good fight," Connelly interjected.

"So, one thing led to another," Ryan continued, "and the next thing we know, the whole city of Boston is bashin' their skulls, and there's no more of those fuckers left! So we went chasin' the rest of them, to see if they wanted a good fight. That's when we ran into Hank. He said he fought with you in New York, and that those Arab fuckers were on their way to take you out. We couldn't let that happen."

"When they arrived in Hartford, Mr. President, I asked them if they knew anyone who wanted to join them," Hank explained. "We spread the word in New England, and here we are."

"How many are you?" Max asked.

"About thirty thousand," Hank answered.

"Thirty thousand, huh?" Max pondered. "Are you ready to keep fighting?"

"Fuck yeah!" Scottie exclaimed.

"That would be a 'yes, sir,' for all of us," Ryan clarified.

"Good," Max said. "Then let's get moving. General Sharpe needs our help in Philadelphia. We can be there in roughly two hours." He paused to assess the damage left by the battle. Satisfied that it was minimal, he said, "I am leaving New York in your capable hands, Colonel Barrington."

* * *

None of Sharpe's men had ever experienced weather as fierce as Hurricane George. The winds blew the rain so hard that it pelted them horizontally. The sea wall from the Delaware River rose high enough to douse them as they tried to tie themselves to the bridge's metallic stanchions. Lightning and thunder abounded, yet for some fortunate reason that defied all scientific laws and principles, it did not strike the bridge. The men struggled for a few hours in those conditions, and it was not a simple task to fight off the wind and the rain but, to their credit, they managed to establish their positions on the bridge as Sharpe ordered. Sultan's men were nowhere in sight.

"All of the men are on the bridge, sir!" Gonzo yelled to Sharpe.

"What?" was all that the general could shout back.

"All of the men are on the bridge, sir!" Gonzo reiterated.

"Good," Sharpe acknowledged holding onto his rope for dear life as the wind struck them head on; fortunately, he was tied to Chatty's mammoth body, which was anchored to the bridge.

"What do we do now, sir?" Chatty asked.

"We wait for the eye of the storm!" Sharpe answered.

* * *

"Keep it steady, Johnny," Ryan said to Murphy when

he nearly lost control of the truck as the caravan entered the Philadelphia city limits. They followed the route that Sharpe outlined in blue ink on the map the general left behind in the trailer at Ground Zero. Max knew all along that it would come in handy; it was not by mistake that he asked Sharpe to outline the route.

"I'm trying, Sean," Murphy replied. "It's not exactly easy to drive this thing in a fuckin' hurricane!"

"Easy, boys," Max pleaded. He had been listening to them pick on each other for just over two hours. "Take this road straight into the center of the city, and when the storm subsides, we'll be able to launch our assault."

The rain pelted the windshield, and although the wipers were furiously working at maximum speed, Murphy was having difficulty seeing the street. The same was true for all of the vehicles; between the lack of visibility and the extremely high winds, it looked as if each was being driven by a drunk. Suddenly, a flash of lightning was accompanied by a rumble of thunder that rocked all of the vehicles. The drivers came to a complete stop so that they could recover their vision before proceeding.

"What the fuck is that?" Scottie asked pointing to something ahead in the road.

Hank opened his window and stuck his head out into the pouring rain. "It's a tree," he reported.

"Great," Max sighed. "Everyone stay here. I'm gonna go have a look."

"But, Mr. President, it's a hurricane out there," Hank protested.

"I know," Max said. "I'll be alright." He opened his door, which was no easy task given the resistance from the wind, and jumped from the cab of the truck. He shielded his face from the rain with his right hand, and kept his useless left hand on the hilt of his sword. He approached the tree to see that it was still smoldering from the lightning strike even though it was being doused by the heavy rain. It was an oak tree, and a large one at that; the size and weight of the wood made it impossible to consider removing it from the road, especially in the current conditions. Frustrated, Max looked up to the sky. "Why?!" he screamed.

Then, through the rumbling of thunder as lightning flashed around him and over the howls of the wind and pummeling of the rain drops on the pavement, Max heard an unfamiliar sound. It was a horse's whinny coming from a shed next to the park across the street. He ran to it and pushed open the door to find a white horse in a stable next to a handsome cab. The beast was obviously affected by the thunder and lightning, and Max approached it with caution. "Easy, big fella," he said as he extended his hand to pat the horse's nose. The animal quickly calmed. "There, there," Max said stroking the horse's mane. "It's okay. It's just a little thunder and lightning." He looked over the beast and noticed that there were markings on its saddle. They were bolts of lightning that surrounded the letter, "Z." "Alright, Zee," Max said as he placed his left foot in the left stirrup. "Let's get out of here."

Max mounted Zee with ease. He placed the reigns in his left hand; it took all of his strength to use the deadened arm and drew his sword from its sheath with his right. "H'yah!" he yelled as he snapped the reigns against the horse's neck, and Zee galloped out of the stable and into the stormy street. Max led him next to the cab of the lead truck before pulling back on the reigns; he winced in pain from exerting his left arm.

Murphy rolled down the driver's window. "We can't move the tree," Max explained. "We're going on foot from here."

"Now?" Ryan called from the front passenger's seat.

"Yes, now!" Max scolded.

"But it's raining!" Connelly protested.

"Are you gonna melt?" Max asked facetiously.

"Guess not," Connelly conceded.

"Then get out here, now! That's an order! You're in my army now!" Max shouted.

"Yes, sir!" they acknowledged in unison. They exited the cab and began to go car to car and knock on the windows to explain what was happening. The New Englanders got out of their vehicles with their weapons at the ready and assembled behind Max and Zee, fighting the wind and the rain the entire time.

"To victory!" Max called raising his sword into the air as lightning flashed through the sky, but did not strike him.

"Victory!" the men cried out raising their guns in the air. Max spun Zee around and led him down the street; the army followed. The oak tree continued to smolder as they passed it.

* * *

The winds died down and the rain began to ease. To the east, the sky was blue and peaceful. The eye of the storm finally arrived.

Exhausted and chilled from the soaking rain, Sharpe's troops knew that the time for their attack had come. They waited for the word. Sharpe watched the clouds pass overhead; he was waiting for the exact moment to set his men loose. Unfortunately, Sultan's men decided to move out sooner.

The gunfire came from the western side of the bridge. Tied to the latticework, the Americans were easy targets. Those who had time to react cut themselves loose and returned fire as best they could. The exchange of gunfire was brutal, and casualties began to mount on both sides.

Sharpe's worst nightmare was coming to fruition; his mistake was costing his men their lives.

An unexpected gust of wind roared from the east across the bridge. It grabbed Sultan's men, pushing them backward. Some of the smaller men were bowled over by its strength. The waters below raged one more time; a great wave rose, crashing on the western side of the span and forcing some of the Arab soldiers off the bridge to their deaths in the river below.

Sharpe responded to the turn of events by ordering his men to charge. They did so with vigor. Bullets raced through the air, and blood began to coat the pavement. After several minutes of exchanging fire, the Americans were able to engage their foes in hand-to-hand combat. They had taken the bridge, and momentum seemed to favor them. However, they were greatly outnumbered, and the enemy was able to hold its ground.

Sharpe saw the stalemate, and ordered his men to reform in ranks. It was an order that confused them more than anything, as they were not versed in regimented combat tactics, and they could do nothing more than fight for their own survival. The general was running out of options.

The situation was tenuous, and Sharpe was in danger of losing the battle of positioning. He could not count on heavy gusts of wind, and he pushed his men to the brink of collapse. He saw himself being remembered as a brilliant general in a losing effort until the white horse appeared on the horizon. It brayed, and its rider, dressed in black and wielding a sword, ordered his army to charge into the enemy ranks.

"He's here!" Chatty hollered. The Americans looked up and saw Max leading the charge, riding Zee into the throng of Sultan's men. He was merciless, using his sword to slice through his adversaries with ease. As Sharpe promised, he brought an army with him.

Sultan's men were caught unprepared for an attack from the west, and their casualties mounted more rapidly than the Americans' as the New Englanders fought with a furor that the Arabs could not match. The surviving few surrendered, not caring that they would be branded cowards. The Americans cheered the overwhelming victory.

Max, his face colored red from his enemies' blood, dismounted Zee, and handed the reins to Williams. He greeted Sharpe with a hug. "You made it!" Sharpe exclaimed.

"Did you ever doubt me?" Max asked sarcastically.

CHAPTER 27

Mohammed Ashwan was all of seventeen years old when Ahmed al-Nabu approached him after Friday prayers at his mosque. Al-Nabu told him that a war was coming that would pit all Muslims against the "infidels," and that it was his duty to join the fight in the name of Allah. Mohammed spent years organizing secret meetings and recruiting boys like him to prepare to fight in Allah's name. Nearly a decade later, he was rewarded for his efforts by being assigned to the communications desk in the Hub. Now, it was his duty to report that they had lost all contact with their men in Boston, including the detachment that was sent to reclaim New York, and their men in Philadelphia.

After discussing the news with each other, Mohammed's cowardly superiors deemed it best for him to deliver the news to Sultan, personally. He knew of Sultan's violent mood swings, and of the negative results they often brought for the bearers of bad news. The lump in his throat grew as he walked down the hall to Sultan's office. His heart raced and he perspired to the point where beads of sweat dripped from his now slimy hands. He swallowed hard when he reached the closed door. From just outside, he could hear Susan Teller's voice lauding the glory of President Noble's twin victories on the television in the office; he hoped that Sultan would not hold him accountable for the news as he knocked on the door.

"What is it?" Sultan, clearly perturbed, hollered.

Mohammed opened the door slowly and ambled into the office. He gently closed the door behind him.

"Great Sultan," he said in Arabic, "we have lost contact with our men in Boston and Philadelphia."

Sultan leaned back in his chair and stroked his beard. Mohammed's eyes were fixed on the gun resting on Sultan's desk. Sultan sensed his trepidation, and a rush overcame him. Nothing thrilled him more than striking fear into a human being. He looked Mohammed up and down several times without saying a word. The young man's apprehension grew with each scan. Until this moment, Sultan tormented millions of people in the United States. Now, his ability to torture was waning, but was not yet gone.

Without warning, Sultan grabbed the gun and squeezed the trigger three times. The bullets tore through Mohammed's chest and shattered the glass in the door to Sultan's office; Mohammed's blood splattered on the door as his body collapsed in a heap.

Harmon opened the door and walked into the office shaking his head at the carcass on the floor, which was oozing blood into a puddle beneath it. "You!" Sultan cried, as he sprang from his chair and raised his gun to Harmon's forehead.

"Now, take it easy, Sultan," the general calmly said. "You're still in command."

"Why is it that every time I listen to you, I am in a worse position?" Sultan grumbled. "You tell me to guard New York's bridges, and they attack us through the train tunnels!"

"That was your brother's fault!" Harmon protested.

Sultan pistol-whipped Harmon across the face knocking him to the ground. "Don't you dare disrespect my brother's memory by trying to blame him for your shortcomings! He didn't tell me to send half of my men from Boston to New York only to have them all fail! He didn't tell me that we would defend Philadelphia easily!

Those words came from you, General!" He paused as he pointed the gun at Harmon again. "Are you sabotaging me, General? Is that what this is?"

Harmon, pressing his khaki military uniform-tie to the right side of his face to soak up the blood Sultan's blow drew, wobbled as he stood. Sultan kept his weapon pointed at him the entire time. "With all due respect, Sultan, those were your men who faltered in the heat of battle, not mine! They are the ones who were overrun by a smaller, younger and less experienced army! You don't allow me to communicate with anyone in the outside world! So, don't go accusing me of sabotage when your insecurities grab hold of you! I'm the highest ranking American military officer – always have been! That's why you've kept me around! And despite whatever consequences I may face I have advised you as I would have the President of the United States. If you lose your power to Noble, I will be tried and killed for treason, for sure. My survival is now, and has always been, tied to your success."

Sultan relented and lowered his gun. Several of his men gathered at the doorway in response to the shouting. "Maybe so," Sultan conceded. "But you are no longer to be trusted." He looked passed Harmon toward his men at the door. "Tie him up!" he ordered in Arabic. "He is a prisoner of war, now."

* * *

In a wooded area just south of Philadelphia, Sharpe ordered the army to make camp. The victories in Boston and Philadelphia emboldened the men. Max's presence in the camp gave them further inspiration. Only months earlier, the prospect of marching an army into Washington, D.C., seemed unlikely to Sharpe; now, the mission was in its planning stages.

Sharpe rewarded Ryan with the rank of colonel, and commissioned him to command the New England regiment. As a street fighter, Ryan had to be taught to utilize the chain of command. He assigned Connelly the rank of major, and the elder Murphy the rank of captain. Chatty and Gonzo worked relentlessly with them to teach them the necessary obedience and authority officers were expected to exhibit. Sharpe realized that it would take time. He could not lead a coordinated attack if a large percentage of his men were undisciplined. Training was needed, and the battle for the capitol that could end the war would have to wait.

Max, meanwhile, took the opportunity to call Armstrong. SBN was running constant coverage of the victories, which it dubbed the "Battle of the Bridges," Armstrong explained; Barrington granted Susan a full hour-long interview, in which he praised Max's poise and leadership during the confrontation. The President's popularity was greater than ever.

Max told Armstrong to reconvene the evacuated council, and to recall Judge Vineri from Europe to chair the council sessions in his stead. Armstrong promised that he would, and ended the conversation with, "Remember to call Roxy, Mr. President."

"Will do," Max promised. He ended the call on his cell phone and retreated into the privacy of his personal tent. A cot was set up in the tent, a luxury not afforded to the average soldier. Max sat on the edge of the cot and sighed before dialing his house on Long Island to speak with his wife.

The phone rang. It rang again. Halfway through the third ring, Roxy answered, "Hello."

"Hi, Honey," Max replied.

"Oh, Max, thank God it's you!" She began to cry.

"Is everything okay?"

"Yeah. Yeah, we're fine." She paused to weep. "Zach keeps practicing with his arrows in the backyard. He says that he can't wait to grow up so he can be a hero like you."

"Oh, Rox, I hope he never has to go through what I have been through."

"Me, too," she laughed. "Me, too."

"How are the guys treating you?"

"They're great! Boots brought his family over. I really like his wife, Tracy. She's a trip! Tough as nails."

"I would think she has to be to put up with him."

"Ha! You're right."

"And how are you doing?"

"I'm fine, Max."

"Are you?"

"Sure."

Max sensed the hesitation in her voice. "Rox, are you?" he asked in a deeper voice to indicate his disbelief.

She cried again. "I miss you, Max. You're my husband, and I love you. And every time we have the chance to be together, you've got to go run off to a meeting, or worse! I just want to spend as much time with you as possible. We're a family, and we need to act like one."

"I agree. I love you and Zach more than anything. And I want to spend as much time with you as I can. But I'm not coming back to New York just yet."

Roxy began to bawl. It was the last thing that she wanted to hear. "When will you be home?"

"I don't know. We're going to go after Sultan in Washington, but Sharpe says that the men aren't ready yet. We're going to be in Philadelphia for a few weeks." He knew that his wife was disappointed, and her sobbing ate away at him. "I'll tell you what," he offered, "why don't you and Zach come down here? This way, we'll be able to move right into the White House when we get to Washington."

"You want us to be there with the army?"

"Sure," Max said. "It will be good for the men to see us together. It will remind them of their families and what they're fighting for."

"Is Sharpe okay with that?"

"He will be. I'll take care of it. I really want you here with me."

Roxy's mood changed. "I'll tell Zach to pack his bags."

"Make sure he brings his bow and arrows, seriously."

"Okay, I will. Oh, Max! I can't wait to see you!"

"Same here. I love you."

"I love you, too."

PART IV

The Peace at Dawn

CHAPTER 28

Autumn brought cooler temperatures and colorful foliage to the heavily forested woods of Pennsylvania. At Sharpe's request, Takinawa and his senseis journeyed to meet the army at their camp so that they could train the Demons and Ryan's men as they had the Long Island army. The process took several weeks, which gave Sharpe the time he desired to properly prepare for the Washington campaign.

Unlike the New York and Philadelphia campaigns, in which Sultan had the advantage, Sharpe had the upper hand this time. In the weeks since the Battle of the Bridges, insurrection spread throughout the nation. Using Max's plea to the people to join his cause as inspiration, citizens from Seattle to Los Angeles to Houston successfully evicted Sultan's men from their cities. Sultan sensed his eventual demise, and reacted by recalling his remaining men to Washington to establish a defensive position. If there was to be a final assault against him, his capture would be no easy feat.

In the wake of Sultan's withdrawals, the Americans heard from SBN's newscasts that Max was no longer available for interviews because he was preparing for the next battle with Sharpe's army in Pennsylvania. The rebel armies from across the nation travelled to rendezvous with them. The thought of being able to fight at Max's side motivated them. He was more than an inspiration to them; he was a hero in every sense of the word. Each soldier knew that he could not look in the mirror to find an equivalent amount of personal anguish. Yet, he bravely fought in the name of a failed nation hoping to restore it as the ideal society imagined by its founders. They allowed him to fight for them without help for too long. Now that he asked for assistance, they could not let him down. Max and Sharpe marveled each morning at how the ranks of their army swelled. They spent countless hours planning for the Washington campaign with Chatty and Ryan. So far, they had not been able to devise a viable strategy.

In New York, the council approved a resolution authorizing Max to, "employ the use of force to remove the enemy threat from the homeland." After lunch with the troops in the mess tent each day, Max retired to his tent to call Armstrong; they conferred about the council's business. Judge Vineri joined Armstrong in the calls to make certain that he understood Max's instructions. Chairing the body, the Judge was the consummate surrogate for Max; no one dared question his qualifications the way they had Max's. He became a familiar fixture on SBN's broadcasts and enjoyed the same popularity as Max. Many credited him with the economy's return to normalcy. His presence and calming influence in the political arena allowed Max to focus on his duties as commander-in-chief.

During the little free time he had in his late afternoons, Max sparred with Boots under Takinawa's supervision. While he tried to strengthen the muscles in his left arm, he could not. He reinjured the tissue that was surgically repaired pulling on Zee's reigns during the storm in Philadelphia. The wound given him by Emir once again made it increasingly difficult for him to flex the arm at all. Boots found himself easing up in their sparring bouts, and Takinawa cautioned against Max's return to action. Only after Sharpe promised that he would not allow Max to engage in actual combat did Takinawa consent in good conscience to Max's presence at the battle.

At the end of every day, after all the military planning,

after all the conference calls with Armstrong and Judge Vineri, after all the sparring sessions, Max returned to his tent where he ate dinner with Roxy and Zach. Despite his title and his hectic schedule, he was able to enjoy a normal meal with his family. That - and that alone - drove him.

Roxy had one rule at the dinner table: No one was permitted to discuss the war. They would speak of their respective activities that day. She would explain how she greatly appreciated that Gonzo made certain to deliver fresh groceries from the mess tent, which he varied depending on the evening's menu, so that she could prepare their dinner in the privacy of their own tent. Zach reported on the book he read that day (Armstrong gave him the books about the characteristics of leadership that he forced Max to learn), and how the Peach and Bam Bam would teach him how to fight with his fists because he would not always be able to use his arrows in a fight. For the most part, Max listened. He never violated Roxy's rule. When he did speak, it was of how exciting it would be to plant a garden in the backyard of his house so that Roxy would be able to grow fresh vegetables.

Despite the excruciating pain his left arm was causing him on this night, he dared not mention it. In truth, he did not have to. Roxy noticed every grimace when he would try to move it. She knew him better than he knew himself. "You need to get that looked at, you know," she said.

"When I get five minutes," Max retorted.

Having eaten his dinner and given his report on Voltaire, Zach asked, "Can I be excused?"

"'May,'" Roxy corrected. "'May' you be excused?"

"Sorry," Zach apologized while rolling his eyes. "*May* I be excused?"

"That's better," Roxy said, satisfied with his response.

"And, yes, you may be excused." Without a word, Zach jumped out of his chair, grabbed his bow and arrows from next to his bed, and darted out of the tent. "I wish he'd stop playing with those things."

"He's a young man now, Rox," Max countered. "You have to let him follow his own path a little."

"He's so confused. School would normally start this time of year. All he's doing is reading those books Jack gave him and playing with those damned arrows."

"At least he's reading. And what's wrong with his hobby? He's getting good at it."

"He needs some direction. Can't you talk to him about it?"

"What type of direction am I going to give him? Tell him to stay out of jail like his father?"

"No!" Roxy forbad. "Besides, his father's not in jail."

"I thought you said that Derek shot a deli clerk and was serving a life sentence?"

"I lied," she deadpanned. "He never shot a deli clerk. I lied about it all. I never married him, either. In fact, Derek never existed."

Max was flabbergasted. "I don't understand. Why did you lie to me?"

"For Zach's sake," she answered. "I didn't want to complicate things for him. It was just easier for him to think that he had a father in jail."

"But I'm your husband! You're supposed to be truthful with *me!*"

Max's tone brought Roxy to tears. She cried, "I'm telling you now! The truth is that I changed my name shortly after you went back to school!"

"Rox, I'm sorry," Max offered as he moved closer to her to console her.

"That's not all, Max. There's more. Much more."

"What is it, Rox? Whatever it is, you can tell me." Roxy sobbed even more. "The truth is that there is no father listed on Zach's birth certificate. I did everything I could to hide his father from him because I didn't know if his real father was mature enough to be a father!"

"Don't you think he deserves to know the truth?"

"Who? Zach or his father?"

"Both," Max insisted.

"You're right," Roxy conceded. Once she composed herself, she said softly, "You should tell him that he's your son."

"My son?" Max asked in awe. "He can't be my son. I mean, we were both drunk at that party, but we used a condom. He can't be my son!"

"Well, it must have broken, Max! You were the only man I slept with at the time! That makes you his father!"

In truth, Max was relieved. He wanted to adopt Zach when the war was over anyway. A sense of pride overcame him. "He's really my son?" he asked calmly.

Roxy nodded. "Yes, Max, he's our son."

A tear streamed from Max's right eye. "Why didn't you tell me you were pregnant all those years ago? And why did you hide him from me this long?"

"You weren't ready to be a father. You had your whole life ahead of you, and I didn't want to hold you back. I was afraid that if I came to you, you would only push me away. When I heard about what happened to Valerie, I knew that you needed support. And who better to give it to you than your family – your whole family."

"Wow, Rox. I – I'm still in awe."

"Do you hate me?" Roxy asked with a hint of insecurity in her voice.

"No, Rox, I don't hate you. I love you more than ever," he said just before he kissed her passionately. He opened his eyes after the kiss and looked deeply into hers. "I'll tell him when the time is right. I promise."

* * *

Max strolled casually into the morning's military briefing only to find that a shouting match had erupted amongst Sharpe, Chatty and Ryan. Apparently, the planning for the Washington campaign was not going as Sharpe intended. Upon his entrance, the men stood and in unison said, "Good morning, Mr. President."

"Good morning, boys," Max said. "As you were. I am only here to observe today."

"Very well, Mr. President," Sharpe said. He turned to Ryan and picked up the argument where he left off. "I don't understand why you can't get your men to follow simple instructions, Colonel Ryan!" Sharpe chastised.

"It's not that they can't follow orders," Ryan pleaded, "it's that they're bored with the damn 'March!' 'Halt!' and 'Stand at Attention!' bullshit! They want to see action!"

"They're not ready for action!" Chatty yelled in defense of his general.

"They were ready in Boston!" Ryan countered. "And let's not forget that we saved your asses in Philadelphia!"

"Major Gonzalez," Sharpe called. "When do you think that Colonel Ryan's men will be ready for combat?"

"Colonel Ryan's men are at least two weeks away, sir, and the men from the western states' militias are at least three weeks away," Gonzo answered. "No offense, Colonel," he said to Ryan, "but your men are a danger to the rest of the army if they are not properly prepared for organized warfare."

"How hard is it to shoot the guys with the fuckin'

towels on their heads?" Ryan asked sarcastically. "They're ready!"

Chatty was quick to insist, "No, they're not! If they can't be trusted to follow the simplest order such as 'March!' or 'Halt!' then they can't be trusted to carry out the General's orders at all. Welcome to the world of organized warfare! There's a chain of command here, and you need to get used to it!"

Ryan's fair skin turned beet red in anger. "There's a chain of command, alright! And the last time I checked, *Colonel*, you and I fall on the same rung of the ladder!"

"That's enough, Colonel Ryan!" Sharpe intervened. "The bottom line is this: We're at least two weeks away from being ready to move out, if not more. Let's use the extra time to formulate our strategy. In the meantime, Colonel Ryan, I want your men to be ready in two weeks. If they're not, then we're leaving them behind. It is your responsibility to get them to that point. I am assigning Major Gonzalez to oversee the western militias' training. Is that clear?"

"Yes, sir," a dejected Ryan answered.

"Crystal clear, sir," Gonzo confirmed.

"Good," Sharpe acknowledged. "Now that we've squared that away, we need to address the fact that we don't have any intelligence on Sultan's defenses as of yet."

"May I suggest a scout team, sir?" Williams asked from his seat at the table.

"That's a fine idea, Captain," Sharpe answered. "Are you volunteering?"

With a wide smile he said, "Of course, sir. Special ops are my specialty."

"My men and I would like to volunteer, too, General," Hank offered. With an equally wry grin he said, "We excel at covert ops as well, General."

"Indeed you do," Sharpe agreed. "Then it's settled. Lieutenant Youseff and Captain Williams, you will form a scout team to gather as much intelligence as you can. Stick to back woods of Pennsylvania and Maryland to maintain your cover. My gut tells me that we will march the army along that route to avoid being spotted. Report back your findings immediately; I want to know every detail. If there's so much as a hobo living in those woods, I want to know what time he takes a shit and where. Colonel Chatham will provide you with the necessary communication devices and codes. The end of this war is near, and victory is within reach. Let's make it so."

CHAPTER 29

The bright white light emanating from the flickering incandescent light bulbs felt like needles piercing Harmon's retinas. Sultan ordered him locked in the empty room, where the lights were kept on. He had lost track of time, and could not sleep. His hands were bound together and raised over his head as the rope was strewn over the metal flag holder near the ceiling. He was given two slices of bread and a glass of water as his three meals of the day. Dried blood coagulated from his swollen lip in the white scruff that lined his face. He was taken to the facilities to relieve himself four times during the day. Only now did he understand why the rules of the Geneva Convention were established to protect prisoners of war; Sultan knew not of them.

With his arms raised for such long stretches, breathing became difficult. It felt as though a fifty-pound weight had been placed on his chest. *The Romans were merciful,* he thought. *They wounded Jesus to speed his death. I wish he would come for me.* He was not so lucky. Instead, he was visited by Sultan.

The guard opened the door and Sultan entered the room slowly. Without warning, he struck Harmon across his legs with a metal pointer that was hidden behind his back. The blow sliced through Harmon's pant leg and drew blood. Harmon cringed, but did not scream. "What do you want?" he asked.

Sultan did not answer immediately. He scanned the prisoner up and down. "It is only a matter of time before your countrymen arrive," he said.

"Yeah, so?"

"What do you think they will do with you when they find you here?"

"That depends on you."

"Really?" Sultan asked with a laugh. "How so?"

"Well, if you kill me, they will give me a hero's burial and name a monument for me. If you let me live, they will question why. After a formal inquiry, they will understand that I had no choice but to cooperate with you to preserve our country's military secrets until they arrived. Either way, I win."

Sultan scratched his beard. "Have my men said anything to you about the current situation?"

"Yeah, we're best friends," he said sarcastically.

"So, you are aware that I have recalled all of my men and we are preparing to defend our position here?"

The smirk on Harmon's face disappeared. "No, it must have slipped their mind."

Sultan made his way toward the door. Before he left, he turned to Harmon and said, "Now you know. They have their country back. My cause is lost, no thanks to you. This will be our last stand. When the final shot is fired, this much I promise you: Even if I am to meet Allah, there will be no monument for you."

Harmon nodded in acknowledgment. He closed his eyes as the guard slammed the door shut. "Please, Jesus, come for me," he said softly.

* * *

The scout team slogged through the muddy Pennsylvania woods and over the Maryland border in four days' time. Although he outranked Williams, Hank instructed his men to follow the captain's lead; as a special ops soldier, Williams was better equipped to give the orders on this mission. Sharpe demanded regular reports from the crew. Using the phones Chatty rigged for them, they called almost hourly to describe their present coordinates and to confirm that they had not come across anything noteworthy. "Not even a hobo takin' a shit," Williams reported to Chatty at one point. What the team did not know was that back at their camp, Sharpe instructed Chatty to map their route with the coordinates. The general planned on marching his army in their footsteps; the Philadelphia campaign taught Sharpe not to leave a single detail of his plan to chance ever again.

The hiking was beginning to take its physical toll, and their pace slowed. On the afternoon of the fifth day, after not having made much progress at all, it began to rain. The ground had not yet recovered from the soaking rains that tortured the nation during the summer; the oversaturation made continuing near impossible. They decided to make camp for the night, and that they would pick up again early in the morning to make up for the lost time. Upon hearing of their decision, Sharpe expressed displeasure with it, but he ultimately agreed that it was in the mission's best interests. With his blessing, they pitched their tent and dug a pit in which to set up a campfire.

Most, if not all, of the wood around their campsite was soaked and unusable. However, with their clothes wet and night approaching, they knew they had to find kindling and make a fire for heat. Hank assigned one of his men to guard the camp, and ordered two to search for wood to the west; he and Williams scoured the forest to the east.

"Where do you think we are?" Hank asked Williams as they trudged eastward.

"If our coordinates are correct," Williams began, "we're not more than fifteen miles outside of Washington."

"The general will be pleased with our progress, especially if we can make it to Washington in the next day or so."

"He should be," Williams said as he bent down and picked up a small log that had been buried underneath some heavy brush. He examined it thoroughly, and ultimately tossed it aside. "Too wet," he determined and explained to Hank.

They continued on their quest for dry wood stopping occasionally to examine potential specimens. Out of the thirty or so pieces they scrutinized, they found three logs and a twig that Williams felt were dry enough to burn. They needed much more.

When they had wandered nearly a quarter mile from their campsite, a familiar odor filled the air. It was the scent of burning wood. "Do you smell that?" Williams asked.

"Of course!" Hank answered. "It seems to be getting stronger. It must be coming from over there," he said pointing slightly to the south.

"Shhh! Do you hear that?" Williams sought to confirm holding his index finger to his lips. He grabbed Hank at the forearm and lowered them both into a squatting position, their eyes scanning the trees in the direction of where Hank pointed. There were voices coming from that direction, but they were too far and intelligible. They looked at each other. Williams pointed his index finger and his middle finger at his eyes, then pointed at Hank, then to the east, then to himself, and finally to the west, to signal that they would split up to survey the origin. Hank nodded, and they went their separate ways.

* * *

Chatty was sitting next to the radio in his tent staring at a picture of his cousin that brought him to the verge of tears. His murder was a retaliation killing. *Stupid gang dispute*! Chatty thought. It pained him greatly, but the giant would not allow himself to remember the loss except in the privacy of his own quarters.

"Bluebird to Eagle's Nest! Bluebird to Eagle's Nest!" Williams' voice called over the radio.

Chatty, startled, quickly composed himself, wiping the tears from his eyes and clearing his throat. "This is Eagle's Nest, Bluebird," he responded. "I thought you were tucked in for the night? Is there a problem?"

"Negative, Eagle's Nest. But the sparrow and the hawk should fly to Bluebird's new home at dawn."

"The sparrow and the hawk?" Chatty repeated. "Are you in danger, Bluebird?"

"Negative, Eagle's Nest. But there's a huge worm, and the sparrow and the hawk need to be here to eat it."

"Understood, Bluebird. Message will be delivered to the sparrow. Await further instructions before proceeding."

"Ten-four, Eagle's Nest. Bluebird out."

"Ten-four, Bluebird. Eagle's Nest out." Chatty replaced the radio's receiver in its cradle, and darted out of his tent. He ran quickly to Sharpe's tent. When he arrived, he paused outside the tent's opening flap to catch his breath before announcing, "General Sharpe, it's Colonel Chatham requesting permission to enter."

"Come in, Colonel," Sharpe responded. Chatty entered and saluted. Sharpe returned the gesture and said, "At ease, Colonel." He pulled a chair over to his table and both men sat. "What is it?"

"Bluebird called," Chatty began.

"I thought they were out of commission until the morning?" Sharpe interrupted.

"As did I, Sir. But Captain Williams said that something has come up. He said that you and the president need to meet them at their last location, immediately."

"Do you think it's an ambush?"

"No, Sir. I asked him twice if there was trouble. He spoke in code, said that there wasn't any, and never used our 'safe' word."

Sharpe thought about the scenario for a moment. "I don't like it. Something's not right. What were his exact words when you pressed him the second time?"

Chatty thought hard for a moment, wishing he had written the conversation down. When it came to him, he said, "He said . . . um . . . he said, 'There's a huge worm, and you and the president need to be there in person to eat it.'" He was paraphrasing, but Sharpe got the idea.

"What do you make of the 'worm'?"

"I . . . I don't know, Sir. They've obviously found something."

"Or, it's a trap and the 'worm' is the bait! I don't like it."

"What should we do, Sir?"

Sharpe sat silently for a moment. If it was a trap, they could not fall into it. However, the only way to find out if it was indeed a trap was to spring it. It would not be an easy decision to make. After pondering the question, he said, "We take it to the President. I'll warn him of the danger. But, ultimately, it's his call."

Sharpe and Chatty left the general's tent and proceeded to Max's abode. Max was sitting outside with Roxy, Boots, Bam Bam and the Peach; all were watching Zach's display of his archery skills. Max took pride in his son's skill; although, he did not let it slip that he was the boy's father. The sound of the arrows cutting through the air mesmerized him like music soothing the beast. He focused so that he did not notice Sharpe and Chatty arrive.

"Mr. President, we have a situation," Sharpe reported

without acknowledging the others.

"Is it urgent?" Max asked.

"Yes, sir. It seems that way," Chatty confirmed.

"You want we should leave you alone?" Boots asked.

"No, you can stay," Max answered. "We're all friends here."

"Very well, Mr. President," Sharpe said. He was perturbed by the decision to allow nonmilitary personnel to stay, but the matter was pressing and there was no time to argue. "We've received a message from Captain Williams. He said that they found something," he explained without using any of the code words. "He said that you and I need to meet him and his team as soon as possible."

"What did they find?" max asked.

"We don't know, sir," Chatty answered. "He was speaking in code, and he could not say what it was."

"Interesting," Max admitted. "What do you think, General?"

"Could be a trap, Mr. President," Sharpe answered honestly. "There's only one way to find out."

"Is there any reason to suspect that the message was made under duress?" Max inquired.

"No, sir," Chatty answered. "He never used our 'safe' word to indicate trouble."

"Our 'safe' word?" Max asked for clarification.

"Yes, sir," Chatty explained. "The team was instructed to use the word, 'vulture,' in the event of forced communication. Had he used it, we would have known that the team was in trouble."

"But he didn't use it?" Max wanted to confirm.

"No, sir, he did not," Chatty corroborated.

"Then we have nothing to fear, General," Max told Sharpe.

"Very well, Mr. President," Sharpe acknowledged. "You and I will set out in the morning."

"What about us?" Roxy asked.

"You and Zach will stay here," Max said. "Bam Bam and the Peach will watch you. Boots, you're coming with me."

"Mr. President, is that appropriate?" Sharpe questioned.

"He's my bodyguard," Max insisted. Boots angrily stared at Sharpe.

"Very well," Sharpe agreed. "We should take one more of my men for protection, too."

"I'll go, sir," Chatty volunteered.

"Can't be you, Colonel," Sharpe answered. "I need you to lead the army down to meet us when the coast is clear. Major Gonzalez is training the new recruits, so he's out, too."

"What about Ryan?" Max asked.

Sharpe bit his lower lip. He did not want to validate Ryan any more than he had to, but taking him on the mission would remove his pessimistic attitude from competing with Gonzo's training techniques. "Alright, Ryan is in," he said. "We'll have him drive us down there so that we can make contact tomorrow."

"And where do we go when the army moves out?" Roxy asked.

"We'll let you know," Max said with a smile. "Bam Bam? Peach?"

"We'll wait to hear from you, Boss," Bam Bam acknowledged. "You got it."

"Yeah, you got it," the Peach parroted.

"Don't leave without saying goodbye," Roxy said with a soured look on her face.

"I won't," Max promised.

"Very well," Sharpe said. "We'll move out at eight hundred hours. Colonel Chatham, tell Ryan to meet me in my tent."

"Yes, sir," Chatty acknowledged.

CHAPTER 30

Just before dawn, Max awoke. The days were getting noticeably shorter, yet his sleeping pattern had not changed. If not for the darkness and the considerably cooler weather, he would not have been able to identify the days with the season. Roxy was curled in the fetal position underneath the blankets that covered the bed; Zach unconsciously mimicked her in his bed. Their faces appeared so tranquil. Max yearned for the day he would awake in the White House to find them resting comfortably in its elegance. Then, he would have peace of mind.

In the meantime, duty called. Max left his tent and surveyed the camp. Again he found only peace. A light frost covered the grass and tents as the morning fog slowly lifted; it blended with the smoke rising slowly from the smoldering ashes of the night's campfires. For the first time in a long time, Max could see his breath when he exhaled as it condensed in the cold Appalachian air. His deadened left arm ached in the cold weather, but he ignored it as usual. The birds began to chirp merrily unaware of the human conflict in the world. He envied them, and he was almost certain that if his army was awake, his soldiers would, too. The war itself was brief, yet all those involved aged so rapidly; the boys he spoke to from the roof of the truck in the rail yard on Memorial Day were now men, if not physically certainly at heart.

Max knew that he, himself, had grown. He used the war to shield his grief for Valerie's death; had he been left to ponder that night's events, guilt would have consumed him. Instead, he chose a path he had never imagined. It was a violent and bloody one rife with difficulty. His heart had been hardened by it. The only remaining compassion belonged to his family. However, given this opportunity to think about it, he discovered anger within that Roxy had kept Zach's existence from him for all these years. *How could she keep my son from me?* he thought as his rage expanded. *He's my son, too! She had no right!* Indeed, the remainder of his soul was disappearing as Judge Vineri warned it would, and Max knew it was happening. "Who will save me when I am done saving them?" he asked aloud. The birds' chirping grew louder. His question went unanswered.

"Oh, you're up already, Mr. President," Sharpe suddenly said as he approached.

Caught by surprise, Max said, "General, you startled me. I was just enjoying the peace at dawn."

"Ah, yes. It can be refreshing. There's nothing like the start of a new day."

The crest of the sun rose over the eastern horizon illuminating the camp. "It's funny, you know," Max began. "Even with all the scheduling and planning we do in our lives, you never know what each day will bring or how you will handle it. It's almost like you never know who you will be at the end of the day."

"I'm sorry, sir. I don't think I follow," Sharpe said. For a structured and calculating man like Sharpe, the thought of not knowing who you would be at the end of the day was preposterous.

"It's okay, General. I don't know either. Just something I was thinking about before you got here."

"Mr. President, is everything okay? Is there something you want to talk about? I mean, I know that we have a very formal relationship with you being the Commander-in-Chief and all, but if you need to get something off your chest, I hope you know that I consider you a friend, as well."

At that moment, Max wished he could tell Sharpe everything. But he remembered what he learned from Armstrong and Dalton: A leader cannot show weakness else the army will not follow. "I consider you a friend, too, General. And I promise you, I'm fine. Heavy is the head that wears the crown, that's all."

"Very well, sir. I'll see you at eight hundred hours."

"Indeed, General. Today is a new day," Max said as he saluted Sharpe, who returned to his tent to prepare for their departure.

Max continued to watch the sunrise. He could feel the star's heat as it warmed the ground beneath him. Slowly, the frost melted into the morning dew. The daybreak invigorated him; however, as much as he was enjoying it, he knew that there was work to be done. He retired to his tent and began to prepare.

The black uniform Dalton made for him was hanging next to his sword by the foot of the bed. It was worn, and the sword had become blunted, but with a significant army behind them this time, Max knew that his warrior's image was only a façade. He dressed quickly, and ate some of the bread that was left over from the previous night's dinner for breakfast. Despite it being stale, it was filling.

The time had come to rendezvous for his mission. He knelt down and kissed Roxy on the forehead to wake her gently from her slumber. When she opened her eyes, he said, "Good morning."

"Hi," Roxy replied with a yawn. "What time is it?"

"Time for me to go," he replied. "But it shouldn't take us long to get there since we're taking Ryan's truck. Once we get this thing sorted out, we'll call Chatty. He'll let you know when Bam Bam and the Peach should start to move you guys."

"Sounds good. Do you have everything you need?"

"I'm all set."

"I can't wait to get to the White House, you know?"

"It's just a house, Rox. I'm already the President."

"True. Just remember your promise, Mr. President."

"I know. I'll tell him when this is all over. I promise. I don't want to upset him while I'm off in battle."

"I guess so," she said lowering her eyes. It was clear that, despite her renewed enthusiasm, she was worried about her husband heading into another battle.

"I gotta go," he said, and then kissed her. "I love you."

"I love you, too."

Max began to leave, but stopped and knelt next to Zach's bed. He kissed the boy on his brow, and said, "I love you, too, son." He turned and smiled at Roxy, and left the tent.

* * *

Ryan commandeered one of his men's sport utility vehicles for the mission. It was more comfortable for him to drive than his truck, and less suspicious, too. Sharpe occupied the front passenger's seat, while Max sat behind the general, and Boots behind the driver. Their ride would be brief; what took the scout team several days by foot would take them only a matter of hours.

Max mostly stared out the window at the foliage. The vibrant reds and yellows were giving way to rustic browns. The trees were beginning to shed their leaves. The shortened days, the cooler weather, and the falling leaves all meant one thing. Autumn arrived, and soon the bitter winter cold would return. He thought of snow sprinkling the White House, and of sipping hot cocoa with Roxy in its warmth while Zach built a snowman on the South Lawn. Maybe then the heartless warrior within would wander away from his soul to return him to his tender, nurturing self. In the meantime, his soul was disappearing and it disturbed him terribly.

In an attempt to distract himself from his inner turmoil, Max asked, "What do you think they've found?"

"Tough to say," Sharpe answered.

"Could it be a weapon?" Ryan asked.

"Nuclear?" Boots expanded the question.

"Possibly," Sharpe said. "Colonel Chatham didn't even know what the 'worm' was, and he invented their code."

"It has to be something good, right?" Ryan asked. "I mean, they were usin' all this bird talk, and a worm is food for a bird, right?"

"Hmph, Ryan," Sharpe commented. "I didn't know you were that astute."

"I'm probably not," the Bostonian answered. "But I have my moments."

"Ha!" Boots laughed. "Even the sun shines on a dog's ass some days!"

"Oh, yeah, ya fuckin' Guinea?" Ryan began angrily. "What's that supposed to mean?"

"At ease, Colonel!" Sharpe ordered. "He was kidding around. We're all friends here, and I will not tolerate racial slurs in my ranks."

"Yeah, ya fuckin' Mick," Boots goaded.

"That's enough!" Max said sternly.

"Right," Boots acknowledged. "Sorry."

"Now you," Sharpe ordered Ryan waving his finger from Ryan to Boots. "Apologize."

"Shit!" Ryan exclaimed. "Sorry! I'm fuckin' sorry! Ya

happy now?"

"What's your issue, Colonel?" Sharpe asked. "You've got the heart of a lion, but you rarely exude its majesty. Why is that?"

"I don't know?" Ryan answered honestly. He never looked at himself introspectively before. "Maybe it's because my old man thought it was funny to drink his paycheck away very Friday night, and then beat on me and my ma when he came home. Maybe it's because I got tired of hearin' him say that I was the biggest mistake of his life! Maybe it's because my ma spent years prayin' to Jesus to come save us, and then when she got sick he never showed up, so I had to live with that mean old fuck when she died. Where was Jesus, then? Huh? Tell me! Where was Jesus then? Was he there when my old man died? No! That fucker drank himself into a fuckin' puddle! I was fourteen, and on my own. No ma. No pa. No fuckin' Jesus, either. So, what did I get instead? I got to live with Murphy and his brothers, and for what? So that we could fight in the streets of South Boston for a fuckin' dollar to buy a pack of smokes! What kind of life was that, huh? Then this fuckin' guy shows up and takes over our city, our country, my fuckin' home! Where the fuck is Jesus? Huh? What was my ma prayin' for all these years? So, why should I care about all your discipline and bullshit? I should pull over right here and make all of you walk! I don't fuckin' need this!" The car swerved slightly as he wiped tears from his face.

Sharpe was shocked. He did not expect Ryan's outburst, and certainly was not prepared to respond right away. There was an awkward moment of silence until Boots said, "Hey, man. It's okay. Look, my old man used to come home and beat on me and my brothers, too. But then I met Don Vito, who taught me about discipline. He taught me how to dress like a man, how to act like a man, and how to talk like a man. He showed me that

Jesus was there all the time, but that we only see him when we need him to survive. I've never seen him either, but you know what? I don't need to. It's called faith, and it's the ultimate discipline."

"Look, Ryan," Max added. "If you don't want to be here, then let us out. We'll make our way. But we want you with us. Listen to Boots. Jesus is with you, you just don't realize it. Life is a series of choices. You chose to lead the fight in Boston. You chose to join me and fight on in Philly. You chose this life, not your old one. General Sharpe is just trying to help you. That's all. The choice remains yours."

"Yeah, man," Boots said. "You have something here with your life that you may never have had, and that's an opportunity. Make something of yourself. Be proud, man! Take advantage of what's right in front of you."

Ryan said nothing. He glanced over at Sharpe through his tears. The car swerved again, and he quickly placed his attention back to the road.

"A disciplined soldier will survive a war, Colonel," Sharpe finally said. "Loose cannons won't. I want you fighting by my side in this battle, Ryan. More importantly, I want you fighting by my side after it. What do you say?"

Ryan pulled the car off to the side of the road. He raised his hands to his face, and bawled incessantly for nearly a full minute. "I'm sorry, General," he finally said. He looked up at Sharpe. "No one has ever asked me for anything. No one ever said they wanted me to be anywhere near them. I've gotten this far on my own."

"Let us out here, then," Max said.

"No, wait!" Ryan continued. "I can't go any further without you. I know that, and it freaks me the fuck out! I guess I'll have to do it your way, General," he said with a salute. "Maybe Jesus will help me to decide what to do with my life someday, but for now, you're right, Boots.

This is the only opportunity I got. I can't walk away."

"That's the spirit!" Sharpe said. "Now, let's keep going. I want to know what this 'worm' is!"

Ryan composed himself using his sleeves to dry his eyes and wipe his nose. It was the first time he embraced his emotions, and he was impressed by the relief it brought. A moment like this was uncommon in South Boston. But now he understood that he had a purpose. Refreshed, he continued to drive his comrades to the rendezvous.

* * *

Williams turned to see the vehicle approaching the scout team's campsite. He noticed Sharpe sitting in the front passenger's seat and said, "They're here."

Sharpe observed Williams speaking with several men who were donning military uniforms as the car came to a halt. He saw that one of the men had three stars on the shoulders of his jacket. "Officers," he commented. "Ryan, come with me. Mr. President, you should wait here. I'll wave you over once I am confident that it is safe." Looking at Boots, he said, "You take the wheel, just in case it's not."

Sharpe exited the vehicle slowly. Ryan followed, and Boots stepped out to move from the back seat to the driver's seat. Sharpe and Ryan ambled over toward Williams and the officers with whom he was speaking. Hank and the rest of the scout team quickly emerged from their tents to join them. They all saluted Sharpe, who returned the gesture and then shook the hands of the officers.

"Seems like they're old friends," Boots said to Max.

"Looks can be deceiving," Max said carefully watching Sharpe's body language as he engaged in conversation with them. Sharpe appeared confident throughout his discussion. The man with three stars on his uniform pointed to his left, and Sharpe craned his neck to follow. Sharpe nodded affirmatively several times, looked at the car, and raised his right arm and waved.

"Must be safe," Boots said. "Wait there. I'll open the door for you." He walked around to the passenger side of the car and opened the rear door. Max emerged, and followed Boots to join the group.

The soldiers all saluted Max, who returned the honor. "Mr. President," Sharpe said. "This is General Chet Rogers. He used to serve under General Harmon at the Pentagon."

Max extended his hand to Rogers, who gratefully shook it. "It's an honor to meet you, Mr. President."

"Likewise," Max confirmed. "How long has it been since you served under Harmon?"

"Several months, sir," Rogers answered. "My men and I escaped shortly after the Chicago incident, as soon as it became clear to us that General Harmon was not acting in the nation's best interests."

"Really?" Max asked, surprised. "How so?"

"Well, sir, he was advising Sultan as he should have been advising you," Rogers answered. "From the beginning of the invasion, my men and I were suspicious about his orders to obey Sultan, but we trusted in his rank and judgment. Once he ordered me to launch the nuclear warhead on our own soil, it became apparent that he either could not, or would not, support your heroic efforts, sir."

Max stoically responded, "So *you* were the one who actually launched the warhead?"

Rogers looked at the ground in shame before returning his gaze to Max's. "Yes, sir. And I am prepared to accept whatever punishment you see fit to administer."

"I see," Max said. "Make no mistake, General, there

must be severe punishment for causing a nuclear holocaust and the deaths of millions of innocent civilians. But I gather that there is more to your story or else your own men would have shot you dead already. I suppose that General Rogers is the 'worm?'" he asked.

"Not exactly, sir," Williams interjected. "The 'worm' is in our custody over there," he said pointing to an elderly man who was kneeling, bound and gagged, before one of Rogers' men.

"Who is he?" Max asked.

"He is one of the traitors, sir," Sharpe answered. "General Rogers and his team apprehended him."

"Alright, General Rogers," Max said. "I have several questions for you before I determine your fate. First, who is the prisoner? Secondly, where did you find him? How did you escape from the Pentagon? And how did you and your men get here? Answer honestly."

"Well, sir," Rogers said before hesitating. As a military officer, he knew that he had a duty to report to his commander-in-chief. As if speaking to a tribunal, he reported, "After General Harmon gave the order to launch the nuclear weapon on Chicago, my men and I discussed our options. It was clear that we had to escape. We lured General Harmon to the Secretary of Defense's office, where we subdued him. We then escaped through the fallout tunnels."

"The fallout tunnels?" Max asked.

"Yes, sir," Rogers confirmed. "During the Cold War, fallout tunnels were constructed beneath Washington and the surrounding area to allow for the government's survival in the event of a Soviet nuclear attack. There are four secret entrances into the tunnels. One is in the Situation Room at the White House to allow for the President's escape; one is located in the Secretary of Defense's office to allow him to communicate with the military; one is located in the CIA Director's office so that he can gather intelligence; and the last entrance is hidden in the woods about one-half mile southeast from here. These locations are highly classified. I am only aware of them having served as the Secretary's personal aide, sir."

Max nodded, fascinated that such a system existed. It was pure military genius. "Harmon was not aware of it?"

"No, sir," Rogers answered.

"Interesting," Max commented.

"As I was saying," Rogers continued, "my men and I entered the fallout tunnels through the entrance in the Secretary's office. We took shelter there for nearly six weeks when we became suspicious of an intruder as our food stores were often being raided. We feared that Sultan became aware of our presence, so we heightened our defenses, and set a trap by placing a net in the pantry. Sure enough, we caught the prisoner."

"Who is he?" Sharpe asked.

"That," Rogers said pointing to the elderly captive, "would be President Cole's Director of the CIA, William Dixon."

"The CIA?" Max asked.

"Dixon?" Sharpe asked simultaneously.

"General Rogers, did you know that Sultan gathered intelligence on the State of the Union through a Secret Service agent named Ben Arnold?" Max asked.

"No, sir," Rogers said.

"Well, as it turns out, Agent Arnold was approached by a member of the CIA, who offered two hundred and fifty thousand dollars to cooperate and provide information and access to the President and Congress on that night. Did you question Mr. Dixon at all?"

"No, sir. He said that he was hiding from Sultan, but in the interest of our own survival, we felt it necessary to arrest him."

"Well, then, it seems that a formal questioning is in order," Max said as he drew his sword.

"A word in private, Mr. President?" Sharpe requested.

"Certainly, General," Max granted. The two men walked away from the group, and came to a halt once they were out of earshot. "What is it, General?"

"Sir, there's something you need to know about Dixon before you question him. It relates to me, too. I don't speak very much of this incident, and it has been a blemish on my record that has prevented me from advancing past the rank of colonel until you promoted me."

"I'm all ears, General."

"As you know, Mr. President, I served with Bob Dalton in Vietnam; I was his lieutenant. One night, in the jungle outside of Quy Noh'n, we were ambushed. I mean there was Charlie everywhere. We lost half of our platoon that night. I was wounded," Sharpe pointed to the scar on his cheek as he explained. "But I managed to pull three men to safety that night, Dixon and Dalton among them. When we returned to camp, our C.O. was a real cuss; he berated all of us for losing half the unit and not being able to keep the line. That man was Colonel Daniel Harmon. Dalton had a bullet go through his hand, and still had to be restrained from killing Harmon, as you can imagine."

Max chuckled at the image in his head. It warmly reminded him of the time he tried to fight Dalton in his house during his training.

"Anyway, Dalton told Harmon what happened, and that I deserved a Purple Heart. Harmon said he would consider it. In the meantime, Dixon was badly injured.

He took a bullet in the thigh that must have hit an artery, and he nearly bled to death. Harmon grabbed him and helped him to the medical tent, where the docs saved him. At the time, we saw nothing wrong with it, since Dixon was the most badly injured of all of us.

"Several nights later, Dixon was discharged by the docs. He would be sent back Stateside the next day. We were thrilled. Every man I pulled from that battle survived. Dalton accompanied me to the Harmon's tent to submit my report of the incident. Bobby was going to sign the report to attest to my actions so that Harmon could nominate me for the honor. But we were not prepared for what we saw when we got there. Dixon was lying on Harmon's bed, and . . . ." Sharpe paused.

"What, General? What happened?"

"I . . . I don't know, sir . . . I shouldn't . . . It's just that . . . ."

"Say it, General! That's an order!"

Sharpe looked at the ground and shook his head before divulging, "Harmon was on his knees at Dixon's bedside, sir. He was performing fellatio on Dixon, sir."

Max's jaw dropped. He did not expect Sharpe's answer. "Seriously?"

"I'm afraid so, sir. If Bobby was here, he'd back me up. He and I apparently interrupted the two lovers. Harmon was mortified. He pulled his gun and nearly shot both of us on the spot. He only resisted the urge because Dixon pleaded with him to spare our lives since we saved his. Harmon acquiesced, but he swore that our military careers were over. We were both transferred to separate units the next day. I didn't see Bobby again until he showed up to recruit me for this war. In the meantime, Harmon declined to submit my version of the report, having doctored it so that one of the men who died appeared as the hero. He branded me as having disobeyed a direct order, and as he progressed through the ranks, he made sure to hold me back. I'm sure of that."

"That's quite a tale, General."

"I know, sir," Sharpe admitted. "I haven't seen Dixon since that night, but it is no coincidence that he and Harmon are wrapped up in this. There is a connection there, Mr. President. If you are going to question Dixon, make sure you find out what their connection is."

"Agreed," Max concurred. They walked back to the group, and Max asked the men to accompany him to question Dixon. They surrounded the prisoner.

Dixon ogled Max skeptically, but was obviously intimidated by the soldiers around him. He tried to stand, but he did not realize that the rope around his wrists, which were tied behind his back, was also tied to the rope around his ankles. Unable to balance himself, he toppled to the ground as quickly as he rose. Rogers' men chuckled until Max leered at them, immediately silencing them. Max knelt down and quickly ripped off the duct tape covering Dixon's mouth. Dixon screamed in pain as blood trickled from his upper lip; part of his moustache was attached to the tape in Max's hand.

Crumpling the tape into a ball and throwing it to the ground, Max said, "My name is Max Noble. I am the President of the United States. And who might you be?"

"Ha! You know damn well who I am!" the seething prisoner replied.

"I think I know who you are, but I want to hear you say it," Max taunted.

Dixon did not answer at first. Instead, he rested his head on the ground. "Go fuck yourself!"

Max laughed. It was a sinister laugh similar to the one he uttered when his father had his heart attack in front of him a decade earlier. "Fuck myself?" Max punched Dixon on his cheek, and the prisoner spit out two teeth and the blood that accompanied them. "I don't think so," Max whispered in his ear.

"Torture is prohibited under the Geneva Convention, you know," Dixon replied.

"Yes," Max assured him. "But the Geneva Convention applies to warring factions. Either you're on my side, in which case the Geneva Convention doesn't apply to you, or you're my enemy, in which case you are guilty of treason. So, I ask you, who are you?"

Dixon pondered the question before answering. "William Dixon," he said, spitting blood inadvertently in the process. "I'm director of the CIA."

"Good," Max said. He grabbed Dixon by the shoulder and pulled him upright to a kneeling position. "Now, why were you stealing General Rogers' food?"

"I was hungry. I've been living in the fallout tunnels for months, and my food was running out."

"Why not just ask for help?"

"They weren't gonna help me. They work for *him*."

"Who is *him*?"

"That prick bastard, Sultan!"

Max eyed Rogers and his men carefully. He did not know if Dixon was being truthful. "What do you know about Sultan?"

"What's to know?" Dixon asked. "He's a sadistic prick with an overdeveloped ego – a real sociopath. He's just what this country needed." Max detected his sarcasm.

"How did Sultan get here?"

"How the fuck should I know?" Dixon asked defiantly.

"It would seem to me, Mr. Dixon, that the director of the CIA would have been privy to such information.

Unless, of course, you were entirely inept at your job," Max needled.

"Fuck you!" Dixon hollered before spitting blood in Max's face.

Unfazed by the warm blood and saliva dripping down his face, Max drew his sword and jabbed it into Dixon's shoulder. He twisted the blade to inflict as much pain as possible; Dixon screamed and writhed in pain as blood oozed from the wound.

"Don't ever do that again!" he chastised Dixon while continuing to torment the prisoner. "I know it was you who bribed Ben Arnold to give Sultan access to the Capitol that night!" Max pushed the sword deeper into Dixon's shoulder.

Surprised by Max's statement and feeling more agony than before, Dixon said through clenched teeth, "I don't know what you are talking about!"

Max pulled the sword from Dixon's shoulder. "Don't you? Didn't you offer a Secret Service agent named Ben Arnold two hundred and fifty thousand dollars to let Sultan and his men into the Capitol to murder President Cole?"

"No, it wasn't me!" Dixon cried. Max bashed him on the head with the butt of his sword, opening a gash that gushed blood down Dixon's face in the process. The prisoner cried like a baby as he collapsed to the ground.

"Liar!" Max called. "If it wasn't you, who was it? Was it Harmon? Was it your fearless lover? What's his role in this?!" Rogers and his men were stunned by the accusation.

"How do you know about Daniel?" Dixon cried.

Just then, Sharpe, who had been standing behind Dixon, walked around and revealed himself to his old comrade. "Hello, Billy," he said.

Dixon was astonished. The sight of Sharpe rattled him. His secrets were no longer safe, and he knew that meant certain doom. "You told him?" he asked Sharpe.

"Had to, Billy," Sharpe confirmed. "It was a secret I kept for far too long."

Angered, Dixon cried, "Damn you, John! Okay, Noble. You got me! So what? What do you want to know? That I'm a fuckin' fag, and Daniel is my lover? We've been together and hiding it from the world for decades. They call this the land of the free, but you know something, it's only free if you're a white, male, heterosexual Christian! It's wrong, and you know it! So Daniel and I decided to do something about it! I had my operatives get him in touch with Sultan, and they figured out this perfect plan, as long as they could get the President to get all of the government people in one room at the same time, we could wipe them all out. Fuck this country! It's bullshit, anyway! Cole, that arrogant bastard, jumped at the opportunity to show the world just how big his dick was when Daniel approached him with the idea of doing it at the State of the Union so the whole world could see it! Then I got that hayseed to breakdown faster than a captured French spy, and the plan was set in motion. But then that fuckin' dumbass kid went and killed your wife. I underestimated you at that point, though. I thought for sure that after the invasion, you would run for the hills; you were no threat to us. But you persevered, and here we are. Good for you, Noble. Fighting for a country built on lies and hypocrisy. It figures that a fuckin' Jew would be the thorn in my side. I watched from my television in my office as the missile annihilated Chicago, and then as you withstood the political attacks. As you made your speeches, I knew that Daniel was losing his grip. I took refuge in those tunnels, hoping that Daniel would join me for one last tryst before we were discovered. When he didn't show, but these others did, I knew the end was near. And now, Noble, you know how it began. The only question left for history to answer is 'How will it end?'"

Max stood next to Sharpe. "What do you think, General?"

"I'd call a confession of overt acts against the nation in front of all those present a confession of treason, no?" Sharpe said to the soldiers.

"What next then? Is he the guy called, 'Our Man,' that Sultan's men refer to?" Max asked.

"You idiot!" Dixon interrupted. "He's not saying 'Our Man!' That's how he pronounces 'Harmon!' It was right in front of you this whole time, and you didn't even know! Ha!"

Ignoring Dixon's outburst, Sharpe answered, "He should stand trial. He'll sign a confession to be entered into evidence, and his treason will be punishable by death."

"Trial, hmm," Max considered. He looked at Rogers, remembering that he had warned Rogers of the punishment for treason earlier when accusing him of the same crime for his launch of the nuclear warhead. "General Rogers, come here please."

Rogers obeyed. "Yes, sir."

"General," Max addressed Rogers, "Your capture of Mr. Dixon was an act of heroism. Our nation is fortunate to have a man of your honor and courage in its military ranks. Your treason is hereby pardoned," he said placing one hand on Rogers' shoulder.

"Thank you, Mr. President," Rogers said.

Turning to the kneeling Dixon, Max announced, "Yours, Mr. Dixon, is not."

"Fuck you, Noble! Go ahead, put me on trial! Even with the death penalty, I'll bet I outlive you! Daniel will take great pleasure in killing you, and I will laugh when I see the pictures of your funeral on TV as your pretty little wife weeps over your grave!"

"What did you say?" Max asked.

"You heard me!" Dixon replied. Without warning, Max plunged his sword into Dixon's sternum. He looked into Dixon's eyes. He focused on the white part surrounding the irises. They slowly turned red, matching Dixon's blood covered face. For the first time, Max found the sensation of killing a man exhilarating.

"No!" Sharpe cried as he tried to pull Max away. His efforts were too late, and Max pressed the sword deeper into Dixon until the tip of the blade came through his back. Dixon coughed and gurgled blood as all signs of life left his eyes. Max pulled the sword from his body, and the corpse slumped to the ground.

Max walked away from the group and replaced his sword in its sheath. Sharpe chased after him, and when they were far enough from the group so as not to be heard, he said, "That was a mistake, sir. He was an unarmed prisoner of war. With all due respect, he should have lived to stand trial."

Max paused but kept his back to Sharpe. He felt no remorse; he felt nothing. He was soulless and empty. "Punishable by death, General. That's what you said."

"After a trial by a jury of his peers," Sharpe emphasized.

"We are his peers, General," Max explained. "We decided his guilt based on his confession. I chose to carry out justice today."

"Who do you think you are?" Sharpe asked, walking around to look Max in the eye. "What happened to the man of great conscience I once knew? God does not show mercy to murderers."

"I don't know, General. I just don't believe that there is a god out there who deserves a say in the matter."

CHAPTER 31

As soon as Gonzo told him that the troops were ready for battle, Chatty gave the order to move, beginning the march to Maryland. Sharpe's orders were clear that they were not to allow anyone near Washington's city limits; the scout team's findings were less than encouraging. Chatty understood, and did as ordered.

Roxy was not as accepting. She and Zach were passengers in a van headed for the forests of Maryland. This was supposed to be a day she long anticipated: The day in which she would be able to begin living her normal family life. Yet, once again, that life was preempted by the war. She wore her disgust with the situation on her face. Bam Bam, who was driving the van, and the Peach, who was playing *Go Fish* with Zach in the back seat, both tried to make small talk in an effort to cheer her up, but to no avail.

When the van arrived at its destination, Max hurried to greet his wife. She walked passed him without saying a word and headed into his tent, which he spent the morning preparing as their new temporary living quarters. Zach, on the other hand, greeted Max with a hug. "Good to see you, champ," Max said. "Why don't you and Peach go set up your archery target over there?" he suggested pointing to a nearby tree.

Zach agreed, and collected the target and his arrows from the van. The Peach, having thrown his belongings in Boots' tent, hurried to watch the young lad. Although he would never admit it, Zach was becoming one of the Peach's better friends. Maybe it was his own immaturity, but regardless of the reason, he was developing a bond with Zach.

Bam Bam continued to unload the van. Max approached him and asked, "What's her problem, now?"

"Don't know, sir," Bam Bam answered. "She was quiet the whole ride down here. I think she's ready for this war to end."

"Aren't we all?" Max scoffed.

"Listen, my old lady can be a real pain in the ass. I know what you're going through. Just remember that it ain't easy on her either. Let her say her piece, get it off her chest, and when she's done, she'll feel better."

"Thanks, Bam Bam. Does that work for you and your wife?"

"Fuck, no," Bam Bam adamantly answered. "My wife's the biggest bitch in the world! She fights with me for no reason just to piss me off! But, your old lady, she's alright, you know? She's kind and she cares a lot about you. That's what's important."

"You have a little thing for her, there?" Max chided.

"No, sir," Bam Bam said defiantly. "I'm old school. In my neighborhood, they cut your pecker off for lookin' at another man's wife the wrong way. I like my pecker right where it is, if you know what I mean. Just tryin' to help you out, that's all."

"Well, I appreciate the honesty, Bam Bam."

"Just part of my job, sir. Now, go in there and clear the air between you two."

"Thanks," Max said. "Boots is out collecting firewood. It's starting to get real cold at night. Once you're settled, you should do the same."

"Will do," Bam Bam said.

Max took a deep breath before taking Bam Bam's

advice. He entered the tent with caution. Roxy was pouting while she unpacked. "Is everything alright, Rox?"

"That's a loaded fuckin' question and you know it," she quipped.

"I'll take that as a 'No,'" he retorted.

"You're goddamned right, that's a 'No!'"

"Do you want to talk about it?" he asked. Although, he secretly hoped she did not.

"What's the use? You don't keep your word, anyway. You're just another politician who can't be trusted."

Max was irate. They had argued plenty, but this was the first time that she elevated their discussion to the point of questioning his character. "That's not fair! You don't even know what's going on!"

"You're right, Max, I don't! And *that's* the fuckin' problem! You're out gallivanting into heroic battles while I'm stuck waiting for you to come home safely so we can live our life together. *That's* what's not fair!"

"Where did all of this come from? I don't get it!"

"Where? Ugh! You can't be that blind!"

"Well, maybe I am!"

She paused, giving him the benefit of the doubt, and explained, "Why are you still fighting this war? There are plenty of people willing to put their lives on the line so that you don't have to! When do we get to be a normal family, Max? I'm tired of living in the woods and waiting for that magic moment."

"I have to fight, Rox," he explained while grabbing the satchel with Dalton's ashes that hung from his belt. "I can't explain why. It's just something that I have to do. It will all be over soon."

"When, Max? It's almost Halloween! I mean, is it so unrealistic to think that we won't be able to have a

Thanksgiving turkey at the White House?"

Max shook his head. Calmly, he said, "No, it's not unrealistic. In fact, it looks very likely that Thanksgiving will be right here."

Roxy's face turned to stone. "You're kidding," she said, shaking her head in disgust.

"I'm afraid not," Max explained. "The scout team reported from Washington. Sultan's men are occupying the city. Sharpe thinks that we have to take to urban warfare and house-to-house combat to take it back. He said that once we gain control of the streets, we'll be able to go after the Pentagon. But, urban battles don't happen overnight like surprise raids. Sharpe says it could be as much as six to eight weeks before we take back the city."

Roxy sat on the bed and began to cry. "Well, that's just fuckin' wonderful," she said sarcastically.

"I know," Max said, echoing her sentiment. He curiously kept his distance.

"You could at least show some compassion and come over here."

"I don't think so, Rox. Something's happened to me. Compassion isn't high up on my list of priorities anymore."

"What's that supposed to mean?" Roxy asked, confused and angry at his refusal to comfort her.

Max proceeded to divulge to her the events surrounding his murder of Dixon; he elaborated as to how he felt when he killed him. He told her of how, at first, he was angry with Dixon for his hatred of others. But after he pummeled the unarmed man and it became clear that he had not broken him, Max said he was excited by plunging the sword into Dixon's shoulder; he became more electrified with each twist as he inflicted more pain. Finally, he explained, he was elated to watch him die.

Roxy was horrified. She saw a blank stare on her husband's face that she did not recognize. This empty shell of a man standing before her was her husband, but in body only. "What's happened to you, Max? Where is the man I married? The sweet, compassionate and caring man I love? I know he's in there, but where?"

"I don't know, Rox," Max said, hanging his head in shame. "Help me bring him back," he pleaded.

"I don't know how," she fretted.

"Me neither," Max warned.

CHAPTER 32

The weeks passed slowly. Sharpe and Rogers coordinated the Washington campaign. Chatty and Ryan led their respective divisions into battle. Sporadic gunfire echoed throughout the nation's capital on a daily basis as the two armies clashed in the streets using the buildings for cover. Unlike the New York and Philadelphia campaigns, the strategy this time did not call for a quick strike. Sultan had too many men stationed throughout the city to allow for such an onslaught. Instead, it was a methodical invasion that would chip away at their control of the city one block at a time. Patience was the secret weapon.

Halloween came and went. Rumors swirled that Max had been killed in action because he had not appeared on television for an extended period of time. Armstrong arranged for Susan to interview Max at the Maryland camp. Although Max initially resisted Armstrong's call for the broadcast, he finally agreed. When the piece aired, the autumn scenery itself reassured the viewers that the images of Max were recent. Max led Susan on a tour of the camp, where she also interviewed several soldiers who professed their determination to end the war shortly. Sharpe granted an interview to discuss the military's morale and strategy. It was perfect: the whispers of Max's death were quashed at home, and Judge Vineri even reported to the council that foreign leaders who saw the piece were relieved to know that an American triumph was at hand.

With the economy beginning to recover, donations to the cause poured in. The money was used to purchase more than artillery. Ammunition, of course, topped the list of necessities and was purchased in abundance, but blankets and warmer uniforms were also delivered, as were fresh supplies of food. The council approved the expenditures, but there was no debate. The politicians knew that if they wanted to secure their role in the new republic after the war they could not stand in the military's way.

SBN also aired special coverage on Veterans' Day. Few troops remained in the camp that day, as most were engaged in the fierce fighting in Washington. Max's brief speech to the troops was followed by the soldiers reading the names of their comrades who had been killed in the line of duty since the war began. Max read the first twenty-five names of the soldiers killed in action, and then returned to read the names of those killed at the State of the Union speech. The last name he read was President Cole's.

The emotional broadcast rallied the American public further. In addition to monetary donations, people began donating turkeys and cans of cranberry sauce so that the soldiers would have a decent Thanksgiving meal. By the time the commemorative holiday arrived, most of Washington had been reclaimed. The American forces encountered pockets of resistance from Sultan's soldiers, but they were becoming fewer and farther between.

At Max's Thanksgiving dinner table, Sharpe declared that he expected to have eliminated the last remnants of Sultan's regime from the city proper within the week. A roar of victory filled the tent, and smiles abounded on all of their faces. Boots, Bam Bam and the Peach gave each other "high fives." Max shook the general's hand to congratulate him on a job well done. Sharpe reminded him that victory was not complete until Sultan and Harmon were captured at the Pentagon; but, he ultimately admitted that regaining control of the capitol made victory that much more imminent.

Max hugged Zach tightly, and they howled like wolves baying at the moon. It was a moment of bonding for the father and the son, only the latter did not yet know of their genetic connection; Max still had not fulfilled his promise to Roxy. He kissed Roxy on the cheek, and she smiled politely. This was not the Thanksgiving meal she planned.

On the Tuesday after Thanksgiving, Chatty reported to Sharpe that Washington, D.C., was entirely under American control once again. Sultan's men had either been killed or retreated to the Pentagon. Upon hearing the news, Max dispersed Boots, Bam Bam and the Peach to the White House to ensure that it was safe for his family. Sharpe ordered Chatty and Gonzo to accompany them, in case there were any signs of trouble. After a thorough inspection, Chatty reported that it was safe for Max and his family to return. Roxy quickly packed their belongings and was anxious to settle into their new home.

That night, Bam Bam returned with the van. He and Max loaded the first family's things into the back. Before they set off for the White House, Max told Sharpe to arrive at the Oval Office at nine o'clock the next morning. The general saluted his commander-in-chief, beaming with pride. The presidential residence would be vacant no more.

* * *

Omar Qaferi had managed to keep the city of Atlanta under his control, but returned to the Pentagon with his men when Sultan ordered the retreat. He was rewarded for his success by being named Sultan's second-in-command.

"Sultan! Sultan!" one of the aides called in Arabic. "You must see this!" He pressed a button at his console in the Hub and the SBN broadcast appeared on the main screen.

Susan appeared in her signature red glasses. "We interrupt this program to bring a message to you from the President of the United States," she said.

The screen cut to an image of Max, donning a navy suit, light blue shirt and a red tie with thin, white diagonal stripes, sitting at the President's desk in the Oval Office. Sharpe stood behind him just to his right. "My fellow Americans," Max began. "It is with great pride that I speak to you this morning from a most hallowed place: The Oval Office. It has been a privilege to fight with America's bravest soldiers, and an honor to live amongst them during these difficult times. It is only through their efforts that I have been fortunate enough to arrive here today.

"General Sharpe deserves most of the credit for our victories as the architect of our strategies. We were blessed to have him in our midst during this conflict. It is only because of his leadership that we have been able to reclaim our cities, and now, I am happy to inform you, our capitol as well." Max turned his head to the general and nodded. "On behalf of all Americans, General, I thank you."

"It is an honor, Mr. President," Sharpe replied.

Turning back to the camera, Max continued, "But our job is not yet complete. We have been able to unravel most of the mystery of how Sultan managed to invade our homeland. He is no great tactician. He is no military genius. He is no inspiration to his men. It is with a heavy heart that I report to you that we were betrayed from within our own ranks. The former Director of the CIA, William Dixon, and General Daniel Harmon conspired to orchestrate a plot in which they failed to report intelligence to the necessary powers that be at the Secret Service, and in which they passed information to Sultan that allowed him and his men to access the Capitol on the night of the State of the Union. These two high-powered officials acted alone in their treason. The burden of guilt was too much to bear for Mr. Dixon, who took his own life."

Sharpe stood stoically as Max uttered his lies to the American public. He always detested politicians for their dishonesty, only this time he felt guilty for abetting Max's. While it weighed heavily on his conscience, he neither said nor did anything to contradict Max's version of events. He vowed to take the truth to his grave, and he hoped that his good deeds would be enough to counter his silence when his soul was to be judged.

"It is believed," Max continued, "that General Harmon remains at the Pentagon, where he continues to assist Sultan in some sort of advisory capacity. The Pentagon remains the last bastion of Sultan's control. My fellow Americans, it is only a matter of time before his presence ends. Dead or alive, Sultan and General Harmon will be brought to justice for their crimes against the United States of America. Make no mistake, vengeance will be ours.

"My fellow Americans, today is a new day for our nation. We will drive our enemies from our lands. We are restored as a people. May God bless you and your families. And may God bless the United States of America."

The image of Max was replaced by the presidential seal, and then by Susan's image. "Well, ladies and gentlemen, there you have it. President Noble, live from the Oval Office, reporting that the former CIA director and General Daniel Harmon are responsible for the events of the past year . . . ."

The screen suddenly went black as Sultan pushed a button on the console. "So," he said. "Noble knows."

"What should we do, oh mighty Sultan?" Qaferi asked.

"Prepare to meet Allah," Sultan answered.

* * *

The Situation Room in the White House had a cold feel to it. It was a solemn place; levity was taboo. Armstrong shut and locked the door once the meeting was to begin. A bright light shone over the conference table illuminating it. The rest of the room remained dark, shrouded in secrecy. Those sitting at the table instinctively knew that they were to lean forward into the light so that they could be seen. Otherwise, the shadows would consume them.

Max sat at the head of the table, with Rogers and Chatty to his left and right, respectively. Sharpe sat across from Max at the table's other end, flanked on his left by Gonzo, and on his right by Ryan. Armstrong stood in the corner of the room, hidden in the darkness; he had been instructed by Max to say nothing, and to take copious notes with his eyes. The meeting was classified as "Top Secret," and Sharpe ordered no written record be made of it. Still, it reminded Max of the strategy sessions they held at Dalton's house during his training exercises. Only Dalton was gone, and Max was not the naïve whelp he once was.

Max broke the silence shortly after the men gathered. "As you are aware, gentlemen, I have spent the last three days shoring up the nation's government. Compared to where we were prior to Sultan's arrival, we are currently operating at forty percent of our payroll capacity. Essential services, such as the Post Office and the Treasury Department, have been restored to full capacity. The Departments of State, Transportation, Agriculture and the Interior are running at fifty percent efficiency, give or take. The Departments of Justice and Homeland Security are coming along. The rest can wait until a full Congress is elected. In the meantime, the council has been put into recess, but its last act was to . . . What was it Jack? I want to get the quote right.

"They granted the Office of the President quote, 'absolute power to secure the homeland and eliminate the intruding enemy force,' end quote," Armstrong said from his post by the door, his voice being heard but his person remaining invisible. "The law also requires that a new Congress be elected within sixty days of victory."

"Thank you, Jack," Max acknowledged. "So, the time has come to finish this and move forward. General Sharpe, I understand you have a proposal for my consideration."

"Yes, Mr. President," Sharpe confirmed. He touched the screen on the monitor built into the table in front of him, and on the wall behind him, an architectural schematic of the Pentagon appeared. He rose from his seat and approached the diagram. "General Rogers and I have developed an offensive strategy, that I believe is indefensible, sir. The enemy has fortified the Pentagon against a possible assault from all directions," he said pointing to artillery stations on the roofs of each of the building's iconic five wings. "It is our intent to launch the attack on the twenty-first of December."

"Why that date, General? It's over two weeks away," Max interrupted.

"Yes, sir, we are aware," Rogers interjected. "But, as General Sharpe will explain, we intend to use the darkness of night to our advantage, and the twenty-first is the shortest day of the year."

Max nodded. "Continue," he said.

"Thank you, General," Sharpe noted. "Our intent is to launch the initial assault at dawn. One battalion will attack from the north, and must be able to withstand heavy shelling all throughout the day. Needless to say, casualties among this battalion will be heavy." Sharpe grew silent at the thought of inevitably sending young men to meet certain death. "We anticipate that the sustained assault from the north will cause Sultan to utilize his remaining defenses to fortify the north wing," he continued, "thereby weakening the defenses at the remaining wings, particularly the south wing.

"Shortly after dusk," he proceeded, "under the cover of darkness, our remaining battalions, who will have surrounded the Pentagon from an unnoticeable distance, will attack the less fortified wings, with the heaviest assault to come from the south."

"Sounds brilliant, General," Max commented. "But what if the enemy is able to repel our forces?"

"I defer to General Rogers," Sharpe said.

"Thank you, General Sharpe," Rogers cordially responded, as he rose and joined Sharpe at the Pentagon schematic. "While General Sharpe is coordinating the surrounding assault, I will lead a battalion of our men into the fallout tunnels through the entrance in the Maryland woods. We should arrive at the entrance to the Secretary of Defense's office at midnight. We anticipate that after approximately sixteen hours of constant bombardment from our troops outside, the inner defenses will be almost entirely forgotten." He pressed a button on the remote control in his hand, and the image changed to a floor plan of one of the wings. Pointing to a room, he said, "We will then enter through the Secretary's office, and proceed to the Hub, where I suspect we will encounter Sultan, his personal guards, and of course, General Harmon. Once we have neutralized Sultan, we will proceed to the roofs to take the artillery stations. And then . . . ."

"And then, what, General?" Max asked impatiently.

"Victory, Mr. President," Rogers answered.

"I see," Max said. "Do you have your personnel in place?"

"Not yet, sir," Sharpe answered. "I would like to brief the men, first. I believe it best for morale to ask for volunteers only for the northern assault. But they must be made aware of the great risks they will be facing." In truth, he was trying to lessen his own guilt for ordering them to meet their maker.

"No need for that, General," Ryan suddenly said. "I am volunteering my men for the northern assault."

"You may feel the need to be macho, Colonel," Gonzo challenged, "but let your men decide for themselves if they should put themselves in the face of certain death."

"Are they ready for battle, Major?" Ryan demanded.

Without hesitation, Gonzo replied, "Yes, they are."

"Then let me worry about their well-being," Ryan retorted. "Mr. President, these are my brothers. They love to fight the tough fights. It would be an honor for them to tell their grandkids that on the day when the United States was officially reborn, they were the biggest reason why. They're ready. I'm ready. Please, Mr. President, I beg of you."

Max pondered the request.

"What of the men who don't get the chance to have grandkids?" Chatty asked. The quiet colonel possessed a knack for asking the difficult questions.

"Just give 'em that chance, please," Ryan whispered to Max, ignoring Chatty's question.

"Alright, Ryan," Max said. "The northern assault is yours, on one condition."

"Anything!" Ryan declared.

"You obey every order General Sharpe gives you," max directed. "If he orders you to pull back, or even to retreat, you trust his judgment. Do you understand?"

Ryan looked at Sharpe and nodded. "Yes, Mr. President. What the general says goes."

"Good," Max said. "General?"

"Of course, Mr. President," Sharpe acknowledged.

"I assume then that Colonel Chatham and Major Gonzalez will be leading the remaining forces in their assault at dusk?" Max asked.

"That is correct," Rogers responded.

"Good luck, gentlemen," Max said to Chatty and Gonzo.

"Thank you, sir," they said in unison.

"I suppose, then, that I am the only one unassigned to a role in this battle?" Max asked.

Sharpe and Rogers looked at each other. Neither prepared an answer to the question. Finally, Sharpe said, "Mr. President, with all due respect, there is no need for you to join this battle. Victory is at hand, and your place is here, now. You and I will be in constant communication during the bat . . . ."

"Nonsense!" Max interrupted. "I started this war, and I am going to finish it! I am joining General Rogers' team. I will bring Sultan and General Harmon to justice myself! I want their blood for they've done!"

Dismayed, Sharpe softly replied, "Mr. President, you're already a hero. This country owes you more than it could possibly repay you. Please don't allow your anger toward Harmon and Sultan to cloud your judgment. You are better than that."

"Nevertheless," Max replied, "I am going to accompany General Rogers. I will have revenge, General!"

CHAPTER 33

The nation was abuzz in the weeks following Max's speech from the Oval Office. Political pundits returned to the television airwaves wondering "When is this guy going to act on his words?" or, as one conservative commentator phrased it, "What the hell is he waiting for?" Max largely ignored them, and made certain to appear before the reestablished press corps in the White House briefing room at least once each day. He rattled off his daily reports about the status of each department of the government, and sidestepped all questions about his plans for Sultan and General Harmon. Since most of the questions were about the latter, some of the talking heads on television began to refer to Max as "The Artful Dodger," for his constant avoidance of answering the burning questions.

Max had become a very good politician. Armstrong beamed in his office where he watched each press conference like a boxing promoter watching his prize fighter in the ring. "Nice one!" he would say every time Max frustrated a reporter. He was proud of his creation.

Roxy was settling into her role as First Lady. She issued statements, all of which were crafted by Armstrong, as to which charities and causes she would support during Max's presidency. Most of them related to helping families and rebuilding homes devastated by the war. But more than anything, she was exhilarated by the normalcy that returned to her life. She was sleeping in the same bed as her husband, and their son's room was just down the hall.

They enjoyed a trip to the different national

monuments as a family; they visited the Lincoln, Washington and Jefferson Memorials, with the press corps in tow, to introduce Zach to American history. Max pointed out the Capitol building to him, but said that they could not visit just yet. In truth, the decomposing bodies of the State of the Union victims had first been removed several days before. Max visited the site himself to survey it. The stench of death inside was nauseating. The bloodstains remained throughout, reminding him of Sultan's disregard for his victim's lives; in turn, Max's desire for revenge grew stronger. Max ordered the building be fumigated for rats, cockroaches and other vermin that had come to feast on the decaying human flesh. After one week of constant exterminating with rodenticides and pesticides, he was told that the building would be safe to reenter. However, it was anticipated that the chamber would not be entirely renovated, and the scars of that horrific night would finally be removed, until shortly into the New Year before the new Congress was to be sworn in. Max would not subject Zach to the sight of the Congressional chamber in its current condition.

Nevertheless, the nation was rapidly returning to its pre-invasion condition. The government was operating at sixty-five percent of its capacity, and the economy was returning to a state of positive growth as money began to flow freely through the banking system. Schools were back in session, and even professional sports teams were preparing to resume competitive play. Max was keeping all of the promises he made to the council that day he defeated Thomas in the election.

Yet, Max still had not kept his promise to Roxy. She thought he might have done it by now. Indeed, he and Zach were spending ample time alone together. She was dismayed to learn that instead of telling Zach that he was the boy's father, Max chose to help him with his archery, discuss the books he was reading, and talk to him about the difference between being a boy and being a man.

Two days before the next battle was to begin, Max even gave Zach his own cell phone with Max's private cell phone number preprogrammed into it. "I'm going to be fighting in another battle soon, but I won't be far away," he said. "If you sense any trouble around here, I want you to text me, okay?"

"Is the Peach going with you?" Zach asked, very concerned that his good friend might be joining Max in battle.

"No, the Peach will be here with you, Boots, Bam Bam and your mother," Max assured him. "But when I am gone, I want you to be the man of the house. You're my eyes and ears around here, and I want you to let me know if anything unusual happens. Can you do that for me?"

Zach nodded excitedly, giddy that Max trusted him with such a responsibility. Under different circumstances Roxy would have lauded Max's paternal influence, but why he had not yet explained that he was Zach's actual father escaped her. And that, in and of itself, irked her.

* * *

The night before the winter solstice, was brutally cold. Temperatures that night dropped into the teens, and the day of the battle was supposed to be even colder. Roxy tucked Zach into bed, and then joined Max in the White House library. They sat in separate chairs by the fire that crackled in the fireplace. The sweet smell of the burning firewood was comforting. They said nothing to each other, but were perfectly content just to enjoy each other's company.

A soft knock at the door interrupted their meditation. Boots peeked into the room and said, "You wanted to see us, sir?"

Max jumped out of his chair and answered, "Oh,

yes. Hold on, I'll be right out." He turned to Roxy, and assured her, "I'll be right back."

She nodded as Max left the room. In the hallway, Boots was waiting with Bam Bam and the Peach. Max hurried the three men into his private study in the next room, where he told them of his intention to fight the battle at the Pentagon without them. "I'll be with General Rogers' men," he explained. "I'll be fine without you guys. But I still consider you my closest friends, which is why it would mean more to me for you to stay here, at the White House, and guard Rox and Zach during the battle. I'll be able to concentrate better if I know that they are safe."

"No problem, Boss," Boots said. "Bam Bam will watch Roxy, and the Peach will stick with Zach while you're away. I'll bounce back and forth between them."

"Yeah, Boss," Bam Bam agreed. "The Mrs. will be just fine."

"Zach, too," the Peach added. "That kid can take care of himself, you know. But don't worry; I'll make sure he's alright."

"Thanks, guys," Max said wholeheartedly. "I meant it when I said that you guys were my closest friends."

"Each of us would be honored to take a bullet for you, Mr. President," Boots said.

"Let's hope you never have to," Max replied. He hugged each of them, and returned to the library to join his wife. "Sorry about that," he said to Roxy as he sat in his chair.

"What was that all about?" Roxy asked.

"That? Oh, nothing big, really. I just told them that I didn't want them to join me in the battle tomorrow. So, they'll be here with you and Zach instead."

"I get so nervous when you go into battle, you know?"

"I know, Rox. But this is the last one, I swear. Tomorrow, we'll finally bring this thing to an end, and I'll be home as soon as it's over. I know it's been rough, but you can't say it hasn't been worth it. I mean, look at us. We're a family. Isn't this what you've always wanted?"

Roxy looked away from Max and into the fire. "Of course it's what I wanted. It's what I've always wanted ever since the day I met you. But what if you don't come home?" she asked concernedly. "What are Zach and I supposed to do, then? We love you, Max. We need you."

"Zach's growing up, Rox. You can't treat him like a little boy anymore," Max insisted.

"He's not a man yet, Max. He needs a father – his father. Have you told him yet?" She already knew the answer.

Ashamed, Max said, "Not yet."

"What are you waiting for, Max? When are you going to tell him?"

"When the time is right," he offered.

"And when will that be? Let me guess, after the war!" she chided sarcastically.

"Precisely!" Max declared. "Just let me finish this, and then I'll be able to focus on making amends here at home."

"Alright," Roxy conceded. "But it has to be the first thing you say to him when you come home."

Max got out of his chair and kneeled before hers. "Thank you, Rox. I love you, you know that, right?"

"I do. And I love you, too," she said.

Max responded with a passionate kiss, and Roxy returned it with matching intensity. They made love on the Persian rug in front of the fireplace, and there they held each other tightly for nearly an hour without saying a word before retiring to the bedroom for the night.

* * *

Ryan assembled his men at the staging area, which was a field located just over one mile north of the Pentagon, at five o'clock in the morning, nearly a full two hours before dawn. The entire army made camp there the night before, and tents were huddled around campfires for heat in the bitter cold. With his troops gathered around one of the larger fires, he and Connelly briefed the regiment as to their role in the assault on the Pentagon. However, the orders were not well-received.

"Who signed us up for this suicide mission?" a soldier with a thick moustache yelled.

"Yeah! I volunteered for a fair fight, not to be bait!" another exclaimed.

Soon, commotion erupted among the battalion, and Ryan and Connelly were losing their men before the battle would even have a chance to begin. Although he would not admit it, Connelly agreed with the troops. They looked at each other in despair.

But Ryan knew that the mission was imperative to the battle's success. He never second guessed his instinct to volunteer his men or his insistence in the face of Chatty's warning. Moreover, Sharpe was counting on him to deliver, and he could not let his general down.

"Now, wait a minute!" Ryan declared. "These aren't the streets of Boston anymore. And you guys aren't just another bunch of dumb and poor Southies. We're soldiers in the United States Army, and we need to act like it! I'm the one who volunteered us for this mission! Right here," he said pointing to himself. "It was me. And I did it because we are the best men for this job!"

"Why?" the mustached soldier asked. "Because we ain't got nothin' to lose? Well, no offense, Colonel, but my life is all I got, and I don't wanna lose that either!"

"No," Ryan responded. "I know that our lives are all we got. But what good are they if we just sit back and let this fight happen around us? What would happen if we were in Boston right now, and your best friend got jumped in the street? You would get your boys and you find who did it and kick their fuckin' asses, right?"

"Yeah," the men answered collectively.

"Well, this is the same fuckin' thing. Our countrymen from the north, south, east and west are about to get into a rumble. Someone has to throw the first punch, and be tough enough to take a few until we get control of the fight. Well, boys, I don't know about you, but I say there ain't nobody better in a fight to do that than a bunch of Southies. Yeah, we're gonna take our lumps. And I can't guarantee that we're gonna make it out of there in one piece, if at all. But let me ask you this," he said approaching the mustached soldier. He came to the challenger face-to-face, looked him square in the eyes and asked, "Are you the gutless puke that runs from that fight? Or are you the guy who throws the first punch?"

"I throw the first punch," the mustached soldier said shoving Ryan.

"Exactly," Ryan said. "We're the guys who get it started. We're the wreckin' crew! We may not march in a straight line, but this army needs us! Without us, this mission would be an absolute disaster because nobody else is crazy enough to do it! Gentlemen, our country calls us to help her. Are we gonna answer that call?"

"Sir! Yes, sir!" the men declared in unison.

"Good," Ryan approved. "Now, eat your breakfast. We move out at dawn, and we will present ourselves to the enemy at eight hundred hours. Dismissed!"

The battalion dispersed, but Connelly remained to talk to Ryan. "What did they do to you in that car ride to

Maryland? Brainwash you?"

"What do you mean?" Ryan asked Connelly to clarify.

"You sounded like one of them, that's all."

"I don't know. It just seems like this is it. This is our moment to do something with our lives. Not just you and me, but them, too. They have an opportunity here to be heroes."

"Yeah, but racing into oncoming artillery fire? It's crazy," Connelly cautioned.

"Get that fear out of your head, Patty. If you let it get to you like that, you'll never make it out of there alive."

"Says you!" Connelly protested. "Do I have to remind you who kicked your ass in the third grade? You ran away like a scared little bitch! I ain't afraid of this."

"Good," Ryan said. "Then just follow my lead and do what I tell you, when I tell you."

"Yes, sir!" Connelly said indignantly as he sarcastically saluted Ryan.

"Fuck you, Patty!"

"Whatever. I'm gonna eat something."

"Fine, Patty. But when this is over, I want a rematch. Fifty bucks says I kick your ass this time!"

"You're on!" Connelly agreed.

* * *

The dawn light illuminated the bedroom and woke Max from his slumber. Roxy was unfazed by it. Max went to the kitchen, prepared two eggs and toast for breakfast, and ate it in silence. He slurped his coffee as he ate, and then gulped down a glass of orange juice to finish the meal.

After the meal, he went to the bathroom, where

he shaved. He paid particular attention to every hair, making sure not to miss any. He wanted to be certain that when he finally met Sultan in person, he was perfectly clean shaven as if to flaunt his bare face; it was a symbolic gesture of his freedom more than anything. He then took a hot shower for longer than usual. He enjoyed the feel of the near scalding water on his skin. He emerged cleansed, refreshed, and ready for victory.

Once he dried himself, Max returned to the bedroom to get dressed. He took his uniform, the same one that Dalton made for him, and that he wore for the New York and Philadelphia campaigns, and put it on. Roxy had washed it by hand and ironed it as best she could; she wasn't entirely sure of the proper way to clean a Kevlar vest. Max examined himself in the mirror. The uniform was perfect: Black as his heart with small tears in certain places. He attempted to flex his left arm, but he could not bend his elbow more than forty-five degrees. It was more useless now than ever before, but his enemies did not – and could not – know that.

He pulled his sword from the top of the closet, and removed it from its sheath, running his finger along the blade to test its sharpness. It was dull, and still had some of Dixon's dried blood on it. He took the sword to his study, where he sharpened it and polished it. Satisfied with its effectiveness and appearance, he replaced it in its sheath and placed the sword on his belt. Finally, he tied Dalton's ashes to his belt one last time.

Ready for battle, he returned to the bedroom and kissed Roxy on her forehead. "I love you," he whispered in her ear. She smiled and rolled onto her side.

He then made his way to Zach's bedroom. Zach was waking, and groggily said, "Good morning."

"Hey, there," Max said.

"Are you going to fight the war today?" Max asked

inquisitively.

"Yes, I am."

"I wanna come!"

Max chuckled. "I'm sure you would. But this war isn't for you."

"Sure, it is," Zach contended. "I have my arrows. I'm ready."

"Maybe so," Max agreed. "But your mother would kill me. So, hang tight today. The Peach will be here with you."

"Can I play hide and seek with him?" the disappointed child asked.

"Of course you can. This place has plenty of rooms to hide in."

"Okay then."

"Good. Well, buddy," Max began. "I have to go. Remember, keep your phone on you and set it for silent mode at all times in case we have to talk to each other, okay?"

"Okay, Dad," Zach assured him.

"Good. I love you, Zach."

"I love you, too, Dad."

Max left Zach's room and wiped a tear from his right eye. *A tear!* he thought as he inspected the moisture on his finger. *I haven't felt a tear in so long. I haven't felt anything in so long. Your son said he loves you. Of course you felt that.*

He continued to the Oval Office, where Armstrong was waiting for him. "Good morning, Jack."

"Good morning, Mr. President. How are we feeling today?"

"It's the best day of my life," Max answered thinking of his exchange with Zach. "Is everything in order?"

"Yes, sir. General Sharpe is waiting for you at the staging area. He says that you only need to be seen by the troops as they set off, and then you will join General Rogers in Maryland to enter the fallout tunnels."

"Good. And the departmental progress?"

"Getting back to normal, sir. Nothing changes quite overnight."

"Understood," Max acknowledged. "Our allies abroad?"

"Have told Judge Vineri that they are excited to celebrate your victory," Armstrong said.

"Excellent. What is it, Jack?" Max asked noticing Armstrong's facial expression. "I can tell when something is bothering you."

"It's nothing. I just wanted you to know that I am truly enjoying our working relationship, sir."

Max smiled. "Me, too, Jack. We've come a long way in a short period of time."

"Indeed, sir. But answer me this. Why are you risking everything we have accomplished? Your presence is not needed. Rogers' men can handle this without you. Stay here, and govern. That is how you will serve this country best."

"Did Roxy put you up to this? You sound just like her."

"No, sir. We just happen to agree that your insistence on joining this battle is . . . well, it's ludicrous!"

Max grew angry. "It's not ludicrous, Jack! Just because you don't think it is necessary doesn't mean it is ludicrous. The reality is that it is something that I have to do. I need to finish this myself. I don't know why. Maybe it has something to do with what the Judge told me about this war consuming me. I just feel like I won't be able to rest until I know that the war is over. It's my choice!"

"Very well, Mr. President. But just know that I expect to continue our work on restoring the government of this country as soon as you return."

Max smiled. "As do I, Jack. As do I."

CHAPTER 34

Three of Sultan's sentries occupied the Pentagon's north guard house. They huddled closely together inside for heat when they were approached by a man, who appeared drunk. "Is this the potty?" the elder Murphy asked them, his breath crystallizing on the guard house glass in the morning cold.

One of the guards pulled his handgun from its holster on his belt. "Who are you?!" he demanded.

Unfazed by the weapon, Murphy said, "I'm me! Who are you?"

"I will pull this trigger in a heartbeat if you do not tell me who you are!" the guard said.

"I'm Batman!" Murphy declared as he spread his arms wide and bowed. "But you can call me, 'Bruce,' if you like."

"What do you want, Bruce?" one of the other guards asked.

"I want to use your potty," Murphy answered.

"You can't!" the sentry with the gun forbade while cocking the gun's hammer.

"Why not? You're not out of toilet paper, are you?" Murphy quipped. "I don't need any. It's just a number one," he said as he unzipped his pants.

"That's enough!" the armed guard shouted. "If you expose yourself, I will shoot dead right here. Now, go!"

"But I can dance real nice," Murphy said as he poorly emulated a circus clown's dance for the Arabs. He fell, unintentionally, and smacked his head on the parking lot concrete. The guards stepped out of the guard house to watch the drunk's spectacle more closely. They were amused by his antics as he continued to prance around. "You wouldn't want to hurt me so that I can't do this anymore, would you? I'm an entertainer."

"I am going to count to three," the armed sentry warned. "One!"

"Two!" Murphy shouted, eliciting a laugh from the unarmed guards.

"I'm not kidding!" the armed guard said sternly. "Two!"

"And, three!" a new voice counted from behind the guards. By the time the three Arabs turned to see who had dared to finish the count, they were being tackled, bound and gagged by a small group of Ryan's men. "That was easier than I thought it would be," Ryan continued. He entered the guard house and pulled down a lever that turned off the electricity running through the chain-link north fence. He pulled his walkie-talkie from his belt and called through it, "New England has a first down on its own twenty yard line."

"Hold the line of scrimmage," Sharpe's voice replied through the radio. "Runs and screen passes, Coach. No Hail Mary's just yet. Save those for the end of the half."

"Eagle, right, twenty-three," Ryan answered Sharpe. Turning to Connelly, he said, "Bring the boys up here and tell them to cut through that fence. It's five hundred yards to the building, and we're gonna get there one inch at a time."

* * *

A feeling of all-too-familiar dread descended upon the Sultan's men in the Hub as alarms sounded. The video from the Pentagon's security cameras appeared on the center screen. The black and white images were clear: Ryan's men were cutting the chain-link fence in preparation for their assault.

"Go get Sultan!" Qaferi ordered one of the younger men in Arabic.

The young soldier ran out of the room and returned shortly with Sultan. The other young men in the room were amazed that their comrade was still alive. "What is it, Omar?" Sultan demanded to know. "It sounds like a carnival in here. Turn these alarms off, now!"

"It seems that the Americans are coming through the north fence, Sultan," Qaferi explained.

"I thought it was electrified," Sultan wondered aloud.

"It is, but they must have cut the circuit for the northern section," Qaferi answered.

"No matter," Sultan said. "This was expected. How many of them are there?"

The man sitting at the center screen's console panned the area with the security camera. The image revealed several tanks positioned in front of Ryan's soldiers; they were prepared for an invasion. "Thousands, Sultan," the man answered.

"Send ten thousand men to the north wing. Tell them to assemble in front of the building but do not advance. Let them bring the fight to us," Sultan ordered.

"What about the artillery, Sultan?" Qaferi asked.

"Tell them to open fire when the Americans are in range. Aim for the tanks first. Once they are eliminated, send the men out for the slaughter."

"As you wish, Sultan."

* * *

"Look at that," Connelly said to Ryan pointing to the seemingly never ending slew of Sultan's men that were positioning themselves in perfect regiments in front of the Pentagon's North Wing. He, Ryan and Murphy established a command post at the center of the combat formation. "They outman us two-to-one."

"All we have to do is hold up our end over here until dusk," Ryan replied. "Send the tanks out fifty yards."

"Yes, sir," Murphy replied. "Get the blockers five yards downfield," he said into his walkie-talkie.

The tanks moved into position fifty yards ahead of the Americans as ordered. Their turrets scanned back and forth so that the gunners inside could acquire targets when the order to fire was given. Once they came to a halt, Ryan checked his watch. It was a quarter to ten in the morning, and although it remained frigid, the sun shining alone in the cloudless sky was beginning to warm the men.

"Here we go," Ryan said to Murphy. "One shot at acquired targets for now."

"Hit them on skinny posts . . . just once," Murphy said into the radio.

The tanks opened fire. Most of their rounds slammed into the ranks of Sultan's men. Black smoke rose from the ground where the shells landed, and the bodies that once occupied the surrounding areas were tossed into the air. Successful shots all of them, each with noticeably confirmable kills, yet the mass of Sultan's troops remained.

"Now what?" Connelly asked.

"Let's see how they respond," Ryan said. Suddenly, the three artillery stations atop the north wing fired; explosions erupted in front of the tanks positioned in the center of the line. One of the tanks was blown backwards and landed on its turret; another two caught fire, and their crews were fortunate to escape alive.

"Did you see that?" Ryan asked.

"Yeah, we must be on the cusp of their range," Murphy confirmed.

"Move our guys back twenty-five yards," Ryan ordered.

"Sir, but then we'll be out of firing range," Connelly reminded him.

"I know, but they're sitting ducks right now," Ryan insisted. "Pull 'em back, Murph!"

Murphy looked at his walkie-talkie, and said into it, "Holding penalty boys. Bring it back ten yards."

"I said twenty-five!" Ryan shouted.

"Tack on fifteen for a personal foul," Murphy added into the radio.

Ryan pulled a pair of binoculars from his belt. He looked through them to survey the damage the tanks' fire caused. He removed the binoculars and scanned the line of tanks now only twenty-five yards in front of him. "It's gonna be a long day," he stated.

* * *

Max appeared at the staging area, which was approximately two miles south of the Pentagon, to oversee the remaining army's departure, joining Sharpe in saluting the troops from a makeshift platform as they marched by. When the last of the army passed by, Sharpe told Max, "This is where we part ways, Mr. President. Private Green will drive you to your rendezvous with General Rogers," he said pointing to a young, scrawny boy standing by a black sedan at the side of the road.

"How old is he?" Max asked.

"He's young, sir. Not much good in a fight, but determined to contribute to the cause."

"Very well," Max conceded. "Good luck, General. I am looking forward to celebrating this victory with you," he said while extending his hand to shake Sharpe's.

"As am I with you," Sharpe concurred, embracing Max's handshake. "It has been an honor to serve at your pleasure, Mr. President," he said with a firm salute for his commander-in-chief.

"You're a good friend, John," Max reminded Sharpe as he returned the gesture.

Sharpe turned and joined the army. He looked back at Max to see him standing alone on the platform. He was unsure which man he knew that stood there: Was it the compassionate, gentle man he first met, or was it the cold-hearted, lying murder he saw in the Maryland woods? The answer was not immediately available, and he knew that at the end of the day, the man that stood on the platform would be branded a hero in the eyes of all Americans. Sharpe could only hope that the hero was not the villain he had come to know.

Max stepped down from the platform and joined Green by the car. "It's an honor to serve you, Mr. President," the boy offered as he held the rear door open for Max.

"Just drive," Max said as he took his seat in the car. Green closed the door behind him, and took his seat behind the wheel. Max never felt as alone as he did on this particular car ride. He could not wait to meet up with Rogers. Revenge was only hours away.

The car pulled into the Maryland woods, and Green drove as close to Rogers' men as possible. When the car came to a halt, Green quickly shut the engine, and left his seat to open the door for Max. Max was not as patient, and let himself out of the vehicle.

"How are we doing so far?" Max asked the approaching Rogers while ignoring Green altogether.

"Well, Ryan's in a battle for positioning right now," Rogers replied. "He's lost three tanks, but only a handful of men so far. But he said that they've been able to take some of Sultan's men in the process."

"Does it look good?" Max asked.

"Hard to say," Rogers answered honestly. "He's not going to be able to advance until he can take out their artillery stationed atop the Pentagon, and he's going to have a hell of time doing it from the open field in broad daylight. They're sitting ducks as soon as they enter the artillery's firing range."

"Where does that leave us?" Max asked.

Rogers looked at his watch. "Right now, we're on schedule. It's almost twelve hundred hours. We're going into the tunnels at sixteen hundred hours. We should reach the Secretary's office at approximately twenty-two hundred hours."

"Are we able to pull out if the attack fails?" Max asked.

"No, sir," Rogers somberly replied. "We'll lose communication with General Sharpe once we enter the tunnels."

"So, that's the point of no return," Max said pointing at the tree containing the tunnel entrance.

"Yes, sir," Rogers replied. "Come this way, sir. You and will be briefed by Lieutenant Youseff and Captain Williams as to your role in this mission," he said leading Max to a secluded area away from the rest of his men.

"What are they doing here?" Max asked. "Why aren't they with Sharpe?"

"The general felt it best for us to make certain that you survived the battle," Hank said.

"Naturally," Max said as he saluted Hank and Williams. "I hope you two are ready for a good fight. I have no intention of being a wallflower in this one."

"General Sharpe has requested that we ask you to refrain from engaging in combat, if possible," Rogers explained.

"That's correct, sir," Williams further explained. "We will be positioned in the rear of the battalion. Our combat role will be limited to your defense, Mr. President."

"We'll see about that," Max said with every intention of revising Sharpe's orders. "The last time I checked, General Sharpe answers to me."

* * *

"Cease the artillery fire for now," Sultan ordered. "We've been at a stalemate with them for hours, and it is useless until their tanks are in range. Send the men into the field of battle. Let's see if the Americans are ready to fight at close range. Draw them in, and then crush them!"

"As you wish, Sultan," Qaferi said. He spoke the orders in Arabic through the microphone on his headset.

On the center screen, the image of the field of battle appeared from the Pentagon's point of view. The Americans were hiding behind their tanks. Every so often small streaks of light became visible from bullets being fired in both directions. Sultan's men began to march toward the center of the field.

* * *

"They're advancing, Colonel," Connelly said.

"Then it's time to move out," Ryan admitted. He quickly scanned the line of tanks in front of him. There was a noticeable gap in the center of the line where the three destroyed tanks were originally positioned. "Send the tanks out on the left and on the right. Then send half our men to follow them."

"What about the middle of the field?" Connelly questioned.

"Get the tanks close enough to take out the artillery stations up there," Ryan said pointing to the roof of the building. "Then flood the center with the rest of our guys."

Murphy nodded, and ordered into his walkie-talkie, "Listen up! Blockers set out in dual wedge formation. One left, one right. Blockers, go for the quarterbacks on the roof. Alpha and Beta Companies follow the blockers on the left. Charlie and Delta follow on the right. Edward, Freedom, Gamma and Henry Companies line up under center until the ball is snapped."

Organized chaos erupted among the New Englanders. Company commanders began barking orders at their men, who responded by readying their weapons. The tanks began to roll out in two distinct V-shaped formations; the companies assigned to follow them, respectively, did.

The gunfire intensified as the two armies closed in on each other. The Americans had the advantage of using the tanks as cover, and were able to fire freely into the oncoming Arabs. Despite taking on heavy casualties, Sultan's men continued their advance.

Approximately three hundred yards from the Pentagon, the tanks stopped. Their turrets began to rise to a higher angle. They opened fire. Most of the artillery shells slammed into the north wing of the Pentagon exploding with great force and sending flames and black smoke into the air. However, one of the shells fired from the right wedge hit its target, and the rocket launcher on the right side of the roof exploded in flames. Several enemy soldiers caught fire and jumped to their deaths. A loud cheer erupted from the American ranks.

The celebration was short-lived. Two loud explosions rumbled through the American lines as two of the tanks on the left erupted in flames. The detonations created monstrous craters where the tanks once were, and shrapnel tore through hundreds of men in the vicinity.

The tanks fired again. The north wing erupted in flames with each strike. Flames from one of the explosions stretched high enough to engulf the area surrounding the center artillery station.

Through his binoculars, Ryan watched as the center rocket launcher burst into flames. He smiled as he saw Sultan's men scrambling to bring the artillery stations from the east and west wings to replace those that his men destroyed. He looked at his watch. "Almost sixteen hundred," he commented. The giant red sun was setting on the western horizon. "It's working," he said. Over the sounds of the continuing explosions and gunfire, he shouted, "Keep the guys on the left firing at the roof. I want the tanks on the right to fire into the enemy lines. And send the rest of our men up the middle."

"Yes, sir," Murphy said. He then repeated the order into his walkie-talkie without using any football references as code this time. The tanks did as commanded, and the American shells began to tear through the rank and file of Sultan's men. A surge of American forces charged up the center of the field; they were stymied slightly by a blast from the enemy's surviving artillery canon, but shortly after it, they continued their surge. Sultan's lines began to falter, and soon the Americans were only two hundred yards from the Pentagon.

Ryan took his walkie-talkie off of his belt. He switched the signal, and said into it, "Beta Two to Alpha One! Beta Two to Alpha One! The east and west wing defenses are softening, General. You're primed, and ready to go!"

"How bad are your casualties, Colonel?" Sharpe asked over the airwaves.

"Several hundred so far. But we're gonna be okay. We can hold 'em for a little bit longer."

"You do that, Beta Two," Sharpe ordered. "We're

starting our approach. We'll be there soon to help. Alpha Two, did you copy?"

"I did, Alpha One," Rogers' voice chimed in. "We're heading in now. See you on the other side."

* * *

Max trudged through the dark catacombs of the fallout tunnels surrounded by Hank, Williams and Green. They stayed about fifty feet behind the battalion at all times; a precaution to allow for a quicker retreat in case an ambush was encountered. Rogers stayed at the front of the group, joined by Norton and the rest of his officers.

"How old are you, Private?" Max asked to initiate conversation.

"Seventeen, Mr. President," Green answered with trepidation in his voice.

Sensing the hesitation, Williams pounced, "How old are you, really?"

Green hung his head. "Fifteen," he answered quietly.

Max laughed. "Is this your first battle?"

"Yes, sir," the boy answered.

"Don't know what to expect, do you?" Williams teased.

"No, sir. No, I don't," he responded.

"Nervous?" Max wondered.

"A little, Mr. President," Green admitted.

"Just stick with your comrades and you'll be okay," Max assured him. "I was nervous before my first battle, too."

"How old were you?" Green asked inquisitively.

Hank, Williams and Max laughed. "It was the battle of New York earlier this year," Max said. "I'm thirty-three."

"Wow!" Green said in awe. "I ran to join up after your speech to the Council. I wanted to be great warrior like you. I thought you've been in thousands of battles. I guess I was wrong."

"No, son, he is a great warrior," Williams said in Max's defense. "But if you've seen one battle, you've seen them all. War has a way of changing a man."

"It's certainly changed me," Max noted.

"With all due respect, Mr. President, I disagree," Hank objected. "You're still the same man you were the first time I met you. Your perspective is different, that's all."

"Trust me, Hank," Max insisted. "I'm not the same. I don't know why I keep fighting anymore. But I know that I must."

"I don't have that curiosity," Hank affirmed. "I joined this fight to stop Sultan from denigrating Allah. He manipulates the sacred teachings, and he must be removed from this Earth. Allah will not have mercy on his soul. Certainly, there are no virgins waiting for a man as cruel as Sultan."

"Only someone as cruel as Sultan on our side can stop him," Max said. "Maybe that's my role."

"Allah would not send cruelty to battle cruelty, Mr. President," Hank professed. "No, he would send its exact opposite to conquer it. You are capable of great compassion, and Sultan is not."

"Not anymore, Hank," Max pressed. "Where was that compassion in the woods?" he asked, referring to his murder of Dixon.

"A lapse in judgment, Mr. President," Hank argued. "Allah does not judge us based on one action, and He does not judge us until we are ready to be judged. You are a young man, Mr. President. Surely there will be a time when your compassion will save you; Allah will show you mercy."

"I hope so, Hank," Max said. "How much longer do we have until we get there?"

"About three hours," Williams confirmed.

"Can we talk about something else?" Max pleaded. "What do you know about women, Private?"

* * *

The sun having set allowed the temperature to drop rapidly. Gusts of wind began to sweep across the battlefield, and Ryan's men were beginning to allow the elements to get the better of them. They advanced to within one hundred yards of the Pentagon, but their resolve was beginning to ebb. The surviving rocket launcher on the roof of the north wing changed its targets from the tanks, which continued to bombard the north wing, to Ryan's soldiers, who were engaged in fierce hand-to-hand combat with Sultan's men; the launcher's operators showed no regard for the lives of their own comrades, and with each blast, men of both sides were instantly incinerated or shredded by shrapnel.

"The men are freezing to death, Colonel, and we haven't been able to take out that last launcher just yet," Connelly complained over the deafening explosions of the battle. "We have to pull out. This is suicide!"

"We're staying just a little longer, Patty," Ryan declared. "Sharpe will be here!" He looked at his watch; it was already eight thirty. "If he's not here by twenty-one hundred, we'll pull back."

Connelly nodded, but cautioned, "If there's anyone left to pull back."

The battle raged on. The rocket launcher blasted another pocket of soldiers from both sides, leaving a fiery crater smoldering thick black smoke. Blood rained down upon the combatants who were fortunate enough to survive its blast. Three blasts pummeled the north wing's façade, which now resembled a piece of Swiss cheese; it was becoming structurally unsound, and began to make loud noises as the concrete and metal began to crumble and break. Suddenly, flames shot up behind the rocket launcher, and there was a great crash as the artillery station was swallowed by the hole in the roof that expanded as the north wing began to collapse.

The Americans cheered, and their vigor returned. The elements no longer bothered them. On Ryan's orders, the tanks rolled forward allowing the New Englanders to approach within fifty yards of the Pentagon. Ryan surveyed the commotion that ensued on the rooftops of the remaining four wings through his binoculars, which he enhanced with night-vision lenses. Sultan's men were scrambling to the east and west wings to reposition their artillery for strikes to the north. It was a lengthy process, and time was the Americans' ally.

Bright flashes of light green nearly blinded Ryan through his night-vision binoculars. He quickly flinched, and when he returned his naked gaze to the Pentagon, he saw flames rising from the east and west wings. There were two more blasts followed by pillars of fire rising from the two southernmost wings.

"He's here!" Ryan exclaimed. "Sharpe's here! We did it!"

Murphy grabbed his walkie-talkie and ordered the New Englanders to press into Sultan's men guarding the western and eastern wings. "Fourth quarter, boys! It's now or never!"

* * *

When Rogers reached the entrance to the Pentagon that led into the Secretary's office, he ordered his men hold silent. He placed his ear on the door to hear if there was anyone just outside of it. All he could hear was the rumble of explosions that were rocking the building. Dirt loosened by the vibration fell from the ceiling. Rogers nodded to his officers, and his men readied their weapons. Next to the door was a keypad that resembled a simple calculator. Rogers typed in a series of numbers, and the red light atop the keypad changed to green. The door began to slide open.

The soldiers poured into the Secretary's office anticipating enemy resistance; however, it was empty. They opened the office door that led them into the hallway. Sultan's men were visible running through the halls, and paid no attention to the Americans. Rogers' men stealthily weaved through the hallways opening every office door, only to find it empty. They continued their search for Sultan by going room to room.

Rogers, with his handgun raised in case he needed to fire it, reached for a doorknob of an unchecked room. He turned it, and pushed the door open and pointed his gun at the room's only occupant: a haggard and disheveled man sporting an American officer's uniform was handcuffed and hanging from a hook on the wall by the handcuff chain. Rogers recognized Harmon immediately, and let the door close behind him.

"You can put away the gun, General," Harmon said. "As you can see, I'm not going anywhere."

Keeping his gun aimed at Harmon, Rogers replied, "It's over, Harmon. We know all about your grand scheme. Your lover confessed to everything. How could you?"

"Hmph," Harmon sounded in disgust. "How is William?"

"Dead!"

Harmon's face turned to stone and his eyes welled up as his lip quivered. "No! How can that be?"

"He went too far. He practically dared the President

to do it."

"Noble?" Harmon asked already knowing the answer. "You're lying. Noble would have insisted on a trial. He wouldn't kill William without a verdict. He doesn't have the balls for it."

"It's the truth. Sorry, Daniel, but you're going to pay for you've done to this country! I won't let the President allow you to get off so easily. You will stand trial for your treason! And I will be first in line to testify against you!"

"Rogers, wait!" Harmon pleaded.

The prisoner's plea fell on deaf ears. Rogers opened the door and grabbed one of the younger soldiers who happened to be passing by, pulling him into the room; it was Green. "Guard him!" Rogers ordered pointing at Harmon.

"Yes, sir," Green answered with a salute. Rogers did not return the gesture. Instead, he stormed out of the room into the hallway, closing the door behind him.

Several minutes passed and not a word was uttered by either Harmon or Green. The building shook as the blasts from the battle outside continued to pulverize it. Finally, Harmon begged, "Can you at least take me off this hook? Just slide me that chair over there, and I'll be able to step down," he said pointing to a desk chair with his foot.

"I have strict orders from the general to guard you," Green replied.

"You'll still be guarding me, son. I just want to be able to protect myself if the roof caves in. General Rogers wants me alive. Besides, it's not like I can do anything with these cuffs on, and you've got a gun in case I try anything."

Green nodded; to him, Harmon's plea was rational. He kicked the chair toward Harmon gently, but kept his assault rifle pointed at him at all times. Harmon stepped on the chair, and using the new leverage lifted the chain off of the hook. He sat down on the chair and sighed.

"There, that's better," Harmon said in relief. "First mission?"

"Yes, sir," Green answered. "Just signed up a few months back, after the President took Philadelphia."

"Good. Welcome to the military life," Harmon said. Pointing to the rear corner of the room, Harmon said, "Now, can you do me a favor and hand me that canteen over there. I'm terribly thirsty."

Green glanced over his shoulder and saw a canteen on the floor next to a tray with crumbs on it. He looked back at Harmon and said, "Sure." He turned and walked over to the canteen. As he bent down to pick it up, he suddenly saw a reflection of light from something metal that flashed in front of his eyes. Before he could identify what it was or where it came from, Harmon secured the handcuff chain around his throat and began to pull its ends together until he heard it snap the boy's trachea.

Harmon released the chain and Green's corpse slumped to the ground. He reached down to Green's belt and pulled the handgun from its holster. Quietly, he moved toward the door and pushed it open slowly to see if anyone heard the struggle. The hallway was empty.

Another blast rocked the building. Harmon closed the door, turned out the light, and hurried toward the window sill. Outside, he saw the carnage from the battle. Bullets flew through the dark of night. Artillery shells rained down from the roof above into masses of soldiers. The impact caused the building to shake as if there was an earthquake.

He placed the handcuff chain on the window sill. With one hand on the gun's trigger and the other holding the chain in place, he placed the gun's barrel against one of the links of the chain and fired. The shot severed the chain, and with his hands independent of each other, he reached toward the ceiling and laughed a sinister laugh. He looked out at the battle and saw one of the tank's turrets aimed directly at him. He knew that time was short.

Gathering Green's assault rifle, Harmon ran out of the room just as an artillery shell struck its outer wall. The force of the explosion lifted him into the corridor wall, and he fell to the floor with a thud. A piece of shrapnel lodged itself in his left calf muscle. He looked up and saw that there was no one in sight. Carefully, he made his way to the Secretary's office, leaving a trail of blood behind him.

The door to the Secretary's office was open, as was the secret entrance to the fallout shelter where the bookcase used to be. Harmon chuckled. "This isn't over yet, Noble," he said as he ducked into the darkness of the tunnel.

* * *

"We've lost our artillery defenses on the north and east wings, and we're down to just one launcher on one of the southern wings," Qaferi reported in Arabic as the barrage of explosions continued to rock the Pentagon. The main screen of the Hub displayed only "snow," indicating that all systems were non-functioning. "It's time to surrender, Sultan! We can't take much more of this."

"Surrender is not an option!" Sultan yelled in Arabic. "We shall fight until the death!"

"Please be reasonable," Qaferi pleaded in English. "Allah will be merciful, Sultan, if only we . . . ."

Gunshots rang out in the Hub. Rogers and his men barged into the room with guns blazing. They fired freely at anything that moved.

Sultan's men instinctively returned fire. It was an

ambush they did not expect. The American presence stunned and confused them.

There were no discernable targets for either side. Bullets tore through bodies. Blood ran like red rivers into lakes on the floor; the tributaries did not discriminate between the nationalities of their respective originators as they commingled with each other.

Some men died quickly, others were merely injured. Qaferi was less fortunate. A bullet ricocheted off a computer console and struck him in the lower back. It did not exit his body; instead, it shredded his internal organs. He tried to fire as many shots as he could, but he could not stabilize himself to get off more than two rounds. A second bullet pierced his left breast and instantly collapsed his lung. Another one shattered his right forearm. The pain was unbearable, and he crumpled at Sultan's feet. Blood rapidly filled his lungs, drowning him at his leader's side.

The loss of yet another closely trusted advisor and friend infuriated Sultan. He stood in the puddle of blood at his feet, and wildly fired his machine gun in the Americans' direction. He screamed in anger as he unloaded the bullets from the magazine cartridge. He had no specific target.

Sultan's men soon realized that their cause was lost; many began to throw down their weapons and raise their hands to the air in an effort to surrender. "No!" Sultan shouted in Arabic. "No! Keep fighting!" he ordered. But, his men looked at each other, and they realized that surrender was their best option.

Abandoned, Sultan kept firing. "So, General Rogers, you decided to come back for me," Sultan antagonized as he fired randomly keeping the Americans in a defensive posture. "That's funny. I always thought that your great President, Max Noble, would be the one to come for me."

"I'm right here," Max announced from the Hub's entranceway. He was flanked by Hank on his right and Williams on his left. "I wouldn't miss this for the world," he said drawing his sword from its sheath.

"Come and get me, Noble," Sultan prodded, as he turned his fire toward the entranceway. Max, Hank and Williams dodged for cover. "Send me to Allah. He will reward me for killing millions of your infidel brethren."

"No, he won't!" Hank disagreed. Max raised his right arm to signal to Hank not to do anything rash. In Arabic, Hank shouted, "My name is Hakim Youseff. I am a willing servant of Allah."

"You are an infidel!" Sultan roared back in Arabic. "You aligned yourself with the infidels! You are not a loyal servant of Allah, and you should die along with them!" His gun ceased firing as he ran out of bullets. He pulled the magazine from the weapon and tossed it aside. Grasping a new one from his belt, he attempted to insert into the gun when a bullet caught him in the side of his left thigh, causing his leg to give out from underneath him.

"Drop your weapon!" Rogers hollered as Sultan collapsed.

With blood oozing from his leg, Sultan hollered, "Never!" He sat up, and began firing at Rogers. Another bullet caught him in his right shoulder, and he dropped his gun.

Hank dashed from Max's side, and approached Sultan with an intense vigor and his gun drawn. "Allah is generous and glorious! You have disgraced his sacred teachings! This is for Allah, praised be He!" Hank fired his gun. The bullet entered Sultan's skull just above his left eye. It exited his head close to where the spine meets the skull splattering blood and brain tissue onto the console behind him. His eyes rolled back, and his body dropped to the ground. Blood pooled beneath the corpse. Sultan's reign was finally at its end.

Rogers shook his head. "Nobody move!" he ordered. "Are you alright, Mr. President?"

"I'm fine," Max called.

Hank stood over Sultan's corpse, staring in disbelief and trying to catch his breath as his adrenaline level subsided. "May Allah show you no mercy," he said in Arabic while bending down to close Sultan's eyelids.

Rogers pointed to Sultan's men, who remained like statues with their hands in the air. "You men are all under arrest," he said. Addressing his men, he ordered, "Take them into custody, and lock them in the room with General Harmon. It's down the hall, seventh door on the right," Rogers said.

"Yes, sir," one of the soldiers responded. They kept their weapons pointed at the prisoners, and marched them out of the Hub.

"Do you hear that?" Williams asked.

"I don't hear anything," Max said.

"Exactly," Williams confirmed. "No gunfire. No explosions. No vibrations. The battle outside is over, too."

Rogers grabbed his walkie-talkie from his belt. "Alpha Two to Alpha One. Alpha Two to Alpha One," he called. "Sharpe, are you there?"

"I'm here. What's your status, Alpha Two?" Sharpe's voice replied.

"Mission accomplished, sir," Rogers reported. "General Harmon is in custody. Sultan was killed in combat. What is your status?"

"Excellent!" Sharpe proclaimed. "All surviving enemy combatants are in custody. Please tell the President that it's over. Victory is ours!" Cheers and applause ignited in the Hub as the Americans congratulated each other.

CHAPTER 35

There were many reasons that the Peach never settled down with a woman, but first among them was his tendency to snore horribly loudly. He sounded like a chainsaw having its motor revved. It was a clear case of sleep apnea, only he was too stubborn to have it diagnosed. Instead, he would awake each night on at least two occasions because he was choking on his own phlegm. This night was no different; the first awakening occurred shortly after midnight. Just over two hours later, he choked himself awake again.

Normally, he cleared his throat after waking and immediately reentered his slumber. Such was the case for the first awakening, but not the second. The latter was more violent; he coughed vigorously for a few moments. Unable to fall back to sleep, he decided to tour the White House to ensure that all was in order. If nothing else, it gave him peace of mind. He slipped his gun into his robe pocket out of habit and began with the bedrooms upstairs.

He cracked open the door to Zach's room and peered inside. He must have woken the boy, who waved to him. "Are you okay?" Zach asked.

"Yeah, yeah," the Peach whispered. "Just checkin' on you. You're cool?"

Zach nodded affirmatively.

"Okay, I'm gonna go check out the rest of the house. Go back to sleep."

"Can I come?" Zach asked eagerly.

"Nah, it's too late," the Peach replied. "Plus, I'm gonna check outside and it's freezin' out there," he explained, even though he had no intention of venturing into the cold night.

"Okay," a dejected Zach answered. But when the Peach closed the door and left, Zach hopped out of bed. He wanted to join his friend, and he did not care what time it was. The weather did, however, concern him. He grabbed his coat and his shoes, followed by his bow and arrows. His plan was to startle the Peach by shooting an arrow at him, but not to hit him; he figured that he would tail the Peach outside and while his back was turned, he would fire the arrow at one of the White House pillars. It was the type of prank only a thirteen-year-old boy would find amusing. For some reason, he thought the Peach would see the humor in it, too.

Zach admired himself in the mirror. He looked like a young soldier with his weapons at the ready, and he felt like he was prepared to fight a battle like Max, but he was missing something. He looked around the room for a hint. He thought of what Max told him about fighting in the war; he could hear Max explaining to him that a soldier has to be responsible for his family first, and that bravery was a part of that responsibility. Then, he remembered: Max told him that he was responsible for the family when Max was at war. He saw the cell phone that Max gave him lying on his night stand, and immediately picked it up and turned it on. He made sure that the ring tone was sent to "silent" so that the Peach would not be able to hear him approach from behind in the off chance that someone actually contacted him during the prank.

The door creaked slightly as Zach opened it a bit to see where the Peach was. To the detriment of his plan, the Peach was coming out of Roxy's room when he heard the door. "I told you to go to bed!" he chastised Zach. "I mean it!" Not wanting to tip the Peach off as to his plan,

Zach immediately shut the door, jumped into his bed with his gear on, and pulled the covers over himself. He realized that he would have to wait a few minutes, giving the Peach a head start, if he was to be able to get the drop on his target. Having rethought his strategy, he stayed in his bed.

Satisfied that Zach and Roxy were safe, the Peach looked in on Bam Bam. His colleague was sound asleep in the recliner with the television running an infomercial for a new type of fishing lure. Across the hall, Boots slept in his room with his hand on his gun, which was adjacent to his face on the pillow. Since all seemed to be copasetic, the Peach continued his tour of the residence.

Many people visited the White House each year, prior to Sultan's invasion, to appreciate its grandeur. The year of neglect had taken its toll; cobwebs needed to be removed in certain rooms, and the entire house needed a fresh coat of paint. One room had two crossed sabers on the wall; a picture of Theodore Roosevelt adorned the adjacent wall, but the Peach could not make the connection. He inspected each room briefly, hoping that his stroll would have tired him. Since it had not, he decided to make his way toward the West Wing; he hoped that a quick patrol of the Oval Office would fatigue him.

Only one word came to the Peach's mind to describe the Oval Office: Intimidating. The curvature of the walls was so unusual that it discombobulated him. Many presidents considered the office to be the best "home field" advantage for negotiations because of its design. The Peach stood in the center of the room, standing upon the Presidential Seal displayed in the carpeting. He admired the leather chair behind the President's desk, but he did not dare to go near it; he knew that the chair brought with it a great deal of responsibility of which he wanted no part.

Suddenly, he heard a faint noise permeating the wall.

He immediately pulled his gun from his robe pocket. The wall had a hinge, which he surmised meant that it was a door. He gently pushed it open, and walked slowly into the dark corridor before encountering another door in front of him; a flashlight would have prevented him from walking directly into it. He composed himself, and opened the door slowly. It was too dark to see anything, so he probed the wall of the interior room for a light switch. Finally, he felt a metallic panel, and lights began to illuminate the conference room table in the center of the room.

This was the Peach's first time in the Situation Room. He glanced at the table, which was the only visible object in the room. "Anybody in here?" he asked aloud. There was no response; further investigation was needed, he determined. He began to circle the table while looking for anything out of the ordinary when the door slammed shut. The Peach pointed his gun in the direction of the noise. "Who's there?" he demanded to know.

The answer came in the form of a blow to the head that he never saw coming. He was knocked to the ground and stunned, losing his gun in the process. The door quickly opened, and the Peach saw the silhouette of his attacker against the moonlit Oval Office limping down the corridor. The Peach gathered himself, and quickly ran to tackle the man. He grabbed the assailant's leg, and quickly recognized that it was wounded from the blood that dampened the pant leg. The two men rolled on the ground trading blows all the while.

"Where do you think you're going?" the Peach asked as he landed a punch to his attacker's body. The attacker dropped the assault rifle he had been carrying, with which he presumably used to strike the Peach, and responded by grabbing and squeezing the Peach's testicles, sending a searing pain throughout his body. He released the perpetrator who, in turn, let go of his gonads and began to limp away. The Peach ignored the pain momentarily, and was able to trip him by grabbing his wounded leg, which began to ooze fresh blood as he fell on the Oval Office carpet.

Determined not to allow his attacker to escape, the Peach tried to follow. He stumbled onto the carpet but could not endure the pain emanating from his testicles any longer. His attacker disappeared into the White House as the Peach struggled to ease the pain.

He rolled onto his back and elevated his legs. His eyes closed tightly as he groaned. When he opened them, his attacker stood above him holding one of the sabers that the Peach recognized from the wall in the room with Roosevelt's portrait.

"Does it hurt?" the attacker asked.

"Not as much as yours will when I'm through with you, you stupid fuck!" the Peach warned.

"Isn't it amazing that a simple squeeze of the balls, even as small as yours, can be excruciatingly painful?"

"Fuck you! Guy, I am warning you! You have three seconds to run before I cut your fuckin' nuts off!"

"No you won't," the attacker calmly stated as he plunged the sword into the Peach's lower abdomen. Slowly, he pulled the sword upward through the Peach's bowels, stopping once he reached the base of the rib cage before removing the blade from the Peach's now-limp body. The pain was too much for the Peach to bear, and although he began to react to the initial strike, he lost consciousness from the shock before he had a chance to scream. "What a pity," the attacker lamented. "I would have enjoyed torturing you. But since I can't have you telling anyone how this happened . . . ." The assailant used the blade to slit the Peach's throat. Without a sound, the Peach died on the Oval Office floor as his blood spouted out of his severed jugular veins.

The attacker quickly departed the Oval Office. He did not notice Zach, who heard the altercation while hiding under the desk of the President's personal assistant, as he limped by. Zach waited until he heard the opening and closing of the outer door leading into the famed Presidential Rose Garden before leaving his position. Confident that the intruder was gone, he darted into the Oval Office only to find his friend's lifeless body lying in a pool of its own blood.

Zach's eyes welled with tears, and he felt nauseous. He cried for a few moments until he remembered how Max described losing the Aryan in the Empire State Building. *We can't stop to mourn our friends who are taken from us in the heat of battle,* Max's voice sounded in his head. *We must honor them by avenging them instantly. There will be plenty of time to mourn them when the new day dawns.*

The words inspired Zach, and he wiped his eyes as he composed himself. He looked around the room: First, he saw the open door leading to the Situation Room; then, he stared at the Peach's body; lastly, he stared at the blood-soaked carpet. He watched as the pool of blood slowly expanded toward the doorway through which the murderer escaped. It slowly enveloped the trail of blood that the intruder left behind. Zach immediately realized that the culprit did not take the time to cover the trail; thus, he would be easy to find.

He reached into his pocket and took out the phone that Max had given him for emergencies. He began typing a text message:

> Peach is dead . . . We're OK . .
> . Killer getting away . . . I will
> follow . . . Will text where he is
> when I find him . . .

* * *

"General Rogers," the young corporal called as Rogers and Max approached the room where they believed Harmon was being held. "General Harmon is nowhere to be found."

"What do you mean, Corporal?" Rogers asked for clarification.

"It looks as though the room was struck by a shell during the battle," the corporal reported. "His guard is dead, but the general's body is missing."

"I want to see this," Max insisted.

"Let's have a look, Corporal," Rogers ordered. He and Max followed the corporal into the room. The smell of gunpowder overtook them as they entered. A large hole gaped in the outer wall. All of the furniture was lying haphazardly by the inner wall, smoldering. A soldier's body was pinned underneath a desk. Max bent down and looked at the soldier's face.

"Shit!" Max exclaimed.

"What is it, sir?" Rogers asked.

"This is Private Green," Max answered. "He was fifteen years old, and this was his first battle. He had his whole life ahead of him. And we killed him, damn it!"

"I'm sorry, Mr. President," Rogers offered. "War is chaotic. God does not discriminate among its combatants. All of our men knew the risks associated with battle."

"They knew them, General. But did they truly understand them?" Max countered.

"General Rogers," the corporal called from the hall. "We've found something."

"What is it, Corporal?" Rogers asked as he and Max rushed to the hallway.

"This trail of blood leads from here to the Secretary of Defense's office," the corporal explained pointing to the blood on the floor. "It could be General Harmon's."

"Or it could be any one of our wounded," Rogers said skeptically.

"It's a lead," Max cautioned.

"Yes, sir. It is," Rogers agreed. "Send a search party into the fallout tunnels, Corporal."

"Yes, sir," the corporal said with a salute.

Suddenly, Max felt a vibration in his pocket. He reached his hand inside and felt that his cell phone was the source. The outer display screen was alit, notifying him that he had a text message. He flipped open the phone, and read the message.

"General," Max said. "I need a ride."

* * *

Zach followed the trail of blood through the White House. There was no time to alert Bam Bam or Boots about the Peach's death; he had to act quickly if he was to catch the murderer. The trail led him outside through the Rose Garden, and onto Pennsylvania Avenue.

Zach hurried east tracking the blood. In the shadows about one hundred yards ahead of him, he saw the silhouette of a man limping. He knew that he had his man, and so he continued his pursuit. Maintaining his distance so as not to be detected, Zach made a conscious effort to stay hidden in the shadows. He ignored the cold, and kept his breathing to a minimum; he did not want the condensed air from his breath to be seen in the moonlight and give him away.

The killer led Zach to the Capitol building, which Zach recognized from his tour of the city with Max. As the killer struggled up the stairs, Zach took out his cell phone. Although he struggled to open the door to the building, the killer managed to pry it ajar using the stolen sword and squeezed into the abandoned iconic edifice.

Zach looked down at his phone, and although he spelled it wrong, he texted one word to Max: "Capital." He gathered his things and quietly climbed the stairs. Once he reached the still slightly ajar door, he peeked in. Through the huge rotunda, he could see into the Congressional chamber where the Peach's killer was preoccupied limping from seat to seat, pulling wires from the electronic voting consoles located at each Congressional member's seat. The killer never noticed Zach slip into the building.

* * *

Williams drove as quickly as he could. Rogers told Max to take whoever he wanted as a driver; Williams, being the first man Max approached, immediately volunteered for the mission as soon as he sensed the urgency in Max's voice. Max shared Zach's text message with him as they drove back into the city. "Where are we headed?" Williams asked.

"I guess we'll head back to the White House if we don't hear from him," Max said.

"Do you think it was Harmon?"

"Who else could it be? He better not have laid a finger on my family, though. Not that I need another excuse to kill him after everything he's done to the country, but especially now that he's killed my friend."

The phone vibrated in Max's pocket again. He reached in and pulled it out. "The Capitol," he said as he showed Williams Zach's new text message.

"Isn't the word, 'Capitol,' spelled with an 'o?'" Williams asked.

"C'mon he's thirteen. Cut the kid a break. I just hope he's smart enough not to follow Harmon into the building."

"We'll be there in five minutes, Mr. President."

"Good. Drop me off when we get there, and then check around outside for Zach. Take him back to the White House and check on Roxy as soon as you can."

"Yes, sir," Williams said.

The car approached the Capitol building and Williams drove onto the sidewalk, coming to a halt at the base of the stairs. Max jumped out, without saying a word to Williams. He dashed up the stairs, pulling his sword from its sheath as he ran. When he reached the door, he kicked it fully open from its slightly ajar position.

The violent swing of the door caught the killer's attention in the Congressional chamber. He looked up from underneath one of the seats holding some wires in his hand. His eyes locked with Max's, and he dropped the wires and limped up the aisle, raising the stolen sword to greet his intruding adversary.

Max recognized the disheveled man instantly; the four stars on his uniform gave away his rank and identity. "So, it is you, Harmon," Max said. "It's over. Surrender, now!"

"Noble," Harmon replied. "You just don't know when to quit. I'm going to enjoy watching you die."

"What were you up to with those wires in there? Covering your tracks?"

"Why, I don't know what you mean," Harmon said with a hint of sarcasm. "It's an old building. I wouldn't want an electrical fire to break out or anything."

The two approached each other in the center of the rotunda. Like gladiators preparing to battle in the Roman Coliseum, each looked the other over to determine his opponent's strengths and weaknesses. Harmon quickly noticed that Max presented his sword only with his right arm, and that the left arm dangled, practically limp. At the same time, Max focused on Harmon's injured leg; he knew that the fresh wound would slow Harmon considerably.

"Why'd you do it, Harmon? What did this country do to you that was so wrong?" Max asked.

"What difference does it make? I can never live the life that I wanted to now that you've taken William from me."

Max moved in to strike first. He wielded his sword at Harmon with a downward thrust. The general responded quickly by raising his sword horizontally, holding off Max's strike. They each stared into their nemesis' eyes across the glistening metal of their perpendicular blades. "You destroyed your country for your love of one man?" Max demanded to know.

"It destroyed me!" Harmon insisted. "I just felt the need to return the favor. All men are created equal, my ass! The hypocrisy of American freedom needed to be corrected! The only way to do that is to tear it down and start from scratch!" He backed away from Max, causing him to stumble forward. As Max struggled to regain his posture, Harmon attacked. He swung his sword upward, downward and upward again. Max was fortunate to dodge the first two attempts, but the third one caught him on the left shoulder. He groaned in pain, but was relieved that the blow landed on his useless arm.

"And how was Sultan's vision supposed to help you?" Max wondered aloud. "Freedom means having the ability to choose. You were so blinded by your hatred that you didn't even think of how much less freedom he would have given you!"

"That was never the point!" Harmon said as he lunged forward; Max was able to paré the strike. Harmon retracted his sword and lunged again. Max spun to his left, dropped to one knee as another swing of Harmon's sword grazed his scalp, and kicked at Harmon's leg wound. The pain dropped Harmon to the ground, and Max used the opportunity to reestablish his positioning.

"What was the point?" Max asked.

Harmon composed himself and said, "You should have tried to finish me, Noble. Never allow your opponent to recover. Mercy is a sign of weakness."

"Don't worry, General. I wasn't merciful when I killed your precious William. So, answer me! What was the point?"

Enraged, Harmon attacked. The clang of metal repeatedly echoed in the rotunda as the two men traded blows. They repositioned themselves after each blow as if dancing a waltz. Tiring, they backed away from each other. As they both gasped for air, Harmon exclaimed, "I wanted this country to suffer as I have suffered, knowing that the worst thing you can do to a person is tell them that they are free but never actually let them experience freedom! I've spent my entire life fighting for other people's freedom, only to be denied my own!"

"A callous traitor like you doesn't deserve to live," Max said gravely.

"Nor does a heartless murderer like you," Harmon countered. He attacked again, this time ferociously striking on Max's left side. Max could only survive the furious onslaught by raising his sword defensively. The clang of their swords rang out strike after strike. The rhythm was interrupted when a series of extra clangs rang out; Harmon paused, and Max noticed that his sword, the one that may or may not have belonged to General George Washington, was lighter in his hand. They both looked at his blade to find it shattered approximately eight inches above the hilt, the longer piece of the blade having slid into the corner of the room.

Maintaining his aggressive stance, Harmon smiled

and said, "Prepare for your death, Max Noble." He swung his sword wildly, slicing through the cotton material covering Max's Kevlar vest as Max attempted to retreat. Max had taken three steps back when he felt the blade of Harmon's sword cut through his entrails just under the Kevlar plate.

Max dropped the remnants of his sword and reached for his abdomen. He looked down at his hands; they were covered in his blood. The president fell to the ground, and rolled onto his back.

"Now, Noble, your heroics are at an end," Harmon said. He lifted his sword above his head while standing over Max. Max prepared for a fatal strike, and closed his eyes. An image of Roxy flashed in his mind followed by an image of Zach; the image of her face every time he told her he would keep his promise about telling Zach that he was the boy's biological father was engraved in his mind. Suddenly, an image of Dalton flashed in Roxy's place, and then one each of Armstrong, Sharpe, Rogers, Judge Vineri, and finally, one of Zach and Roxy, together, again. Then there was darkness interrupted only by a sound, a familiar sound, like a buzzing in the air, followed by a thud.

Max opened his eyes. Harmon stood before him, his sword raised over his head, but slipping out of his hands. Blood began to run from the corner of his mouth down his uniform to the hole in the center of his chest from which an arrowhead protruded. A loud clang echoed through the rotunda as Harmon's sword hit the ground. His body collapsed next to it. Max squinted upward toward the rotunda balcony to see Zach standing with his bow in his hand.

"Hold on, Dad!" Zach yelled as he ran down the stairs. He joined Max in the rotunda, and knelt at his side not caring that his knees were becoming soaked by the growing pool of Max's blood.

"Zach, there's something I have to tell you," Max said. He coughed blood, much the way Dalton did on that fateful night months earlier. "You're my son."

"I know," Zach said as he began to cry.

"No, I mean, you're really my son. You're a Noble, like me. Make sure you tell your mother that I told you. And make sure you tell her that I love her."

"Hang on, Dad! You can tell her yourself!"

Williams barged into the rotunda. He saw Max on the ground and the blood surrounding him. "Mr. President!" he cried.

"Get help!" Zach yelled.

"Right away!" Williams replied. He turned and ran outside.

Max coughed more blood. "Zach, listen to me. I was not the man everyone thinks I am. I was a man, flawed the same as any other. You will be, too. Only . . . ."

"What?" Zach asked as Max gurgled and spit out blood. "Only, what?"

"Only don't let your anger get the better of you as mine did me. I was so angry that lost my ability to think clearly. I even lost my faith in God. I chose this fate. Remember that, for someday, you will choose yours," Max professed. A feeling of relief overcame him, as if the weight of the world was lifted from his shoulders. He gasped for air. "I feel cold," he explained.

"Here, take my coat," Zach insisted.

Max waved his hand to signal that he did not want the garment. "I haven't felt anything since the first time I saw you and your mother on my driveway. It was warm then, but it's cold now," he said thinking of how the cold did not affect him on that frigid January day. Max coughed and began to choke on his own blood again.

The sun began to rise, and a ray of sunlight illuminated the rotunda through the open doors. Max noticed the light and said, "I love . . . the dawn, Zach," he said gasping for air. "It's so . . . quiet . . . . It's the . . . start of . . . a new . . . day . . . ." Max exhaled his last breath, dying in his son's arms on the marble floor of the hallowed rotunda of the Capitol where many presidents' caskets often laid in state upon their deaths.

CHAPTER 36

Williams ran back into the rotunda after calling Sharpe to inform the general of Max's injury. He felt Max's neck for a pulse, but found none. Cardiopulmonary resuscitation did not help, but he continued to try until help arrived.

The ambulance came to a screeching halt in front of the Capitol. Two paramedics jumped out of the vehicle's cabin and ran up the stairs; a third emerged from the back of the truck holding a defibrillator, and he, too, hurried into the rotunda. They pushed Williams and Zach out of the way, removed Max's Kevlar vest, and began to attempt their own resuscitation. The defibrillator paddles jolted electricity into Max's body, but there was no change in his response.

Upon arriving, Sharpe took inventory of the situation. He lifted Zach and held him tightly as the boy wept on his shoulder. The paramedics continued their work to no avail. Sharpe nodded at them to indicate that their services would no longer be necessary; they left momentarily, only to return with a stretcher and a black, vinyl body bag. Max's corpse was placed in the bag, which was zipped, placed on the stretcher and taken to the ambulance for delivery to the morgue. Sharpe ordered Williams to accompany and guard the body until the funeral arrangements were made.

In the meantime, the general delivered Zach back to the White House. He was greeted by an irate Armstrong, who was in a panic from discovering the Peach's body in the Oval Office. He told Sharpe that everyone slept through the incident; although, he was confused as to why Zach was with the general and covered in blood. In turn, Sharpe delivered the news about Max. Armstrong was overwhelmed; he sat on the White House lawn and cried for several minutes. He could not believe that his good friend and protégé was gone. After composing himself, Armstrong took it upon himself to notify Judge Vineri, and to arrange for the Judge to be sworn in as the next President.

While Armstrong was arranging to place the nation in the Judge's stewardship, Sharpe took Zach to the master bedroom, where the two woke Roxy with the devastating news of her husband's death. It was news she dreaded, but was surprisingly prepared to hear. She was furious at first, then inconsolable. She hugged Zach tightly as she wept uncontrollably; the realization that she was now a widow was a heavy burden to bear. Being a single mother again did not bother her, for she had done it for so long before. However, losing the only man she ever truly loved hurt more than any pain she experienced in her life. Her sobs did not cease, except that when Zach told her that Max explained to him that he was Max's son, she laughed through her tears. "He always kept his promises to me," she said. "And I'll always love him for that."

"He wanted you to know that he loved you, too, Mom," Zach said.

"Of course he did," she said. "Of course he did."

* * *

"This is Susan Teller with an SBN Special Report," Susan said, wearing her signature red glasses while anchoring SBN's broadcast. Her eyes were bloodshot and puffy, as if she had been crying. "President Max Noble was killed earlier this morning in a duel with General Harmon in the rotunda of the Capitol building. General Harmon was also killed in the fight. Just moments ago,

Arthur Vineri took the Oath of Office to serve as President of the United States. Here, now, to describe the events of last night and this morning is President Vineri."

The broadcast cut to a picture of Vineri approaching a podium adorning the Presidential Seal in the White House Rose Garden; the original venue of choice, the Oval Office, was a crime scene that was filled with police. His eyes were filled with tears, and it was unclear if his nose was red from his sobbing or the frigid temperature.

"It is with a heavy heart that I stand here before you this morning to deliver both the greatest and worst of news," he began. "Sadly, only a few hours ago, my good friend, President Max Noble, was killed in a duel by a sword wielded by General Harmon, the same traitor who attempted to destroy this nation. However, while the general managed to kill our leader, he could not defeat our cause. Brave men, most of them boys themselves, under General Sharpe's command have defeated Sultan and his army once and for all. America is the land of the free once again!

"Sultan, we are told, was killed during the battle, and his soldiers are now being held as prisoners of war. General Harmon, too, was killed during the battle. More specifically, as I will describe to you shortly, he was killed following his duel with President Noble. President Noble will always be remembered as a defender of freedom and the hero of this great American restoration. For all that President Noble gave for our freedom, he shall be honored by being buried in a private ceremony tomorrow at Arlington National Cemetery.

"Let history record that President Noble's undertaker was stricken from this earth by his victim's son, Zachary. Zachary, too, deserves similar recognition, for a boy aged a mere thirteen years acted bravely and, poetically, nobly in ensuring that the treacherous General Harmon would not escape to regroup and return his reign of terror to us. For that, Zachary Noble will become the youngest recipient of the Presidential Medal of Honor.

"And so, my friends, we must now look ahead. Zachary tells me that his father's last words were, 'Today is a new day.' Indeed, President Noble was correct. Today *is* a new day. This nation is in need of new leadership. In sixty days, we shall have a national election, in which we shall elect a new President, a new Vice President, and a new Congress. I shall act only as an administrator to ensure that essential government services remain available until our new leaders can return our nation to its glory. I will not be a candidate for any elected office, and I will cede power to my rightfully elected successor.

"My friends, today is a new day. And yet it is bittersweet. May God bless you and your families. And may God bless the United States of America."

* * *

The funeral was a small, private affair. The procession to Arlington National Cemetery included a hearse that left directly from the funeral home, where a brief memorial service was held; Sharpe and Armstrong spoke of their friendship with Max, and how they could not imagine the future without him. Roxy could not bring herself to address the gathered guests; among them were President and Mary Vineri, Don Vito, Takinawa, Morris, Susan, Bard, Barrington, and most of the members of the Council (although, Thomas was conspicuously absent). Alas, there was no grand spectacle for the public to see. The only images captured on camera were those of his casket, draped in an American flag, being carried by its pallbearers: Boots, Bam Bam, Chatty, Gonzo, Ryan, Hank and Williams.

Graveside, Roxy wept. Zach stood in front of her, and she pulled him close by his shoulders. Armstrong and Sharpe flanked them, and took turns placing a hand on Roxy's shoulder to console her. Rabbi Schonberg conducted the brief service, which was followed by a twenty-one gun salute. The coffin was lowered into the ground. The rabbi handed Zach a shovel and instructed him that it was his responsibility as Max's son to place the first bit of dirt on his father's casket. Zach composed himself and shoveled three heaping piles of dirt from the mound sitting next to the open grave onto the coffin containing Max's carcass. A deep thud rattled Zach's core each time the dirt landed on the lid. The shovel was passed to each of the others in attendance until each person had placed a shovel's worth of dirt into the hole. The professional gravediggers completed the burial once each attendee had his or her turn.

They left the cemetery in an orderly fashion. President Vineri insisted that Roxy and Zach sit *shivah* at the White House since the widow had not yet been able to gather her thoughts, let alone her life and belongings. Roxy and Zach rode in the first limousine with the President, Mary, Armstrong and Sharpe. The pallbearers' limousine immediately followed, and the remaining attendees ensued.

"Do you think he made a difference?" Roxy asked.

"Absolutely, my dear," President Vineri answered. "He saved us all."

Roxy began to sob. "What are we going to do now?"

"Well, Mrs. Noble," Sharpe said. "If it's alright with you, I would like you to serve as First Lady during my administration. And I would like to recommend Zachary to continue his studies at any one of the finest military academies that this country has to offer." Turning to Zach, he said, "Someday, the keys to the kingdom will be yours, and you must learn what to do with them."

"Wait," Roxy interjected. "You're running for President?"

"Yes, Ma'am," Sharpe answered.

"Against who?" Zach wondered.

"Thomas declared his candidacy this morning," Armstrong answered. "He is so despicable! He has the votes for the Democratic nomination all locked up."

"If Thomas is going to be the Democrat's nominee, then who's going to run your campaign?" Roxy asked Sharpe.

"I am," Armstrong said with a smile. "I may never get to be the chair of the Democratic Party. But at least I'll be able to sleep at night knowing that the country will be in good hands."

"You'll be campaigning for the Republican candidate, Jack?" Roxy asked. "Max will roll over in his grave!"

"Actually, no," Sharpe answered. "The Republicans are going with Jim Parker from Virginia."

"Oh," she said in utter confusion.

Armstrong offered an explanation. "The Democrats are going to run to the left. The Republicans are going to run to the right. It's that division that tore this country apart and created opportunity for wicked men like Harmon. So, we're starting a new party, one that will be based on the principle that freedom is only effective when people have choices, and that a strong, united central government has a responsibility to provide people with the necessary protections so that they feel safe to make those choices. So, we're reaching back into history and bringing back the party of Washington, Hamilton and Adams: the Federalist Party."

"I see," Roxy acknowledged. "And you want Zach and I to be part of all this?"

"Absolutely!" Sharpe insisted. "I am a childless widower. Every president needs a family, and let's be honest here, we're all that we've got."

Roxy smiled. She felt comforted by the notion that, after a year of hell on earth, she and Zach would have people around them to share happy occasions. Indeed, they were family. But the decision could not be hers alone. "Thank you, General. If you don't mind, I think that Zach and I should talk it over first. We'll let you know before you announce your candidacy."

Zach looked out the window as the limousine turned onto Pennsylvania Avenue. The dome of the Capitol occupied his entire sightline. He thought of Max's parting words. *I chose this fate. Remember that, for someday, you will choose yours,* he heard his father say.

"Very well, Mrs. Noble," Sharpe replied.

The limousine, along with the rest of the funeral procession, arrived at the White House. The mirrors were covered, as Jewish custom prohibited mourners from looking at their own image during the mourning period. Roxy and Zach spent the day sitting on wooden crates and talking to their guests about Max and his heroics. The repetitive conversations made them numb.

At the end of the night, as Zach was getting ready for bed, Roxy asked him, "What do you think of the General's proposal? Should we join him?"

"I don't know," Zach answered. "One of the last things Dad said to me before he died was that we get to choose our own fate."

Roxy smiled, knowing that it was something her late husband would say. "That's right, Zach. We do."